Fo: JENNA

THE
SULTAN
OF
SARAWAK

Hope you Enjoy

THE SULTAN OF SARAWAK

AN AVA LEE NOVEL
THE TRIAD YEARS

IAN HAMILTON

SPIDERLINE

Published in Canada in 2022 and the USA in 2022 by House of Anansi Press Inc.
www.houseofanansi.com

House of Anansi Press is committed to protecting our natural environment.
This book is made of material from well-managed FSC°-certified forests,
recycled materials, and other controlled sources.

House of Anansi Press is a Global Certified Accessible™ (GCA by Benetech)
publisher. The ebook version of this book meets stringent accessibility standards
and is available to students and readers with print disabilities.

26 25 24 23 22   1 2 3 4 5

Library and Archives Canada Cataloguing in Publication

Title: The sultan of Sarawak / Ian Hamilton.
Names: Hamilton, Ian, 1946- author.
Series: Hamilton, Ian, 1946- Ava Lee series.
Description: Series statement: An Ava Lee novel ; book 14
Identifiers: Canadiana (print) 20210273194 | Canadiana (ebook) 20210273208 |
ISBN 9781487010157 (softcover) | ISBN 9781487010164 (EPUB)
Classification: LCC PS8615.A4423 S85 2022 | DDC C813/.6—dc23

Cover design: Lucia Kim
Text design: Alysia Shewchuk

*House of Anansi Press respectfully acknowledges that the land on which we
operate is the Traditional Territory of many Nations, including the Anishinabeg,
the Wendat, and the Haudenosaunee. It is also the Treaty Lands of the
Mississaugas of the Credit.*

*We acknowledge for their financial support of our publishing program the Canada
Council for the Arts, the Ontario Arts Council, and the Government of Canada.*

Printed and bound in Canada

For Don and Gloria Baxter, Rick Burgess and Brenda
Bowlby, and Stephen Gross and Dona Matthews —
wonderful friends all, and constant, caring Zoom
companions for us through the worst of the pandemic.

PROLOGUE

Kuching, Sarawak, Malaysia

IT WAS NINE O'CLOCK ON A MOONLESS NIGHT WHEN the unmarked car came to a stop on a poorly lit street in a small industrial park. Two men dressed in black exited the vehicle and quietly surveyed the area. They were the only people in sight, and the few nearby buildings were in darkness. One of the men produced a large athletic bag from the back seat, and then together they set off in the direction of a large two-storey warehouse.

As they approached the building, they could see the words KOTA KINABALU LUMBER COMPANY on a sign that stretched across three sets of double doors. To their right was a single entrance door, which opened onto stairs that led to a second floor containing offices. They looked up and saw a light shining from one of the office windows.

"Do you think someone's there?" the man with the athletic bag asked.

"I can't imagine anyone would be working this late," his partner said. "The light was probably left on by accident."

"Still, we should be quiet."

"I'm always quiet."

The two men walked to the set of double doors farthest from the office entrance. A padlocked chain was strung through two large handles. The man with the athletic bag took out a pair of bolt cutters and severed the chain, then opened the doors just wide enough for them to enter. Inside, he produced a flashlight from the bag and swept the warehouse with its light. The space was stacked from floor to ceiling with various cuts and types of lumber.

"How do you want to handle this?" he asked.

"Let's spread out the bombs evenly. We'll toss the Molotov cocktails as we're leaving."

"I don't know why fireballs are necessary. The bombs should do the job."

"Those are our orders, and you know how the boss is about obeying orders."

"Okay, fine. Let's get to it."

The two men laid five bombs across the expanse of the dirt floor. When that was done, the man with the bag took out two bottles, their tops tightly wrapped in layers of plastic and aluminum foil. He put the bottles on the floor, removed the wrappings, and pushed long rags into the necks.

"Are you ready?"

His partner nodded and took a lighter from his jeans pocket. They each picked up a bottle and walked towards the door. When they reached it, they lit the rags and then in unison threw the bottles as high and as far as they could. The bottles didn't explode when they landed on the floor, but as the men backed out of the building, they could see flames leap into the air and begin to spread.

They walked hurriedly back to their car, still the only people around. At the car, the man reached into his bag and took out a timer, put his thumb on the trigger, and pushed. The five bombs went off simultaneously, and they watched as most of the warehouse flew up and out into the night.

"We used more nitro than was needed," his partner said.

"Better to be safe than sorry."

Taipei, Taiwan

THE OVERWHELMING SOUND OF TANKS ROLLING DOWN
the street filled Ava Lee's ears. She couldn't see them, but
she knew they were there from the roar of their engines
and the clanking of their treads digging into concrete. She
stood behind the camera and sound operator as they cap-
tured the dark images and the noise. They were in a Taipei
neighbourhood that was substituting for Beijing, filming a
re-enactment of the events of June 4, 1989, when more than
200,000 People's Liberation Army soldiers marched into
Tiananmen Square to crush a mob of protestors demand-
ing reform in China. The film was to be called *Tiananmen*.

Despite knowing they were making a film, Ava felt a touch
of fear as she watched the tanks approach. *How horrible the
reality must have been*, she thought, and reached for the hand
of May Ling Wong, her close friend and business partner.

Lau Lau, the film's director, whispered directions to the
camera operator and then shouted to Pang Fai, one of the
film's stars and Ava's lover, "Fai, we're coming to you."

Fai stood partially hidden in the entranceway to a store with her back pressed against the wall, facing the approaching army. From her vantage point she had a clear view of the street. Protesters were being herded in her direction, some of them running, others stopping to shout and throw bricks and Molotov cocktails at the advancing soldiers. Their efforts were futile. Protestors were shot, falling dead on the street, and the tanks rolled over everything in their path. Fai raised a camera to her eye and began to take pictures of the carnage. Even from a distance, Ava could see her hands trembling.

As the lead tank drew close to Fai's position, Lau Lau shouted, "Cut," and the action came to a halt. Lau Lau walked towards Fai. He said a few words in her ear, then put his arms around her. They hugged, the diminutive director's head barely reaching her chin.

"There's nothing to that man," said May Ling. "He can't weigh more than a hundred and thirty pounds."

"You should have seen him before he went into rehab," Ava said. "He was even thinner, and his skin was waxy and pale."

"Lau Lau always loses weight when he's making a film he cares about," a man's voice said from behind them.

Ava turned to see that Chen Jie had joined them on the set. He was the film's producer, and until recently he had been the agent for both Lau Lau and Fai. Chen had sold his agency when he made the decision to produce *Tiananmen*. The man was in his early sixties, rotund and of medium height. He was always clean-shaven, kept his nails manicured and his steel-grey hair cropped close to the scalp, and was never seen in clothes that hadn't been ironed.

"Lau Lau is intense," Ava said. "When he was filming in Beijing, I thought his nerves were on edge because we didn't have approval from the government. Now I see it's just his natural state."

"It might have been a combination of both. We have to remember that he's not long out of rehab. It must be difficult for him to do this without falling into old habits," Chen said.

"What was it like filming in Beijing?" May Ling asked. She had been with them only since arriving in Taipei the day before from her home in Wuhan, in Hubei province.

"It was tricky," Chen said. "We were shooting exterior scenes surreptitiously in and around the Square, but Lau Lau found ways to slip Fai and Silvana in front of the camera. We were questioned only once by the police, and they bought our explanation that we were making a film to promote tourism. If they had known what we were really doing, we would likely be in jail today, and all our equipment and film would have been destroyed."

Ava knew from experience that no feature films could be made in China without the approval of the China Movie Syndicate, and it was inconceivable that the Syndicate would have approved *Tiananmen*. As far as the Chinese government was concerned, neither the protests nor the massacre at Tiananmen Square had occurred. All information about them had been removed from public records, and any mention of them was forbidden. In fact, Chen was convinced that if the government knew they were filming in Taiwan, it would still try to shut them down somehow.

Financing the film had been a risky move on the part of Ava, May Ling, and their third partner, Amanda Yee. If the Chinese government learned of their involvement, there was a justifiable fear that it might take action against their businesses in China. But, with the help of a lawyer in Hong

Kong, and using money that could not be traced back to them in any way, they had been able to establish a production company based in the U.K., its ownership hidden behind layers of lawyers.

The idea for the film had originated with Lau Lau, Pang Fai's ex-husband and once China's most respected film-maker. Ava knew and loved Lau Lau's work, but when she first met him in Beijing, he was a shell of a man, crippled by his addictions and certain that public knowledge of his sexuality would make him unemployable in the Chinese film industry. His pitiful situation had touched Ava, so she enlisted Chen's aid to get Lau Lau into rehab and commissioned him to write a film script. *Tiananmen* was the product of that agreement.

"Here comes Fai," May said to Ava.

In the film, Fai was playing the role of a general in the People's Liberation Army who opposes the use of armed soldiers to end the protests. When her arguments are ignored, she goes into the streets to record the events of June 4 for posterity. She returns the following day and meets the mother of a student protester who failed to come home the night before. The mother was being played by Silvana Foo, a Hong Kong actress known for her work in soap operas. Together the two women try to locate the son, and in the process they uncover the full, brutal extent of the atrocities.

In the scene they had just finished filming, Fai was wearing civilian clothes, jeans and a loose-fitting white blouse. Even dressed so simply, wearing no makeup and with her hair hanging loose around her shoulders, Ava thought she looked stunning. Fai was tall, about five foot ten, and willowy; she moved with a languid grace. Ava considered her acting equally graceful. It was understated and nuanced, raw emotions expressed by the slight quiver of a lip or a fleeting glance from eyes that hinted at latent tears.

"You looked genuinely frightened when the tanks approached," Ava said to her as they hugged.

"I was. Those tanks are scary. Can you imagine what it must have been like for those unarmed people as thousands of soldiers were coming at them?"

"I hope this doesn't mean you won't be able to enjoy dinner tonight," said Chen, moving alongside them. "I had to make this reservation over a month ago. I don't know how many Michelin three-star restaurants there are in Taipei, but Le Palais is supposed to be spectacular."

"What time is the reservation?" Fai asked.

"It's for ten o'clock. If you join us we'll be six people: you, Ava, May Ling, Silvana, and me."

"No Lau Lau?" May asked.

"I invited him but he declined. He plans to spend most of the evening going over today's footage and planning tomorrow's shoot. If he eats, it will likely be instant noodles or some street food," Chen said.

May Ling glanced at her watch. "It's just past eight now. I'd like to go back to the hotel and freshen up before dinner."

"The restaurant is close to the hotel. Why don't we head back to the Mandarin and reconvene in the lobby at quarter to ten," Chen said.

"Perfect," Ava said.

"I'll call for the driver."

Five minutes later they were all bundled into a Toyota SUV and heading for the Mandarin Oriental Hotel in downtown Taipei.

"I've never been on a film set before. Is it always so chaotic?" May Ling asked Fai.

"It just looks that way. In reality, it's well organized. Lau Lau has surrounded himself with some very capable people. We should thank Chen for arranging that. They don't come cheap, but on the technical side of the film industry, you generally get what you pay for."

"And in case you're wondering, we're still within budget," Chen said to Ava with a smile.

"Even after leasing all those tanks and employing hundreds of extras?" May asked.

"We can thank the Taiwanese government for the tanks — and they're not charging us," said Chen. "And many of the extras are soldiers in the Taiwanese army. Again, the government was very generous."

"They must like the idea of supporting a project that will cause Beijing distress," Ava said.

"That sentiment was certainly conveyed, if not in those exact words," said Chen.

The Mandarin Oriental appeared in the distance, and a moment later the Toyota stopped at the entrance.

"I'm going to the business centre, but I'll meet you back here in an hour," Chen said as they walked into the lobby.

Ava, May Ling, and Fai got into the elevator together. They had suites on the same floor, and when they exited, May said, "If you two get changed fast enough, come to my suite for a drink."

"What are you going to wear?" Ava asked.

"For a Michelin three-star restaurant, I think a Chanel suit will be perfect."

"I brought the little black dress Clark made for me," Ava

said, referring to Clark Po, the creative genius behind the
PÖ fashion line, which was partly owned by the women's
investment company, Three Sisters.

"You two are going to make me feel like the ugly duckling,"
Fai said. "All I have with me is a couple of sundresses."

May looked at Ava and they both began to laugh. "You
could wear a rice bag and still look better than us," May said.

Fai smiled. "I just hate to feel underdressed, especially
when Chen has gone to such trouble booking the restaurant.
He's been talking about it since we were in Beijing. He had
to pre-order the barbecue pork and crispy duck days ago."

"Then we'd better be dressed smartly enough to do the
food credit," Ava said. "I suggest we get started."

2

THE THREE WOMEN MET CHEN AND SILVANA FOO IN THE lobby at quarter to ten. Silvana hadn't been on set that day, and May hadn't met her the night before when she arrived in Taipei. Chen introduced them to each other.

"It's such a thrill to meet you," May said. "I've seen you so often on television and read so much about you that I feel I know you already."

Silvana, who was short and somewhat plump, had made a career of playing doughty mothers and aunts. Her personal life, though, wasn't anywhere near as ordinary; she was often featured in the Hong Kong tabloids, usually connected to a variety of men. "Don't believe everything you read," she said to May with a wink.

"But I want to! I admire women who take charge of their lives and don't give a damn what anyone else thinks," May said.

Silvana grinned and turned to Chen. "I like this one already. How did you get lucky enough to surround yourself with so many smart women?"

"I have good taste," Chen said, grinning as well. "Now we should get going."

The Toyota was waiting for them outside. Chen sat in front with the driver while the four women squeezed into the back. Ten minutes later they arrived at the Palais de Chine Hotel, which housed Le Palais restaurant. When she got out of the car, Ava found herself looking at a building that seemed slightly contradictory. The front was a stark unbroken façade of windows and steel, while the revolving door leading into the lobby was made of intricately carved wood. Above the door was a massive bright red sign with the hotel's name written in gold letters in both English and Chinese.

Chen led them inside, and when they reached the lobby, the contradictions intensified. The lobby was a riot of colours, with huge painted urns filled with flowers and wildly decorated carpets. One wall was covered in gold silk shot through with streaks of silver. In the middle of the lobby was a collection of cushioned chairs and loveseats that Ava thought looked out of place.

"This is spectacular," May said.

"It's certainly different," said Ava.

"Palais de Chine has a style all its own. When I was here with a friend a few years ago, he told me it was rococo, but I think it pays homage to several eras of interior design," Chen said.

The lobby was busy, and as Ava and the others stood taking in the decor, she noticed they had attracted the attention of a group of women. "I think Silvana and Fai have been recognized," she said.

"Let's get into the elevator before they descend on us," said Chen.

The restaurant Le Palais was on the seventeenth floor of

the hotel, and as they approached the entrance, Ava saw that its decor was faithful to the mix of styles they'd seen in the lobby. They walked past a gigantic ceramic pot infused with subtle hues of light blue towards a minimalist glass entrance framed with black steel posts.

Chen gave his name to the host and said, "I was told I'd be put on the waiting list for one of the private dining rooms. Was I fortunate enough to get one?"

The host shook his head. "I'm sorry, sir. It's rare for anyone to cancel a reservation."

"Then seat us wherever you can, please," said Chen.

Their table was in the farthest corner of the restaurant from the entrance, and as they followed the host past packed tables, Ava saw many eyes turn their way. May Ling wore a pink Chanel suit trimmed in blue and had raided her jewellery box for diamond earrings, white jade bracelets, and a pearl-and-diamond necklace. Silvana wore a Mao-style jacket over a pair of black silk trousers, but the jacket — red silk shot with gold and fastened with pearl buttons — was unlike anything Chairman Mao's wife would have worn. Ava had on the black dress that Clark Po had made for her when they launched the fashion line in Shanghai. She seldom wore dresses, but this one was special. Clark had designed it to show off her curves, and whenever she wore it, Ava felt especially sexy. Fai was the most plainly dressed of the four, but in a powder-blue sundress and flat shoes, with her hair pulled back and fixed with a gold chignon pin, she outshone them all.

They sat down on padded chairs with ornate wooden arms and legs.

"Are you going to order for us?" Fai asked Chen.

"Only if no one objects," he said. "I had to pre-order the barbecued pork and crispy roast baby duck in advance, so I'm afraid you're stuck with those."

"You are a cruel man," Silvana said with a smile.

She's flirting with him, Ava thought. *I can't wait to see how this plays out.*

"How about I start by ordering drinks. Is everyone going to have wine?"

They agreed on white. When their server arrived, Chen ordered two bottles of a French Chardonnay, then said, "I pre-ordered the barbecued pork and crispy baby duck. We'll also have the braised sea cucumber and abalone, vinegar-marinated jellyfish, two ghost crabs, stir-fried prawns with ginger and scallions, and the stir-fried lily buds with wood-ear mushrooms. We'll start with the sea cucumber and jellyfish."

"Excellent choices, sir," the server said. "I'll be back in a few minutes with the wine."

When the server left, Silvana leaned towards Chen. "Tell me, have you ever heard a server say that your choices were terrible and an embarrassment to good taste?"

Chen laughed. "Why have we never met before this film?"

"I guess fate decided to wait until now," Silvana said.

Ava felt Fai kick her under the table. "I know," she said under her breath.

After the wine was poured and several toasts had been made, the food began to arrive. They were just starting to eat when Ava's phone rang. She saw Amanda Yee's name on the screen and felt a touch of anxiety. Amanda knew about their dinner plans, and it wasn't like her to interrupt.

"Hey, is everything all right?" Ava asked quietly.

"No, it's the furthest thing from all right," Amanda said in a rush. "I'm so glad I was able to reach you."

"Slow down," Ava said, rising from her chair. "I'm in a noisy restaurant, so I'm going to move to a quieter spot. Give me a minute."

What's up? May mouthed.

"It's Amanda," said Ava. She left the restaurant and found a suitable alcove. "Now I can concentrate. Tell me what's happened."

"There's a problem in Borneo," Amanda said, her distress obvious.

"In Kota Kinabalu?" Ava asked.

"No, in Sarawak, in Kuching, at our new warehouse," said Amanda. "Or rather, what *was* our new warehouse. It burned down tonight. There's nothing left of it."

"What? How?"

"I don't know. I just spoke to Chi-Tze, who heard from Aisyah. It happened about an hour ago."

"Was anyone hurt?"

"Yes," Amanda said, and then fell silent for a few seconds. "Jamilah Daeng was working in her office, which is attached to the warehouse. She's been taken to the hospital, but we're still waiting for news of her condition."

"Jamilah was hired by Aisyah to manage the warehouse, yes?" Ava asked. Aisyah Tengku managed all their operations in Borneo. Several years before, Three Sisters had purchased a furniture business in Borneo, near Kota Kinabalu in the state of Sabah, from Chi-Tze and her siblings. Chi-Tze had gone to business school in the U.S. with Amanda and was now managing the PÖ fashion business in Shanghai.

"Yes, she's an old friend of both Aisyah and Chi-Tze."

"Does Aisyah have any idea how it occurred?"

"No, but she's getting ready to travel to Kuching. She'll get there early tomorrow morning. Maybe by then some information will be available."

"Is there anything we can do to help?" Ava asked.

Amanda hesitated. "No, but Chi-Tze wants to go there to do what she can. I was reluctant to say yes, but she told me her brother Mamat lives in Kuching and has some excellent contacts there. She's already reached out to him and he's eager to help."

"That's a surprise. When we had all that trouble in Kota Kinabalu, Mamat was completely useless. As I remember it, he and his brother Tambi basically abandoned Chi-Tze," said Ava.

"Well, a few years have passed since then. Chi-Tze's sister, Ah-Pei, and the two brothers are all the family she has left. There's been a reconciliation of sorts with the brothers, but of course not with the sister."

"Where is Ah-Pei?" Ava asked.

"I've never asked Chi-Tze. I thought it better not to reopen old wounds."

"That was wise," Ava said. "And when it comes to Borneo, there are a lot of old wounds."

The Three Sisters' furniture business in Kota Kinabalu had run into problems when Ah-Pei conspired with a Dutchman to bleed the company dry. Amanda had gone to Borneo to try to keep the business intact, but soon after her arrival, she and Chi-Tze were attacked and badly beaten by men hired by Ah-Pei. Amanda still bore a scar over her right eye as a reminder. Ava had flown in to help and was abducted and abused by the same men. Only a violent intervention by Ava's triad friends had saved her. It had been an experience that made Ava feel nauseated whenever she thought of it.

"I certainly haven't forgotten mine," said Amanda. "But Chi-Tze wants to join Mamat and Aisyah in Kuching as soon as she can."

"I don't like the idea."

"Me neither, but she's insistent. And remember, she still owns a minority share in the furniture business, so she has a stake in this."

"I guess, if she's with Mamat, she'll be safe enough, but it still makes me nervous."

The line went quiet. Ava was wondering if their conversation was about to end when Amanda said abruptly, "I think I should go to Kuching as well."

"No," Ava said instantly.

"I knew that's how you'd react," said Amanda. "But that's you treating me like your *da sou,* not your business partner. I'm responsible for that company. Aisyah reports to me. She needs support, as does Chi-Tze, and I'm the first person they should be getting it from."

Ava knew Amanda was right, but she found it emotionally difficult to accept. She loved Amanda like a sister, and in all the years they'd known each other they had never had so much as a minor falling-out. *This isn't the time to start,* Ava decided. "When would you leave?" she asked.

"Thank you for understanding how I feel — I didn't want to argue with you," Amanda said. "I'll be leaving tomorrow morning. I'll have to go through Kuala Lumpur, and I'll be in transit for about twenty-four hours."

"Send me your itinerary and contact me whenever you hear something about Jamilah or the situation in Kuching.

I don't care what time it is," said Ava. "And Amanda, you and Chi-Tze should stay in the background. Let Mamat get out front and be helpful for once."

"We'll be careful."

Ava sighed. "I'm having dinner with May and some people from the film. I think I'll hold on to this information until May and I have some privacy. Safe travels, and give Michael a hug from me."

3

AVA COULD SEE MAY LING EYEING HER AS SHE WALKED back to the table. "There was a business issue in Borneo that Amanda wanted to discuss," she said before May could ask. "She's handling it."

May looked at her questioningly but said nothing.

"What kind of business can you have in a place like that?" Silvana asked.

"We own a furniture manufacturing company in Kota Kinabalu, in the state of Sabah," said Ava. "The warehouse is in Kuching, in the state of Sarawak."

"I've never heard of any of those places," said Silvana.

"I hadn't either until I had a reason," Ava said. "Sabah is one of two Malaysian states on the northern side of the island. The other is Sarawak. Between them is Brunei, which is an independent sultanate. The southern portion of Borneo is an Indonesian territory called Kalimantan."

"Do you go there often?" Silvana asked.

"As little as possible," Ava said.

"Why's that?"

"It isn't an easy place to get to. Besides, we have capable

employees on the ground, and the last thing they need is us looking over their shoulders," May interrupted, and then nodded at the platter being placed on the table. "I hope that pork tastes as good as it smells."

It did. In fact, the entire meal was fabulous, rivalling anything Ava had eaten before in Taipei. Despite the food, however, she couldn't stop worrying about what was going on in Borneo. She kept looking at her phone for texts or missed calls.

When dinner ended, they headed back to the Mandarin, the four women again squeezing into the back seat of the Toyota. As the SUV pulled away from the Palais de Chine, Chen turned towards them. "Can I interest any of you ladies in a nightcap when we get back to the hotel?"

"Truthfully, I'm rather tired, and Ava has promised me a full day of sightseeing tomorrow, so I'm going to call it a night," May said.

"Me too," said Ava.

"I have to be on set and ready to work by eight, so no more alcohol for me," Fai said.

"I don't have to be on set until noon," Silvana said. "I'll join you."

"Wonderful."

Fai elbowed Ava, who under different circumstances would have laughed.

When they reached the hotel, Chen and Silvana said their goodnights and headed to the bar. Ava, May, and Fai got into an elevator. As the doors closed, Ava said to May, "Why don't you join me in our suite for a drink while I tell you about Borneo."

"Is it the kind of problem that requires a drink?"

"It sounds like it."

The elevator stopped and they walked silently to the suite. "I think I'll shower now and get ready for bed," said Fai.

"We're not going to discuss anything you can't hear," Ava said.

"I know, but I do have to be up early. You can fill me in later."

"I won't stay long," May said.

"Don't rush away on my account. I suspect you have lots to discuss."

Ava poured cognacs from the mini bar for May and herself.

"So, what happened in Borneo?" May asked as Ava sat down next to her.

"The new warehouse and distribution centre we built in Kuching burned down a few hours ago."

May flinched. "What happened?"

"Amanda couldn't say, but I'm not ready to rule out anything."

"Was anyone hurt?"

"Jamilah Daeng, who manages the operation, was in her office when it happened. She's been taken to a hospital, but that's all Amanda knows. Aisyah will be in Kuching in the morning, and both Chi-Tze and Amanda are joining her."

"Is it necessary for all of them to be there?"

"They all have their own reasons for going. I tried to talk Amanda out of it, but she's determined."

May finished her cognac. "Is there another one in the mini-bar?" she asked.

"Yes, I'll get it," said Ava.

"I wish we hadn't bought into that furniture business,"

May said as Ava poured her a second glass. "It's caused us more trouble than all our other investments combined."

"It was Amanda's recommendation. Her friendship with Chi-Tze, going back to their university days in the U.S., contributed to the decision, but the numbers made sense. I thought it was a good decision at the time, and after we got that nonsense with Ah-Pei sorted out, the business has been a solid earner."

Ava's phone rang. She took it from her LV bag and glanced at the screen. "Speaking of Amanda…" she said as she put the phone on speaker mode and placed it on the table. "Hey, I'm here with May. We're on speaker. I've just finished telling her about Borneo."

"And I just finished speaking with Aisyah. She's really shaken."

"Has she heard anything about Jamilah?"

"Yes, and it's bad," Amanda said, her voice trembling. "She has burns covering much of her body, but it seems her face was spared. Aisyah says we should be thankful she's alive. According to the fire official she spoke to, there isn't much left of the warehouse or the office. Those structures weren't built to survive a strong explosion."

May's face paled and she reached for Ava's hand. "Did you say *explosion*?"

"The official said it looks like we were bombed, but they didn't give Aisyah any further details. That will take another day or two to figure out."

"Are the police involved?" Ava asked.

"Yes, but Aisyah wasn't able to speak with them. She tried, but no one has returned her call, so Chi-Tze has asked Mamat to see what he can find out. He has a friend in Kuching who is a lawyer with strong police connections. Kuching is a small place; everyone in legal circles seems to be connected in one way or another."

"If we've been bombed, that means it was deliberate. Why would someone attack our warehouse?" May asked.

"Aisyah doesn't know, although she did say some local businesspeople have expressed their displeasure that we're selling imported lumber at a lower price than the local supplier. But that's just business, right? I can't believe that would drive anyone to violence," said Amanda. "Maybe by the time Chi-Tze and I get there, things will be clearer. I'm already at Chek Lap Kok. I managed to book an early morning flight to Kuala Lumpur with a connection to Kuching. I'll be there in time for a late lunch. Chi-Tze is doing the same from Shanghai."

Ava sighed. "We're worried about you. You need to be careful, Amanda, especially if someone is targeting our businesses."

"I know, and I appreciate that. But you and May made me a partner because you trusted me to run the business. Now you have to stand back and let me do my job."

"I can't argue with that, but I'll still worry. Be careful," Ava said.

"Who were you telling to be careful?" Fai asked as she emerged from the bathroom.

"Amanda. She's flying to Borneo to deal with our problem."

Fai sat down next to Ava. "If you're telling her to be careful, I think it's time you filled me in on what that problem is."

THE IDEA HAD BEEN FOR AVA AND FAI TO WAKE UP AT six-thirty so they would have time for breakfast together before Fai caught her ride to the set at seven-thirty. That plan fell apart when Ava woke to find Fai staring into her eyes.

"Is something wrong?" Ava asked.

"Just the opposite — I dreamt about us. We were making love," Fai said, offering her lips for a kiss.

Half an hour later they were disentangling. "I enjoy everything about sex in the morning, except when it makes me late for the rest of the day," Fai said as she slid from the bed. "Now I have to rush my shower if I'm going to catch that ride."

Ava stayed in bed, her face turned towards Fai's pillow. She breathed deeply, taking in the smell of her lover. *I have never been so happy*, she thought, and then felt a slight shiver. Ava had always held the power in every relationship she'd been in. How would she handle it if Fai left her? "Don't even think it," she muttered to herself.

When Fai emerged from the bathroom, Ava joined her in the sitting room. They made coffee and sat looking out at the street below.

"It's going to be a long day for me. The shoot will go until nine tonight," Fai said. "I'm glad you're spending the day with May. I know you'll both be thinking about Borneo, so having each other's company will be a distraction. Besides, being on set for that long would be the ultimate bore for you."

"I would have managed on my own, but I am glad she's here. We don't see each other as often as I'd like. The demands on her in Wuhan never let up. Taking even two days away can be difficult."

"What are you going to do today?"

"There are a couple of decent museums, and the Taiwanese are fond of memorial halls. There's one for Sun Yat-sen and another for Chiang Kai-shek. Also, May is Taoist and might like to visit the Longshan Temple. If none of those options appeal to her, we can always just go shopping."

"The girls on set were talking about the night markets here. They recommended Shilin and Raohe. Apparently, the Raohe market also has lots of good food options."

"A night market might interest her, and she's never been a snob about food. Going from a Michelin three-star restaurant one night to night-market food the next shouldn't be an issue."

"If you like the market, we'll go back there together after May leaves," said Fai.

"It's a date."

Fai checked her phone for the time. "I should get going. Lau Lau is very punctual these days — which is a lovely change. I remember back when he was starting to decline. There were days when he wouldn't even make it to set."

"Text me if your plans change," Ava said.

As Fai left the suite, Ava thought about her morning. She

had arranged to meet May at Café Un Deux Trois in the hotel at nine-thirty, which gave her some spare time. She used an hour of it for a leisurely shower and two more coffees before sitting down at her laptop. She found a website that gave her access to virtually every English-language newspaper in the world. To her surprise, eight were identified as Malaysian, one of which was the *Sarawak Daily Journal*. Ava selected that day's edition and found a two-paragraph mention of the warehouse fire in Kuching. There was no mention of a bomb or anyone being hurt. The story ended with THE SARAWAK POLICE ARE IN THE EARLY STAGES OF THEIR INVESTIGATION.

Ava thought about phoning Amanda but remembered she'd still be in transit. Instead she opened her email. She had been away from her home in Toronto for six weeks, three weeks in Beijing and now three weeks in Taipei. It was the longest continuous time she had been absent from Canada. She loved being with Fai, and spending time on the set had been fascinating, but she was starting to miss the people back home, particularly her mother.

Marcus Lee, Ava's father, had taken three wives. Ava's mother, Jennie, was the second. Marcus had four sons with his first wife, Elizabeth, the oldest of whom was Michael, Amanda's husband, and a son and daughter with the third. Ava had met all her half-brothers from the first marriage but none of the Australia-based children from the third.

Jennie and Marcus had met and married in Hong Kong, but their relationship soon turned contentious, and Jennie and her two daughters — Ava and her older sister, Marian — were sent to live in Canada. They originally settled in Vancouver, but Jennie despised the weather, so they relocated to Richmond Hill, a city north of Toronto with a large Chinese-Canadian population.

Marcus continued to provide for the family, spoke to Jennie every day by phone, and visited her for at least two weeks every year. Although he was an infrequent physical presence in their lives, as far as Ava and Marian were concerned, he was their father in every other way. As Ava grew older, she and Marcus became especially close. In her former career as a debt collector, she had even helped Michael — and, by extension, the rest of the first family — weather a financial crisis. That event had brought Ava into contact with Amanda, and their friendship quickly developed to the point where Ava was asked to be maid of honour at Michael and Amanda's wedding. Within the first wife's family it caused a minor controversy, which abated only after Elizabeth Lee thanked Ava at the wedding dinner for the help she had given the family.

As complicated as her family structure seemed to some outsiders, to Ava it was completely normal. She had never felt deprived of love, attention, or support, and Jennie Lee was the main provider. Fiercely proud of her daughters, Jennie had pushed them to succeed. She had also ensured that Marcus made money available for a multitude of extra-curricular activities, private schools, and later university. Marian had earned a law degree but, to Jennie's mild disappointment, became a stay-at-home mother. Ava had several accounting degrees, including one in forensic accounting from Babson College in Massachusetts that had served her well during her debt-collection days.

Jennie hadn't worked since arriving in Canada. Raising her two daughters had been her priority, and once they were grown, her daily life began to revolve around a wide network of friends — many of whom were second or third wives like her — and endless games of mah-jong and trips to the casino.

Ava looked at the time. It was almost eight-thirty, which meant it was the middle of the evening in Toronto. She expected her mother would be playing mah-jong but tried her phone anyway. It went to voicemail. "Mummy, this is Ava calling. I'm still in Taipei. The film is coming along very well. Everyone is full of hope that it will be a success. I'll try to call back when it's late morning in Toronto. I love you and I'm missing you."

She had no sooner put down her phone when it rang.

"Good morning," May said.

"I thought we were meeting at nine-thirty," said Ava.

"I couldn't sleep. I kept thinking about the fire."

"It's been on my mind as well. I was just searching the internet and found a small article in the *Sarawak Daily Journal*."

"What does it say?"

"There's no mention of a bomb or anyone being hurt. It says the police are investigating, but nothing more."

"Maybe the police are withholding information until they figure out what happened."

"That's possible. But there's no reason not to disclose the fact that Jamilah was injured. Surely someone getting caught in an exploding building isn't an everyday occurrence in Kuching."

"So what now?"

"I'm going to text Amanda to tell her about the story. Maybe Mamat's contact can find out what the police are saying. Also, I'm sure Amanda and Chi-Tze will be able to find out more once they arrive."

May sighed. "That was another reason I couldn't sleep. I'm worried about them. I know I said we should let them go, but the idea of a bomb and Jamilah's situation was nagging at me all night."

"We're drawing conclusions from limited information. Let's give the girls a chance to get some real facts," Ava said.

"I know you're right," May said with another sigh. "When will you be ready for breakfast?"

"I'm ready now. Knock on my door when you get here."

A few minutes later they rode the elevator down to the ground floor. The café was designed in a contemporary style, with a high ceiling and plenty of windows and mirrors, and furnished with white acrylic tables and white chairs. Various paintings, sculptures, and ceramic pots and bowls were scattered throughout. A rhino head hanging on one wall had jarred Ava during her first visit, and she asked to be placed so she didn't have to look at it.

The café wasn't busy, and Ava and May were quickly seated. The menu was international. During her stay Ava had tried traditional Western dishes as well as Japanese, Taiwanese, and Chinese cuisine. The Chinese dim sum selection was limited but the quality was superb. She recommended it to May, and they ordered double servings of har gow, siu mai, and a vegetable-mushroom dumpling.

They drank copious amounts of coffee as they slowly worked their way through the dim sum. The conversation was comfortable and intimate. Ava felt blessed with the friends she had. They were intensely loyal and supportive, but May was possibly the most loyal of them all; on several occasions she had risked her personal safety to help Ava. They didn't have many secrets between them, but there was one subject Ava felt uncomfortable talking to her about, and that was Xu, the leader of the triad gang in Shanghai.

Ava's partner and mentor in the debt-collection business had been an elderly Hong Konger whom everyone called Uncle. He and Ava were like family. When she was working for him, she had heard rumours about Uncle's triad past, and gradually she learned he had been a Mountain Master — the leader of a gang — and had served as chairman of the Hong Kong Triad Societies. What she didn't know until he died was that for many years Uncle had been mentoring Xu, who was the son of one of his oldest friends. That friend had been the Mountain Master in Shanghai, a role Xu assumed when his father died.

After Uncle's death, Xu had made himself known to Ava and they had forged their own unique relationship. Now they were as close as brother and sister, and in fact he often referred to her as his *mei mei*, which meant "little sister," and she called him *ge ge*, "big brother."

May had met Xu several times, and Ava couldn't help but notice that they were attracted to each other. But May was married to Wong Changxing, the wealthiest man in Hubei province. They were childless, and Ava knew they were as much business partners as husband and wife. Xu had never married, but Ava's fear that Xu and May might one day take their feelings beyond casual flirting had nothing to do with their marital status. Rather, it had everything to do with friendship. She dreaded the idea of their getting into a relationship because she was worried about what would happen if it turned out badly. The last thing she wanted was to have to choose one friend over the other. Her way of preventing that was to keep them apart as much as possible and not discuss them with each other.

So when May asked "How is Xu? Has he recovered from that bout of meningitis?" Ava hesitated before replying.

"He still has some bad days, but he's well looked after."

May nodded. "Changxing has a business meeting in Shanghai next month. He wants me to go with him. I was thinking I could see Xu if I did."

"Truthfully, May, he's not really seeing visitors right now. He conducts most of his business by phone, and Auntie Grace tries to limit even that to a few hours a day." Auntie Grace was Xu's former nanny, now his housekeeper. Ava felt a touch of guilt for exaggerating his condition and invoking her name.

"If that's the case, I won't bother going. The air there is horrid anyway."

"Next time we speak, I'll tell Xu you asked about him," Ava said.

"Please do. And tell him how much we wish for his good health."

"I will, May, and I know he'll appreciate it."

May turned to look out the window. "It looks like it's going to be a lovely day. What do you have in mind for us?"

Ava repeated the options she'd discussed with Fai.

"I like the idea of going to Longshan Temple," May said. "I often think about going to the temple in Wuhan, but something always seems to interfere."

"Then we'll start there."

"I don't want to go to the memorial halls, though. I have no interest in Sun Yat-sen or Chiang Kai-shek."

"That's fine —" Ava was starting to say when her phone rang. She took it from her bag. "Hi, Fai. Is everything all right?"

"No. Lau Lau has been trying to reach Chen, but he isn't answering his phone."

"Why does he need Chen?"

"Some local gangsters showed up on set. They told Lau Lau he can't keep filming without security, and that they're here to provide it. They want thirty thousand new Taiwan dollars a day."

"I thought we already had security people."

"Ava, they're a couple of old men who look like they're doing the work for extra retirement income," Fai said. "Besides, the gangsters ran them off."

"What does Lau Lau want Chen to do?"

"I don't know, but he'd better do something, because Lau Lau is getting more anxious by the minute. The last thing we need is for him to lose focus."

"How many of them are there?"

"Four."

"Okay, I'll try to reach Chen. If I can't get him, May and I will come to the set."

"What's going on?" May asked as Ava ended the call.

"There's trouble on set. Some local gangsters are trying to extort protection money from Lau Lau," said Ava. "He's been trying to reach Chen."

"He's probably still with Silvana."

"That would be my guess, and I really don't feel like interfering in their romantic arrangement right now. I think we should just go to the set. There's an ATM in the lobby. I'll stop on the way out."

THE FIRST THING AVA NOTICED WHEN THE TAXI ARRIVED
at the set was Lau Lau sitting on a canvas chair talking to
his cameraman. Even from a distance she could see he was
agitated. One of his feet kept bouncing up and down, and he
pointed repeatedly towards the camera. When Ava looked
in that direction, she saw four men gathered around it.

Fai rushed towards them. "I was hoping you'd find Chen,"
she said.

"I didn't bother," Ava said. "You can let Lau Lau know that
I'll get this sorted out. I'll talk to those guys myself."

"Ava!"

"Please, it will be easier this way," Ava said, and she began
to walk towards the four men. They were all dressed in jeans,
running shoes, and a variety of T-shirts. Two were heav-
ily tattooed, one had a modified mohawk haircut, and the
fourth had a shaved head.

"Which of you is the boss here?" Ava asked.

"Who wants to know?" the one with the shaved head
grunted.

Ava eyed him. He was short and thickset and scowling

at her. "I guess it's you, then," she said. "I brought the thirty thousand dollars. As soon as I give it to you, I want you to leave and not come back."

"Who are you to give us orders? We said thirty thousand a *day*. We'll be back tomorrow, and every day you're here."

"This is all you're going to get," Ava said, reaching into her LV bag and taking out the money.

"You aren't listening," he snarled.

"No, *you* aren't listening. This is all you're going to get," Ava said, offering the money.

"You bitch!" he shouted, and took two steps forward, one fist clenched and the other hand reaching for Ava's arm.

Ava moved quickly to one side. His hand grazed her arm, and before he could attempt anything else, she pivoted and drove the extended first knuckle of her right fist into his ear. He groaned and his knees buckled, but he didn't fall to the ground until Ava hit him again with even more force. The other men stood frozen to the spot, staring in disbelief. Before they could recover, Ava put her heel in the middle of the man's back, grabbed his arm, and twisted it so the palm was facing skyward.

"If any one of you takes so much as a step towards me, I'll snap his arm. And then I'll do the same to the other," she said.

"We won't move, okay? Just let him go," the one with mohawk said.

"We have to talk first," said Ava. "Are you triads?"

The man with the mohawk seemed surprised but nodded.

"Who is your Mountain Master?"

"Tsai," he said, showing even more surprise.

"If you phoned him right now, would he answer?"

"Probably not, but he'd pick up for Wang," he said, pointing to the man on the ground.

Ava looked down and saw Wang's phone sticking out of his back pocket. He was semiconscious and no threat, so she reached for the phone and tossed it to the other man. "Call Tsai, and when he answers, tell him the *mei mei* of Xu, the Mountain Master of Shanghai, wants to talk to him."

The man looked doubtful.

"Do it, or I'll give this arm an extra twist," she said.

He tapped the phone twice and held it to his ear. Seconds later, he repeated what Ava had instructed him to say. He listened and then said, "He can't talk. She has him on the ground and she's threatening to break his arms." After a short wait he took a couple of steps towards Ava with the phone extended. "The boss wants to speak to you," he said.

"This is Ava Lee," she said.

"What do you think you're doing?" Tsai asked gruffly.

"I'm the *mei mei* of Xu in Shanghai. If you have any doubts about that, call him."

"I know Xu, and I've heard stories about his *mei mei*. But that doesn't answer my question. What are you doing?"

"Your forty-niners came to this movie set to extort protection money from the director. My partners and I are financing the film, which means they're trying to extort money from me."

There was a pause. "We didn't know you were involved."

"I know, but now you do."

"Ava," a familiar voice said behind her.

She turned and saw that Chen had arrived and was standing with Fai and May. "Wait one minute, please," she said to Tsai, and pressed the phone against her leg. "Chen, the men you hired from the security company ran away as soon as these guys showed up. What were you paying the company?"

"Twenty thousand NT dollars a day."

"Thanks," Ava said and put the phone back to her ear. "I have a proposal for you. The film could use some real security. Can you keep two men posted here for as long as they're needed? We'll pay you twenty thousand a day."

"Yeah, I could do that. And that way there'll be no hard feelings."

"Thank you for being reasonable, Tsai. Now I'll pass the phone back to your man. After you've explained the deal, I'll let Wang go."

A moment later the mohawked man nodded at Ava. "Okay, we understand what we're supposed to do."

"Good," Ava said, and released her grip on Wang's arm. He groaned and rolled over onto his back. "You'll be unsteady on your feet for a while, but it will pass," she told him. "I just spoke to Tsai and we've worked out an arrangement. Your friends can explain it to you."

The other two men helped him to his feet. Wang wobbled, and the men grabbed his arms to steady him.

"Do you see the man in the grey suit and the man sitting on the chair over there?" Ava asked, pointing at Chen and Lau Lau. "Whatever they tell you to do, you do it."

Wang looked questioningly at the man with the mohawk, who said, "Tsai said to do whatever she says."

"You are now officially hired as security on this film. I don't mind paying you if you work for it," said Ava. Then she smiled and walked over to Lau Lau, where she was quickly joined by Chen, Fai, and May.

"In case you didn't hear, I've hired these men as your new

security team. They'll do whatever you and Chen tell them," she said to Lau Lau, then turned to Chen. "Fire that other outfit. We don't need security guards who run away at the first sign of trouble."

Lau Lau looked up at Ava and shook his head gently. "That was amazing."

"No, it was bak mei. Luckily I have a mother who believes her daughter should know how to defend herself."

"I've seen her do much worse," May said.

Ava smiled at her. "Why don't you and I get out of here and let these people get back to work."

AT SIX O'CLOCK AVA AND MAY WERE SITTING AT THE central island of the art deco M.O. Bar in the Mandarin. It was happy hour, but since they intended to eat at the Raohe Street Night Market, they were trying to be careful about how much they drank. Still, May was on her second gin martini and Ava her second glass of Chardonnay.

After the hectic morning on the film set, the rest of the day had been uneventful. First they had spent an hour at the Longshan Temple, where they said prayers for Jamilah. Ava had been raised Roman Catholic, but the Church's position on sexual orientation had turned her away. She still retained vestiges of her upbringing, though, and during times of stress she would often pray to Saint Jude, the patron saint of lost causes. But if asked to define her religious beliefs, Ava would say she had more in common with Buddhist or Taoist views of the world and beyond.

After Longshan they went to the Bopiliao historic area, a walking street only a block from the temple. It was a restored version of a Qing Dynasty street and featured work by local artists. Ava had no eye for art, but May did, and she bought two small paintings that she arranged to send directly to Wuhan. They lunched at Din Tai Fung, a restaurant recommended by the hotel concierge. It was famous for its soup dumplings, and as Ava dipped her last *xiao long bao* into a concoction of soy sauce, vinegar, and ginger, she thought the reputation well deserved.

Given options for what to do after lunch, May chose to shop. By the time they returned to the hotel in the late afternoon, she had three bags containing clothes and shoes in each hand. Ava found shopping boring but she enjoyed May's company, and the afternoon had gone well enough. During their visits to the shops, May had asked several staff members where they could find the best local food. The Raohe Night Market was always suggested, and when May showed an interest, the salespeople would mention some of the more famous street vendors and their specialties. Ava wasn't sure that spicy stinky tofu, beef ribs stewed in herbal medicine, or black pepper meat buns would be her thing, but she was willing to give them a try.

When they returned to the hotel, they went to their rooms to freshen up and get ready for the evening. The night market was only four kilometres from the hotel, and Ava had persuaded May to walk there. Given the dress code of the bar, Ava couldn't wear her Adidas jacket or pants, but she did put on her running shoes. May didn't own running shoes, so she wore Gucci leather loafers.

During the day, Ava and May had been checking their phones continually for messages. Amanda had texted twice, once to say she had safely arrived in Kuching, and then a second time to say she had met up with Chi-Tze and they were staying at the Riverside Majestic Hotel. She promised to call later, after they had spoken to Mamat and Aisyah.

"I'm always suspicious of a hotel that describes itself as majestic," Ava had said to May when she got the second text.

They finished their second drinks at M.O., slid down from the bar stools, and were starting towards the lobby when Ava's phone sounded. "It's Amanda," she said to May, and switched to speakerphone. "Hey, we got your texts. Glad you got there safely. How is it going?"

"I'm not sure. It's all very confusing," Amanda said.

"How is Jamilah?"

"That's part of the confusion. The hospital isn't allowing visitors, and they wouldn't give Aisyah any information about Jamilah because she's not immediate family," Amanda said. "Aisyah has been trying to reach the family, but they live in a village several hundred kilometres from Kuching and don't have a phone. She finally convinced the local police to contact them, but she still hasn't heard back."

"What else?"

"Mamat met with his contact this afternoon and was told that the police will be releasing a statement tomorrow morning. They've decided the fire was caused by a bomb that was deliberately set. There may also have been an incendiary device. A group called the Sarawak United Front has supposedly claimed responsibility."

"Who are they?"

"According to the police, they're a radical environmental group opposed to logging activity in Indigenous people's traditional territories, a lot of which is rainforest. Aisyah says that's crazy."

"Which part?" asked Ava.

"All of it. To begin with, our company here and in Kota

Kinabalu has been a leader in opposing that kind of logging. We've refused to buy timber that comes from rainforests, and that's why we've been importing and selling foreign timber in Sarawak and Sabah," Amanda said. "On top of that, Aisyah tells me that Jamilah is an active member of Friends of the Earth, an environmental group in Borneo, and has a good reputation with the other environmental groups here. Our company would be the last place targeted by radical environmentalists."

"Why did you say they 'supposedly' claimed responsibility?" asked Ava.

"Because we're not sure they actually exist," said Amanda. "Aisyah has never heard of them, and she insists she knows every environmental group in Borneo. She also spent the past hour calling friends who are involved with the movement, and none of them have heard of this Sarawak United Front either."

"That is strange. Maybe when we can talk to Jamilah, she can shed more light on the situation."

"Just a minute," Amanda said suddenly. "It sounds like Mamat is at the door. Chi-Tze has gone to let him in."

"What do you think of all this?" Ava whispered to May.

"I don't like the sound of it."

"I wonder if I should go to Kuching."

"It's something to consider," May said.

There was a scream from the phone. "What the hell was that?" Ava said. "Amanda, are you still there?"

There was a long pause. Then Amanda said, "I'm here. I just wish I wasn't."

"What happened?"

"Mamat's contact just phoned him," Amanda sobbed. "Jamilah is dead."

7

IT WAS ALMOST NOON WHEN AVA WALKED INTO THE arrivals hall at Kuching International Airport, a new but much smaller version of the efficient modern airports being built all over Asia. She had flown from Taipei to Kuala Lumpur the night before, spent several restless hours trying to sleep at an airport hotel, then caught a mid-morning Malaysian Airlines flight to Kuching.

As soon as Amanda told her about Jamilah's death, Ava made the decision to travel to Kuching and moved quickly to make the arrangements. May had wanted to join her, but she had obligations in Wuhan that couldn't be put off. That she was available by phone was enough, Ava told her.

Fai took the news well. She knew Amanda and understood how close she and Ava were. "Just be careful," Fai said. "And stay in touch."

When she landed in Kuala Lumpur, Ava called Amanda to give her the ETA of her flight into Kuching and to get an update. Amanda told her the police hadn't yet made a public pronouncement about Jamilah, and Mamat's contact hadn't been able to provide any more details. "She's dead — that's all we know," Amanda had said, still very emotional. "Aisyah can't stop crying, and Chi-Tze seems to be traumatized. I'm so glad you're coming. We need someone to take control."

"A sudden death is always a shock, and the circumstances make it even worse," Ava said. "But we can't do this alone. We'll need their help if we're to get to the bottom of this. Explain that to them as gently as you can."

"I will."

"I've been searching the Web for any mention of this Sarawak United Front, but I haven't been able to find a single reference," Ava said. "There's lots of material, though, about that timber issue you mentioned. It seems to be a very controversial — and corrupt — business in Borneo."

"I'll let Aisyah explain it to you when you get here, assuming she's calm enough to talk. But she has told me it's both of those things, and no one in power seems to care."

"Ava!" a voice shouted as she entered the arrivals hall. She turned to see Amanda walking towards her with arms outstretched. Ava was five foot three and weighed about 115 pounds. Amanda was the same height, but even slimmer. She had just celebrated her thirtieth birthday but looked younger. She had fine features, eyes that were normally lively and friendly, and long hair worn loose that she was constantly tucking behind her ears.

When they had first met, Amanda used a lot of cosmetics, wore nothing but designer clothes, and was seldom seen without expensive jewellery around her neck and wrists. Now, like Ava, mascara and a touch of lipstick was enough makeup for Amanda, her only jewellery was her wedding

ring, and jeans and shirts were her everyday wear. May
Ling had been amused by the transformation from what
she called "Hong Kong princess to working-class girl."

"I'm so glad you're here," Amanda said as they hugged.

"Where are the others?"

"They're waiting for us at the hotel. It isn't far from here,
about a twenty-minute drive."

"Any news?"

"Nothing, but Mamat phoned Chi-Tze this morning to
tell her he's meeting his contact. He seems really committed
to helping her."

"As he should be," Ava said. "But that's water under the
bridge."

"Ava, it was Ah-Pei, not Mamat, who hired the goons that
beat up Chi-Tze and me."

"I know, but her brothers helped create the situation that
allowed it to happen, and then they acted like cowards after
the fact."

"Remind me never to get on your bad side," Amanda said.

Ava touched Amanda lightly on the arm. "I'm sorry.
I shouldn't be cynical about Mamat's need to atone. Uncle
always said I carry grudges too long and too hard. In fact, if
he hadn't intervened so forcefully, I might still be carrying
one towards May Ling."

"She told me that story," Amanda said.

"One day you can tell me her version of it," Ava said. "But
now we should get going."

Amanda took Ava's Shanghai Tang Double Happiness bag
and said, "Follow me." They got into a cab and Amanda told
the driver, "The Riverside Majestic Hotel."

"What's the hotel like?" Ava asked.

"It's okay. It would be a three- or four-star in Hong Kong, but it overlooks the river and there's an esplanade nearby. I went for a walk on it this morning. There were lots of joggers."

"If I can find the time, I might go for a run later. I didn't exercise much in Taipei."

"How's the film going?"

"From everything I saw, it's going well. But who really knows until it's done?" Ava said. "You should try to spend a couple of days on set before shooting ends."

"I might have been able to before this mess."

The conversation dwindled, and Ava looked out at the passing city. From the little research she'd done, she knew Kuching had a population of about 300,000, almost the same as Kota Kinabalu. And, like KK, it didn't have much of a skyline. "This is where the 'white rajahs' ruled," she said to Amanda.

"The who?"

"I saw it online when I looked up Sarawak. In the 1800s an English adventurer named James Brooke did something to earn the gratitude of the Sultan of Brunei. The Sultan gave him the land that became Sarawak. The Brooke family ruled here for decades. Conrad's novel *Lord Jim* was based on Brooke."

"I haven't heard anything about white rajahs, but I know about the Brookes from my walk this morning. I saw a palace on the other side of the river, and when I asked the concierge about it, she said it was built by the Brookes. The governor lives there now," Amanda said. Then she bit her lower lip and lowered her head slightly. That was usually a sign that Amanda had something she wanted to say but was reluctant to do so.

"Is there something you aren't telling me?" Ava asked.

"No," Amanda said quickly. "But I've been thinking that maybe we should consider selling the furniture business once all this trouble is settled. We've made some money, and I'm sure there's been some appreciation in value, but I don't think it's worth all the bad luck it has brought us."

"What would Chi-Tze say to that?"

"She would probably like the idea. She loves living in Shanghai and working with the Pos. She's told me many times that she'd never live in Borneo again. Until now she hasn't even come back for a visit."

"Discuss it with her," Ava said. "If she's agreeable and we can find someone willing to pay a fair price, I'm not opposed to selling. The business has always been a bit of an outlier anyway."

"I know. I should never have proposed buying it."

"You were trying to help a friend, and it was a good deal at the time. Besides, that was early days for us. We hadn't yet figured out where best to invest our money," Ava said. "Neither May nor I have any regrets that we followed your recommendation."

"I'm so fortunate to have partners like you."

"We're a team. You're as much a part of it as May and me."

Amanda bit her lip again.

"I meant what I just said, Amanda."

"I believe you; I wasn't going to question you. I was going to talk about Michael," Amanda said. "When I spoke to him this morning about Jamilah, I was crying. He didn't want me to come here in the first place, and he immediately asked me to fly back to Hong Kong. When I told him I couldn't, that I have responsibilities here, he said my first responsibility is to him and our marriage....I can't believe he said that."

"The men in the Lee family — starting with my father — find it difficult not to come across as paternalistic. Every so often they see us women as something close to equal, but then all the old prejudices resurface. I ignore my father when he's like that. You should do the same with Michael."

"I did more than that. I told him I'm part of a strong sisterhood that owns businesses many times bigger than his, and that if he can't handle that, he should find himself another wife."

Ava spun towards Amanda. "How did he react?"

"He went quiet and tried to change the subject," Amanda said with a smile. Then she pointed to a plain white building. "There's the hotel."

A minute later the taxi stopped in front of a set of glass doors. Ava got out and waited on the curb while Amanda paid the driver. She immediately felt the humidity. Kota Kinabalu had a steamy tropical climate, and she knew she was in for more of the same in Kuching. Amanda got out of the taxi and they entered the hotel.

"Chi-Tze and Aisyah are in the lobby waiting for us. We should say hello to them before you check in," she said.

Ava was accustomed to being among the smallest women in any room, but as Amanda guided her towards Chi-Tze and Aisyah, Ava felt almost tall. Chi-Tze was perhaps five foot one, and Aisyah was at least an inch shorter.

"Ava, it was so good of you to come," Chi-Tze said. "I'm sorry it was necessary."

"There's no need to apologize; it was through no fault of yours," Ava said, and then looked at the other young woman. "You must be Aisyah. I'm Ava Lee. It's a pleasure to meet you."

"I'm honoured to meet you, Ms. Lee," she said.

"No one calls me Ms. Lee. I'm Ava."

"I'm honoured to meet you, Ava, but I'm sorry it's because of these events."

"Well, why don't I check in and freshen up, and then we can meet somewhere to discuss the events," Ava said.

"The café on the first floor?" Chi-Tze asked.

"Perfect. I'll see you all in half an hour."

Amanda had booked a suite for Ava, which was spacious and tastefully furnished. Ava unpacked her bags, set up her laptop, and headed for the bathroom. She showered, put on black linen trousers and a white button-down Brooks Brothers shirt, and applied a touch of lipstick. She texted Fai and May Ling to let them know she had arrived safely, then opened the laptop to check her email.

Her mother had written. I was expecting you to call this morning. I can't remember the last time we were apart for such a long period of time. I have to say I'm really missing you. Marian calls every other day, which I appreciate, but her life never changes. Call me when you can. I can't help worrying. Love, Mummy

Ave wrote back. Sorry about not calling. I had to leave Taipei and was in transit to Borneo on a business matter. The film is going well, and with any luck we'll be finished in two weeks. After that, my plan is to take a short trip to Shanghai to catch up with Xu and Auntie Grace, and then fly home from there. Fai will be with me. We've become almost inseparable. That's a new experience for me, and I have to confess I'm really enjoying it. Love, Ava

She clicked Send, closed her laptop, and headed for the door.

* * *

The café was full, but Amanda and the others had secured a table overlooking the river. Three heads turned in Ava's direction as she approached.

"For a second you looked like you were expecting someone else," Ava said.

"Mamat just called. He's on his way to see us," Chi-Tze said.

"Does he know I'm here?" Ava asked.

"Yes, and he sounded relieved to hear it."

A server appeared at the table. "Can I get you something to drink?" she asked.

"Water will be fine," Ava said.

"And are you going to order something to eat? These women have been waiting for you to arrive."

"We're going to share a couple of orders of pad thai, shrimp spring rolls, and chicken satay," Amanda said.

"That sounds fine to me," Ava said.

The waitress poured water into Ava's glass and left.

"The food here is quite good," Amanda said, as if Ava needed reassurance.

"I'm so hungry I'll be satisfied if it's warm," Ava said.

Amanda started to reply when Chi-Tze interrupted. "There's Mamat."

Ava barely remembered Chi-Tze's brother. She had met him only briefly at the end of several days of emotional upheaval and wouldn't have recognized him if Chi-Tze hadn't pointed him out. Mamat was about five foot six, slim like his sister, and wore a Lacoste polo shirt and designer jeans. He and his brother, Tambi, had made a career out of going to university in Kuala Lumpur and then theoretically working in the family furniture business. From what Ava had been told, the brothers did as little work as possible, letting their parents and then their sisters carry the load. They had, though, pocketed a lot of money when Three Sisters bought into the company.

Ava had been rather nasty to the brothers when they met. She wondered now if that was why Mamat looked so uncomfortable as he approached the table.

"Mamat, let me reintroduce you to Ava Lee, our boss," Chi-Tze said when he reached them.

He gave Ava a wan smile and offered his hand. "I'm pleased to see you again," he said.

The hand was damp and his grip limp. Ava shook it vigorously. "Thank you for helping us with this problem," she said.

"Take a seat," Chi-Tze said. "We've ordered food, and there's enough for everyone."

"I've eaten, but I will sit with you," he said.

"How was the meeting with your contact?" asked Amanda.

Mamat's face fell. "Upsetting ... and confusing."

"Why's that?"

His eyes flickered and he licked his lower lip. "I would like some water," he said.

"Take mine," Chi-Tze said, passing him her glass.

"Thank you," he said, and gulped down half the water. Then he drew a deep breath. "My contact told me that Jamilah suffered a severe brain injury in the explosion. That's what eventually caused her death. He also said she was so badly burned that maybe it was a good thing she didn't survive."

"Oh my god," Aisyah said.

Amanda and Chi-Tze lowered their heads, and Ava knew they were fighting back tears. She leaned towards Mamat. "That is very upsetting," she said softly. "But where's the confusion?"

"When the police issue their statement later today, they're going say that, until her death, Jamilah had been a 'person of interest' in their inquiry. They mean to imply that she planted the bomb herself."

8

THE TABLE FELL SILENT, THEN AISYAH BEGAN TO SOB.
As the tears coursed down her cheeks, Amanda and Chi-Tze
began to cry as well.

"I'm sorry to bring you bad news like this," Mamat said,
his discomfort obvious as he averted his eyes from the crying women.

"This isn't bad news. This is absolute madness!" Aisyah
shouted.

Ava reached towards her and gently touched the back of
her hand. "I am sure Mamat is only repeating what he was
told," she said, and then turned to him. "Tell me, who is this
contact, and how reliable is his information?"

Mamat hesitated and looked to his sister to intercede.

"We're here to work together as a team. There can be no
secrets between us," said Ava.

"Please, Mamat, tell Ava what she wants to know," Chi-
Tze said.

Mamat looked slightly undecided, then blurted, "He's a
criminal lawyer. I went to school with him in Kuala Lumpur.
We kept in touch over the years. He knows people in the

police department and the Ministry of Justice."

"Did this information come from the police or the Ministry?" Ava asked.

"He said it was the Ministry, and I have no reason to doubt him."

"Are his contacts paid for their information?" asked Ava.

"That's what he tells me."

"And you're paying him?"

"I am. Is that an issue?"

"No, not in the least. In fact, I've often found that paying for information is the best way to ensure it continues to flow," Ava said. "And I'm prepared to repay whatever you've spent, and give you more if it helps us understand what's happened here."

"I don't want your money. This is my way of saying I'm sorry for Kota Kinabalu."

"We appreciate that," Ava said, sending a little smile in Chi-Tze's direction before turning back to Mamat. "You obviously trust your friend. Does he have the same level of trust in his contacts?"

"He's known them for years. He says they've never lied to him, especially when money is involved."

"I like that distinction," said Ava. "Did he suggest why the police want people to believe Jamilah set the bomb?"

"He isn't one hundred percent sure, but he thinks they may have been instructed to plant that seed, and that people at the Ministry might be involved too."

"Instructed by whom?"

"He didn't say, only that he finds it strange that the police reached that kind of conclusion so quickly, especially when the fire officials won't have had sufficient time to complete their investigation," Mamet said. "That makes him suspect someone wants this case closed."

"And he didn't tell you who he thinks that might be?" Ava asked. "He didn't mention a name at all?"

"No, but Sarawak is a small place. There aren't many people with that kind of power."

"I see," Ava said slowly, her eyes fixed on Mamat.

"In truth, I didn't push him very hard. I was still absorbing the news that Jamilah is dead and that the police are trying to blame her," he said.

"I understand what a shock it must have been for you, but we're going to have to go back to your friend," Ava said. "We need a better understanding of how the system works here, and he's the only person we can trust who's in a position to tell us."

"Do you want to meet with him personally?"

"Yes."

Mamat looked at Chi-Tze.

"Ava is an expert at this kind of thing," Chi-Tze said. "She'll know better than any of us what questions to ask and what actions to pursue. I think it's a good idea."

Mamat nodded. "Okay, then, when do you want this to happen?"

"As soon as possible. In fact, this afternoon would be ideal," said Ava.

"I'll see what I can do."

"Great, and don't hesitate to offer more money. Right now we need all the information we can get."

"I'll do everything I can to make it happen."

"Thank you," Ava said, just as the food began to arrive.

"I've lost my appetite," Aisyah said.

"Me too," said Chi-Tze.

"You should try to eat something. Who knows what kind of day lies ahead?" Ava said.

"I agree," Amanda added. She picked up a spoon and served herself some pad thai, a spring roll, and a skewer of chicken satay.

Ava joined in, and then Aisyah and Chi-Tze followed suit.

"Did you find out anything more about the Sarawak United Front?" Ava asked after a few minutes.

"Who are you asking?" Aisyah said.

"All of you. Does it exist?"

"We don't know," Aisyah replied. "I haven't been able to find the name in the usual lists of environmental organizations, and no one I've talked to in the movement has ever heard of them."

"They could be more concerned about the rights of Indigenous peoples than the environment," Chi-Tze said.

"Either way, why would they target us? We're opposed to illegal logging, not for it. And we've actively supported protection of Indigenous territory," Aisyah added.

"It seems to me that the whole thing is bogus, simply a smokescreen," Ava said.

"To what end?" Amanda asked.

"I don't know. That's why we need to speak to Mamat's contact," Ava said, and turned to him. "Why haven't you called him yet?"

"I was waiting until you finished lunch."

"I know you're trying to be polite, but there's no need. Please call him now."

"Excuse me," he said, taking a phone from his pocket and leaving the table.

Ava nodded and spooned another helping of pad thai onto her plate. "This food is quite good," she said.

The other women followed Ava's example, and by the time Mamat returned, all the dishes on the table were empty.

"Did you reach him?" Ava asked.

"He can meet with us anytime this afternoon."

"Excellent. Do we have far to go?"

"No, his office is nearby, no more than a five-minute taxi ride."

"Do any of you want to join us?" Ava asked the others.

Aisyah shook her head. "We don't know if the police have informed Jamilah's family about her death, and even if they have, we should try to get in touch with them."

"We spoke about this earlier," Amanda said. "The company was planning to pay Jamilah's medical expenses and keep her on the payroll at full salary until she was ready to come back to work. What should we do now?"

"Her father is a labourer who earns very little money, and there are three younger sisters, her mother, and a grandmother at home. Jamilah was their primary source of income, and their main hope for the sisters to get an education," Aisyah said.

"What do you recommend?" Ava asked.

"We should pay her funeral costs. She had a small insurance policy, but as for the rest..."

"Let's look after the family properly," said Ava. "The three of you can decide how much to give them, and I don't care if it's one lump sum or a monthly stipend. You make the arrangements. No amount of money will bring Jamilah back, but we should do what we can to ease the financial strain on her family caused by her death. And we should make sure her sisters get that education," Ava said.

"I'll contact the family today," said Aisyah.

"Is there anything else you'd like us to do in the meantime?" Chi-Tze asked.

"Yes. After you speak to Jamilah's family, you and Aisyah should compile a list of her friends and then talk to as many of them as you can. Ask them about the Sarawak United Front. Ask if Jamilah seemed worried recently. Ask them if they can think of anyone who might want to harm her."

"She is — was the sweetest person. I can't imagine anyone wanting to hurt her," Aisyah said.

"That may be true, but it would be irresponsible of us not to ask," said Ava. "There has to be a reason why our business was attacked, and even though I'm inclined to think her death was accidental, I'd still like you to speak to as many people as you can and ask as many questions as you can. I know you've been in contact with some of the environmental groups; go back to them, and then go outside that circle if you have to."

"Okay, we'll do that," Aisyah said.

Ava stood up. "Good luck. I'll see you back here later today."

Mamat stepped back to allow Ava to pass, then followed her from the restaurant. When they reached the taxi stand outside the hotel, he moved to open the back door of the first cab in line for her.

"You don't have to be so attentive," Ava said.

"I'm just trying to be respectful," he said.

Ava thought of a sharp rejoinder and then bit it back. He did seem sincere, and maybe she should leave it at that. "Thank you."

Mamat slid into the back seat next to Ava and gave the driver an address.

"What is your friend's name?" Ava asked as the taxi pulled away.

"Douglas Brooke."

"That's a famous name around here. Is he related to the white rajahs?"

"I've been told — though not by him — that he's related to Charles Brooke, who succeeded his brother James as rajah. I'm not sure if he's a direct descendant, though."

"I may ask him."

"I'm sure he won't mind; I just never thought to. When you're students from Borneo at university in KL, your instinct is not to talk about where you're from, so you can avoid having to answer stupid questions about headhunters and the like."

"Were the other students that insensitive?"

"Given the chance, I'm sure they would have been," Mamat said. "Even Chi-Tze didn't identify herself as being from Borneo when she was at Brandeis. She told everyone she was Malaysian."

"What did you tell Mr. Brooke about me?"

"I told him you're one of the owners of the furniture business and that you're here to investigate the bombing."

"Which is true enough."

The taxi slowed and then came to a stop in front of a three-storey red-brick building. "We've arrived," Mamat said, passing several bills to the driver.

The ground floor of the building housed a Starbucks, and they had to walk through the coffee shop to get to a small, white-tiled lobby. On the wall next to the elevator was a directory. Ava saw that the law offices of Brooke and Samuels were on the third floor, along with four or five other firms.

"How many lawyers work with Mr. Brooke?" she asked Mamat.

"From what I've seen, it's just Douglas and Richard Samuels, his partner — and brother-in-law."

"They can't be that busy if he can make time for us on such short notice."

"I think he's between cases right now. He jokes that there are lots of lawyers in Kuching and not enough criminals to keep them busy."

They got out of the elevator on the third floor and walked to a wooden door at the end of the corridor. A brass plaque on the door read BROOKE AND SAMUELS — BARRISTERS AND SOLICITORS. Mamat knocked on the door and waited several seconds before opening it.

"Welcome back," a young woman said from behind a desk just inside the door.

Ava saw two other desks in the open area, neither of which was occupied. Behind them were two closed wooden office doors.

"Could you let Mr. Brooke know I'm here?" Mamat said.

"Certainly," said the young woman, reaching for a phone.

A moment later, one of the office doors opened and a tall, pale man stood in the frame. His blue eyes were bloodshot and sunken, with dark shadows below them. His thin sandy hair was combed from just above his left ear across his scalp, though it didn't do much to cover his baldness. He wore a double-breasted linen suit that was slightly wrinkled and had some sort of stain on the right lapel.

"Douglas, this is Ava Lee," Mamat said.

"It's a pleasure. Mamat has told me that you're a very successful businesswoman," Brooke said, offering his hand.

Ava took it and was surprised by the firmness of his grip. "My partners and I have done reasonably well, although this affair in Kuching has set us back. Perhaps more emotionally than financially."

"It is a shocking business," Brooke said, stepping back. "Come inside and take a seat."

Brooke's desk was massive, looked to be made of oak, and showed signs of considerable age. In front of it were four green leather armchairs, and on either side wooden bookcases rose from floor to ceiling. It was an office that spoke of class and serious intent. Ava wondered if it was Brooke's appearance or his office that best represented the man.

"Would either of you care for something to drink before we begin?" he asked.

"No, I'm fine," said Ava, sitting down in a chair directly across the desk from his.

"Me too," Mamat said.

"Good. Now, what can I do for you?" Brooke asked, settling into his chair. "I told Mamat everything I've been able to uncover so far. I'm not sure what there is to add, but I'll listen."

"Are you certain the police are going to imply in their official statement that Jamilah Daeng set the bomb that killed her?" asked Ava.

"That's what I've been told, but we'll be able to confirm that soon enough. Their announcement is scheduled for later this afternoon."

"Have you seen the actual statement?" she asked.

"A draft was read to me over the phone."

"Does it include an explanation for why she might have set the bomb?"

Brooke shifted in his chair, his eyes wandering to the bookshelf on his right. "Not specifically."

"I don't mean to be rude, but that's a very careful use of the word 'specifically.'"

He looked directly at her, as if seeing her for the first time. "What did you do before you got into business? Were you in law?"

"I'm a trained forensic accountant. My partner and I chased money that had gone astray. It was often a lot of money, and we were often successful."

"Then it's safe to assume you're an inherently skeptical person with an eye for detail and a nose for falsehoods."

"Yes, I think that's a fair assessment. And right now I'm skeptical about your use of 'specifically.' I'd like to know what it is you aren't telling me," said Ava.

Brooke looked at Mamat, and Ava knew immediately that whatever money Mamat had paid him wasn't going to be enough. "Mr. Brooke, I would like this to be a productive meeting, and that means I'd like you to be absolutely candid with me," she said. "I'm not asking that as a favour. I know we're imposing on your time, but I'd also like to impose on your knowledge of how things really operate in Sarawak. I don't expect either imposition to come free of charge. I'm prepared to pay you for your time and knowledge. What do you think is an appropriate amount?"

"You get straight to business, don't you," he said.

"I do," Ava said. "And along those lines, tell me how much Mamat has paid you for the help you've given him so far."

"A thousand U.S. dollars," Brooke said without hesitation.

"I'll give you another thousand for the next hour of your time."

"You have a deal, Ms. Lee," said Brooke.

"I don't have the cash on me, but I'll arrange to have it sent to you before the end of the day."

"I trust you on that."

"Thank you. And now tell me why you're being so coy about the police statement."

"I was told the draft I was read probably won't be the final version. They were still working on the final wording."

"Why is that? If they're secure in their facts the wording shouldn't be an issue."

Brooke cocked an eyebrow at her and smiled as if sharing a secret joke. "They want to say definitively that Jamilah set the bomb herself, did so badly, and was killed as a result," he said. "But they have two problems. The first is that they have no physical evidence and thus no way of proving it. And second, they haven't been able to find a logical motive for why she would do such a thing. So, having failed on both those grounds, my contact expects they'll resort to innuendo and suggestion."

"Is he suggesting that the police will invent evidence?"

"No, I don't expect them to go to that much trouble. They'll issue a statement that will be strong enough to implicate your associate but vague enough not to be challenged. I imagine the term 'person of interest' will be used, on the assumption that it will be interpreted to mean Jamilah was guilty but, now that she's dead, there's no point in pursuing things further. Case closed."

"And your contact inside the police department was certain about this?"

"I never said my contact is with the police department. In fact, he isn't," Brooke said. "He's a dear friend who works at the Ministry of Justice. He actually believes in true justice — even here in Sarawak. Senior officers in the police department are obliged to keep him briefed on any case that might involve the Ministry at some future date. And please don't ask me for his name, because I won't give it to you."

"I won't. But can you tell me what he said about the Sarawak United Front? How will the police handle their claim of responsibility for the bombing? I can tell you that we haven't been able to locate the Front or even find anyone who's heard of them."

"The police are in the same predicament, but that won't stop them from mentioning the group in connection with Jamilah. They know she was a supporter of Friends of the Earth. If questioned, they may try to portray her as a radical environmentalist who might have had ties to the Front."

"Is there a Sarawak United Front?" she asked.

"How would I know?"

"Would you look into it for us? If it does exist, there has to be a record of it somewhere," she said.

Brooke pursed his lips. "I'll look into it, but it will take some time. At some additional cost."

"I'll pay you another thousand."

"I'll drop everything else I'm doing," he said with a slight smile.

Ava sat back in her chair as she gathered her thoughts, and then leaned forward abruptly. "Why would the police be so quick to imply that Jamilah was the cause of her own death?"

"I imagine someone put them up to it."

"Who has that kind of influence?"

"We're getting onto squidgy ground here," Brooke said slowly.

"That's why I'm paying you. I need you to get your shoes dirty."

Brooke hesitated, then said, "You know, I think I need a glass of water. I'll just go and get one. Can I bring back something for you?"

"Yes, you can bring back an answer to my question," Ava said.

9

"WHAT DO YOU THINK OF HIM?" MAMAT ASKED AS soon as Brooke had left the office.

"Ask me that again in half an hour," said Ava.

"I know he looks a bit wasted. He drinks too much, and his mind may not be what it once was, but he's still sharper than most. I think he's going to be helpful."

"Can we really trust him?"

"I believe so, yes. Though I've never had reason to put that much trust in him."

Ava turned to look at Mamat. "You know, I'm starting to like you." She thought she saw him begin to blush, but before it went further, Brooke returned with a glass of water.

The lawyer took his seat behind the desk, sipped his water, and said, "I was thinking about your last question. Would you object if I rephrased it?"

"Not at all."

"Assuming someone else planted the bomb and Jamilah's death was a tragic accident that the police are trying to cover up, we're still left with a question. Why was the bomb planted in the first place?"

Ava hesitated. "I'm told Jamilah was involved in opposing illegal logging operations, and our company imports timber from other countries to sell into this market. Perhaps someone wanted to stop those activities?"

"If that's true, who in Sarawak might object to your company's activities?"

"How would I possibly know?" said Ava, with some irritation.

"Apologies. I was being rhetorical," Brooke said, and sipped from the glass again. "You couldn't know, of course."

"Are you going to answer your own question?" Ava asked.

Brooke looked at Mamat. "I know you can be indiscreet, Mamat. This is a time when complete confidentiality has to be maintained. If I tell Ms. Lee what I suspect, I can't have it repeated. Will you swear to keep it within this office?"

"Of course."

"Don't say that so quickly. I'm deadly serious."

"I'll repeat nothing. Not one word. I swear to God."

Brooke nodded and looked at Ava. "I am going to give you a name. I'm not saying the people associated with it are guilty of anything, but my colleague at the Ministry made a vague reference to them, and it's been on my mind ever since."

"I'm waiting," Ava said, her patience with Brooke's penchant for drama beginning to wear thin.

"The name is Chong. They don't own Sarawak, but they have a disproportionate amount of control over everything that happens here. The family's patriarch is Sulaiman Chong. He happens to be chief minister, the head of our state cabinet, and head of our legislative branch. Nothing of importance happens in Sarawak without his approval."

"Even illegal logging?"

"Especially illegal logging. The Chong family have been up to their armpits in it for decades, and their timber company is by far the largest in Sarawak. The money Sulaiman made from it helped secure his political base. Now he uses that base to protect his son, who runs the logging and palm oil business here, and his daughter and her husband, as they build the family's overseas investment portfolio."

Ava nodded. "Sulaiman Chong? That's an unusual name."

"Chong's mother was Malaysian and his father was a third-generation Chinese Malay. They decided to split the difference when it came time to name him. Given some of the cultural biases in Borneo, it could have been a problem for him, but from where he sits, it gives him a foot in both camps," Brooke said. "His nickname is 'the Sultan of Sarawak.' We don't have Sultans — only Brunei does — but Sulaiman has just as much power."

"What are his children's names?" she asked.

"The son is Ahmad. The daughter is Laila."

"You mentioned her husband."

"His name is Martin Bowles. He's English, Cambridge-educated. He met Laila in Hong Kong, where he was working for a British bank. In a sense they both hit the jackpot. The Chongs needed someone who understood international finance, and Bowles needed someone with a lot of money to invest."

"Mr. Brooke, you're telling me all this with an almost overwhelming air of confidence. What makes you so sure the Chong family could be responsible for what happened to Jamilah?"

"Please, call me Douglas."

"All right, Douglas, why are you so confident?"

"Obviously I have no proof. I'm just connecting the dots and exercising a bit of logic. There's less than a handful of people in Sarawak who could influence the police in this way. Sulaiman Chong is at the very top of that list. There are only three or four major players in the logging business, and the Chong family is by far the largest. Finally, whoever gave the order to bomb your warehouse has no qualms about using violence to meet their objectives, and that's been part of the family's modus operandi for as long I can remember."

"Are there no other people who come to mind?"

Brooke shook his head. "None who match all those criteria."

"And you're not exaggerating about how much power Sulaiman Chong exerts in Sarawak?"

"I'm deadly serious. I'm sorry if that sounds like a pun; I don't mean it to be," Brooke said. "As I said, Sulaiman Chong is Sarawak's chief minister. He appoints and dismisses cabinet ministers at will — everyone in the cabinet is beholden to him. This gives him ultimate control over many government departments, including Forestry, Regional Development, Agriculture, and Natural Resources. Some chief ministers in the past had a more relaxed approach and gave their ministers latitude to make decisions. But that's not Sulaiman's style. He runs a tight ship."

Ava took a small notebook from her bag. "Do you mind if I make a few notes?" she asked.

"Go right ahead."

"Could you spell the names of his son and daughter and her husband?"

Brooke did. After recording them, Ava asked, "You

mentioned that Laila met her husband in Hong Kong. Where do they live now?"

"Hong Kong. They never left. My understanding is that Bowles has invested billions of dollars in real estate there, and across the border in Shenzhen."

"Billions of U.S. dollars?"

"That's what I've been told."

"Is there really that much money in logging?"

"Yes, especially when you don't pay for the timber or the land rights. Sulaiman has never paid so much as a dollar," Brooke said. "He was always a rough operator. He'd send bulldozers into the rainforest with armed guards and simply start taking down trees. When he finished, there wouldn't be a single native tree left standing, and then he'd replace them with imported palms. Where once there were Indigenous homelands, all we have now is those goddamn palm oil plantations."

"Don't the plantations provide employment for the local population?" Mamat asked.

Ava turned to look at him. She had been so absorbed by Brooke's account that she had almost forgotten he was there.

"The rainforest was home to the Penan people before the loggers arrived," Brooke replied. "They're nomadic hunters who live off the land. When Sulaiman and others like him destroyed their traditional territories, they were forced to relocate to other parts of the forest. I've heard estimates that as much as seventy-five percent of our magnificent rainforest has been destroyed, so the surviving Penan are being squeezed into an ever-tightening living space. The question is, how much longer will it be before the loggers take down all the rainforest and destroy an entire Indigenous culture?"

"You make it sound inevitable," Ava said.

Brooke shrugged. "I'm sentimental about Sarawak's history. I'd like to see the older cultures and customs preserved. But I'm also a realist, and I know this government doesn't care about those things."

"Is your sentiment rooted in your family's long-standing connection to the place? I'm assuming you're related to the so-called white rajahs."

"My great-grandfather was the brother of Charles Brooke, so there is a direct link to the great man himself."

"I'll have to read more about Charles," Ava said, then glanced at her notebook. "Where does Ahmad Chong live?"

"In Kuching. He has a penthouse apartment along the river."

"Is he married?"

"No, and I'll be surprised if he ever settles down. He's Sarawak's most famous playboy, and he relishes the reputation. I'm told he has a private garage in the basement of the Chong office tower, where he keeps more than twenty of the most expensive sports cars in the state," Brooke said. "He's famous for his parties. He flies in food from KL, wines and booze from Hong Kong, and women from all over Southeast Asia."

"Have you ever been to one of his parties?"

"A few, but that was when I was between marriages."

"Does he work?"

"Oh yes, he works, but not as hard as he plays. He has a very competent second-in-command who handles much of the day-to-day details of his business. His name is Arven Saad. Both men have a reputation for being ruthless and unfeeling. Those are easy traits to flaunt when you never have to worry about the consequences," Brooke said.

Ava looked at Mamat. "Do you have any other questions for Douglas?"

"Not right now."

"I don't either, but I'm sure some will come to mind as soon as I leave," Ava said.

"Here, take my card," Brooke said, sliding it across the desk. "Call me anytime, within reason."

Ava put the card in her notebook and slipped it into her bag. "Please don't forget the Sarawak United Front," she said.

"I'll start working on it as soon as you leave."

"Thanks, and I'll get the money to you later this afternoon."

Ava stood up. Mamat and Brooke followed suit.

"I hope you don't mind my asking, but how do you intend to proceed from here?" Brooke asked her.

"I want to see the police statement, and if it's what you say it is, I'll speak to someone in authority there," she said. "I don't expect they'll change their opinion, but I want them to understand that they're not dealing with naïve fools."

"I think that's the best you can hope for," Brooke said.

"After that, I'll digest what you've told me and then I'll start gathering more information about the Chong family."

"To what end?"

"I want to know if they ordered the attack on our warehouse."

"And suppose you find out they did, then what?"

"I'll try to bring them to justice."

"I was afraid you'd say something like that," Brooke said. "I was hoping, after everything I've told you about them, you'd realize there's no chance of that happening here. They're the ones who decide what is just and what isn't. You'd be wasting your time."

"Maybe, but I still want to get to the truth."

"Then be very careful," Brooke said sharply. "I wasn't kidding when I told Mamat that I don't want my name associated with this."

"We'll keep your name out of it, I promise you."

"You need to be careful on your own behalf too. The Chongs do not take kindly to outsiders poking around in their affairs. A large number of politicians and business-people in this state thought otherwise and came to regret it."

"I know how to be unobtrusive."

Brooke shook his head. "This is a small place, more town than city. People love to gossip here, and there isn't anything juicier than the Chong family. If you start making inquiries, you should assume that word will get back to them. So, I repeat, be careful."

10

AMANDA, CHI-TZE, AND AISYAH WERE SITTING IN THE lobby when Ava returned to the hotel. Mamat had left her outside Brooke's office but told her he would be available. She had thanked him and said she would get in touch through Chi-Tze if more help was necessary. But truthfully, she thought his introduction to Douglas Brooke would be the extent of it.

"How did it go while I was gone?" Ava asked as she joined the other women.

"Aisyah spoke to Jamilah's family. They asked if we could make arrangements to send her body to their village. We told them we would as soon as the police released it," Amanda said. "The police had already told them they thought she planted the bomb and in effect caused her own death. They're a very religious family, so that was piling trauma upon trauma. In their minds, if Jamilah set the bomb herself, it was the equivalent of committing suicide, which is strictly forbidden in their religion. Jamilah's father told me a suicide is condemned to hell and can never get to heaven. If what the police are saying is true, in their minds their daughter has been killed twice — physically and then spiritually. The idea that they will meet their daughter in heaven would have been some comfort. Now even that has been taken from them."

"That's horrible," Ava said.

"Jamilah's father said he will never get over such grief," Aisyah said. "When I mentioned that we're going to send money, he said that's kind of us, but it didn't sound to me like he really cared."

"Is the family Muslim?" Amanda asked.

"No, they belong to a Christian fundamentalist church. Unlike the rest of Malaysia, Christians are in the majority here. I didn't know that until I mentioned Jamilah's parents to Celia Ng," Aisyah said.

"Celia was Jamilah's closest friend. She's coming here to meet us," Chi-Tze said.

"She's involved, like Jamilah, with Friends of the Earth and some other local environmental groups," Aisyah added.

"How is she?" Ava asked.

"She told me she has cried herself dry," said Chi-Tze.

"Did you tell her that the police are going to imply that Jamilah planted the bomb herself?"

"No. She seemed eager to talk to us, and I didn't want to say anything that might jeopardize that," Chi-Tze said.

"That was smart," Ava said. "When do you expect her to arrive?"

"Anytime now. She said she'll be wearing a red silk blouse."

"Then I'll wait here with you."

"How was your meeting?" Amanda asked.

"I think it was productive. Mamat's contact seems to know how things work in Sarawak," Ava said. "He confirmed that the police will imply in their official statement today that Jamilah set the bomb."

"Does he know who's behind this?"

"No, but he offered some theories that I think are worth pursuing — albeit carefully. He stressed that we need to be careful," said Ava. "He mentioned a family named Chong. Evidently they control a great deal of what goes on in the state. Aisyah, have you heard of them?"

"Yes, of course. Jamilah mentioned them often in connection with their ownership of Sarawak's largest illegal logging business. That's all I know, though. I'm sure Celia will have more information."

"The patriarch, Sulaiman Chong, is also the chief minister of Sarawak. He's the top man in the government."

Aisyah shrugged. "I've never concerned myself with the politics of this place."

Ava turned to Amanda. "The family also has a Hong Kong connection. Sulaiman's daughter, Laila, is married to a Hong Kong banker named Martin Bowles."

"Are you joking?" Amanda asked.

"No. Why do you look so surprised?"

"I know both Laila and Martin."

"How?"

"Through my father. Martin Bowles is a member of the Jockey Club and raced three horses last season. I first met them in the members' dining room at Sha Tin, and then a few times after that."

Ava knew Amanda's father, Jack Yee, very well. On two occasions she and Uncle had collected debts for him, and during the second job had saved his life. He was an ardent horseracing fan and had been an active member of the Hong

Kong Jockey Club for decades. "What did you think of them?" she asked.

"They have a house on Victoria Peak, and they make sure everyone knows it. He's a bit of a snob, not rude or overbearing, just rather pleased with how well he has done in business. She dresses expensively and smiles a lot, but she's a cold fish. I have never seen her express a real emotion; everything is surface level. I get the sense she would be difficult to deal with if you crossed her."

"You say that as if you've thought about it before," said Ava.

"That's because I have. After Michael and I met them, Martin seemed intent on making us best friends. Michael, to his credit, was hesitant. I wasn't. I wanted nothing to do with them outside of the race meetings."

"Could you change that attitude if I needed you to?"

"What do you mean?"

"Could you get close to them? My understanding is that the family is a tight-knit unit and that they're all in business together."

"I think I could, if I really had to," Amanda said.

"I note your lack of enthusiasm. Don't think any more about it right now; I'm jumping ahead of myself."

"There's Celia," Aisyah said, rising to her feet and waving in the direction of a slim woman in a red silk blouse.

"She's gorgeous," Ava said.

"And really clever. Jamilah told me she's in an environmental sciences doctoral program in Singapore," Aisyah said.

Celia looked very nervous as she approached them. As if in response to her body language, Aisyah walked towards her with arms extended and spoke to her. The women hugged, then Aisyah turned and said, "Celia, these are our friends and business associates Ava Lee, Chi-Tze Song, and Amanda Yee. They have travelled here to help us uncover what happened to Jamilah."

"Someone killed her, I know it," Celia said, her voice breaking.

"We agree. And now we need to find out who did it and why," Ava said. "Come and sit with us."

The women formed a small circle with Celia in the middle. "Can we get you anything?" Ava asked.

"No, thank you."

"Before I say anything else, let me tell you how much we grieve Jamilah's passing. She was part of our family," Ava said. "We want to get to the truth of what happened, but none of us are from Sarawak and know next to nothing about it. We need your help to understand this place."

Celia nodded. With noticeable effort, she said, "What do you want to know?"

Ava reached for her hand. "If this is too much for you, we don't have to do it now."

"No, I want to help."

"Okay, why don't you start by telling us if Jamilah seemed upset or concerned lately."

"I wouldn't say she was upset, but she certainly seemed worried over the past six months or so."

"Did she say why?"

"Not at first. She brushed it off when I asked if something was bothering her. It wasn't until about two months ago that she told me she had been getting threatening phone calls. They weren't frequent, but she said that made them worse in a way, because of their unpredictability," Celia said, her voice catching.

"Take a deep breath. Take your time. There's no rush," Ava said.

Celia closed her eyes, breathed in deeply, and a few seconds later said, "I'm okay now. Let's keep going."

"What kind of threats were being made?" asked Ava.

"A man — or maybe men, because she thought the voice was different more than once — told her she would be hurt if she kept doing what she was doing."

"Hurt how?"

"They never specified."

"And what was it they wanted her to stop doing?" Ava asked.

"Importing and selling foreign lumber. They said she was damaging local businesses, that she was a traitor to Sarawak."

"Did she report these calls to the police?"

"She thought about it, but when nothing happened after the first few times, she decided not to. Besides, this is one of the most male chauvinistic places on earth, and the police reflect those attitudes. She doubted she would be taken seriously."

"Why didn't she tell me about the calls?" Aisyah asked.

Celia shrugged. "She was so happy when she got this job, and so eager to prove that your trust in her wasn't misplaced. She wanted to show you she could run the business and handle all the challenges that came with it. She didn't want to look weak."

"That's the last thing she would have looked," Aisyah said.

"I know, but Jamilah was very proud. She had a stubborn side," Celia said, and then looked at Aisyah. "She ran the business well, didn't she? She told me she'd increased sales for five consecutive months."

"She ran the business very well," Aisyah said.

"Too well for somebody," Celia said.

"But who?" Ava asked.

"I've been thinking about that," said Celia.

"And what did you come up with?"

"I don't have a name, but given the nature of the threats, I can't help thinking it has to be someone connected to the lumber business."

"I've been told that Jamilah was quite active in the environmental movement," Ava said. "Do you think it's possible there's a connection?"

"I would be surprised, since environmentalists are basically ignored here. We kick up as much fuss as we can, agitating about illegal logging and destruction of the rainforest, but no one pays us much attention."

"I was told that seventy-five percent of the rainforest had been destroyed," Ava said.

"More like ninety percent. And the loggers haven't stopped. I suspect they won't until it's all gone."

"How can the government allow that to happen?" asked Ava.

Celia shook her head. "The man who controls the government made his fortune from illegal logging. He'll never stop while there's still money to be made."

"Sulaiman Chong?"

"Yes, he's the one. His son, Ahmad, is coming up right behind him. When the old man steps aside or becomes governor, his son will likely succeed him as chief minister."

"Do you know them? Have you met them?"

"I only know of Sulaiman from television and newspapers, but I have had dealings with Ahmad."

"How did that happen?"

Celia looked slightly uncomfortable. "He asked me out. One of the girls I went to high school with works for him. I met her at their company headquarters for lunch, and he saw me, came to our table, and introduced himself. I was polite, nothing more, but the next thing I know I'm getting phone calls and texts from him asking me to join him for dinner or a weekend trip to KL. He wouldn't take no for an answer. The last time we talked, he invited me to a party at his penthouse. When I refused, he acted insulted and asked why I wouldn't give him a chance. I told him I'm a committed environmentalist and deplore everything his company is doing to the rainforest. He laughed and said that gave us something to talk about. When I still refused, he called me a stupid bitch and said I was wasting the opportunity of a lifetime."

"Someone told me he's quite the playboy," Ava said.

"That's what my girlfriend says as well. If you work at the company and are young and attractive, sleeping with him is the fee you pay to keep your job."

"Is that behaviour condoned by his father?"

"I told you this is a chauvinistic place. A father can pass on his Malaysian nationality to a child born abroad, but a mother can't. There's no law against marital rape. Family law is different for each state, and here Muslim men can have four wives but a woman must have only one husband. Boys can't marry until they're eighteen, but girls can do it at sixteen, and even younger if an Islamic judge approves. And those are just laws I'm talking about, not to mention the everyday discriminatory practices against women."

"I hope you don't find this rude of me, but why do you stay here?" Ava asked.

"I don't. I go back and forth between here and Singapore, where I'm in a PhD program. I wouldn't come here at all, but I have ailing parents who need me. And when I finish school, I'll be looking for work outside of Malaysia."

"I hope you didn't find my question insensitive."

"Not at all. One of the many things Jamilah liked about working in your company was that everyone is free to be open about their thoughts and feelings."

Aisyah leaned towards Celia. "When Jamilah told you about the threats, did she mention any names?"

"If she did, I would remember."

Ava knew there was no point in pursuing that line of questioning any further. "I'm sure you would, so let me ask you two unrelated questions," Ava said. "First, have you ever heard of the Sarawak United Front?"

"Not until I saw the name in the newspaper and that they were claiming responsibility for the bomb. There are several organizations fighting for the rights of the Indigenous peoples of the region, but none by that name."

Ava nodded. "I know you may have answered this already, but I want to be sure. Did Jamilah have anyone in her personal life who might want to cause her harm?"

"No. I'm certain of that."

"Thank you. Thank you for coming and speaking with us, Celia."

"What are you going to do next? You can't leave it like this," Celia said.

"We won't," Ava said. "But we have to think about the path forward. There is no simple answer."

"Whatever I can do to help, I will. All you have to do is ask."

"Thank you again. We'll keep that in mind," Ava said as she stood up.

Celia hesitated, then got to her feet.

"I'll walk with you to the door," Aisyah said.

As the two women left, Ava turned to Amanda and Chi-Tze. "I need to clear my head. I think I'll go for a run. While I'm gone, can you arrange for us to meet with the local police?"

"We'll do what we can," Amanda said.

"Tell them we're family, which isn't far from the truth."

11

WHEN AVA WAS AT HOME IN TORONTO, SHE USUALLY ran eight kilometres four or five times a week. On the road she tried to maintain the same schedule, but she was often sidelined by other demands on her time. That had been the case in Taipei, where she had managed to get in only six runs during her entire three-week stay.

She left the Majestic Hotel in running shorts and the lightest T-shirt she had with her. She normally avoided running in overly humid climates — and Kuching certainly qualified as one — but she hadn't misspoken when she told the others she wanted to clear her head. For Ava, physical exercise was the surest way of achieving that. Her hope was that there would be a breeze coming off the Sarawak River to diminish the mid-afternoon swelter.

The esplanade ran alongside the river for two kilometres. It was wide enough to accommodate eight people walking side by side, and at that time of day there weren't many people around, which gave Ava a clear path. The hotel was at one end of the esplanade, which meant twice back and forth would be eight kilometres. But as Ava started to jog, she immediately felt the past few weeks' inactivity hit her. She didn't have that burst of energy that normally accompanied the first kilometre, and she couldn't find a rhythm. She pushed on, hoping to find her legs.

Ava concentrated on the day. Jamilah's death was upsetting, but it hadn't affected her as deeply as it had the other women. Ava had seen a lot of death in her time and never wanted to take it for granted, but she hadn't been close to Jamilah. What had troubled her more was Aisyah's description of the pain that Jamilah's parents were experiencing. Their lives had been shattered, and if the official reason for her death didn't change, there would be no way forward for them.

Ava tried to think about other things as she ran past food stalls and restaurants, some of them shuttered for the afternoon. Across the river she saw the Brooke palace and a building that looked like a fort. Her mind wandered. Ava thought about the Brooke family. How had a family from Britain carved out such a presence in this place? How did someone earn a title like "white rajah"?

By the second kilometre, Ava's legs were beginning to feel stronger. She believed in back conditioning, that all the runs she'd made over the years had laid a foundation that she could call upon. She felt the same way about bak mei. The hours of practice she'd spent with Grandmaster Tang were never lost; when she needed speed and power, her muscle memory kicked in. At least, it had until now. Would a day come when it would fail her?

Ava's mind returned to thoughts about Borneo. Her experiences on the island had been almost uniformly bad. She had been extricated from the situation in Kota Kinabalu only because Xu had sent a small army of triads to rescue her. If the Chong family was behind the bombing in Kuching, what might they do to prevent the truth from emerging? *Don't get ahead of yourself,* Ava thought suddenly. She still had no evidence that the Chongs were involved. All she had were Douglas Brooke's insinuations.

Ava hadn't brought a facecloth from the hotel with her, and she began to regret it as sweat began to run down her brow and into her eyes. She wiped at it with her hands, but that wasn't very effective. She didn't want to quit, but the sweat was almost too irritating for her to continue. She lifted up the bottom of her T-shirt to her face and used it like a towel. This exposed her sports bra to two gaping men, but she didn't care, as it absorbed enough sweat that she managed to run another complete length before she'd had enough.

When she entered the hotel lobby, the air conditioning hit her like a polar vortex. But even though it made her shiver, the cool air didn't stop her from sweating. The other women were still in the lobby, and Ava walked over to them. "Did you contact the police?" she asked.

"After a bit of a runaround I spoke to a Sub-inspector Yusop," Amanda said. "He refused to meet with us. He said there's no point, and even if we were family — which he emphasized we aren't — they won't be in a position to say anything until their investigations are complete."

"They've already decided to imply that Jamilah caused her own death. What else is there for them to complete?"

"Ava, they just don't want to talk to us. If it wasn't that excuse, it would have been another."

"I need to call Douglas Brooke and pressure him to get us through the door," Ava said. "I'll call him from my room before I shower. Wait here for me."

Celia's remark about Sarawak's ingrained chauvinism came back to Ava as she rode the elevator to her floor. The sub-inspector may have brushed off Amanda because of her sex. Ava had experienced the same dismissive behaviour from police in Indonesia and other places in Southeast Asia. She was sure Brooke's request would find a more receptive audience.

"Brooke and Samuels," the receptionist answered.

"This is Ava Lee. I met with Mr. Brooke earlier. Could you put me through to him, please?"

"Just one moment."

Ava carried her phone into the bathroom as she went to get a towel. She laid it across her shoulders and wiped her face with one end as the sweat kept coming.

"Ms. Lee. I didn't expect to hear from you so soon," Brooke said.

"We asked for a meeting with the police and they turned us down. I need you to make some calls."

"I expected that would be their reaction, but I didn't want to say so in case you thought I was trying to be obstructive," Brooke said. "I'll get you an audience. But when I do, don't mention the fact that I'm in your partial employ, and please don't be overly aggressive. There are fixed opinions in this state about the role of women."

"So I've been told, but I don't care. I was raised to be polite — that won't change. Just get us a meeting."

"Who rejected your initial request?"

"My partner spoke to a Sub-inspector Yusop."

"He can be a pain," Brooke said.

"Then please talk to someone who isn't."

"I'll look after it. Can I reach you at this number?"

"I'd rather call you back in, say, half an hour."

"Whatever you prefer," Brooke said.

"I'll call you then," Ava said, ending the conversation.

She opened her laptop, checked her email, found none that were pressing, and then sat quietly for five minutes. She knew from experience that jumping directly into the shower while she was still sweating would lead to more sweating when she got out. As she waited, she thought about Brooke. *He might have connections, but I'm not sure how much influence he has. I guess I'll find out soon enough. At least he hasn't asked for more money.* As it was, she knew she was overpaying him, but that was one of Uncle's tricks to create a sense of obligation.

She wiped her face with the towel again and felt the sweating begin to abate. A few minutes later she stepped into the shower.

Ava emerged from the bathroom wearing a hotel robe, a towel wrapped around her head and her phone in hand. She sat at the desk to call Brooke and was put right through to him.

"Were you successful?" she asked when he came on the line.

"You have an appointment at five p.m. with Sergeant Kamir. He's junior to Yusop, but I've always found him easier to communicate with," Brooke said.

"Thank you. I assume you told him who we are and why we want to talk to him."

"I most certainly did," Brooke said. "And Ms. Lee, I want to apologize for my earlier remark about not being aggressive. It was uncalled for."

"I didn't take offence."

"Excellent. But I do have to caution you ever so slightly. The Sarawak police force is a contingent of the Royal

Malaysian Police, and they consider themselves — rightly or wrongly — to be true professionals. I have had clients from other countries behave rather disrespectfully towards them; an American client referred to them as 'local yokels' to their faces, and that certainly didn't help his case."

"I'll keep that in mind," Ava said. "Now, where I am going for this meeting?"

"Local headquarters on Jalan Badruddin. It's quite central and won't take you long to get there. Who will be going with you? I need to advise Kamir so he can arrange for entry at the gate."

"There will be four of us: Amanda Yee, Chi-Tze Song, Aisyah Tengku, and me."

"That's quite a contingent."

"Every one of us has a stake in this."

"I can understand how upset you all are, but please don't get your hopes too high. The police seem quite set in their opinion about how your friend died," Brooke said.

"Don't worry, I won't hold it against you if it doesn't go well," said Ava. "I should go now. It's almost four-fifteen and I need to get dressed."

"Good luck," Brooke said.

Ava immediately called Amanda. "We have an appointment at the police station at five. I'll be downstairs in fifteen minutes. I told Brooke we'll all be going, and he'll pass that along to the police."

"We're all wearing jeans," Amanda said. "Is that presentable enough?"

Ava had to smile. Despite her professional business acumen, there were times when Amanda displayed a wide-eyed naivety about life and the world in general. Being concerned about what to wear to a police station was an example of this. "You all look fine," she said.

Ava left the room wearing a white cotton shirt, black linen slacks, and flat shoes. She'd look a little dressier than the other girls, but not by much. The group was already standing by the exit when she entered the lobby. "If we catch a cab now, we'll probably get there early, but I don't think that will matter."

Ten minutes later the taxi pulled up in front of a gate, the entrance to a complex of two-storey white stucco buildings with blue tile roofs. The gate was between two thick pillars; a blue sign overhead read POLIS DIRAJA KONTINJEN SARAWAK. The women got out of the cab and walked over to a sentry box.

"We have an appointment with Sergeant Kamir," Ava said.

"Names, please," the officer said.

Ava spoke for all of them.

"You are on my list," the officer said as he stepped out of the box. He pointed a digital camera at them. "We take pictures of all our civilian visitors as a security precaution. Do you mind?"

Ava felt an urge to argue but didn't want to give the officer an excuse to deny them entry. "I guess not," she said.

It took him only a few seconds to take the pictures, and then he said, "You'll find the Sergeant on the ground floor of the third building over there."

They followed his directions and found an open door into the building. They stepped into a small lobby and were met by an officer coming down a flight of stairs.

"Can I help you?"

"We're looking for Sergeant Kamir," said Ava.

"His office is the second door on the left down that corridor," he said.

"Thanks," Ava said, and led the women down the hallway.

She knocked on the door.

"Yes?" a man's voice called out.

"This is Ava Lee, with my colleagues. We have an appointment."

Seconds of silence passed and then the door opened. Ava looked up at a tall, broad-chested middle-aged man with a bushy moustache. He wore a navy-blue long-sleeved shirt and navy-blue cargo pants tucked into military boots. The word *Polis* was emblazoned on the left breast of his shirt, and on the right was a name tag with a shield and a police service number. There were three stripes on the right arm.

"I'm Sergeant Kamir," he said. "You're early."

"Sorry. We had no idea how long it would take to get here from our hotel."

"No matter, come inside. I'll fetch Constable Lazim. She'll be sitting in on the meeting," he said. "Please, take a seat."

Kamir slid past them out of the office as they entered. There were four metal chairs in a row in front of a grey metal desk. Off to one side was a fifth chair. The women took the chairs in the row.

"He seems pleasant enough," Amanda said.

"We'll see how long that lasts," Ava said. When she saw Amanda flinch, she quickly added, "But you're right. So far, so good."

"I'm actually nervous. I've never been in a police station before," Aisyah said.

"It's an office, nothing more than that. Think of it that way and you'll be fine," Ava said. "My introduction to the police was a jail cell in Shenzhen, China, after I got into a fight with, funnily enough, one of their sergeants. Luckily my former partner had considerable influence in that city, so I wasn't detained long."

"Is that true?" Aisyah asked.

"You can be certain it is," Amanda said. "Ava has had more adventures that any ten people I could name."

"Don't exaggerate," Ava said.

Amanda started to say something but stopped as the door opened. Sergeant Kamir entered with a woman wearing the same uniform; she didn't look older than thirty. "This is Constable Lazim," he said. "She'll take notes."

The policewoman nodded at them and took the seat off to the side.

Kamir settled behind his desk. "So, what can I do for you?"

"I'm sure you have some idea," Ava said.

"I was told you have some interest in the unfortunate death of that young woman who blew herself up."

"The explosion destroyed our business and could cost us millions," Ava said, trying to widen Kamir's focus. "But yes, the main reason we're here is because of Jamilah Daeng."

"Before we go any further, perhaps you could all identify yourselves for the record. Douglas Brooke said you're business partners in the lumber business that was destroyed, but maybe you could provide us with some additional details, such as your names, positions, and where you are from."

"Is that really necessary?" asked Ava.

"As much as I respect Douglas Brooke, we can't share information with people who aren't directly connected to what's happened over the past few days."

"Very well, I'm Ava Lee. I'm a partner in Three Sisters, an

investment firm that is the majority owner of the business that was blown up. I'm from Toronto, Canada," she said. "Next to me is another partner in Three Sisters, Amanda Yee. She's from Hong Kong. Next to Amanda is Chi-Tze Song; she manages one of our businesses in Shanghai but is originally from Borneo and is a minority owner in the lumber business. And last is Aisyah Tengku, from Kota Kinabalu, who is in charge of all our operations in Borneo."

"Who would have imagined that such a small warehouse and distribution operation would have so many international connections," Kamir said.

"It wasn't planned. It just fell into place that way," said Ava.

"Your other business interests are more substantial?" Kamir asked.

"Yes. They're centred in China and Hong Kong. But that's not to diminish our commitment to Borneo. We've been very pleased with the investment we made in Sabah and, up to now, our business here in Sarawak."

"The events of the past few days must have been very upsetting to bring all of you to this part of the world."

"Of course they were upsetting, but it wouldn't have mattered where they took place; our reaction would have been the same," Ava said. "And besides, Sarawak is hardly the end of the world."

"Not everyone would share that view, but regardless, you are here."

"Yes, we are, and we have questions about the bombing and Jamilah's death," Ava said, and saw the constable glance quickly at Kamir.

"We have concluded that the unfortunate young woman in all probability set the bomb that destroyed your business and somehow became a victim of her own actions," he said without hesitation. "A statement to that effect was released to the media an hour ago, although, out of respect for her family, we were careful not to impugn her directly."

"We don't believe she could have done that."

"You disagree with the findings of our experts?"

"Is there an official report we can see?"

"Of course there is a report, but it's restricted to immediate family."

"We can get her family to make the request," said Ava.

"Even then, there might be some reluctance to share such a sensitive document."

Her frustration growing but still under control, Ava pressed. "What about this Sarawak United Front that claimed responsibility for the attack? Have you managed to find out who they are?"

Kamir sat back in his chair, seemingly more relaxed with that line of questioning. "We have done an extensive search but have been unable to confirm their existence."

"Is it possible they don't exist?"

"That has occurred to us."

"But you released a statement saying they had claimed responsibility for the bombing. How could you do that without any proof they're real?"

"Someone representing themselves as part of the Sarawak United Front made that claim, and that information was released," Kamir said carefully. "We made no assertion that the organization is real or that the claim was factual."

"How was the claim made?"

"The police and members of the local media received emails."

"Can we see them?"

"No."

"Which media received them?" Ava asked.

"I'm not at liberty to say."

The constable shifted in her chair. Ava, sensing her discomfort, smiled at her. "Are you writing all this down?"

"Some of it," Lazim said.

She turned back to Kamir. "We're going to ask the family to request a copy of the official report, including the emails sent by the Sarawak United Front."

"You are free to do so, and the family has the right to make that request. But, as I said, I can't guarantee they'll get a positive response," Kamir said, and then leaned forward. "Ladies, I'm trying to be as helpful as I can without stepping beyond certain limits. The sad truth is that all the evidence indicates that your friend, your employee, was responsible for the explosion. I can understand why that may be difficult for you to accept."

"But it makes no sense at all!" Aisyah blurted.

"Our understanding is that she was a rather zealous member of Friends of the Earth and was a supporter of several other environmental and Indigenous rights groups. Our theory is that she targeted your business to draw attention to their cause," he said. "Her commitment to them was obviously stronger than her commitment to you."

Ava noticed that Lazim had stopped writing and watching Kamir. Her head was lowered and she stared down at her hands.

"That's absurd!" Aisyah said loudly. "It's totally illogical."

"There's no need to raise your voice," Kamir said sharply.

"But it's complete bullshit!" Aisyah said, her voice breaking as it continued to rise.

Kamir shook his head. "I'm afraid I'm going to have to end our meeting. It's obvious you have different opinions, and while I respect your right to have them, I can't permit you to behave like this in my office."

"Sergeant, surely you can understand why Aisyah —" Ava began.

"I don't care to listen to you anymore," he interrupted, holding up a hand. "This is over. Constable Lazim will escort you out of the building. Please don't make a fuss as you go."

Aisyah turned to look at Ava as if saying *Do something*.

Ava stood up. "We'll leave now. Thank you for your time, Sergeant Kamir. You will hear from Jamilah's family, and I think we may engage a local lawyer to represent our interests in this matter."

"That is your right," Kamir said.

"Let's go, ladies," Ava said to the other women.

Lazim put her notebook on Kamir's desk and opened the door. Ava joined the constable, with the others falling in behind. "Lead the way," she said to Lazim.

As they started to walk along the corridor, Ava noticed Lazim glancing at her. "Is there something you want to say to me?" Ava asked softly.

"Yes, but not here," Lazim whispered. "Where are you staying?"

"The Riverside Majestic."

"I'll come to the hotel," Lazim said. "My shift ends at eight. I'll call you from the lobby."

(12)

CONSTABLE LAZIM WALKED THEM ALL THE WAY TO THE
entrance gate. She waited until they managed to hail a taxi
before leaving wordlessly.

"What was that about?" Amanda asked as soon as the
taxi pulled away.

"She's coming to the hotel tonight."

"She didn't seem very comfortable listening to the sergeant," said Amanda.

"No, she didn't," said Ava.

"He was lying through his teeth," Chi-Tze said bitterly.

"He was so full of shit," Aisyah added.

"That's obvious, but I do wish you hadn't expressed your
opinion to him quite so quickly."

"I'm sorry, I couldn't restrain myself," Aisyah said. "Really,
I am sorry."

"What do you think is really going on?" Chi-Tze asked Ava.

"He recited what he'd been told — the official position —
and we weren't going to get him to budge from that," Ava
said. "It's even more obvious now that someone higher up

the chain is issuing the orders. We need to find out who. Maybe Constable Lazim will know."

"Do you think she'll tell us if she does?" Amanda asked.

"I don't know, but I'm keenly interested in whatever she has to say," Ava said as the taxi approached the hotel.

On their arrival at the Riverside Majestic, the women gathered in the lobby. "The constable won't be here until after eight, so we can go out somewhere for dinner if you like," Ava said.

"I have no appetite," Aisyah said.

"Me neither," Chi-Tze added.

"Okay, then we'll meet back here at eight," said Ava.

"Do you mind if I come to your room for a few minutes now?" Amanda asked.

"Of course not."

The four women got into the elevator together, and Aisyah and Chi-Tze got out on a lower floor.

"What's up?" Ava asked as soon as she was alone with Amanda.

"Let's wait until we're in your room."

Ava unlocked the door and led them inside. "Would you like something to drink?" she asked.

"A beer would be nice."

Beer was Amanda's drink of choice, and Ava had seen her consume large quantities in the past. She also had a hearty appetite and never seemed to exercise, which left Ava perplexed as to how she managed to remain so slim. Ava opened the minibar. "Carlsberg or Heineken?" she offered.

"Carlsberg," Amanda said as she sat down on the couch.

Ava took out the beer and a small bottle of Chardonnay,

grabbed two glasses, and joined Amanda. After the drinks were poured, she said, "Now, what's up?"

"Aisyah asked me if we're going to rebuild the business here. Both the building and the inventory were insured. The question is, do we really want to continue operating in Sarawak?"

"What is Aisyah's opinion?"

"She wants to rebuild, but when I asked about her reasoning, she was vague and a bit emotional," said Amanda. "It could be she thinks it's a way to honour Jamilah's memory."

"We should hear her out, though I have to say I'm not eager to reopen."

"Chi-Tze is also opposed to rebuilding, but she will go along with whatever we decide."

"Did you discuss the idea of selling the business with her?"

"Briefly, and her initial reaction was what I expected. She's for it, but she isn't sure it will be easy to find a buyer."

"Maybe Aisyah and some of the employees could put together a purchase group. Our cash position is strong, so we wouldn't need a lot of money upfront. I'd be content with letting them buy it over time. It could end up being positive for us in terms of cash flow," said Ava.

"That is a thought. And truthfully, I'll support any plan that lets us put Borneo behind us," Amanda said.

"Then talk it over with Chi-Tze."

"I will," Amanda said, finishing her beer with one large gulp.

"Do you want another?"

"I'd better not," said Amanda, and then hesitated before asking, "Are we going to be able to do anything about the Jamilah situation? It sounded to me like the outcome has already been decided."

"I agree with you about the way the police are behaving, but that doesn't mean we should stop digging," Ava said. "My worry is — if Brooke is correct — that this is the kind of place where the truth can be easily buried."

"Maybe Constable Lazim can help."

"Maybe," Ava said with a sigh, and then stood up. "I have some calls to make before the meeting. I'll see you in the lobby at eight."

When Amanda had left the suite, Ava reached for her phone. She called Fai first, got her voicemail, and said, "It's me. It is just before six in the evening. I have a meeting later tonight, but I should be back in my room around ten. I'll call you then. Love you."

May Ling answered her phone with a soft "*wei*." In the background Ava thought she could hear Lau Lau's voice. "Are you on the film set?" she asked.

"Yes, I've been here most of the day. It's fascinating," May said. "How are things there?"

"Not good. The police are saying that Jamilah set the bomb herself, which is obviously ridiculous. I'm not sure we'll be able to set the record straight," said Ava. "We're all a little discouraged."

"Do they have any proof?"

"Absolutely none. I think they just want to pin it on her and then move on."

"If there's nothing you can do, you should leave that place."

"Not right now. I want to work on this for another day or two, although truthfully, I don't know how much more I can accomplish here."

"Ava, don't be stubborn. Don't stay there if there's nothing to be done."

"I won't. And speaking of staying here, Amanda and I have been discussing the idea of not reopening the business in Kuching and selling the furniture plant in Kota Kinabalu."

"Whatever you decide is fine with me," May said. "I know Borneo has bad memories for both of you."

"Thank you, but the personal stuff shouldn't matter. We'll try to make sure whatever we decide is best for the business," said Ava.

"Stay in touch. I'm leaving for Wuhan tomorrow."

Ava put down the phone and then lay down on the bed. She thought she would try to nap, but her head was too full of Jamilah. Half an hour later she rolled off the bed, refreshed in the washroom, and went downstairs to sit in the bar. She was halfway through a glass of Chardonnay when she was joined by Amanda.

"I was too restless to stay in my room," Amanda said.

Ten minutes later they were joined by Chi-Tze and Aisyah.

"We're all early," said Ava.

"Including Constable Lazim. As I was coming through the lobby, I saw her standing outside," said Chi-Tze.

Ava looked towards the hotel entrance. A young woman who at first glance looked nothing like the constable was standing near the doorway. Her hair was hanging loose around her shoulders instead of being pinned back in a bun. She was wearing a plain white T-shirt, blue jeans, and running shoes. Ava left the table and walked over to meet her. "We didn't expect you so soon," she said.

"It was quiet at the office and I was able to get away," Lazim said.

"Thank you for coming. Do you want to come inside with us?"

"Sure," Lazim said after a slight hesitation.

"Do you mind sitting with us in a public place?"

"No."

"The bar is in the lobby," Ava said. "This is a weeknight, so it isn't very busy. Is that okay with you?"

"Yes. I could actually use a drink."

"Then join us," Ava said.

A server approached as soon as they sat down. When she had taken their drink orders, Ava turned to Lazim. "We appreciate your coming here tonight. Jamilah's death has really upset us, which I'm sure you saw today."

"It upset me as well," Lazim said.

"How so?"

Lazim looked down at her hands, then raised her head to look directly at Ava. "I knew Jamilah. We grew up in the same village and went to school together until we left to go to different universities. When she moved to Kuching to take the job with your company, she called me. We met a couple of times, but our lives were so different that we didn't have much in common anymore, so I didn't follow up. I'm sorry now that I didn't make more of an effort."

"Did you know her family as well?" Ava asked.

"Yes."

"We were told they belong to a Christian sect that believes people who commit suicide are damned to hell."

"They do. The way Jamilah's death is being portrayed must be haunting them."

The server arrived with wine for Ava, beer for Amanda and Lazim, and lemonade for Chi-Tze and Aisyah. "To better days," Ava said, extending her glass towards Lazim.

They sipped their drinks. Ava saw that the constable seemed

anxious and decided not to ease her way into the conversation. "Tell me, do you really believe Jamilah set that bomb?"

Lazim shook her head.

"Then who did?"

"Someone who wanted to shut down your business. Jamilah must have been peripheral damage."

Aisyah groaned and closed her eyes. Chi-Tze reached for her hand.

"Did Sergeant Kamir have that information when he met with us?" Ava asked.

"Of course."

"So he lied to us."

"He did, but judging by your reaction, I think you knew that already."

"Yes, I thought he was lying, but it's still good to have it confirmed," said Ava. "What I don't know is why he would lie. Or, more importantly, why the police are so eager for everyone to believe she was the culprit."

"The Sergeant was following orders."

"Orders from whom?"

"If I tell you, no one can know that I did."

"You have my word that no one will be told, and I guarantee that my colleagues will follow my example," said Ava.

Lazim glanced around at all of them and then nodded. "Almost immediately after it was known Jamilah had died, the Sergeant and three senior staff were given those orders by Deputy Commissioner Hassan."

"How do you know that?"

"I was at the meeting when they were given," she said. "I often take notes for the Sergeant, like I was doing when you met with him today. He is a careful man and maintains records of all his meetings. I've been doing it for so long that everyone, including the most senior staff, is accustomed to my presence. So accustomed, in fact, that they sometimes forget I'm in the room. I'm like a piece of the furniture to them."

"Did Deputy Commissioner Hassan say why Jamilah was to be blamed for the bombing?" Ava asked.

"Not specifically. All he said was that there are issues at play that involve state security, and that it had been decided to put a complete stop to any further investigations into both her death and the warehouse bombing. He then read the statement that was later released to the media."

"Did he say anything more about these 'issues at play'?"

"No, that was left vague, and no one pursued it any further."

"Was the decision to stop the investigations made by Hassan alone?"

"No. Later, when the others had left and it was just him and Sergeant Kamir in the room, the Sergeant asked him how high up the chain of command the decision went," Lazim said. "The Deputy Commissioner said that Commissioner Chik had made the decision, in consultation with Arven Saad."

"The Arven Saad who works for the Chong family?"

"Yes. He's the executive vice-president of Chong Timber Industries."

"Are you saying the police made the decision about Jamilah at Saad's request?"

"I can only repeat what the Deputy Commissioner told the Sergeant."

"That Commissioner Chik and Saad made the decision together?"

"Yes, but I think it's possible that Saad dictated the decision to the Commissioner," Lazim said.

"If that's true, wouldn't the Sergeant think it strange?"

"Not if the Commissioner was involved," Lazim said.

"Did the Sergeant express any reservations at all about the decision?"

"Not to me, and I doubt he ever would. He's a stickler for respecting rank. I've never heard him question an order."

Ava shook her head, then sipped her wine while she gathered her thoughts. "How is it possible for Saad to exert that much influence over the police department?" she finally asked.

"You obviously don't know much about Sarawak."

"That's true, I don't. But I did hear some things about Chong earlier today, and I'm already making assumptions."

Lazim nodded. "The Chong family controls most of what goes on in this state, through a combination of money and politics. Arven Saad is perhaps the most powerful man in their organization outside of the family itself. If he met with the Commissioner — and I don't doubt he did — it would be at the direction of the family."

"Has the Chong family, directly or through proxies, interfered with police business before?"

"Not that I know of, but I wouldn't be surprised to find they had."

"Let me change the subject for a moment. What has Sergeant Kamir told you about the Sarawak United Front?"

"He doesn't think it exists. He says someone probably invented the name as a cover for the bombing."

"And who does he think really planted the bomb?"

"He hasn't said, but Deputy Commissioner Hassan

suggested that Jamilah might have done it to draw attention to the crusade against the illegal logging going on in
the interior. He said she might have wanted to frame the
logging companies for the attack."

"And no one questioned that?" Ava asked.

"No, just the opposite, as you heard from Sergeant Kamir."

"It's all very convoluted. It seems to me that they've jumped
to a conclusion and are now twisting the facts to match."

"You have to understand their reasoning," Lazim said.
"Jamilah is dead. There is no one left to dispute their conclusions. They can spin any story they want because there's
no one to contradict them."

"No one?"

"Tell me who," Lazim said with a shrug.

"Us."

"And assuming you find facts to the contrary, who's going
to believe you? Who's going to take action?"

"Isn't there anyone who might listen to us?"

"Not in Sarawak. The verdict is already in."

"Are things really that corrupt here?"

Lazim drained her beer and sat back in the chair with a
grim look on her face. "No one thinks of it as being corrupt.
They think of it as being pragmatic, something they're doing
in the best interests of the state."

"And there's nowhere we could turn?"

"You could try going over the Commissioner's head to his
superiors in Kuala Lumpur, but I can tell you from experience there's little chance that would succeed."

"So we should just leave it alone, forget about it," Ava said.

"I won't forget about Jamilah, and I don't imagine you will
either, but that's about the extent of what we can do."

"What if we went to the news media?" Amanda asked.

"Is that a joke? I sure hope it is," Lazim said. "Who do you think owns the media in Sarawak?"

"The Chongs?" suggested Ava.

"Of course."

"Do they control everything?"

"Most of the things that matter, and that includes the courts. So if you were thinking about hiring a lawyer to pursue this, I wouldn't bother."

"Good grief, I thought the days of the Raj were over," said Ava.

"They are, but they've been replaced by the days of Sultan Sulaiman."

Ava turned her head and looked distractedly around the bar. She tried to conjure up more questions but couldn't think of any that would elicit helpful answers. Looking towards Lazim again, she finally said, "From what you're telling me, it seems we've reached a dead end."

"I think you have."

"So why did you come here at all? Why tell us anything if it's pointless?"

Lazim ran her tongue over her lips, and a tear escaped from one eye. "I wanted someone besides me to know the truth. Also, the times I did meet with Jamilah, she spoke very highly of Aisyah and your company. She said you treated her properly, and that's a rare thing for a woman in Sarawak. When I met you earlier today, it seemed to me that you're also the kind of people who will keep digging into her death, and I wanted you to understand what a bad idea that is. You would only be putting yourselves at risk."

"I appreciate your concern for our well-being," Ava said.

"Please, take me seriously when it comes to that."

"I do, and I apologize if I sounded ungrateful," said Ava. "I just find it all very frustrating."

"Well, I've said what I came to say, so I should be heading home," Lazim said, rising to her feet.

Ava stood and held out a business card. "Thank you for coming. We'll talk among ourselves and decide what's to be done. In the meantime, if you find out anything else you think we should know, you can reach me at this number."

The two women shook hands. Lazim nodded at the others, then left the bar.

"Well, that was discouraging," Ava said as she sat down again.

"It fits with everything I've been told about this place," Aisyah said.

"Can any of you think of anything we could do to change this situation?" Ava asked.

The three other women glanced at each other, then shook their heads.

"I can't think of anything right now either, so I guess that's it," Ava said. "What else can we do except make plans to leave?"

"We have a meeting with the insurance company tomorrow morning at nine," Aisyah said. "They want to do it at what's left of the warehouse."

"We should all be there for that," Ava said. "Shall we meet for breakfast and go together?"

"That sounds like a plan," said Amanda. "How about we meet at seven-thirty?"

"That's fine with me," Ava said, and then surprised herself with a yawn. "You'll have to excuse me, ladies. It's been a very long day and I'm ready for bed."

Amanda stood up. "I'll share the elevator with you."

They left the bar and were starting across the lobby when Amanda said, "I don't remember the last time I was this angry. I tried to contain it in front of Aisyah and Chi-Tze, but I'm boiling mad. And what makes it worse is knowing there's nothing we can do."

Ava stopped and turned to face her. "There's always something that can be done. We just haven't discovered it yet."

13

DESPITE HER WORDS TO AMANDA, AVA FELT HELPLESS — more helpless than she'd felt in years. As she entered her suite, she turned on her phone, collapsed onto the bed, and hit Fai's number.

"Hi, baby," Fai answered. "I wasn't expecting you to call so soon."

"Am I disturbing something?"

"No, I just thought your meeting would go longer."

"It wasn't much of a meeting," Ava said.

"You sound discouraged. That's not like you."

"The meeting depressed me. In fact, this place depresses me," Ava said. "Our warehouse and office were blown up, our local manager was murdered, and all I hear is lies and veiled threats that we should just walk away."

Fai paused. "This is *really* not like you."

Ava slid from the bed and took a small bottle of cognac from the mini bar. "I'm pouring myself a drink," she said. "I'll be with you in a few seconds."

"There's no rush."

Instead of returning to the bed, Ava went to sit in a chair

by the window, which overlooked the Sarawak River. "Are you still there, Fai?" she asked.

"Of course."

"The only other time I can remember feeling so helpless was when I was abducted by a gang of creeps in Kota Kinabalu. That was the time when Amanda and Chi-Tze were attacked. We were all so vulnerable — emotionally, psychologically, and physically. I'm not sure any of us would have survived if it hadn't been for Xu."

"You know Xu will do anything for you. He's still there to help if you need him now."

"This is different. We're not contending with a gang; we're dealing with a powerful family that has this place completely under its thumb. That includes the police, the government, and the legal system. Even Xu can't take on an entire state."

"You will come up with something. You always do."

"This time, I'm not so sure," said Ava. "Amanda thinks Borneo has brought us nothing but bad luck, and I'm starting to believe she's right. Maybe we should just put it behind us and move on."

"I'm all for that if it means you'll return to Taipei sooner."

Ava started to respond but was interrupted by the hotel phone ringing. "I'll be right back," she said to Fai, and picked up the other line. "Yes?"

"I'm sorry to disturb you, but I thought you should know that the insurance company has cancelled tomorrow's meeting," Amanda said.

"They want to reschedule?"

Amanda hesitated and then said in a rush, "No. At least, not until they have a better understanding of what happened. They've seen the police statement and now believe it is more than possible that Jamilah blew up our business. They say that under those circumstances they have no liability, and that there's no point in meeting until things are clarified."

"This just goes from bad to worse," Ava said.

"I know. Chi-Tze and Aisyah are very upset. They're going out for a walk on the esplanade, and I'm going to join them. It might be reassuring if you did as well."

"I don't feel like taking a walk," Ava said, and then caught herself. "But if you think it will help calm the others, I'll meet you in the lobby."

"Thank you. I'll see you downstairs."

Amanda is becoming a good manager — not just of her staff but also of me, Ava thought as she hung up the phone and returned to Fai. "I have to go, Fai. There's another problem here that needs my attention. It isn't dangerous, but I have to tend to it."

"Call me when you get back. It was an exciting day on set, and I won't be able to sleep for a while."

"Exciting?" Ava said, concern creeping into her voice.

"Yes. All good, so there's no need to worry. Go and do what you have to do."

Ava put down the phone and went into the bedroom. If she was going to walk, she might as well be comfortable. She changed into a T-shirt, Adidas training pants, and running shoes.

The women were once again waiting in the lobby when she stepped off the elevator. "This is so terrible," Aisyah said as Ava reached them.

"Let's talk while we walk," said Ava.

They left the hotel and found their way onto the esplanade. Amanda linked her left arm through Ava's and her right through Chi-Tze's. Aisyah was on Ava's left, and Ava linked arms with her.

"What insurance company are we using?" Ava asked Aisyah as the four walked side by side.

"Jamilah found it. It's the local agency for a large firm with its head office in Kuala Lumpur. I signed off on the policy after Amanda gave me the go-ahead."

"It's a reputable company, and I reviewed the policy and thought it was comprehensive," said Amanda. "It covered the building and its contents, including our entire inventory, for just about everything, even acts of God."

"Maybe we should be speaking to the head office," said Ava.

"I expect they'll take their direction from the local agency," Aisyah said.

"Still, we should make the effort."

"I'll reach out to them tomorrow," Amanda said. "If I have to, I'll involve our lawyers."

"I wonder if it would be wiser to use a local lawyer rather than one in Hong Kong," Ava said.

"Are you thinking of Mamat's friend?" asked Amanda.

"He does seem to be well connected," said Ava.

The esplanade suddenly became quite crowded. It was wide enough to accommodate them, but the area they were in was lined with food stalls. There were lineups at the stalls and people standing at the railings looking across the river. The women unlinked arms and moved to one side.

"It makes me ill to think about how much money we could lose if the insurance company doesn't pay," Aisyah said.

"As much as I dislike losing money, I have to say that isn't top of mind right now," said Ava.

Aisyah shook her head. "For me neither, but it seems as if things just keep piling up, and I'm not sure what to worry about most."

"Hey, ladies," a man said from behind them.

Ava turned to see two men, both at least six feet tall, approaching. They wore jeans and T-shirts that accentuated lean, muscular torsos. Their hair was buzz-cut, they looked neat and orderly, and they carried themselves like soldiers.

The women stopped walking and turned towards the river. The men moved alongside but maintained their distance. The slightly taller of the two reached into his pocket and pulled out a piece of paper, looked it at, and then put it back. "Would you know where we can find the Riverside Majestic Hotel?" he asked.

"Yes, it's over there," Aisyah said as she pointed at it.

"You wouldn't be staying there by chance, would you?" he asked.

"Why would that be of interest to you?" asked Amanda.

"We're on our way to see some women staying there," he said. "Is one of you Ava Lee?"

Ava felt a chill run down her spine. "Let's keep walking, ladies," she said, and began to move away from the men. "Don't look back. Those guys are trouble."

They had gone no more than four steps when the trouble materialized. It started with a gasp from Aisyah as she was propelled face-first onto the ground. Ava turned and saw the taller man drive his fist into the back of Chi-Tze's neck. As she collapsed next to Aisyah, he pulled his arm back to strike Amanda from behind.

"Aiiieee!" Ava screamed, the frustration of the day morphing into rage. She coiled and released her phoenix-eye fist with every ounce of power she could generate. It caught the attacker squarely in the middle of his nose — or what had been his nose, because it seemed to disintegrate as bone cracked and blood flew. He screeched in pain as he reeled backwards. Ava leapt after him, the toe of her shoe knifing into his groin. He stumbled, and she kicked him again, and then again. He fell to the ground, a hand still covering his nose, and she kicked him one more time.

It had all happened so fast the man's partner had barely moved. He stood staring at Ava, his mouth slightly agape, trying to comprehend what was going on. Then he shook his shoulders. "Goddamn you!" he yelled, and started towards Ava.

She waited until he was just a couple of steps away, with his right fist balled and pulled back. When she sensed he was almost ready to throw the punch, she became the aggressor. Ava took one step forward and then her feet left the ground. The base of her right palm caught the man in the middle of the forehead. As his head snapped back, her left fist drove into his throat. The sound he made as he fell to the ground was a combination of grunt, groan, and gargle, like something that would come from a wounded animal. He writhed on the ground, gasping for air.

Ava stepped over him towards the man with the smashed nose. She reached into his pocket and took out the piece of paper. On it were four small photos of Ava, Chi-Tze, Amanda, and Aisyah.

14

THEY SAT IN STUNNED SILENCE IN THE BAR OF THE Riverside Majestic. Chi-Tze and Aisyah had stopped crying by the time they reached the hotel, but Amanda had been too shocked for tears. Ava waved to the server and ordered the same drinks they'd had an hour earlier.

Aisyah started to speak when the server left, but Ava reached out and tapped her hand. "Let's wait. Have a drink. Pull yourself together. We need to think this through."

When the drinks had been brought to the table, almost as one they lifted their glasses and drank.

"How are your heads?" Ava asked Chi-Tze and Aisyah.

"Mine is sore, but I can move my neck okay," Aisyah said.

"Me too, and the double vision is gone now," Chi-Tze said.

"Good," Ava said.

"Who were those guys?" Amanda asked.

"I think they were cops. They had the photos of us taken today at the police station," Ava said.

"Why would the police attack us like that?" Aisyah asked.

"As bad as things are here, I doubt it was sanctioned. They must have been hired by someone else."

"Who? The Chongs?" Amanda said.

"Who else could it be? After our meeting with Sergeant Kamir, I imagine he phoned the deputy commissioner, or maybe even Arven Saad, to say that four nosy women were asking questions about Jamilah. Maybe those men were sent to frighten us off. They weren't armed, so they weren't there to kill us — not yet, anyway." Ava saw Aisyah pale and realized she shouldn't have made that last remark. "I was joking about them trying to kill us," she said quickly.

"You came closer to killing them," Aisyah stammered. "I've never seen anything like that."

"Nothing makes me angrier than men who beat up women. They think they can do it with impunity. That smirk as they raise a hand, and that look in their eyes that says *I own you...*" Ava said, glancing down at her glass of wine. "I don't often lose control like that, but I was thinking of Jamilah, and for a few seconds I thought they could be the men who killed her."

"Do you think they were?" Aisyah asked.

"I have no idea, but it's possible."

"What are we going to do now?" Amanda asked.

"Leave Sarawak," Ava said.

"Do you mean that?"

"Absolutely. There's nothing to be gained by staying here, and as we saw just now, there's a lot to lose. If the Chongs hired those men who came after us today, they can hire more tomorrow," Ava said. "Amanda, when you get to your room, please make arrangements for all of us to get out of here as soon as possible. I'd like us to travel together to Hong Kong. Chi-Tze can connect to Shanghai from there."

"You know there are no direct flights from here to Hong Kong, right?" Amanda said.

"Then find the connection that will get us there the quickest," Ava said.

"But I need to get back to Kota Kinabalu. I can get there directly from here," Aisyah said.

"Until things are settled, I think you should stay out of Sabah," said Ava.

"What about the business?"

"Do you have people in place to run it while you're gone?"

"Yes."

"Then let them run it. I want you to stay in Hong Kong until we're sure there isn't any risk."

"We have a spare bedroom in our apartment. I'm sure my husband won't object to you staying for a little while," Amanda said.

"This is so crazy," Aisyah said.

"Maybe so, but it isn't something we created," Ava said.

Silence descended on the table as they finished their drinks between furtive glances into the lobby. Ava understood the anxiety but thought it was misplaced. She was convinced that whoever hired the men wouldn't be so quick to repeat their mistake. There would be more thinking, more planning behind their next move, and by then she intended to have all the women safely ensconced in Hong Kong and Shanghai.

"Well, I don't know if any of us are going to get a good night's sleep after that, but I think we should give it a try," Ava said. "Amanda will call us when the flights are arranged, and we'll meet at whatever time she says is appropriate. Is everyone okay with that?"

"Yes," Chi-Tze said, while Aisyah nodded.

"Then let's go to our rooms," said Ava.

They linked arms as they left the bar and crossed the lobby. Before Chi-Tze and Aisyah left the elevator at their floor, they shared an intense group hug. "I'll call you as soon as I've made the flight arrangements," Amanda said to them.

When the elevator door closed, she turned to Ava. "I'm kind of surprised by how I reacted when I saw you attack those men. I keep thinking it should have upset me, but it didn't. Instead I found it kind of thrilling. Is that wrong of me?"

"When I'm in the moment, I never think about right or wrong. Later I may think I went too far, but just as often I think I didn't go far enough," Ava said. "I don't know what that says about me."

Amanda held out her arms. "Give me a hug. I was so lucky the day you became my *da sao*."

"I feel the same way about you," said Ava.

The elevator doors opened to interrupt their hug. Amanda held Ava's hand as they walked along the corridor. "I'll organize the flights as soon as I get to my room," she said.

Ava entered her suite and stood distractedly near the door for several seconds as she tried to decide what to do first. She wanted to call Fai and May Ling, but she wasn't sure she was quite ready to tell them everything that had happened. *A shower will help*, she thought. *A full-bore shower with the water as hot as I can bear it will wash away the day's unpleasant memories.*

She stepped into the shower and turned the water to its maximum intensity. She stood still for the next ten minutes, her body relaxing under the powerful stream as the tension gradually began to ease. She turned off the shower, slipped on a terrycloth robe, wrapped a towel around her head, and went into the living room. She picked up the small bottle of cognac she'd started drinking before going for the walk and sat down at the desk. There were no messages on her phone, so she assumed Amanda was still putting together their travel schedule.

Fai or May Ling? *Better put business first,* she thought, as she called her friend.

May's phone rang five times before she answered, and Ava heard a public address announcement in the background. "Where are you?"

"I'm at the Taipei airport. I'm leaving for Wuhan tonight. Where are you?"

"I'm in my hotel room," Ava said. "Today was a complete disaster."

"What happened?" May asked, instantly becoming anxious.

"The police have decided to cover up Jamilah's murder. They want the world to believe she set the bomb and mistakenly killed herself in the explosion."

"That's horrible!"

"Yes, but there's more," Ava said. "Given the police's position, our insurance company has decided to hold off on paying our claim. Frankly, I think we'll have to accept that they'll probably never pay."

"We need to get our lawyers involved," May said.

"Yes. Amanda and I discussed that earlier, and she'll get on it tomorrow, but there's more," Ava said. "An hour ago we were out for a walk near the hotel when we are attacked by two off-duty policemen. I think they wanted to frighten us so we'd stop poking around. It went badly for them, but it shook up the others. I've told Amanda to book flights out of here as soon as possible. I want to get all of us to Hong Kong, where we'll be safe.

"We'll talk to our lawyers when we're back, but I honestly don't care about the insurance money. I also don't want to reopen this business. Let's just write it off, and while we're at it, let's get rid of the furniture company. I'm done with Borneo."

"You know I'll do whatever you think is best, Ava, but I have to say this attitude isn't at all like you," May said.

"I think what got me to this point, May, is seeing Aisyah and Chi-Tze get punched from behind and the same goon getting ready to attack Amanda. I've always felt guilty about what happened to Amanda and Chi-Tze in Kota Kinabalu. They never blamed me, of course, but I put them in a position that turned out to be vulnerable, and now I feel I've done it again. It took them weeks to recover physically, and while I like to think they got past the emotional trauma, I can never be certain. I won't let them go through anything like that again."

May paused, then said softly, "We'll do exactly what you want."

"Thank you, May, for your love and support."

"Just stay in touch. I won't relax until you're all in Hong Kong."

Ava put down her phone and reached for the glass of cognac. She was finishing a second sip when the room phone rang. "Hello," she said.

"Hi, this is Amanda. The fastest way to Hong Kong is through Kuala Lumpur. I've booked us on a flight leaving here for KL at seven a.m. tomorrow. We land around nine and have enough time to catch a ten-o'clock flight to Hong Kong. We'll get in around two in the afternoon."

"Perfect. Let the girls know. What time should we meet in the lobby?"

"Five-thirty should give us ample time."

"I'll see you then. And Amanda, thanks for doing this."

"*Mei wenti,* boss. No problem."

Ava sighed and reached for her phone to call Fai. "It's me again," she said when Fai answered.

"You don't sound any cheerier."

"Things haven't changed much," Ava said, deciding not to discuss the attack on the esplanade. "But the good news is I should be in Hong Kong tomorrow afternoon and headed for Taipei not long after that."

"That's wonderful."

"Now, absolutely no more about me. Tell me about your day. You said it was exciting."

"Not exciting in the sense of action. It was actually a quiet thing, but Lau Lau handled it brilliantly, and Silvana was amazing."

"You can't stop there."

Fai laughed. "We were shooting the scene where the mother and the general meet for the first time. They're in a street close to Tiananmen, both for different reasons, but the street is deserted and it's dangerous for them to be there. When they see each other, they're immediately suspicious, but they're so driven that they can't help making contact, just in case the other person has information they want or need. When they start to talk, it's in half-sentences, each of them afraid to speak openly about why they are there. Lau Lau had us slowly circling each other, like vultures waiting for their prey to die."

"I can't wait to see it."

"We're shooting the same scene again tomorrow, so who knows what it will look like when Lau Lau is finished. All I know is that he's found his stride. Even Silvana commented on how good he is; she said it's been years since a director forced her to dig so deep."

"I'm so happy for him, and for you."

"Ava, this is going to be a fantastic film."

"I'll trust your judgement on that."

"It will be very good, I promise you."

"And I promise you I'll be back in Taipei in a day or two."

"That sounds like you're saying goodnight," Fai said.

"I am tired, and we have a very early start tomorrow," Ava said. "I should try to get some sleep."

"Then go and get it," Fai said. "I love you."

"I love you too, and I'm anxious to get back to you," Ava said, and put down the phone.

She towelled her hair. It wasn't completely dry, but it was good enough. She carried her phone to the bed, set the alarm for five, and for good measure called the front desk and asked for a five-o'clock wake-up call. With that done, she took off her robe and climbed into bed. Her eyes closed and she felt herself slipping quickly away.

Ava was never sure if Uncle came to her when she was deep in sleep or when her mind was wandering in the grey area between sleep and consciousness, but he did visit her often in her dreams, usually during times of stress and uncertainty. He came to her that night, sitting in the chair by the window, partially hidden in shadow. Only the glow of his cigarette illuminated his face.

I am not used to seeing you like this, he said.

It has been difficult.

I know it is worrisome, but you cannot let it become too much for you.

What can I do? I'm in a place where absolute power is concentrated in the hands of one family. If I take them on, I'll be putting my partners and employees at risk. I can't do that.

Protecting your partners and attacking the Chong family don't have to be linked. Once your people are in Hong Kong, they will be out of reach of the Chongs, said Uncle. *Remember, they may run Sarawak, but this place is not much more than a pimple on the ass of the world.*

What do you mean by that? she asked, surprised by his crudeness.

No one cares what happens in Sarawak, not even the Chongs. They have already pillaged the state, so there is not much left for them to steal. The question you need to ask yourself is, what have they done with all the money they have stolen?

Amanda says a lot of it is in Hong Kong.

That makes them vulnerable. You cannot hide assets in Hong Kong. Someone always knows what you have and where it is, said Uncle.

Amanda thinks they've invested most of it in real estate.

Even so, I guarantee there will still be cash somewhere, he said. *Chinese families value liquidity.*

I don't understand what you're trying to tell me, she said.

Ava, you cannot just walk away from what these people have done. It runs contrary to your character, and you will always regret it if you do not seek justice for yourself and your friends. If you cannot get it in Sarawak, look elsewhere.

Hong Kong?

Uncle nodded, took a deep drag of his cigarette, and then butted it out in an ashtray.

But I know virtually nothing about their businesses.

You will figure it out.

Uncle — she said, but he was gone, and all she could hear was the ringing of phones.

15

THE WOMEN WERE QUIET WHEN AVA JOINED THEM IN the lobby at five-thirty. She didn't know if they were tired or lost in thought, but she was grateful for the silence. She was still trying to make sense of Uncle's late-night visit. It had disturbed her, and she couldn't stop thinking about it.

There wasn't much talk during the trip to the airport, and the check-in and boarding processes were equally subdued. The flight was almost full, and because Amanda had purchased the tickets so late, the women were scattered around the plane. Ava was in business class; she was grateful for the extra space as she curled up against the window, waved off breakfast service, and closed her eyes.

She might have dozed, but for most of the trip her mind remained focused on Uncle. He had been correct; it wasn't in her character to cut and run, and it bothered her that she had been thinking that way. Now any thoughts about accepting what had happened in Sarawak were gone. Instead she knew she had to find some way to correct the wrongs. As that decision took hold, her mind started to clear.

The plane landed in Kuala Lumpur on time. Ava waited

at the gate for the others, and then they made their way to the far end of the terminal to catch their connecting flight. Pre-boarding had started when they arrived. Ava was in business class again and could have gone onto the plane, but she hung back with the others. Everyone's mood seemed to have lightened, and Amanda was talking to Aisyah about taking her to dinner at a hotpot restaurant in Central when Ava's phone rang. She glanced at the screen and saw the Malaysia country code, but she didn't recognize the number.

"Hello?" she said tentatively.

"This is Lydia," a woman said.

"I don't know anyone named Lydia."

"Lydia Lazim, Constable Lazim."

"Oh, hi. What can I do for you?" Ava said.

"You need to leave the hotel. You have to find a place to hide, and then you need to get out of Sarawak," she said in a rush.

"Why?"

"Two men claim you beat them up last night and have filed assault charges against you. Sergeant Kamir is sending a squad to your hotel to arrest you. If you're taken in, there won't be any access to bail, and if you end up in prison, it won't go well for you there."

"Those men attacked *us*. I responded only after they struck Chi-Tze and Aisyah."

"I'm sure that's true, but no one here cares about your version of events."

"Is that because those men are police?"

"They were once, but not anymore," Lazim said. "They work in security at one of the Chong family's companies."

"They had copies of the photos taken at the police station."

"That doesn't surprise me," Lazim said. "But listen, we're spending too much time talking. You only have about twenty minutes before the squad arrives. You need to get out of there now, and if possible, you should get your colleagues to leave with you. I don't think they're in any immediate danger, but it might be prudent for them to lie low as well."

"I appreciate this," said Ava.

"Just go," said Lazim, and hung up.

"You'll never guess who that was," Ava said to Amanda.

"Who?"

"Constable Lazim, telling me I'm going to be arrested for assault and that I should get out of Sarawak as soon as possible."

"You're joking!"

"No."

"Thank god we decided to leave this morning. That was great timing."

"Wasn't it. But I'm not going to feel safe until we land in Hong Kong, so let's get on that plane and get out of here," said Ava.

Ava sat back as the plane left the tarmac, and smiled as she thought about the phone call from Lazim. Had the tide started to turn in their favour? Maybe so, but it was still going to need help.

Halfway through the flight Ava walked back to the economy section to find Amanda, who was sitting by the aisle with an empty seat next to her. Ava slid past her and sat down.

"I can't stop thinking about how the police will react when they get to the hotel and find you gone," Amanda said.

"They aren't going to be happy, that's for sure. And they'll be even less happy when they discover I'm not even in Sarawak, or any other part of Malaysia," Ava said.

"I don't imagine you came back here to talk about that, though," said Amanda.

"No. I wanted to ask if your father is still connected with the Hong Kong Jockey Club."

"He's been chairman of the membership committee for the past five years. You don't get much more connected than that."

"I thought that was the case," Ava said. "As I recall, to become a member you have to lay open your financial and personal life."

"Yes, they do quite thorough background checks. You can't just walk in, sign an application form, plop down a wad of money, and become a member."

"So there would be files of some sort on all the members?"

"I believe so, yes."

"I'm very pleased to hear that," Ava said. "I want you to know I'll be calling your father when we land."

Amanda's brow furrowed. "Why would you do that?"

"I have a favour to ask of him. I was going to ask you to call him, but I think it will be better if it comes from me. It makes it less personal, and he does owe me a lot of favours."

"What's the favour?"

"I want him to provide me with information on Martin Bowles, his wife, and their businesses."

Amanda blinked and then smiled. "I knew you would do it," she said.

"Do what?"

"Go after the Chong family. I knew you wouldn't let them get away with what they've done to us."

"I can't do anything without information," Ava said. "That's why I need Jack's help."

"He'll ask why you want it."

"I'll tell him what we went through in Sarawak, and in general what my intention is, but I can't be specific, because truthfully I don't know what I'll do. All I know is that I have to start somewhere," said Ava.

Amanda turned to face her. "You don't have anything in mind?"

"Not yet, but I'm working on it. And, Amanda, I don't want you to mention any of this to Chi-Tze or Aisyah."

"I won't. But I want to help. I know my father owes you several favours, but even without access to the Jockey Club information, I can find out a lot of what you're looking for."

"I know you can, and I won't hesitate to ask. But before we go down that road, let me find out what Jack can provide," said Ava. "I just hope it isn't too much to ask. I know he puts tremendous value on his status in the Jockey Club. He might not want to breach the trust they've put in him."

"After everything you've done for him, you could ask him to stand naked in front of the Peninsula Hotel and he'd do it," Amanda said.

"That's something I'd rather not see," Ava said. "Luckily, he can do this for me with his clothes on."

16

CHI-TZE STAYED AT HONG KONG'S CHEK LAP KOK
Airport to catch a connecting flight to Shanghai, while the
other women planned to take a taxi to the Central district
on Hong Kong Island. Ava had tried to persuade Chi-Tze
to spend a few days in Hong Kong, but she was anxious to
return to Shanghai and the fashion business she managed
with the Po siblings. Despite Chi-Tze's lack of experience in
the clothing industry, Amanda had pushed May Ling and
Ava to offer her the job, arguing that her education, intelligence, and drive made her the perfect candidate. Amanda's
assessment had been proven correct again and again.

But as she pulled Chi-Tze aside to say goodbye, Ava's
thoughts weren't on her work. "How are you feeling?" she
asked.

"I have a slight headache, nothing more," Chi-Tze said.

"If it persists, see a doctor. You might have a concussion,
and those can be tricky — I say that from experience," Ava
told her.

"Don't worry, I will."

After leaving Chi-Tze at the transfer desk, the women

made their way to the taxi stand. Normally Ava would have been met by Sonny Kwok. A former triad, Sonny had been Uncle's bodyguard and driver for many years, and before Uncle died, he had asked Ava to hire Sonny. Uncle's fear had been that an unemployed Sonny would get into serious trouble, so Ava hired him, and she was glad she had. Whenever she was in Hong Kong, he was available twenty-four hours a day and ready to take on any request. When she wasn't in the city, he drove for her brother Michael and her father, Marcus.

As soon as the taxi had left the airport, Ava phoned the Mandarin Oriental Hotel in Central and booked a suite. She then checked her messages and finally sat back for the ride across the two-kilometre-long Tsing Ma Bridge. Crossing the bridge always made Ava feel like she was coming home — her second home, but a home all the same.

During the years she spent in business with Uncle, Ava had often come to Hong Kong. Nearly their entire customer base had been in Asia, and most of it in Hong Kong. But even if business took her elsewhere, she was still in and out of the territory frequently, as it was the most important air hub in Asia. The most consecutive time she had spent in the city was when Uncle was dying. She lived there for more than three months, meeting him every morning for congee and joining him on the long, slow walks he enjoyed. The last month had coincided with Amanda's wedding to Michael, and her role as a bridesmaid had absorbed some of her attention. It had also introduced her to her three other half-brothers and Marcus's first wife, Elizabeth. The wedding had been enjoyable and Ava genuinely adored Amanda, but everything happening in her life at the time was coloured by the knowledge that she was in Hong Kong waiting for Uncle to die.

As the taxi left the bridge, Aisyah mentioned that it was her first visit to Hong Kong. She started asking Amanda questions about the city, which Amanda was happy to answer.

At one point Aisyah looked out the window and said, "I never imagined there could be so many apartment buildings in one place."

"We're a city of apartment buildings. I read somewhere that there are fewer than a thousand single-family homes in all of Hong Kong," said Amanda.

"Those must be expensive."

"About forty-five percent of all housing is public or subsidized, but the rest is very expensive, especially on Victoria Peak. Houses there can sell for more than two thousand U.S. dollars a square foot," Amanda said. "We'll go there one night. The view of the harbour is spectacular."

"Amanda and her husband, Michael, live on the Peak," Ava said.

"She's teasing. We have a modest two-bedroom apartment that's halfway up the Peak. The prices rise dramatically as you go higher," Amanda said.

"It's a very nice apartment, and you do have a view of Victoria Harbour," Ava said.

"A sliver of a view," replied Amanda.

They reached Central and the taxi headed towards the Mandarin Oriental on Connaught Road. At one time the hotel had been right next to the harbour, but land reclamation had put a couple of city blocks between the building and the water.

"When will you call my father?" Amanda asked Ava.

"As soon as I'm settled, but I don't have his home number. Can you give it to me?"

Amanda reached into her bag and took out a business card. "His home and cell numbers are on here."

"Thanks."

"Will you join us for dinner tonight?"

"I don't think so. In addition to your father, I want to talk to Sonny, and I have an important call to make to Toronto," Ava said. "Maybe I'll be able to join you tomorrow night."

"Would you be up for hotpot?"

"Sure! Say hello to Michael for me, and tell him I'll be happy to see him if he wants to have dinner with us."

"I will. Um, do you want your father to know you're in the city?"

Ava hesitated. Her relationship with her father had become somewhat uncomfortable. It was one thing to know there was a first wife, but it had been another to meet her. Now, whenever she was with him, Ava found herself tiptoeing around the subject of Elizabeth and her half-brothers. Listening to him talk about them almost felt like betraying her mother. "Tell Michael I'd prefer to be the one who lets Marcus know I'm here. I'll do so when I feel ready."

"Okay," Amanda said as the taxi stopped at the front doors of the Mandarin.

"You two have a relaxing evening. Goodness knows you've earned it," Ava said. "I'll talk to you tomorrow."

"I intend to go into the office as usual. I'll take Aisyah with me so she can meet the rest of the staff."

Ava waved goodbye to them and turned to enter the hotel. She had stayed there so often that many of the staff knew her by name, and she wasn't surprised to be greeted by the doorman and the associate at the check-in desk.

Her suite was on the twenty-second floor and overlooked the harbour. In the bedroom she unpacked her clothes and toiletries from her Double Happiness bag, then carried the LV bag into the living area. She took out her laptop and set it on the desk. As soon as she had internet access, she sent emails to Fai and May Ling to let them know she'd landed and was staying at the Mandarin. She thought about sending a similar message to her mother, but she knew that would prompt questions about when she was going to see her father, so she decided to hold off for another day.

Ava took a Moleskine notebook and a Pelikan fountain pen out of the LV bag. During her years with Uncle she had maintained a different notebook for every job. In them she kept names, phone numbers, addresses, and other personal details about the people she was pursuing or had met. She also jotted down any questions and thoughts that came to mind. Her friends thought it comically old-fashioned of her, but Ava didn't care. She believed the act of writing brought clarity to her thought process and engrained facts and figures into her memory.

The front of this particular notebook was filled with observations from her time in Taipei. Ava turned to the back and wrote *CHONG AND BOWLES, SARAWAK* across the top of a page. She then wrote for fifteen minutes, recalling who and what she thought was important about her time in Kuching. When she had finished, she made a short to-do list for herself. At the top was the name Jack Yee.

She tried Jack's home number first, and when no one answered, she called his cell.

"*Wei.*"

"Jack, this is Ava Lee. I hear a lot of noise in the background. Is this a bad time to call?"

"No. We're in a restaurant but we've finished eating. Let me go outside where it's quieter."

"There's no need to rush. I'll wait," she said.

A moment later he said, "Ava, this is a pleasant surprise."

"Have you heard from Amanda?"

"Yes, she texted me to say she's back in Hong Kong."

"Do you know where she's been?"

"We knew she was in Borneo but had no idea what she was doing there. She doesn't share that kind of information with us."

"Well, we had a problem — a business problem — and without getting into all the details, we couldn't resolve it. In fact, things went very badly," she said. "I'm calling to see if you can help turn things around."

Jack went quiet and then said slowly, "Ava, I can't imagine what kind of problem you could have that I might help with."

"We got into a dispute with a family named Chong. They control everything that matters in the state of Sarawak and the city of Kuching. That's where our problem is, but we have little chance of resolving it there," said Ava. "They also have business interests in Hong Kong, and, as it turns out, you have some knowledge of the family."

"I don't know anyone named Chong," he said.

"Amanda tells me you know Martin Bowles," said Ava. "He's married to Laila Chong. She's the only daughter and second child of Sulaiman Chong, the family patriarch and its centre of power."

"I had no idea. She's always been Laila Bowles to us, and I've never heard her or Martin speak of her father or Sarawak."

"The connection is real."

"I don't doubt it is, but where is this leading?"

"I need to learn everything I can about Martin, Laila, and their businesses in Hong Kong. Given your position at the Jockey Club, I'm assuming you know quite a bit already."

"Martin was a banker, but he's been running a private investment firm for as long as I've known him. From what I recall, most of the company's portfolio is connected with Hong Kong real estate," Jack said. "I don't think Laila is involved in the business, though. At least, not that I know of."

"I'm told they live on the Peak."

"Yes, very near the top, in fact. You may also be interested to learn that Martin made a very big splash at the club last month."

"How did he do that?"

"He paid over two million U.S. dollars for a yearling colt that he plans to race here in Hong Kong," Jack said.

"That's fascinating. Amanda suggested he has a rather large ego. Would you agree?"

"Martin likes people to know how well he's doing, and so does Laila. Amanda never took to them."

"Yes, she told me that as well," Ava said.

There was a slight pause, and then Jack said, "I hope I've been helpful."

"You have," Ava said. "But I also need you to do me a favour."

"What's that?"

"When I said earlier that I need to know everything about the Bowleses and their business, I was actually hoping you would be my researcher," Ava said. "I'd like to know where they live — an address — as well as any details you can find about other residences. I want personal and business phone numbers and email addresses. Last, I want as much detail as you can uncover about their businesses. Where they do their banking, account numbers, what types of property they own, and if it's primarily real estate, whether there are mortgages attached to the properties."

"That's an awful lot of information," Jack said.

"You know I wouldn't be asking if I didn't have a good reason."

"You said you had a dispute with the Chong family. What kind of dispute?"

It was Ava's turn to hesitate, but then she thought, *This is Jack Yee I'm talking to. He knows me too well.* "Jack, I'll be honest with you, but I don't want you to share this with anyone."

"Does Amanda know?"

"Of course, but I would still prefer that you don't discuss our conversation with her."

"I'll keep it between us."

"Okay. We opened a business in Kuching that imports and sells foreign lumber. It isn't a large operation, but it was enough of an irritant to the Chong family, who are major players in illegal logging, that they decided to shut us down," Ava said. "They did so by bombing our warehouse and office. A young woman who was managing the business for us was killed by the blast. The police are saying she set the bomb and made a mistake that caused her death. We believe the police are in Sulaiman Chong's pocket."

"Good god!"

"I know it sounds far-fetched, but we're sure of our facts, which leaves us with two questions. Given the power wielded by the family in Sarawak, do we accept what happened and move on? Or, if we decide not to let it go, how can we seek justice?"

"Justice? Or retribution?"

"As I remember it, Jack, when your money was stolen, justice was never your primary objective. You wanted retribution, and we delivered it to you — on two occasions," Ava said. "But in this case I'll settle for justice. I have no interest in exacting an eye for an eye."

"I wouldn't care if you did. I've never known you to be violent for the sake of violence. Everything you do is always for a purpose, and in my case the purpose was saving my money and then saving my life."

"So you'll help us?" Ava asked.

"Of course I'll help, and I'll be pleased to do it."

"There must be a file on Bowles at the Jockey Club."

"There is, though I'm sure you knew that already," Jack said with a laugh.

"Amanda said it was a strong possibility," Ava said. "She also suggested that those membership files are quite detailed."

"Fortunately for you, they are. Equally fortunate is that I have access to them," Jack said. "How soon do you need this information?"

"As soon as possible."

"I'll go to the club offices when I leave here," Jack said. "Bowles's file might not contain everything you're looking for, but it will be a start. Do you want me to email or phone you with what I dig up?"

"Email, please."

"You'll hear from me," Jack said. "And Ava, thanks for thinking of me. I'm glad I can do this for you."

Ava put down the phone with a sense of relief. Regardless of how confident Amanda had been that Jack would agree to help, Ava hadn't been so sure. *One down, two to go*, she thought as she checked the time. It was getting close to four o'clock and she was suddenly feeling hungry. She had skipped lunch and it was too early for dinner. She wanted to eat later at Man Wah, the Cantonese restaurant on the twenty-fifth floor, but she needed something to tide her over. She checked the room service menu and ordered a club sandwich. Then Ava made herself a coffee and sat at the desk to call Sonny.

"Hey, boss," he answered. "Where are you?"

"I'm in Hong Kong. It was a last-minute decision, and I was so rushed at the other end that I didn't have a chance to let you know I was arriving."

"That doesn't matter; I'm just glad you're here. Are you at the Mandarin?"

"I am."

"How long will you be staying?"

"I don't know. It depends on how things go."

"How what things go?"

"I'm not exactly sure about those either, but I'll know more tomorrow. I just want you to be on standby."

"Whatever you need. All you have to do is ask."

"I know, Sonny. Thank you. I'll be in touch," she said, and sighed as she put down the phone. Whatever uncertainty there was in her world, Sonny was always her rock. She didn't know what she had done to earn such loyalty, but she never took for it granted, and she liked to believe she returned it in kind.

17

AVA MADE HER WAY TO THE TWENTY-FIFTH FLOOR AT six-fifteen. Man Wah didn't open for dinner until six-thirty, but she decided to have a drink at M Bar while she waited. She had fond memories of the bar. It was there that she and May Ling had started to mend fences, and it was there she had gone with Fai the night they first connected romantically.

She climbed into a purple chair at the bar and ordered a glass of Chardonnay. While she waited, Ava looked out onto the harbourfront and marvelled at the soaring architecture framing a body of water alive with ships, boats, and ferries. In her mind there wasn't a skyline in the world that could touch it. At night, when the unique buildings were lit up, it was a truly majestic sight.

Her wine arrived. Ava sipped and checked her phone. She still hadn't heard back from Jack Yee, and until she did, she couldn't call her friend Derek Liang in Toronto.

"Would you like some company?" a man's voice said over her shoulder.

She turned, ready to snap, and then froze. "Daddy. I didn't expect to see you here," she said.

"I'm with some colleagues. We're going to have dinner at Pierre in about fifteen minutes. I didn't see you come in, but one of the men I'm with made a comment about the gorgeous young woman who'd just arrived by herself. I looked over and, to my surprise, it turned out to be you."

"Amanda and I flew in just a few hours ago, rather unexpectedly. We were on a business trip to Borneo that was cut short," Ava said, feeling slightly uncomfortable with the compliment.

Marcus sat down next to her and put his glass of Scotch on the rocks on the bar. "I'm really pleased with the way it's worked out with you and Amanda. That girl is fortunate to have mentors like you and May Ling Wong."

"That 'girl' is capable enough to do well without us."

"I wasn't suggesting otherwise. I have a lot of respect for Amanda."

"I'm glad to hear that. How's your business?" Ava asked.

"Boring, but it continues to be profitable. The apartment buildings in Shenzhen are still fully occupied and able to sustain modest annual increases in rent. I've stepped back from any daily involvement, but Peter is running things admirably."

Peter was Ava's second-oldest half-brother. They had met, but she couldn't say she actually knew him. "Amanda tells me that Michael and Simon To keep expanding their noodle franchises."

"The boys are doing well, though Simon is still overly aggressive at times. I've warned Michael not to let him overextend their credit line."

"We don't want a repeat of that fiasco in Macau."

"No, we don't," Marcus said as he picked up his glass. "I'm

going to Toronto next month to spend two weeks with your mother. Did she tell you?"

"She did. She's excited about it."

"Will you be there?"

"I'm not sure. I have business to finish here, and I'm not sure how long it will take."

"Marian and her girls are going to come down from Ottawa. It's been quite a while since I've seen them, and I'm really looking forward to it. The girls must be getting big."

"You should visit Canada more often," Ava said, and then wished she hadn't.

"I do the best I can," he said.

"How often do you visit Australia?" she asked, and immediately wished she hadn't said that either.

"Less often than I visit Canada. Which doesn't make it any better or any worse," he said. "There are days now when I really wish my life wasn't so complicated."

"Well, who made it that way?"

Marcus shook his head. "I know. It's the same question I ask myself when I start missing you and Marian and the children in Australia. But the truth is, I miss you more than any of them. I can't help thinking about what we could have accomplished if we'd been side by side all these years."

"Daddy, it doesn't work like that. I am what I am because of the way Mummy raised me, and because Uncle gave me his guidance and wisdom. If it had just been me and you, I could have turned out to be just another spoiled Hong Kong princess."

"Never," he said, looking slightly pained. He glanced at his watch. "I should rejoin my colleagues. I'm being wooed. They have some real estate holdings that aren't performing very well and want our company to take over their management."

"I hope it works out. You're too young and too smart not to stay active," she said.

He smiled. "On that note I should go, but I have to insist that we have dinner or dim sum while you're here. Maybe with Michael and Amanda?"

"I'd like that. I'll phone you, I promise, as soon as I know what my schedule looks like."

He leaned towards her and kissed her gently on the forehead. "Love you," he said.

"I love you too, Daddy."

Ava watched her father walk unhurriedly across the room to join two other men. She had rarely met anyone who made such a good first impression. He was a bit over six feet, still lean, always impeccably dressed in suit and tie, and with a full head of greying hair that he combed straight back. He always looked distinguished, an impression that was reinforced when you met him by his precise, almost elegant way of speaking. Ava saw him say something to the men, and they looked in her direction. She wondered what he had told them. She hoped it was the truth.

Ava waited until her father and his colleagues had left M Bar before making her way to Man Wah. She had requested a window table so she could continue to enjoy the Hong Kong skyline. A server she recognized from previous visits hurried over as soon as she sat down.

"How nice it is to see you again, Ms. Lee," he said, and handed her food and wine menus.

"Thank you," she said. "I don't need the wine menu. I was

drinking a Chardonnay in M Bar, and I'll continue with that."

"I'll look after it right away," he said.

Ava opened the food menu and almost groaned. As always, there was a surfeit of choices, and this was one place where eating alone was a disadvantage. If she'd been part of a group, they could have ordered a variety of appetizers and maybe six or more main courses to share. But alone, Ava had to weigh what was possible to eat against what was desirable. One of her mother's life lessons was never to waste food. In Toronto that meant cleaning your plate or taking home leftovers. Leftovers weren't an option for Ava at Man Wah, so she had to be realistic with her order.

She had eaten only half the club sandwich she had ordered from room service, so her appetite still had an edge. She decided to have the wok-fried Australian wagyu beef as her main course, with a side of braised bean curd with morel mushrooms in an abalone sauce. The only question left was whether she could handle both hot and sour soup and the shrimp and lemongrass spring rolls. She adored hot and sour soup in all its endless variations, but it was filling, and she didn't want to lessen her enjoyment of the beef.

The server came to the table with a glass of Chardonnay. "Are you ready to order your meal?" he asked.

"Yes," Ava said, and ordered the beef, bean curd, and spring rolls. When the server had left, she sipped her wine, looked distractedly at the lights criss-crossing the harbour, and thought about her father.

She did love him. Despite everything, he had been true to his Canadian family. He had called Jennie every day for as long as Ava could remember, and his annual two-week visits had been as constant as the seasons. He had been a rock, someone they could depend on, and Ava hadn't realized he was having doubts about the way he had led his life and the legacy he had created. *Maybe I should have dinner with him alone,* she thought. *We can both be more open, and anything that helps us better understand each other can only be good.*

Her phone rang, and she paled. Cellphones were discouraged, if not outright banned, at Man Wah. She looked at the screen, saw the name Jack Yee, and knew she had to take the call. She rose from her chair and hurried out of the restaurant.

"Jack, thank you for getting back to me so quickly. What do you have?"

"Martin Bowles's file."

"The entire thing?"

"I have a copy of it. It's only six pages, but there's a lot of detail, including much of the information you wanted."

"That's fantastic."

"I have something else," he said. "In addition to being CEO of the investment company, Bowles listed two other businesses he appears to run. One of them has the word 'Properties' in the title. I contacted some of my real estate friends, they did a bit of research for me, and I now have a list of more than twenty buildings that his companies either own or have a major interest in."

"Jack, you're a whiz!"

"Photocopying a file and having friends who know how to use the Hong Kong Real Estate Registry hardly makes me a whiz."

"Still, I'm very grateful," Ava said. "Where are you now?"

"I'm in Happy Valley. Where are you?"

"I'm having dinner at Man Wah in the Mandarin."

"I'm not far from you, then. Why don't I bring the material to you in person?"

"That would be perfect. In fact, why don't you join me for dinner?"

"My wife had plans for us this evening, but if she knows I'm doing you a favour, I think she'll give me a pass. Let me call her and I'll call you back."

"Great. I'm waiting."

Ava went back into the restaurant and caught the attention of her server. "I may be having company, so could you hold off putting in my order until that's confirmed? It shouldn't take long."

"*Momentai*, Ms. Lee," he said.

Ava put her phone on vibrate and placed it on the table next to her. A moment later it signalled an incoming call. "*Wei*," she said softly.

"I'll be there in twenty minutes," Jack said.

"Come directly to the restaurant."

She turned off the phone, sipped her wine, and contemplated with satisfaction what she had accomplished. If Jack's information was as good as she hoped, all that was left was to get Derek Liang in gear. Derek was married to Mimi, Ava's closest Canadian friend. Among his several talents, he was almost as good at bak mei as Ava. In fact, until he married Mimi, Ava had used him on several jobs where she needed physical backup.

Ava finished her wine and told herself to slow down, but she didn't object when the server offered to get her a fresh glass.

Jack appeared at the entrance to Man Wah. He was a short, thin, cheerful man with a winning personality, which he had needed in the trading business. Outside work, his wife had run his life, and now that he was retired, Ava was sure she ran it twenty-four/seven. But Jack didn't seem to mind; Ava had never heard him complain. Amanda was the only other woman in his life, and he doted on her. It was a constant surprise to Ava how Amanda had emerged from such a spoiled upbringing to be the kind of woman she was.

Ava waved at Jack to catch his attention. He hurried over with a manila folder held tightly in one hand. He smiled as he sat down across from her and placed the folder on the table. Theirs had always been a rather formal business-type relationship, and neither of them felt the need to hug, kiss, or even shake hands. A simple nod to each other was sufficient as a greeting.

"I've ordered spring rolls, beef, and braised bean curd. Is there anything you'd like me to change or add?" she asked, trying not to stare at the folder.

"If you don't mind, I'm not going to eat with you. My wife pushed our dinner back to nine o'clock so I'd have time to see you."

"Thank her for me," Ava said.

"But I will have a beer," he said.

Ava motioned towards the server. "I'll have a Tsingtao," Jack said to him.

"Do you mind if I look in the folder?" Ava asked.

"Go ahead. I brought it here for you."

She opened the folder and saw a colour head-and-shoulders photo of Bowles. His thinning hair was sandy brown, parted on the left and hanging over his right ear. He had a moustache and goatee in the exact same shade as his hair, and his face was split by a broad smile. "He looks like a happy man," Ava said.

"Why wouldn't he be?"

Ava looked at the home address. "He lives on Barker Road. I assume that's quite prestigious."

"These days it isn't in the same league as Severn Road or Pollock's Path, but a house there still runs into the tens of millions. Some might cost a hundred million."

"Hong Kong dollars?"

"No, U.S. dollars."

"Good grief! I knew it was expensive, but that's beyond my comprehension."

"And mine."

Ava scanned the first two pages of the file, then closed it. "I've already seen some very useful information," she said. "The Jockey Club must be very persuasive to get this kind of disclosure."

"If this sounds like I'm boasting, I apologize, but the Jockey Club is the most important organization in Hong Kong. We have more than twenty thousand members at present, but some members are more equal than others. When Martin first applied, he had his choice of a full membership, a racing membership, or a racing club membership. There are different requirements attached to each. He applied for a racing club membership, which would allow him to own and race horses at our tracks. Before his application was accepted, he had to undergo a thorough background check, be interviewed by a panel of members, and have his finances assessed. If he had been rejected, no reason would have been given."

"But he wasn't rejected."

"No, he wasn't. There were no black marks against his character, and his financial situation was incredibly strong."

The server arrived with Jack's beer and poured it into a

glass. "Are you ready to order?" he asked Ava.

"My order will stay the same, but don't put it in until my guest leaves," Ava said.

When the server left, Jack said, "I put the real estate holdings after the Jockey Club information."

Ava opened the folder again. "So, he's CEO of the Chong Investment Corporation, the Chong Family Trust, and Chong Income Properties." Ava turned a page. "They all bank at HKSS. I'm surprised he gave you the account numbers."

"It was required, but it isn't the only place he banks."

"How do you know that?"

"I once went to Martin to get a donation for a charity I support, and he sent me a cheque from a personal account in a Kowloon bank. I found that rather strange."

"What was the name?"

"I don't remember."

"Could you look it up for me?"

"Of course. I might even have a copy of the cheque in my files."

"That would be very helpful," she said as she turned another page. "There's no mention of a car. Do you know what he drives?"

"Laila drives a Porsche SUV of some kind; Martin typically drives a new Bentley. I don't why he feels he has to trade them in every few years, but he does."

Ava closed the folder. "I'll go through this later in more detail, but it's an excellent start."

He raised his glass. "Anything for you and Amanda."

Ava sipped her wine and looked at Jack. "To be fair, I should give you advance warning that I plan to make Martin Bowles's life miserable."

"Do whatever you have to do, and don't worry about me. You know I trust you completely."

"Thanks for all this, Jack."

He took a deep swig of beer and put the glass down on the table. "I should get going. I have to get back to Sha Tin," he said. "I'll look up Bowles's charitable donation when I can. If I can't find a copy of the cheque, I'll send you the bank information."

"That would be great," Ava said, standing up to say goodbye.

She remained standing until he left, and then reached for the folder before retaking her seat. "Jack, you wonderful man," she murmured to herself as she leafed through the pages. Nearly everything she had hoped for was there — home and business addresses, phone numbers, email addresses, banking information, and credit and character references with their contact information. Then, separately, there was the list of the Chong family's Hong Kong real estate holdings.

The server arriving with the spring rolls interrupted Ava's perusal. She closed the folder and for the next half-hour tried to concentrate on her food, but she couldn't help feeling distracted. It was with almost a sense of relief that she finished dinner and headed to the elevator.

It was past eight o'clock when she entered the suite, which meant it was the same time in the morning in Toronto. She'd give Derek another half-hour before calling, she decided as she went into the bathroom. She showered quickly, slipped on a black Giordano T-shirt and her Adidas track pants, and sat down at the desk. She opened Bowles's file and her Moleskine notebook. As she went through the documents, she started prioritizing the information they contained. One

thing that stood out was the list of credit and character references. *These could be valuable*, she thought as she reached
for her phone to call Derek.

Derek was the only child of very wealthy Hong Kong
parents and, like Amanda, he had been completely spoiled,
even after he graduated from the University of Toronto. He
had never bothered to get a job and, aside from helping Ava
from time to time, had put all his energy into enjoying himself. When he and her best friend got together, Ava had panicked. She envisioned Mimi, who worked for an insurance
company, eventually getting hurt. But to her surprise the
marriage had worked, and Derek had gone from carousing
night owl to devoted stay-at-home father. Along the way he
had developed considerable computer skills as well, and any
help he gave Ava now was of a technical nature.

She phoned Mimi and Derek's land line.

"Ava, what's up? Are you still in Taipei?" Derek said when
he answered.

"No, I'm in Hong Kong. I have a business issue I have to
deal with, and I could use your help," she said.

"Sure. What do you want me to do?"

"I need to get into a corporate bank account. I have three
candidates, all related to the same family business."

"Which bank?" Derek asked calmly, accustomed to that
kind of request from Ava.

"HKSS in Hong Kong."

"I know them; my father banks there. Their security system is bound to be top grade."

"I don't expect miracles, just your best effort. I have quite
a bit of corporate and personal information. I was going to
scan it and send it to you," Ava said.

"The more I have to work with, the easier it will be, so send me absolutely everything you've got."

"Thanks. I'll go down to the business centre as soon as I hang up."

"Your timing is perfect. This is Mimi's mother's day with the baby, so I won't have any distractions."

"Great. Give everyone a hug from me," Ava said. She ended the call, picked up the file, and left the suite to go to the business centre.

Fifteen minutes later Ava was back in the room. She looked at the names on the to-do list she'd made earlier and there was only one remaining. She found Douglas Brooke's business card and dialled his cell.

"Hello?" Brooke answered tentatively.

"This is Ava Lee."

"What a surprise."

"I'm sorry for calling so late. Are you able to speak to me?"

"I'm at home and I have people over for dinner."

"This is quite urgent. I'd really appreciate a few moments of your time."

"Okay, let me excuse myself and then I'll go to my upstairs office," he said.

Ava waited as seconds turned into minutes. She was beginning to think he'd lied to her when he came back on the line.

"Sorry for the delay, but I couldn't just walk out abruptly on these guests," Brooke finally said. "One of them is an associate from the Justice Department. If he knew you were on the other end of the line, he'd get very excited. You were quite the topic of discussion at dinner. Who would have guessed you were such a dangerous woman? The police weren't pleased to learn that you and your friends left Kuching this morning before they could get to you. They've been trying to find out if someone tipped you off. They even called me to see if I had anything to do with it."

"I wasn't about to sit around and let the police lay bogus charges against me."

"I don't blame you in the least. But since you have left, why do you need to speak to me?"

"I want to know if the police's final statement about the bombing has changed."

Brooke sighed. "You won't be happy to hear this, but they decided that your business was destroyed and your employee died as the result of what they term a misadventure. They made it very clear that the investigation is over and no charges will be forthcoming."

"Misadventure?"

"I don't have the statement in front of me, but it strongly implies that your employee set the bomb herself. The word 'misadventure' has a specific intent in that regard."

"I haven't had a chance to look at your local media reports. Did they pick it up?"

"They did, and they dutifully parroted the official line."

"So, in addition to her being killed, Jamilah's reputation has been forever smeared."

"Yes, that is the case. And unfortunately there's nothing to be done about it." He paused. "Ms. Lee, if you don't mind my saying it, since it was fortunate that you were able to leave here when you did, perhaps this is an appropriate time to put the entire episode behind you. Cut your losses, so to speak."

"I can't do that."

"Why not?"

"I'll explain that later. For now, I would like to engage you formally as my lawyer and as my company's lawyer in Sarawak."

"I'm not in the habit of turning away business, but what could I possibly do for you?"

"We still have the business in Sabah, but we're thinking of selling it and may need a lawyer to put together an agreement."

Brooke hesitated, then said, "I could do that."

"Then you're willing to accept a retainer?"

"Of course."

"Is a thousand U.S. dollars a month sufficient?"

"It is."

"Then consider yourself retained," said Ava. "I trust this means we're now functioning under the protection of client privilege."

"We were doing that even before I agreed to accept your retainer."

"Thanks for saying that. I wasn't suggesting you don't have principles."

"I didn't take it that way."

"Then let's move on. I'd appreciate your opinions with regard to some other matters."

"Such as?"

"How comfortable are you with representing our interests if it brings you into conflict with the Chong family?"

"What on earth are you talking about?"

"I don't know yet, but as I said to you earlier, we're not ready to cut our losses. We're examining various options that may eventually lead to bumping heads with the Chongs. If it comes to that, are you up to the challenge?"

"Yes, I am."

"Good. Now one last thing. How well do you know Arven Saad?"

"I know him on a strictly social level. We're not friends and we've never done business together. Why are you asking?" Brooke said carefully.

"I've been told by a source I trust that he spoke to Commissioner Chik immediately after Jamilah's death and directed Chik to drop the investigation and issue the statement implying she set the bomb herself. Do you think that's possible?"

"Who is your source?"

"I can't say. And besides, what I want is your opinion."

"Given that he's the Chongs' right-hand man, Saad has considerable influence," said Brooke. "It's assumed he speaks for the family."

"That doesn't answer my question," said Ava.

"It's the best I can do without more information," Brooke said. "Is it possible that Saad gave directions to the Commissioner? Absolutely. Is it probable? I don't know."

"If he did, then I think it's logical to assume that the Chong organization was responsible for the bombing."

"That's a perfectly sensible conclusion."

"And given that, I'm also assuming they invented the Sarawak United Front as a cover."

"That makes sense. But where are you going with this?"

"I don't know yet. I'm still gathering facts. When I've gathered enough, I'm hoping I'll see a path for me to follow."

18

AVA SLEPT WELL, BUT WHEN SHE WOKE UP AT SIX TO GO to the bathroom, she had so many thoughts bouncing around in her mind that she knew she'd never get back to sleep. She made a coffee, checked her messages, and then decided to go for a run.

Victoria Park, near Causeway Bay in Wan Chai, was one of her favourite places in the world to run. The park wasn't large — only about fifty acres, compared to New York City's 850-acre Central Park — but it was one of the few green areas on Hong Kong Island, and it was a magnet for thousands of locals. Ava hoped, as she left the Mandarin and walked to the Central MTR station, that she'd get to the park early enough to avoid the morning crush. Four stops later she got off at Tin Hau station and jogged to the park, only to find it already bustling with activity. Luckily the 600-metre running track wasn't completely jammed; she had been there when so many people were on the track it was impossible to do anything but walk.

Ava began to circle the track, running past knots of people doing variations of tai chi, old men sitting with their birdcages, and people beginning to gather near a stage, where instructors from the city's recreation department would soon be leading them in morning exercises. If she had been running on the southern perimeter, towards Causeway Road, she would have passed soccer pitches and tennis and basketball courts that were in constant use.

As she ran, she thought about the previous night. Ava still hadn't finalized her plans for dealing with the Chongs, but Jack Yee had come through for her, Derek was breaking into the Chong's business accounts, Brooke had been retained, and Sonny was on standby. She had also had long talks with May Ling and Fai. As always, she had told May exactly what she hoped to accomplish and, as always, May supported her. She and Fai had talked mainly about the film. Fai was completely absorbed in the scenes they were shooting, which made it a little easier when Ava told her she didn't know when she would make it back to Taipei.

In between the phone calls and emails, Ava had worked her way through the information Jack Yee had provided. With the exception of the real estate holdings, the data about Martin Bowles was six years old, dating back to when he had applied to the Jockey Club. Ava didn't know if his declared net worth of HK$2.6 billion had changed, but she was able to confirm that his home and office addresses were the same and that at least some of the personal references were still valid.

In the application, Bowles had described himself as CEO of the Chong Investment Corporation, the Chong Family Trust, and Chong Investment Properties, but there were no details about how much money was under his management. Ava had emailed Amanda to ask her to get the credit service used by their trading company to initiate a search. It might not be able to get exact numbers, but an estimate was all she needed.

After Ava had finished with the Jockey Club file, she turned to the list of the Chong family's real estate holdings. She looked up the addresses online and checked out the street views of all the buildings. There were twenty-one in all, and with the exception of two in Central, they were small to medium-sized, typically with a restaurant or retail stores on the ground floor and offices or apartments above. It wasn't an overly impressive group of buildings, but given the astronomical prices Hong Kong commercial real estate demanded, collectively their value would run well into the billions of Hong Kong dollars.

The two structures in Central were a world apart. One was a forty-storey office building with a mall on the ground floor — where the Chong companies were headquartered — and the other was a thirty-storey apartment building. She guessed each would be worth billions. Ava also attempted to check out the house on Barker Road, but the only view from the street was of a brick wall with razor wire strung along the top.

The last thing she had done before going to bed was review her to-do list. When that was done, she started to close her notebook and then realized she had forgotten something. She wrote, *Get information from Jack on Bowles's Kowloon bank.*

As she started her fourth lap of the morning, the fact that Bowles did some banking in Kowloon popped back into her mind. There weren't many local banks there, and if she was lucky — really lucky — Kowloon Light Industrial Bank might be the one. Through Uncle she had an excellent contact at that bank, and he had helped her in the past.

By the sixth lap it was getting more difficult to manoeuvre around the track. Ava had to zigzag in order to keep moving, and twice she had to come to a full stop. That was her signal to call it a day. She walked past the exercise class, where about a hundred people were jumping up and down, and made her way to the Causeway Bay MTR station.

It was not quite eight o'clock when she entered her suite at the Mandarin. She drank two glasses of water, made herself another coffee, and sat down at the desk to phone Jack Yee.

"Good morning. I hope this isn't too early," she said when he answered.

"No, I've been up for a while. Did you have a chance to go over the information I gave you in more detail?"

"I did, and it's going to be immensely useful. I can't thank you enough," she said. "I have a quick question, though. Did you actually contact all the references Bowles provided?"

"Every one of them, and they obviously spoke well of him, or he wouldn't have been offered a membership."

"So they are either friends or professional acquaintances of Bowles?"

"As I remember, most of them knew him through business."

"Excellent. And now one last thing. Did you manage to find the name of the Kowloon bank where he has an account?"

"I found the copy of the cheque. It's the Kowloon Merchants Reserve Bank," he said, and then rattled off the account number.

"Ah," she said as she wrote it down.

"You sound disappointed."

"I was hoping for a different bank, but no matter. I might still be able to use the information."

"Good luck," Jack said.

Ava hung up and debated briefly whether she should shower right away or call Derek. Her curiosity got the better of her, and she phoned Toronto.

Mimi answered. "Ava, how great to hear your voice! It seems like forever since we've spoken. When are you coming home?"

"As soon as they finish filming in Taipei, but that won't be for a few weeks."

"I can't remember your ever being away for so long."

"Me neither. I've been busy."

"I assume you're calling to speak to Derek about that thing you have him working on. He's been going at it all day," she said. "Do you want to talk to him?"

"Please. I'll call you in a few days, when things are calmer here and we can have a proper chat."

"I'll look forward to it. Now let me pass the phone to Derek."

"Hey," Derek said seconds later.

"How's it going? I know I should have waited for you to call me, but this thing has me on edge."

"Sorry, no luck so far. But that doesn't mean I won't get there. The software I'm using has so many variables that sometimes it takes a couple of days to run through them all," he said.

"Well, keep trying," Ava said, hiding her disappointment. "And while you're at it, I have another bank account for you to try accessing. It's Bowles's personal account at the Kowloon Merchants Reserve Bank."

Derek repeated the number back to her, then said, "The file you sent me has lots of information, but it doesn't mention if Bowles has children."

"Do you need that info?"

"It might be useful. Could you find out? And if he does, send me their names and dates of birth. It's surprisingly common to include that sort of thing in passwords."

"I'll see what I can do."

"Thanks. In the meantime, I'll keep working on the HKSS accounts. I'll start the Kowloon one when I'm finished with those."

Ava phoned Jack Yee as soon as she had hung up from Derek. "Sorry to bother you again so soon, but do you know if Bowles has any children?"

"He has a son, Joshua, and a daughter named Sarah," Jack said without hesitation. "I know that because he includes one or the other in all his horses' names.

"Do you know when they were born?"

"Not a clue."

"Don't worry about it. Having the names is a good start. I'll try not to bother you again for a while."

Ava opened her laptop and emailed the names to Derek, but without any confidence that they were going to make a difference. She was starting to feel discouraged again. She needed something, anything, that she could use as leverage against the Chong family, and if Derek came up dry, she had no idea what other options were available. She sighed, picked up the Bowles file, and walked over to the window. She turned a chair to face the harbour and sat down.

Ava closed her eyes and lay her head against the back of the chair. It had been an exhausting few days, and as she replayed them it seemed that all she had been doing was reacting to the Chongs and waiting for other people's help. She felt a desperate need to be proactive, but what could she do that would have an impact on the Chong family? Then, out of the haze of her thoughts, she remembered Uncle's nighttime visit. Had he said something about going after them where they had their cash? No, there was more: he had emphasized assets. Ava sat up and opened the file.

The Chong family's wealth was disproportionally tied up in real estate. Ava smiled. Those were assets you couldn't hide and couldn't move — and they were vulnerable. Ava's smile broadened as another idea came to her. *First things first,* she thought, leaving the chair to get her phone.

"Hi, boss," Sonny answered.

"Do you know anyone competent with explosives?" she asked. "It needs to be someone professional and absolutely trustworthy."

"Jimmy Li is your man," Sonny said without hesitation.

"The sniper?" Ava asked, referring to the man who had provided backup for them during a couple of gun battles in Sha Tin the previous year.

"Jimmy is more than a sniper. When he was in the army, he spent time in the ordnance corps. He's an expert in land mines and bombs."

"I liked working with him."

"He's a good man. I've seen him a few times since our dust-ups last year. He was fed up with retirement, and working with us reinvigorated him. He's always asking if I have another job for him. Working with you again would be icing on the cake."

"Then give Jimmy a call and see if he's available," said Ava.

"If he is, ask him how soon he can meet with us. My whole day is free, and there's some urgency to this."

"Are we going to blow something up?"

"Assuming Jimmy is game and he can find everything he needs, I think there's a distinct possibility."

19

THREE HOURS LATER, AVA WAS WALKING TOWARDS THE entrance of the hotel's Café Causette with the file folder in hand. Sonny and Jimmy were already standing outside. The contrast between the two men couldn't have been greater. In his black suit, white shirt, and black tie, the grim-faced, massively chested, six-foot-four-inch Sonny Kwok was a menacing figure, while skinny, five-foot-five Jimmy, dressed in khaki pants and a light blue polo shirt, looked like a mild-mannered senior citizen.

"Hey, boss," Sonny said when he saw Ava, his face exploding into a broad grin.

"Hi, Sonny," she said, going up onto her toes to kiss him on the cheek. She turned to Jimmy. "And it's good to see you again, Jimmy. Thank you for coming on such short notice."

"Sonny didn't give me many details, but from what he told me, I'm excited to hear what you have planned."

"That's why you're here. I need some expert advice, and Sonny tells me you're the man who can provide it. Why don't we have some lunch and talk it over."

Ava led the two men into the café and over to a table in a

quiet corner. A server poured coffee and water and handed each of them a menu.

When the server returned, Ava said, "Jimmy, you go first."

"A chicken salad sandwich and black coffee," he said.

"I'll have the same," said Sonny.

"A club sandwich with a glass of water," Ava ordered.

When the server left, Ava looked at the two men across from her. "Let me tell you what happened to my friends and me when we were in Borneo," she said. She hadn't quite finished the story when their food arrived. "Let's eat before I say anything else. I don't want any distractions," she said.

"No, please keep going," Jimmy said. "I'd rather listen to you than eat."

"Yes, don't stop," Sonny said.

Ava looked at him and saw that he was trying to control himself. Sonny was quick to anger under most circumstances, especially when Uncle or she was in danger. At those times his anger could turn in a heartbeat into violent rage. She finished her story by describing their escape from Kuching ahead of the police, and then said, "I want revenge on the Chongs. They killed our employee, they attacked me and my friends, and they've cost our business nearly three million dollars."

"We'll take an eye for an eye," Jimmy said.

"In a sense, yes, but not at the cost of a life," Ava said. "Now let's eat and then figure out the best way to approach this."

Sonny and Jimmy nodded and dug into their sandwiches. They finished before Ava and then tried not to look impatient while she ate. Finally she pushed her plate aside and opened the folder. "As I was saying, I want to attack the Chong family, and it seems to me the best way to do this is go after their assets here in Hong Kong. I want them to experience the same sense of vulnerability and loss that we felt after our warehouse was destroyed. Then I want to disrupt their businesses and, if I can, cause them grief with friends, business associates, and banks."

"What's in the folder?" Jimmy asked.

"The addresses of their real estate holdings. I also have the home address and some other personal information about Martin Bowles and his wife, Laila, the daughter of Sulaiman Chong. Bowles runs the Chong businesses and manages their money in Hong Kong."

"Where do they live?" Sonny asked.

"On the Peak, Barker Road."

"Do you want us to target the house?" Jimmy said.

Ava paused. "Does this mean you're willing to help us?"

"Yes, of course I'm in."

"I insist on paying you. I believe last time we agreed to a rate of ten thousand Hong Kong dollars per day."

"That's fine, but money isn't my motivation."

"I appreciate that, though we'll pay you all the same," Ava said. "And when you say you're in, you do understand that we're also expecting you to source the materials that will be needed? We'll pay for them, but you'll need to find them."

"That won't be a problem. I have some friends in Tai Wai New Village, former army colleagues, who are in the demolition business. They'll have what we need."

"Then it appears our team is back together again," Ava said with a smile. "Now, returning to your last question, no, we won't be targeting Bowles's home. The risk of hurting someone is too great. I do want to inflict damage on Chong properties, but I think we should stick to their commercial real estate holdings."

"Have you decided on a target?"

"Not yet. I want to go over the list of their properties with you, but before I do that I want to return to Martin Bowles. I want him to know that we're capable of getting to him personally," she said. "I was thinking that maybe we could deliver that message by blowing up one of his cars. Jimmy, do you think that's doable?"

"If the car isn't under guard, planting a bomb should be easy enough. The bomb can be linked to a detonator that we could set off whenever we chose."

"Is it really that easy?"

"Sure, as long as we have access. We would have to stake out his house and office to figure out his patterns, and then find a time when we could plant the device," Jimmy said. "Hopefully his cars are parked in a driveway or somewhere outside the house."

"I don't know about that. I do know he drives a Bentley," Ava said.

"Does he drive it to work?" Jimmy asked.

"Again, I don't know."

"If he does, he probably parks it underground. That would be the ideal place to plant a bomb."

"I know someone in the vehicle registry office who can supply us with his licence number," Sonny said.

"Good. Contact them when you leave here," Ava said.

"Okay, boss."

"The car will be the first step," Ava said.

"And then the buildings?"

"Yes. Those would be the next targets."

"We'll have to scout them first."

"I'll make a copy of the list of properties for you."

"Do you want Bowles to know who's targeting him?" Sonny asked.

"Eventually, but I'm thinking it might be wise to keep him guessing for now," Ava said, and then looked at Jimmy. "If we're going to bomb Chong properties, we'll have to make sure no innocent people get caught in the crossfire."

"That shouldn't be an issue, though we can expect enhanced security after the Chongs figure out they're being targeted," Jimmy said. He hesitated and then continued. "Ava, I think you should know that we'll have a very tight time frame to accomplish these attacks. Planting bombs in buildings with minimal security is one thing, but once they call in reinforcements, it will become much tougher."

"Do you have any top priorities?" Sonny asked.

"The Chong company headquarters is at the top of my list," Ava said.

"Then we should target it after the car," Sonny said.

"Jimmy, how soon can you get the materials you need?" Ava asked.

"My friends normally have a large inventory. I could probably pick up everything this afternoon."

"Then do that, please," Ava said.

"While Jimmy is in Tai Wai, I'll call my contact at the vehicle registry, then scope out Bowles's house," Sonny said. "I'm assuming you want to move quickly."

"I'd like to start tomorrow."

"Then we'll spend the rest of today gathering info," Sonny said.

"Would you mind if I come along while you scout the house?" Ava asked.

"Of course not," Sonny said.

"How much cash do you need for the materials?" she asked Jimmy.

"We'll sort that out later," he said.

"Okay. Give your receipts to Sonny. I don't want you paying for this out of your own pocket."

Ava signalled to the server to bring her the bill, then said, "Gentlemen, we're dealing with a family who take it for granted that, without consequences, they can do untold damage to other people's lives. That may be true in Sarawak, but this is Hong Kong, and they need to be taught that things are very different here."

20

WHILE AVA SIGNED THE BILL, JIMMY WENT TO THE LOBBY to make a phone call. After Ava and Sonny joined him, they walked together to the exit.

"I just spoke to a friend in Tai Wai. They have everything I need," Jimmy said. "I'll take a taxi to pick up the stuff and then head to my house. I can store the supplies there until we need them. It will also give me a chance to tell my daughter what my schedule will be like for the next few days. I look after my grandkids most days, so we'll have to reorganize things, but I'll work it out."

"Would it be easier if you stayed in a hotel?" Ava asked.

"No. Even if the hours are odd, it's better for me to go back and forth. The girls get anxious if I'm gone for too long," Jimmy said. "My daughter thinks it's funny that they're so dependent on me and that I worry about them so much. When she was growing up, I was hardly ever around."

"I never knew any of my grandparents. They all died long before I was born," Ava said. "The closest thing I had to a grandfather was Uncle."

"You couldn't have done better than him," Jimmy said, and then looked at his watch. "I should get going."

"Call Sonny when you're ready to come back to Hong Kong. Hopefully we'll know where Bowles's car is by then."

They waited for Jimmy to get into a taxi before going back inside. "I have a few things to do upstairs before I'm ready to leave," Ava said.

"There's no rush. I'll call the vehicle registry while I wait."

Ava felt satisfied as she re-entered her suite. There was something comforting about working with competent people that she trusted. With Sonny and Jimmy on her team, her plan felt more likely to succeed.

She sat at the desk and called Amanda.

"Hi, sis," Amanda answered. "How was dinner with Dad?"

"We didn't eat together, but the meeting went very well. He was extremely helpful," Ava said. "But that's not what I'm calling about. Has our credit service finished looking into the Chóngs' companies?"

"I have the information here. I'm not sure what you expected, but all the companies have a top-grade rating, with little debt. Even Chong Income Properties operates with only a minimal amount of mortgage financing."

"Did they give you any idea how much money these companies are managing?"

"They're all private companies, so there's nothing on record, but their best guess is about four billion American dollars," said Amanda.

"That's impressive. The Chong family not only knows how to steal money, it knows how to invest it."

"I wish I had more to share, but Bowles runs a tight operation."

"No matter. We'll find other ways to get where we need to go."

"And I assume you're not going to tell me what those are," said Amanda.

"No, I'm not. But I will tell you what I told your father. During the next few days, ignore everything you hear about Martin Bowles."

Amanda became quiet, and then she said, "I love you, Ava."

"I love you too, Amanda."

Ava made a coffee and went to stand at the window. By any measure, the day had gone well, but now she had to speak with Uncle's former banker. She considered the best approach to take and decided to be blunt. She found the phone number for the Kowloon Light Industrial Bank and dialled.

"Henry Chew, please. This is Ava Lee calling."

"Ms. Lee, it's been a while since we've spoken," Chew said a moment later.

"I need a favour," Ava said.

Chew was silent.

"You can either work with me now or wait until you hear from Xu," she continued.

"There's no need to involve others in our business. What can I do for you?" he asked.

"Do you have any contacts at the Kowloon Merchants Reserve Bank?"

"They are our competitor," Chew said.

"Yes, of course they are, but that's not what I'm asking."

"I know the bank's president, Ronald Ho. We sit on several government advisory committees together. We respect each other as both rivals and colleagues."

"I would like to meet with Mr. Ho. Could you call him and arrange an appointment for me? Late this afternoon or tomorrow morning would work best," she said. "It might be beneficial to mention that I'm connected with some of your more special customers — without naming names, of course."

"I could do that. Is there a reason for the meeting that you'd like me to relay?"

"No, I'll look after that myself."

"Where can I reach you?"

"You can call me back at this number. If I don't answer, just leave a message," Ava said. "And Mr. Chew, I want to thank you in advance. I really appreciate your making this effort for me."

"It's always a pleasure to help you when I can," he said.

When Uncle was alive, he could have asked Chew to burn the bank to the ground and it would have been done without question. But Uncle had been a part-owner of the bank, and his friends owned most of the rest. Evidently Ava had inherited enough of Uncle's *guanxi* to get some favours done.

Sonny was sitting in the lobby when she came back down. As soon as he saw her, he leapt to his feet with a smile on his face.

"What's happened that makes you so pleased?" she asked.

"I have the licence number for Bowles's Bentley. It's registered to Chong Investment Properties, with an address on Jubilee Street in Central."

"Should we check the parking lot there?"

"Yeah, I'd like to. We can walk to the building from here. Jubilee runs off Des Voeux Road."

"Then let's go," Ava said.

It was just past one-thirty when they left the Mandarin. The worst of the lunchtime rush hour was over, but the sidewalks were still busy, forcing Ava and Sonny to move at a slow, halting pace. Still, it took only fifteen minutes for them to get to the building on Jubilee Street. It was narrow, with four-paned windows on either side of a glass revolving door. Above the door in large gold letters, a sign read CIC. Ava looked up. The real estate report had said the building was forty storeys tall. Maybe it was, but to her eye it was a rather unimpressive forty storeys.

"Where's the entrance to the underground parking?" she asked Sonny.

"Over there," Sonny said, pointing to a ramp on the south side of the building.

"There must also be elevator access inside. Let's have a look," she said as she headed for the revolving door.

The door led directly into a mall that housed ten small stores and a coffee bar. Ava checked their business hours and saw that they all closed at either six or seven. There was no security in sight. She saw a sign for the elevators and they followed the arrows to two banks of three elevators each. Again there was no security.

Ava pushed the down button and a moment later they got into an elevator. There were two levels of underground parking. "Since he owns the building, I'm assuming Bowles will park on the first level, as close to the elevator as possible," she said as she chose that button.

They exited into a small glassed-in area that had security cameras facing the elevators. Ava opened the door leading to the parking garage but stopped after she had stepped through, looking at the surrounding walls. There were no cameras visible. She smiled when Sonny pointed to a black Bentley that occupied two parking spots immediately to their right.

"That's his car. I can't believe it was this easy," he said.

"Sometimes fate decides to give you a break," Ava said. "Do you see any CCTV?"

"The only cameras I can see are facing the elevators."

"Which means we shouldn't use the elevators to enter the garage," Sonny said.

"We should check out the entrance ramp," Ava said, and began to follow the signs that indicted the way to the exit.

It wasn't a large garage. The floor they were on couldn't have contained more than sixty cars, and Ava noticed that at least half of those were in spots reserved for building tenants. When she neared the exit, she could see swing gates and machines that dispensed parking tickets. She stopped short of them and noticed cameras mounted on the walls on both sides of the ramp.

"If we used your car, they would get the plate number for sure," she said to Sonny. "They would still have to trace it, but I don't want to risk it."

"What are you thinking?"

"That it's safer to have Jimmy use the customer elevator. He would be almost impossible to identify, and if he was carrying a shopping bag from one of the stores upstairs, he wouldn't seem out of place."

"That makes sense," Sonny said.

"Let's buy something on the way out."

Ten minutes later, Ava and Sonny were back on Jubilee Street. Sonny carried a large plastic bag containing two pillows and bearing the store's name.

"You should phone Jimmy," she said. "Tell him we've located the Bentley."

Sonny nodded and made the call. "Jimmy, it's Sonny. We found Bowles's car. Get back to me as soon as you can."

When they reached the Mandarin, Sonny put the bag in the trunk of his car and said, "What do you want to do now, boss?"

"Why don't we drive up the Peak to look at Bowles's house."

"Okay," he said, reaching to open the back door for her. After Uncle's death, when Sonny started working for Ava, she had once tried to sit in the front seat. He was so offended that she hadn't done it again.

"I can't remember ever being on the Peak during daylight hours," she said as the Mercedes started a climb that would take them up about five hundred metres. "I've been partway up, when I visited Amanda during the day, and to the top at night often enough. I guess you must know it pretty well, since you drive for my father."

"Your father doesn't use me much anymore, except to go to Shenzhen," Sonny said. "I mostly drive for Michael now. He's constantly on the go and likes to work in the car."

"My father still worries about him."

"He shouldn't. Michael and Simon To have things under control. After what happened in Macau, they're far more cautious."

"That's good to know."

Ava turned to look out the back window as the car reached the mid-levels of the Peak. The view was already impressive, and it continued to improve as they climbed higher. Sonny drove carefully, slowing down to take the turns on narrow, winding roads. Most of the traffic was going downhill towards Central — a steady stream of Mercedes, BMWS, Jaguars, Bentleys, and Porsches, many of them chauffeur-driven. Large apartment buildings started giving way to smaller, more luxurious-looking buildings, and then individual homes, some of which were themselves the size of a small apartment building.

"Barker Road," Sonny said, turning left. He drove slowly past gated houses with walls and fences of various designs, many of them topped by barbed wire and some with guardhouses.

"I wouldn't want to try breaking into one of these places," Ava said. "They're like armed camps."

"Speaking of which," Sonny said, coming to a stop, "this is Bowles's house."

Ava looked to her right. The house was separated from the road by a brick wall with a gate that opened onto a paved courtyard with a working fountain in one corner. The wall had pieces of glass embedded in the top, and for good measure it and the gate were strung with razor wire. The house was a broad two-storey red-brick structure with a grey slate roof, leaded windows, and massive dark wood double doors with brass hardware. It looked to Ava like a manor house in the English countryside.

"There are CCTV cameras everywhere, on every wall and fence," Sonny said. "I've been on this street before and never noticed them."

"That's because you didn't have to," Ava said, as she stared through the gate. "The good news is there's a Porsche SUV parked in the courtyard, and the house doesn't seem to have a garage."

Sonny started easing the car forward. "I don't want to stay

too long in one place," he said. "If you want to see more of the house, I'll loop back."

"There's no need; I've seen enough. But Sonny, you shouldn't be using this car," Ava said. "Can you find another one, with licence plates that can't be traced?"

"Yes, that shouldn't be a problem," he said.

Ava's phone rang. She looked at the screen and saw a Hong Kong number. "This is Ava Lee," she said.

"Ms. Lee, this is Henry Chew. I'm calling to confirm your appointment this afternoon at four-thirty with Ronald Ho, president of the Kowloon Merchants Reserve Bank."

"Thank you, Mr. Chew. That's marvellous."

"Ho's office is in Tsim Sha Tsui, above his bank's branch on Haiphong Road. You can walk there from the Star Ferry by going north on Canton Road to Haiphong."

"I'll most certainly take the ferry," Ava said. "How much did you tell Mr. Ho about me?"

"He was reluctant to meet with you at such short notice, until I asked him to do it as a personal favour to me. Then he asked me how I knew you, and I told him you and I have a long-standing history involving Uncle Chow Tung and Mr. Zhao," Chew said. "I invoked Mr. Zhao's name quite deliberately. Uncle may have passed on, but Zhao is still very active in Kowloon. The last thing Ho would want to do is displease him. I told him that Zhao would support whatever request you make. Use that information as you see fit."

"Thank you again, Mr. Chew. If the occasion arises, I won't hesitate to tell our mutual friends how helpful you continue to be."

"That would be appreciated." Chew said.

Ava ended the call. "That was the president of the bank

in Kowloon," she said to Sonny. "He's set up a meeting for me late this afternoon with the president of another bank over there."

"You seem pleased," Sonny said.

Ava shrugged. "During my time in Borneo, nothing seemed to go right. In fact, everything went wrong," she said, "Now, finally, we're catching some breaks."

Sonny's phone rang. "It's Jimmy," he said, and answered.

"I hope I didn't jinx the good roll we're on," Ava said under her breath.

Sonny listened and then said, "That's great. Meet me at the Mandarin, and we can walk over to the CIC Building together so you can see what you're dealing with."

"Are we okay?" Ava asked when Sonny put down his phone.

"Jimmy has everything he needs. After he drops some of it off at his house, he'll meet me at the hotel. We'll scout the Bentley and the CIC Building."

Ava smiled. "I guess I didn't jinx us after all."

21

AVA ARRIVED AT THE STAR FERRY TERMINAL IN CENTRAL just as a boat was departing, but she wasn't bothered. It was only quarter to four, and she knew another ferry would be along in six or seven minutes and that the ride across Victoria Harbour took less than ten minutes. She bought a one-way ticket for the equivalent of forty cents Canadian and joined a queue.

As she waited for the ferry, Ava thought about her upcoming meeting with Ronald Ho. She knew the information she wanted wouldn't be easy to acquire. She needed to persuade Ho to co-operate, and luckily Chew had laid the groundwork by bringing Zhao into the conversation. Zhao was one of the triad Mountain Masters in Kowloon and had been a long-time ally of Uncle, and now of Xu. Ava had met him several times with Uncle and once with Xu and had been impressed. Zhao was a tall, carefully dressed man with long silver hair that hung in a braid down his back. Like Xu and Uncle, there was nothing about the way he presented himself that hinted he was a triad gang leader.

Their encounters in Uncle's company had been social, but

there had been no doubt about the respect Zhao had for him, nor about the bond between the two men. Moreover, Zhao had made it clear that the same respect applied to Ava, as Uncle's valued partner. The meeting with Xu, though, had been more contentious. It had occurred when Xu was trying to extract his Shanghai gang from a difficult situation in Wan Chai and needed the support of the surrounding gangs, of which Zhao's was the most important. Ava had attended the meeting with Zhao at Xu's insistence, and she had managed to help broker a deal that satisfied both men.

Still, she thought as the next ferry approached the terminal, *what if Ho decides to contact Zhao to confirm there's a relationship? I shouldn't assume that Zhao will automatically support me. If nothing else, I should give him the courtesy of a warning that Ho might call.* She took her phone from her LV bag and called Shanghai.

"*Wei*," Auntie Grace answered.

"Hi, Auntie, this is Ava. Is Xu available?"

"He's in the kitchen with Suen. I'll get him."

"To what do I owe this pleasure?" Xu said a moment later.

"I know I've been asking for a lot of favours lately, but I'm sorry, I have to ask for another," she said, shuffling forward in the line to board the ferry.

"'Sorry' is a word you never have to use with me," Xu said. "What can I do?"

"Are you still on good terms with Zhao?"

"Yes, very good terms."

"Could you phone him for me? I'm in Hong Kong and I have a meeting at four-thirty in Kowloon with a bank president named Ronald Ho. I'm going to be asking for information that he won't want to provide. Acknowledgement of my relationship with Zhao, such as it is, might induce him to be more co-operative," Ava said. "But I don't want to use Zhao's name unless he's okay with it. Could you check with him to see if he has any objections?"

"What's the name of the bank?"

"The Kowloon Merchants Reserve."

"I'll call Zhao now," Xu said. "I'll also text you his number in case you want to talk to him directly."

"Thanks."

"*Momentai*. But now you can do me a favour. Call me back later today and let me know what you're doing in Hong Kong and how it went with the banker."

"I'll do that, I promise," Ava said, stepping onto the ferry.

The boat wasn't overly crowded, and Ava took a seat near the back so she could have a clear view of the Hong Kong skyline. As impressive a sight as it was from the Peak, she preferred to see it from the water, expanding endlessly outwards as the shoreline was left further behind.

The ferry was more than halfway across Victoria Harbour on its way to Tsim Sha Tsui when her phone pinged. It was a text from Xu. Spoke to Zhao. He's happy for you to use his name. Zhao's phone number appeared underneath.

In a city that was continually reinventing itself, the Star Ferry was a constant in Hong Kong. But even the ferry had undergone some upgrading, and its terminals on the Hong Kong Island side of the harbour had been moved to new locations. Thankfully the terminal in Tsim Sha Tsui was still at the end of Salisbury Road, where it had been for more than a hundred years. It was as familiar to Ava as any part of Toronto. She disembarked, walked past newsstands selling papers from around the world, bypassed the taxi and bus lines, and started up Canton Road.

Ahead of her, the old Kowloon Station Clock Tower read five minutes past four. If she went directly to the bank she'd be early, so she stepped into a coffee shop near the Ocean Terminal. The place was busy but service was efficient, and she was able to enjoy a double espresso before continuing on to Haiphong Road.

The building that housed the Kowloon Merchants Reserve Bank was a modest six storeys of light brown brick with small windows. The bank branch on the main floor had large-paned windows and a double set of glass doors. The entrance to the building itself was a separate door to the left. Ava walked through into a lobby that had a stained white-tile floor and two small elevators. *What prompted Martin Bowles to do business with a bank that appears so undistinguished?* she thought.

Ava waited for a minute for an elevator that seemed to be stuck on the third floor, then decided to take the stairs. The door to the second floor opened onto a brightly lit corridor. The floor was nicely carpeted and the walls seemed to be freshly painted, and Ava's opinion ticked upwards. The bank appeared to be the only tenant on the floor, and there were arrows on the wall directing visitors to various offices and departments. The office of the president was to the right. She walked to that end of the corridor and came to a set of wooden doors with KOWLOON MERCHANTS RESERVE BANK embossed in gold. There was a sign to the right of the doors that read PLEASE BUZZ TO GAIN ENTRY. She did as directed, and seconds later the door opened.

"Can I help you?" a young woman asked.

"I have an appointment with Mr. Ho. My name is Ava Lee."

"Yes, he is expecting you. Come in," she said.

Ava walked into a small outer office containing a single desk, a couch, a coffee table, and two rows of filing cabinets. The walls were decorated with oil paintings of waterfalls, bamboo forests, and rice paddies — all familiar, if trite, subjects of Chinese office art.

The young woman walked to a closed wooden door, knocked, waited for a few seconds, and then opened it. "Ms. Lee is here," she said, and stepped to one side.

Ronald Ho stood behind a large metal desk. He nodded at Ava and then came around the desk to greet her with an outstretched hand. "Pleased to meet you, Ms. Lee," he said.

His handshake was firm but slightly damp, and Ava noticed a trace of sweat on his upper lip. He wore a grey three-piece suit with a red tie knotted tightly at the neck. Ho was in his mid-forties, she guessed, and of medium height and build. His face was rather round, a fact exaggerated by the long, fluffy hair encircling it.

"Thank you for seeing me," she said.

"How could I refuse?" he said with a wan smile. "Can we get you something to drink? Coffee, tea, water?"

"I'm fine," she said.

"Then why don't we sit at the table," he said, pointing to a round conference table with six green leather chairs.

Ava sat down and Ho took a seat across from her. "It was good of you to see me on such short notice," she said.

"Henry Chew made it clear that you have special friends," Ho said. "That was reinforced ten minutes ago, when Mr. Zhao phoned me."

"I didn't ask him to," Ava said, sensing that Ho was quite nervous.

"Then it's even more striking that he chose to do so of his own accord."

"I've known Zhao for many years," Ava said. "It isn't unusual for him to help his friends."

"You don't seem old enough to have known him very long, but that doesn't matter, does it. He obviously considers you a special friend," Ho said.

Ava didn't like the sly insinuation, and said briskly, "Zhao did business with my former partner, Uncle Chow Tung, and now has dealings with my *ge ge*."

Ho's face flushed. "Anyway, Zhao asked me to give you any assistance you may require, and I promised him I would. But I have no idea what you want of me, or my bank."

"Is this a public bank?" Ava asked. "I hadn't heard the name until this morning."

"No, we are privately owned. We do have one branch open to the public, on the ground floor of this building. My father, who founded the bank, opened it as a convenience for the local residents, and I've kept it open in his memory. Otherwise, all our business is conducted on this floor. We have a select list of clients, many of whom have been with the bank for decades."

"How long has Martin Bowles been a client?"

Ho looked uncomfortable. "Ms. Lee, we have a strict policy of not disclosing client information. That is one of the reasons our client list has remained stable for all these years, and why we have a waiting list of people who wish to become clients."

"Did Bowles find his own way to you, or was he pointed in this direction by his father-in-law, Sulaiman Chong?"

"I find this incredibly awkward," Ho said. "I really do want to help you, but —"

"I have to say I'm disappointed, Mr. Ho," Ava said. "You

promised Zhao you'd give me assistance, and now it appears you're reluctant to answer even my most basic questions."

"We have a policy —" he began.

"Shall I call Zhao now?" Ava interrupted. "Perhaps you'd care to explain the policy to him."

"I'd rather you didn't," Ho said.

"Look, I don't want to be unreasonable. How about I meet you halfway," said Ava. "Tell me what I want to know and I promise you it will never be repeated. I am a woman of my word. If you doubt that, you can call Zhao and ask him to verify."

Ho closed his eyes, pressed his lips together, and furrowed his brow. "You have put me in a most difficult position," he said.

"I apologize for that, but you can make it easier on yourself by trusting me."

He looked across the table at her. "Yes, Martin Bowles is a client."

"How about his wife, Laila, or other members of the Chong family?"

"Sulaiman Chong has had an account here for more than twenty-five years. He and my father were friends. Ahmad and Laila Chong also have accounts."

"Are those personal or business accounts?"

"Personal. The family has always done its business with HKSS."

"What kind of balances are we talking about?" Ava asked.

"They vary, but rarely less than forty million dollars."

"American or Hong Kong?"

"American."

"Have they always had these separate accounts?"

Ho frowned, and Ava knew he was wondering how much to tell her. "It's a simple question, Mr. Ho."

"Yes, but the truth is, those accounts aren't really separate. Money just passes through them before being consolidated in the family's various business accounts at HKSS."

"You're laundering the money for them?" Ava asked.

"No! We would never do anything illegal," Ho said.

"But you said 'passes through.' What else could that mean?"

Ho sighed. "The Chong family, and several other families close to them in Borneo, make their money from timber. The practice has always been controversial, and increasingly so in recent years, as environmentalists equate illegal logging with drug smuggling. Some top-line banks are more sensitive when it comes to the source of the money they accept. In the case of HKSS, they made it clear to the Chong family early on that they wanted no direct connection with the logging trade or any money made from it. So the money starts here, and a year or so later it finds its way to their HKSS account in the form of bonds and other government securities from reputable countries."

"But why do the Chongs need a top-line bank? Why not just place all their money with you and not worry about what anyone else thinks?"

"Sulaiman Chong has a long-term dream of taking the family businesses public. He can't do that with the support of a small private bank in Kowloon. He needs to be affiliated with one of the majors," Ho said. "One thing my father learned about Sulaiman — and something I've seen in Martin as well — is that these are not people who think in the short term. They have plans that extend well into the future, many years from now."

"And those plans are to build a real estate empire and then go public?"

"Hong Kong real estate has always been Sulaiman's favourite form of investment," Ho said. "He has faith in this market, and that faith has certainly been rewarded."

"That's good to know, but you still haven't answered the second part of my question. Has Chong given you any indication when he might take the businesses public?"

"They hired a consulting firm a few years ago to look into it and decided the time wasn't right. I know discussions have been underway since then with HKSS, but I have no idea how far they've progressed."

Ava nodded. "Well, I think you've told me what I want to know. I hope it wasn't too difficult."

Ho furrowed his brow, surprised. "That's . . . all you want?"

"Yes. What did you expect?"

"I thought you might want account numbers and other private information."

"And if I did?"

"I wouldn't have given them to you," Ho said.

"I respect that. As I said, I'm not unreasonable. But that could change if you decide to contact Martin Bowles or Sulaiman Chong to tell them about my visit here."

"Why would I do that?" Ho asked, his face flushing again.

Ava knew she had caught him in a lie. "You might want to curry favour with valued clients."

"I won't contact them. You have my word on that, Ms. Lee."

Ava nodded again. "Eventually I might like you to call Sulaiman Chong on my behalf, but not until the time is right. When it is, I'll let you know. Are you sure you can maintain silence until then?" she asked.

"Of course."

"Don't say that quite so nonchalantly. I'm going to be doing serious business with the Chong family, and I can't risk its being disrupted."

"I promise you, I won't say a word."

Ava stood up and extended her hand. "Thank you for your time, Mr. Ho," she said. "I'll let Zhao know that you were cooperative."

22

AVA LEFT THE KOWLOON MERCHANTS RESERVE BANK feeling satisfied. She now knew how much money the Chong family typically had on hand, and she had a rough idea of Sulaiman Chong's long-term plans. Both were potentially useful pieces of information.

She walked back to the Star Ferry terminal and once again found she had just missed a boat and had to join a queue. She found Zhao's number and called it.

"*Wei,*" Zhao answered.

"This is Ava. Thanks for the help with the bank president. It went well."

"Excellent."

"If there's something I can do for you —" she began.

"There is," Zhao interrupted. "Xu has started producing the latest version of the iPhone. My allocation is less than I'd hoped for. A kind word from you might increase it."

"I'll do what I can," Ava said.

"That's all I can ask," Zhao said. "Now don't hesitate to call me again if there's something else you need while you're still in this part of the world."

Ava smiled as she ended the call. Uncle had taught her that favours granted were many times more powerful than favours received, and that she should always keep the balance on her side of the ledger. With that in mind, she phoned Xu, and to her surprise he answered.

"I'm waiting for the Star Ferry," she said. "I had my meeting, and Zhao went out of his way to make sure it went well. When I thanked him, he mentioned the new iPhone you're manufacturing. He would like to have more of them. Can you do that?"

Xu laughed. "That old man is so shrewd. No wonder Uncle had so much respect for him."

"So you'll give him more iPhones?"

"Yes, I will. Maybe not what he originally asked for, but more than I told him we'd ship. Do you want to tell him?"

"No, I think it would be better if it came from you."

"I'll call him."

"Thank you, Xu. Give Auntie Grace a hug from me and tell her Fai and I will see you both soon."

"Just one second. You were going to tell me what you're doing in Hong Kong. Was it simply to see this banker?"

"No. We had trouble in Borneo again, and one way of rectifying it happens to be here," she said.

"You do know that if you need Suen and his men to get involved, I can have them in Borneo in a heartbeat," he said, referring to his Red Pole, the man who ran Xu's men on the street. "And if you need help in Hong Kong, there's no shortage of men we can provide through friends."

"We aren't at that point, and hopefully we won't get there," she said. "I'm working with Sonny and his friend Jimmy on a plan. If it works, I shouldn't need help. If it doesn't, you'll be the first person I call."

"Okay. Just be careful."

"I will," she said.

The next ferry was approaching the pier and the queue started to shuffle forward. When Ava boarded, she went to the front of the boat. She waited until the ferry had left the dock to call Amanda.

"Have you had dinner?" she asked when Amanda answered.

"More like a late lunch. We ordered in fried noodles and a few other dishes. There's some left if you want to come to the office."

"Is Aisyah still with you?"

"Yes, she's here."

"I'm on the ferry. I'll see you in half an hour," said Ava.

The Yee Trading Company and the Three Sisters corporate offices shared the third floor of a building in Central that was a fifteen-minute walk from the ferry terminal. The trading company, like the furniture factory in Sabah, didn't actually fit the profile of companies that Three Sisters wanted to own, but May Ling and Ava had bought it as a way of securing Amanda's services. And since she regarded it as her father's legacy, there was no way they could sell it.

The companies had separate offices, with the trading company occupying three-quarters of the floor. Ava rarely visited the trading operation, and as usual when she got there, she turned left out of the elevator and headed directly to the Three Sisters offices.

They had a staff of nine, four of them in finance and accounting, two in purchasing, and two young women who helped Chi-Tze and the Po siblings with sales and marketing. With the exception of Amanda, everyone worked in an open office space. All heads turned in Ava's direction when she walked through the door.

"Hello, everyone," she said.

Amanda and Aisyah emerged from Amanda's office as soon as they heard Ava's voice. "The food is on the board-room table. Help yourself," Amanda said.

"Both of you come and sit with me," Ava said.

There were three Styrofoam containers, an empty plate, and chopsticks on the table. Ava opened the containers and dished out fried noodles with beef, a spring roll, and some bok choy onto the plate. "How did you sleep?" she asked when the two women joined her.

"I had trouble. I kept waking up; I couldn't stop thinking about Jamilah," Aisyah said.

"Me too," said Amanda.

"Well, let's see if we can cause the Chong family to lose some sleep too," Ava said, and then saw Aisyah glance furtively at Amanda.

Amanda noticed that Ava had caught the look. "I told Aisyah you wouldn't take what happened in Sarawak lying down."

"That's true, but I don't want either of you to mention that to anyone outside this room," Ava said.

"What are you going to do?" Aisyah asked.

"I'm not ready to talk about that yet, but there's something you can do to make a contribution," Ava said.

"Anything," Aisyah said.

"I'd like you to compile a list of the active environmental and Indigenous rights organizations in Sarawak," Ava said.

"I know some of them, but certainly not all. Celia would be a better source for that information."

"Then you can get it from Celia, and please do so without telling her I asked for it. If I could get the list and some contact information by sometime tomorrow, that would be great."

"Okay."

Ava nodded and began to eat.

"Why don't you try to reach her now? I have a couple of things I need to go over with Ava," Amanda said. She waited for Aisyah to leave the room before turning to Ava. "I hope you aren't disappointed that I said something to Aisyah. She was so down last night and kept repeating how hopeless everything was that I felt I had to try lifting her spirits a little."

"There's no harm done, as long as she keeps it to herself."

"I'll make sure she does."

Ava finished a spring roll. "For food that isn't particularly warm anymore, this is very good," she said.

"I bought it at the noodle shop where Uncle used to go."

"No wonder I found the flavours familiar."

"Are you going to join us for dinner tonight?"

"I'm not sure. I'm working on a project with Sonny and it might keep me busy."

"You have everyone working on something except for me," Amanda said.

"You'll get your chance," Ava said with a smile. "Actually, there is something you could do for me now. I want to know how much insurance we should have been paid for the damage to the warehouse and our loss of inventory. I'm guessing it's about three million."

"The building isn't a total write-off, and with some work we could salvage some of the inventory."

"Since we don't intend to rebuild the business, it's all a write-off as far as I'm concerned."

"Then it would be approximately two point eight million U.S. dollars."

"I wasn't far off, but I think I'll round it up to three million," Ava said. She looked at her phone as it rang. "That's Sonny."

"Do you want me to leave you alone?" Amanda asked.

"No," said Ava, hitting the answer button. "Sonny, I'm at our office in Central. How did it go?"

"It went well. I'm outside the CIC Building with Jimmy. The Bentley is still parked in the garage."

"Good. Now have him check out the front of the building. We want lots of noise and visible damage."

"Okay, boss."

"What will you do after that?"

"I have to go to Kowloon to pick up the replacement car we discussed. After that, Jimmy and I plan to go to the Bowles's house, and then I thought we would scope out some of their other properties."

"Okay, good. You don't need to call me unless there's a problem. I have some work to do, and then I need a good night's sleep. We'll touch base in the morning."

"Lots of noise and visible damage?" Amanda said when Ava put down the phone. "You do know how strange that sounds, right?"

"If you're ever asked, you didn't hear me use those words," Ava said.

23

IT WAS GETTING DARK WHEN AVA LEFT THE THREE
Sisters offices. She took her time walking to the Mandarin,
thought briefly about going to M Bar for a drink, and
then decided to go directly to her suite. The day had gone
much better than she'd expected. Now she wanted to lay
the groundwork that would make the following day just as
successful.

It was too early to call Toronto. The time difference
between North America and Asia seldom bothered her, but
speaking with Derek was her top priority, and Ava hated having to wait. She took a bottle of Chardonnay from the minibar,
poured half of it into a glass, and carried it to the desk. After
a couple of sips she opened the Bowles file and her notebook.

Ava made a list of the references Bowles had given the
Hong Kong Jockey Club. He had provided email addresses
for four of them. Ava went online to see if she could locate
addresses for the remaining two but wasn't successful.
Instead she added Jack Yee's and those of the secretary and
chairperson of the Jockey Club.

Next she visited the HKSS Bank's website and recorded

the email addresses for the customer relations, investor and government relations, human resources, and corporate governance departments. The Hong Kong news media made up her third list, and they quickly became her fourth as well, when she realized she had to separate the Chinese-language media from the English. She'd had no idea how many media outlets there were in Hong Kong and was surprised by the numbers in both languages.

When that was done, Ava took a short break to check her messages and empty the wine bottle. When she returned to the desk, she found the website that listed all the English-language media in Malaysia, accessed as many of them as she could, and recorded the email addresses attached to them.

Ava checked the time, guessed that Derek was probably up by now, but then decided to finish her last list. It was going to be the largest and most complicated. She started with Chong Timber Industries and then worked her way through the companies named on the Jockey Club application. She wrote down every email address she could find, no matter how trivial. There were none for Bowles, Ahmad Chong, or Arven Saad, and certainly not for Sulaiman Chong, but Ava made a note of the template each of the companies used for emails and figured she'd use the same for them.

Finally she turned to the Sarawak state government. She found email addresses for the offices of the governor, chief minister, state secretary, state attorney, state treasurer, and ten other departments and state boards. Ava was about to close her notebook when another thought occurred to her. Ten minutes later the email addresses for the Royal Malaysia Police in Kuala Lumpur and its contingent office in Kuching formed yet another list.

It always amazed Ava how much information was so easily available online. Her challenge now was to use it in a way that would cause the most anger and discomfort in the world of the Chongs. She reached for her phone and called Derek.

"Hey, Ava," he answered.

"Is this a good time for you?"

"Sure, but I don't have anything for you yet," he said quickly. "I inputted the names of Bowles's kids into my software, but I'm still running it through the HKSS bank accounts. I haven't even started on that Kowloon account you gave me."

"That's not why I'm calling," she said. "Can you set up a website for me? It doesn't have to be fancy, just something basic I can use to send and receive email."

"Yes, I can. It isn't that difficult."

"Can you also prevent anyone from finding out who controls it?"

"That's not a problem. Many domains have policies that protect the privacy of the originator, unless of course the site is being used to promote things like racism and violence."

"It would be promoting the preservation of natural habitats, so I assume that's fine."

"I didn't know you were into protecting the environment," Derek said.

"I am now. Do you mind registering the site? I'll pay you back."

"I don't care about the money," he said. "What do you want to call this website?"

"Whatever you think works best. The name of the organization is the Sarawak United Front."

"That's a mouthful for a web address."

"Then make it more concise."

"Okay. We could go with suf.com, or maybe sarawakfront. com. Do you have a preference?"

"I like the second option."

"I'll set it up right way. I'll make you the administrator."

"How soon can you make this happen?" she asked.

"That depends on how much information you want the site to contain."

"What if it has just a generic banner and a one-paragraph description of the Front's objectives?"

"No photos, graphics, or tabs?"

"I don't think we need them."

"It doesn't get simpler than that. I could have the site up and running by tomorrow. But could you confirm by email the name you want on the banner? And I'll need the description of the organization's objectives."

"I'll email you the name now, but the description will take a bit longer."

"*Momentai*. I'll get started."

Ava hung up, immediately emailed the name to Derek, and then called Douglas Brooke.

"Hello?" he answered.

"It's Ava Lee. I hope I'm not disturbing another dinner."

"You aren't. What can I do for you tonight?"

"I'd appreciate some help with something."

"Such as?"

"The Sarawak United Front."

Brooke paused. "You and I and everyone else know there's no such organization."

"But if there were, what would its mission statement be?"

There was an even longer pause before Brooke said, "I know you must have a reason for asking that, but I have absolutely no idea what it could be."

"I'm in the process of setting up a website for the Front, and I'm trying to construct a mission statement. I thought you could help. I don't need more than a paragraph," she said. "I remember, when I met you in your office, how passionate you were about the destruction of the rainforest and the people who depend on it. Can you put that in writing?"

"That's an extraordinary request."

"I have a good reason for making it."

"I'm sure you must. Will you tell me what it is?"

"I think it's better for both of us if I don't."

"Goodness me. You are full of surprises, Ms. Lee. Please assure me I won't be sorry for helping you with this."

"Of course."

"Okay. Give me an hour," Brooke said.

Ava smiled as she ended the call. The plan was taking shape. Its success would still come down to the execution, but she had confidence in Sonny and Jimmy. And then it was up to her to parlay that success into pressure on the Chongs. One thing was certain: Ava was in a far better place than she'd been twenty-four hours earlier.

When she worked with Uncle, he had preached patience and the importance of not making assumptions. "Don't get too far ahead of the reality of the moment," he would say, "but when you are finally ready to strike, go hard and go fast." It was a way of working that was now ingrained in her.

Ava climbed into bed with her phone. She called Fai and they chatted for close to an hour. Ava avoided discussing the specifics of her day and instead asked about Fai's time on set. Fai was happy to share, but as their conversation drew to a close, she asked, "You seem calmer. Have you solved that problem in Borneo?"

"I'm getting there. The next couple of days will tell the tale, but I'm feeling optimistic. I'll tell you all about it when everything is finalized." She hung up feeling slightly guilty for not being completely honest with Fai, but Ava knew she'd only worry, and Fai didn't need distractions so close to the end of filming.

Ava slid out of bed and opened her laptop. Brooke had sent an email with an attachment. I hope this is what you are looking for. I still can't imagine why you want it, but I'm sure I'll find out eventually Ava clicked on the attachment labelled "Mission_Statement.doc" and began to read:

The Sarawak United Front is a coalition of environmental and Indigenous rights groups that have come together to protect what is left of the Sarawak rainforest. It is estimated that as much as 75 percent of the rainforest has already been destroyed by illegal logging. This is a tragedy. The ecological impact is obvious, but less understood is the horrific human cost that has been exacted. The Penan people have called the rainforest home for centuries. As the rainforest is being illegally torn down for profit, their culture and their very lives are being threatened.

The Sarawak United Front is committed to doing whatever is necessary to stop this environmental and human carnage. Not only the illegal loggers but also the government of Sarawak must be held accountable for this abuse.

Help us save what's left of the rainforest. Help us protect the Penan people.

Ava smiled and replied to Brooke: Your statement is brilliant. I love it! Then she forwarded the message to Derek with a note. Here is the mission statement I'd like you to use for the website. Call me when it's set up.

24

AVA WOKE UP FEELING ENERGIZED. SHE HAD GONE TO bed immediately after emailing the mission statement to Derek and had slept for nine hours straight. *Whatever the day holds in store*, she thought, *at least I'll be rested in mind and body.*

She made a coffee, checked her messages, and went to sit in a chair by the window. There were only a few clouds in the sky and the sun bore down on Victoria Harbour, creating the illusion that its oil-streaked waters were a multi-coloured carpet. In the distance Ava could see a Star Ferry churning its way towards Hong Kong Island as myriad boats moved haphazardly around it.

She finished her coffee and went to get another. Before she could return to the chair, her phone rang. "Sonny, how are things going this morning?"

"Good. I'm on my way to pick up Jimmy now. I'm driving a blue Toyota with plates that once belonged to a BMW."

"What are your plans?"

"Jimmy and I are going to the CIC Building again to check on the Bentley, but before that Jimmy was hoping you'd have

ten minutes to meet with us. He's been thinking about timing and has some questions."

"How long will it take you to get to the Mandarin?"

"At least an hour, maybe longer."

"Okay. Call me when you get here."

Ava returned to her seat by the window. It was oddly
coincidental that Jimmy wanted to discuss timing, because
it was something she'd been thinking about that morning
as well. Her initial instinct had been to blow up the car and
leave Bowles in the dark about what was happening. But
finding the Bentley had been so easy that she now wondered
if she should press Bowles sooner. By upping the ante she'd
increase her chances to grab the Chong family's attention.
As she weighed her options, her phone rang again.

"I was hoping you'd call," she said as she answered.

"I don't have any updates yet on HKSS, but I've started running my software on the Kowloon bank account," Derek said.

"Let's hope we have more luck with it," Ava said. "What
about the website?"

"I've registered a site in the name of the Sarawak United
Front and it's now live. For the banner I used a photo of some
rainforest and superimposed the mission statement on it. It's
a great statement, by the way. If you want to look at the site,
you can go to sarawakfront.com."

"And I can send and receive emails through it?"

"I've made you the administrator. To access it, you'll need
to log in using the username mimichiang and the password
amber111chiang. Once you're in, you can send emails from
info@sarawakfront.com. I set it up so any messages sent to
the info address will be forwarded directly to your personal
account. No one will know you're receiving them."

"That's exactly what I wanted. Thank you," Ava said. *Another building block in place*, she thought as she began getting ready to meet Sonny and Jimmy.

An hour later Ava came out of the Mandarin expecting to see the Mercedes parked near the entrance, but then she remembered Sonny had switched cars. She looked for a blue Toyota instead, and as she walked towards it, Sonny stepped out.

"Good morning, Jimmy," she said as she climbed into the back seat.

"Good morning, boss," Jimmy said from the front.

"Unless you want to go somewhere else, we thought we'd meet in the car," said Sonny.

"That's fine with me. Sonny tells me you have the supplies you need," she said to Jimmy.

"They're even better than I expected. My friends had enough Semtex to blow up a parking lot full of cars," said Jimmy.

"I'm not really sure what Semtex is," Ava said.

"I won't get technical, but it's a powerful plastic explosive. A few ounces will destroy the Bentley, and I'll have enough left over to do serious damage to six or seven buildings."

"I'm pleased to hear that. Sonny said you have some questions about timing."

"Yeah. I was thinking it would be safer to hit the car and as many buildings as we can in one go," Jimmy said, glancing nervously at Sonny. "The longer we drag this out, the tighter security will become and the greater the risk that we'll be identified or caught. I have all the supplies to construct everything we'd need."

"Ava, Jimmy isn't afraid to go with whatever you decide.

If you want to do it over a week, he'll do it that way. He's just being cautious."

Ava smiled at Sonny's concern for how his friend's idea might be received. "I appreciate that, Sonny, and I respect your opinion, Jimmy," she said. "In fact, I've been having similar thoughts. My objective is to get the Chong family's total attention, and I'm beginning to believe that hitting them hard right out of the gate is the best way to do it. It will also draw public attention to their businesses."

"So we'll make it a big-bang evening?" Sonny asked.

"Yes, I think we will," said Ava.

"I have to go back to the house to assemble the rest of the bombs," Jimmy said excitedly to Sonny.

"Assuming the Bentley is already in the parking garage, do you want to plant that one before I drive you home?" asked Sonny.

"We should at least try."

Sonny turned to Ava. "Is that okay with you?"

"Of course. And while you're gone, I'm going to pay a visit to some of the other buildings on the list. I'll take some photos and try to put together an action plan for damaging as many of them as makes sense," she said. "Jimmy, you said you have enough Semtex for six or seven more bombs?"

"To be on the safe side, figure on five."

"Okay, I'll identify five potential targets."

"When we get back from Jimmy's place in Sha Tin, we'll have to confirm that the Bentley is still there. I'm assuming you'll want us to tail it when it leaves the garage," Sonny said.

"Yes. I'm hoping Bowles will go directly home from the office, but regardless, we should keep track of the car," she said, and then turned to Jimmy. "Does it make a difference to you if it's dark when we do this?"

"I'm sure the house's courtyard will be lit, but I'll bring my night-vision binoculars just in case."

"And, coming back to timing, do you want to wait until later in the night or do we blow the car the first chance we get?" Sonny asked Ava.

"My objective is to scare the hell out of Bowles," she said. "I think blowing up his car right after he gets out of it might be the best way to achieve that. He'll assume he was lucky to escape with his life."

"I agree," said Jimmy.

"Good, then we have a plan," Ava said. "You two head for the garage and stay in touch. I'm going to visit some buildings."

"Will you be joining us tonight?" Jimmy asked.

"I wouldn't miss it for anything," she said.

25

AVA RETURNED TO HER SUITE AND OPENED THE FILE containing the addresses of the Chong family real estate holdings. *If we're going to bomb five buildings,* she thought, *it should be done in a logical sequence, one that makes the best use of our time and limits our exposure.*

She created a long list of seven Chong-owned buildings in Central, and in her notebook she worked out a route that went from the farthest point from the Mandarin back to the hotel. But geography wasn't the only factor she needed to consider when making her decision. There were also the questions of feasibility and preventing casualties. Until she actually visited the buildings, Ava couldn't decide which five to hit. She checked her watch and calculated that if she left the hotel right away, she should be able to visit all seven buildings before four-thirty.

As she was getting ready to leave, her phone rang. "Yes, Sonny," she answered.

"The Bentley was there and Jimmy planted the bomb," he said. "We're heading to Sha Tin now. When we get back this afternoon, we'll confirm that the car is still there and then find a spot on the street where we can watch the garage until it leaves."

"Call me when you get back. I'll join you in the car," she said.

"Jimmy still has the balaclavas we used in the last job. We're going to wear them when we go up the Peak. Do you want one?"

"No, I have a hoodie I'll wear."

"Then that's it. We'll see you later," said Sonny.

Ava sighed with relief; the last thing they needed was a problem with the Bentley. It seemed that her lucky streak was still alive. She gathered her things and got a taxi to Murray Road. It was the farthest point from the Oriental, and from there she intended to walk back. She arrived at the first building on her list and was immediately disappointed; it was a small commercial property with a restaurant occupying most of the ground floor. The restaurant's hours of operation weren't posted, which prompted Ava to cross the building off her mental list. Uncertainty was something they didn't need.

From Murray Street she walked to Garden Road. She smiled when she saw a ten-storey office building with nothing on the ground floor except a revolving door that led into the lobby. Ava took her notebook from her bag and put a tick next to the address. An hour and a half later she had ticks next to buildings on Duddell Street, Wyndham Street, and Graham Street, plus the CIC Building on Jubilee. Only the one on Pedder Street didn't make the cut, and that was again because of a restaurant.

Ava hadn't heard from Sonny during her walk, so when she returned to the Mandarin at just past four o'clock, she knew she had time to spare. She got two maps of the Central District from the concierge and took them to her room. After freshening up and making herself a coffee, she sat at the desk and marked on each map the route she had just covered. On paper it looked as if moving from building to building, bombing as they went, would be a relatively simple exercise. She knew it wouldn't be that predictable but had confidence that Sonny and Jimmy would help her make the right decisions.

She left the desk and went into the bedroom. She took a black hoodie, which she'd bought the year before at the Adidas store in Central, from her bag and was about to return to the living room when a thought struck her. She dropped to her knees by the side of the bed, closed her eyes, clasped her hands in front of her face, and began to pray to Saint Jude. She never asked Jude to help her achieve a specific end, only that her problem would be resolved in some manner and that no one would be hurt in the process. She asked for that now. When she'd finished, Ava felt calmer and more confident that the evening would be a success.

Ava returned to the living room, saw it was almost four-thirty, and decided she'd better leave for the short walk to Jubilee Road. The office towers in Central were beginning to empty and progress was slow, but at ten to five she finally turned the corner onto Jubilee. She didn't see the blue Toyota at first, then heard a car horn and saw Sonny waving at her from across the street. The Toyota was sandwiched between two trucks about twenty metres from the garage. She walked towards it and Sonny got out and opened the back door for her. She looked right and saw they had a clear view of the exit.

Ava took a map from her hoodie pocket and passed it to

Sonny. "I had a look at the buildings in person. Five of them have offices that should be vacated by seven or so, and none of them have a business on the ground floor that will be open late. I think these are the right candidates for tonight. We can start with the building on Garden Road and then work our way back towards the hotel."

"That sounds good to me. Jimmy's made five more bombs."

"How do they work?" Ava asked.

Jimmy pulled a square box from his bag. "This red button is the detonator for the car bomb. Once I remove the tape, all I have to do is press it down," he said. He then held up a thick metal rod with a patch of black tape across its centre. "This is one of the bombs for the buildings. The switch is under the tape. After the switch is flipped, there's a one-minute delay before the bomb goes off. That should give us enough time to get the hell away from the building."

26

TWO HOURS LATER, THE TRIO WAS STILL SITTING IN THE car and darkness was beginning to descend.

"I'm glad you suggested we wait here instead of some spot along the way," Ava said, after making a second trip to a nearby Starbucks for coffee and water. "I wouldn't have been able to stretch my legs, let alone get a coffee."

"One of the things you learn as a sniper is how and where to wait," Jimmy said.

"How did you get into munitions?" she asked.

"That's where I started when I enlisted, but I found it too random. We'd set a bomb or a landmine with a target in mind, only to have someone else stumble over it. I preferred the precision that came with sniping."

"We need precision tonight," she said.

"Actually, if you weren't approaching it that way, I might not have agreed to bomb the buildings," Jimmy said. "A car is easy to hit without injuring people, but buildings are much more difficult. In a way it's good that Bowles is making us wait. It means there will be fewer people around the other buildings when we're done."

"Speaking of Bowles, I think that's the Bentley coming out of the parking garage," Sonny said.

Ava saw that it was a Bentley, and when it turned onto Jubilee Road, she recognized from his photo that it was Bowles behind the wheel. "Yes, that's him. I'm surprised he doesn't have a chauffeur."

"He's heading in the direction of the Peak," said Sonny, easing the Toyota into traffic.

"I hope he goes directly home and doesn't stop somewhere for dinner," Ava said.

Sonny followed several car lengths behind for a few minutes and then said with a smile, "He's turning onto Magazine Gap Road."

Traffic was heavy, and by the time they reached Peak Road, the last vestige of daylight was gone. Sonny turned onto Peak Road and then, at the entrance to Barker Road, he came to an abrupt stop. "We should put on our balaclavas now," he said.

Ava put her hood over her head and pulled the strings tightly so that it covered most of her face. "This will do for me."

Sonny and Jimmy put on their balaclavas. "Are you ready?" Sonny asked Jimmy.

Jimmy reached down and took the detonator out of his bag. "I'm as ready as I'll ever be."

Sonny turned onto Barker Road. The street itself was fairly well lit, but the houses behind its walls and fences could have been in full daylight. Sonny stopped the Toyota in a darker area that afforded a clear view of the well-illuminated Bowles house and courtyard.

"This is good. I won't need my night-vision binoculars," said Jimmy.

The Bentley was in the courtyard, parked next to the Porsche. Bowles had just left the car and was walking up the front steps to his home.

Jimmy looked around and then sat back in his seat with his head turned away as several cars passed them. When no more traffic was visible in either direction and the door had closed behind Bowles, Jimmy looked back at Ava. "Ready?"

She stared out at the courtyard. "Do it."

Jimmy gently removed the tape, turned again to smile at Ava, and pressed the red button. Ava had imagined the explosion would be loud, but she hadn't expected the intense burst of light, which forced her to avert her eyes. A sustained roar was followed by the clanging of debris as pieces of the Bentley that had been propelled into the air landed on the Porsche and the house. As the smoke cleared, Ava could see what was left of the car lying on its side. The now windowless Porsche had been pushed against the gate.

"That was terrific!" said Sonny.

Ava saw Bowles emerge from the house, gaping in horror at the carnage, before quickly retreating back inside. "We scared the hell out of him," she said.

"If that didn't do it, then he's an idiot," said Sonny.

Ava heard an alarm go off and saw several security guards take careful steps out of other compounds to look in the direction of the Bowles home. "We've attracted some attention. Let's get out of here before they get any closer," she said.

Sonny nodded, did a tight U-turn, and drove off. "Where are we going now?" he asked when they reached Magazine Gap Road.

"Head for Garden Road," Ava said. "Hopefully the offices have cleared out and the street is quiet."

The men took off their balaclavas as they began the downhill drive into Central. Halfway down they heard sirens and saw the cars in front of them pulling over to stop. Sonny did the same. Seconds later a police car sped by with its siren blaring.

"They were quick," Jimmy said.

"Given the type of people who live on the Peak, I'm sure the police patrol it constantly," said Ava.

Traffic started to move again. "After Garden Road, what's the route I outlined on the map?" Ava asked Jimmy.

He held the map in front of his face. "It looks like we'll go from Garden Road to Duddell Street, then Wyndham Street, and then Graham Street, ending up at the CIC Building on Jubilee. Sonny, do you need me to give you directions as we go?"

"No. I know the area like the back of my hand."

When they reached Central, Ava was pleased to see that traffic was relatively light and many of the side streets were quiet. Sonny drove carefully, but with the confidence of someone who knew where he was going. As he turned onto Garden Road, Ava spotted the building that was their next target.

"Stop near the red-brick building on the right," she said to Sonny.

He parked the car about twenty metres short of the building's revolving glass doors. Ava looked through the front window into a vacant lobby. The street was almost as quiet, with only three pedestrians in sight, and they were walking towards the far end.

"Let's do this now," she said abruptly. "The lobby is empty and there's virtually no one on the street."

"*Momentai*," said Jimmy, reaching into the bag at his feet to take out one of the bombs.

"How will you do this?" Ava asked.

"I thought I'd toss it into the lobby after we break a window."

"You said *we*," Ava said.

"I'll need Sonny's help," he said, peeling back the black tape. "There's the switch. Like I told you earlier, after you take off the tape and flip the switch, you have a minute before it explodes."

"How are you going to break a window?" Ava asked.

Jimmy reached into the bag again and extracted a wrench. "I brought this."

"That should do the trick. I'll handle the window," Sonny said as he held out his hand. Jimmy passed the wrench to him.

"I didn't see any CCTV outside the building when I was here earlier, but you should still wear the balaclavas," Ava said.

Both men slipped them on and then Sonny moved the car so it was directly in front of the revolving doors. Ava looked into the lobby again. It was still empty. A car drove towards them from the other end of the street. She watched it pass and then glanced behind her to make sure it kept going. "Now is as good a time as any," she said.

Sonny and Jimmy opened their doors and, without closing them, crossed the ten metres between car and building. The two men spoke for a few seconds, and then Sonny swung the wrench at the window. It shattered, cascading around him. When the glass stopped falling, Jimmy flipped the switch on the bomb, threw it into the lobby, and then turned and ran to the car.

Ava had begun counting silently as soon as she saw Jimmy flip the switch. They got back to the car as she reached twenty. Sonny gunned the engine and began to drive. They had gone maybe fifty metres when Ava heard the blast. It was even louder than the one at Bowles's house.

"Why was it so loud?" she asked Jimmy.

He turned and peered at her through the eye slits in his balaclava. "The body of the Bentley muffled that explosion. This bomb had nothing to interfere with it, and the lobby may have acted like an echo chamber," he said.

Ava saw some pedestrians in the distance walking quickly in their direction. "Can you turn around and go back?" she asked Sonny. "I'd like to see the damage."

Sonny nodded, then did a U-turn. As he completed it, people began to come out of the adjoining buildings. The middle of the street was cloaked in semi-darkness and Ava was quite certain the onlookers wouldn't be able to identify them. All the same, she lowered her head when she saw some of them pointing phones at the car. "We're getting more attention than I would like," she said.

"We made a lot of noise," said Jimmy.

"And we did a lot of damage," said Sonny as he slowed the car to a crawl.

Ava looked at the building. The revolving doors had been blown off their hinges and catapulted into the street. There wasn't a window left intact on the ground floor, and a sofa and set of chairs had been thrown across the lobby, coming to rest against elevator doors streaked with black. Although they had been careful, she searched the area for signs of any-one who might have been caught in the explosion. When she saw no one, she said, "Yes, we did, and we managed to do so without hurting anyone. Now we should get a move on."

As the car left Garden Road, Jimmy and Sonny rolled up their balaclavas, only to roll them back down moments later, when they got to Duddell Street.

"This doesn't look good," Ava said as she looked down the street and checked her notebook. "The next target is that six-storey steel-and-glass building on the left with a pharmacy on the ground floor. The pharmacy is still open. According to my notes, it should have closed at six. There are also far too many pedestrians."

"What now? Do you want to wait or move to the next target?" Sonny asked.

Police sirens blared behind them. Ava turned and saw three police cars speeding by in the direction of Garden Road. "The cops are going to be all over this neighbourhood," said Jimmy. "It might be risky to attempt more than we've already done tonight."

"What do you think?" she asked Sonny.

He shrugged. "You've probably made your point already, but it's your call."

"Well, truthfully, I don't feel like sitting here waiting for the pharmacy to close," she said. "And someone from Garden Road is sure to report a blue Toyota in the vicinity, so the longer we hang around Central, the more likely it is we'll get pulled over by the police."

"So we're calling it a night?" asked Jimmy.

"Yes," Ava sighed. "Sonny, take Jimmy home to his grand-children and get this car back to Kowloon," she said. "I have other ways of causing Bowles pain tonight."

27

IT WAS A QUIET CAR RIDE BACK TO THE MANDARIN Oriental. Ava knew that both men were coming down from the adrenalin high generated by the evening's events. She felt much the same, having experienced surges of excitement she hadn't anticipated. She had been involved in shootouts and other physical confrontations that caused her emotions to spike, but she hadn't expected the hands-on nature of planting explosives to have the same effect. Maybe the uncertainty about the outcome was the reason. Whatever it was, she was starting to calm down and her mind was beginning to focus on the rest of the night ahead of her.

"That was great work, gentlemen," Ava said as the Mandarin came into view. "Jimmy, I can sort out your payment tomorrow. Or, if you prefer, you can wait until I've decided if we're going after another building."

"I'll wait," he said.

"Thank you. I should know in the next day or two."

Sonny brought the Toyota to a halt in front of the hotel behind a red Ferrari.

"I am glad Bowles wasn't driving a Ferrari," Jimmy said. "That car is too beautiful for such a fate."

"Both of you enjoy the rest of your evening. I'll be in touch," Ava said with a smile.

She took out her phone and called Amanda as she walked into the lobby.

"Ava, where are you?"

"I just got back to the hotel."

"We were just sitting down to dinner. Would you like to join us?"

"That's tempting, but I have things I need to do here," Ava said. "Did Aisyah get hold of Celia?"

"She did; and she has the names you want. Do you need them now?"

"No, but it would be helpful if she could send them to me later tonight."

"I'll make sure she does," Amanda said. "How did things go today?"

"Well enough that I hope you'll read about it in the morning papers."

"What did you do?"

"We blew up Martin Bowles's car in the courtyard of his house. We were careful to make sure no one got hurt, but it was a powerful message all the same."

"Oh my god!"

"Don't share this with Aisyah just yet."

"I won't. Do you think Bowles will know who did it?" Amanda asked.

"Not yet."

"Will you tell him it was you?"

"Hardly. But I do want him to know it wasn't an accident,

and that he and his companies are being targeted," Ava said.

"By whom?"

"The Sarawak United Front."

"But that organization doesn't exist," said Amanda.

"It exists now, at least on the internet. Check out www. sarawakfront.com." Ava reached the elevators and saw that one was available. "I'm getting into an elevator and then I'm going to work in my room. Call me when you've finished dinner and we can continue this."

When she got to her suite, Ava headed directly to the bathroom for a quick shower, then bundled herself in a robe and went into the living room. She sat down at the desk, opened her laptop, and was about to start working when her stomach growled. Realizing she hadn't eaten anything since breakfast, she opened the room-service menu and quickly ordered — for the second time in two days — shrimp and lemongrass spring rolls, wok-fried Australian wagyu beef with garlic and black pepper, and a bottle of Sauvignon Blanc from the Twomey Estate in Napa Valley.

With the hunger issue soon to be resolved, Ava returned to her laptop and typed in "sarawakfront.com." She reread the mission statement written by Douglas Brooke, copied salient points into her notebook, and then opened a blank Word document. Now it was her turn to write.

She started with the heading, typing NEWS RELEASE: WHY WE BOMBED A BENTLEY ON VICTORIA PEAK AND AN OFFICE TOWER IN CENTRAL HONG KONG, and continued below that:

For the past thirty years, Sulaiman Chong, Chief Minister of the Malaysian state of Sarawak, has been systematically destroying one of the richest ecosystems on Earth. Along with members of his family, Chong has been doing this without permission, and against international laws and regulations. Why? The answer is simple: greed. The Chongs have decimated the rainforest in Sarawak province for its timber, and they have turned that timber into billions of dollars that they have invested in real estate in Hong Kong and elsewhere.

Their wealth has also come at a terrible human cost. The deforestation perpetrated by the Chongs has destroyed the natural habitat and traditional way of life of the Indigenous people of Sarawak and Brunei, the Penan. The rainforest is home to these nomadic people, and for centuries it provided for them. Now most of their home is gone, and the small part that remains is threatened by the Chong family and the politicians and rich businessmen who support them.

Why is no one holding them accountable? The answer is again simple: Sulaiman Chong is Chief Minister, the head of the Sarawak government. Provincial politicians, businessmen, the media, and even the legal system are beholden to him. He has almost absolute power in Sarawak, just like the sultans in this part of the world until seventy-five years ago. But that power does not extend to Hong Kong, where tonight our organization, the Sarawak United Front, took action against the Chong family.

Sulaiman Chong's daughter, Laila, is married to Martin Bowles. They live in Hong Kong, where Bowles manages the Chong family's ill-gotten money through the Chong Family Investment Corporation, the Chong Family Trust, and Chong Income Properties.

Bowles drove a new Bentley. He won't be driving it anymore. We blew it up tonight as it sat in front of his house on Victoria Peak.

The Chongs own more than twenty commercial buildings in Hong Kong. Tonight we bombed one of those buildings, on Garden Road.

There is more to come. Just as the Chong family has destroyed our natural habitat in Sarawak, we will destroy theirs in Hong Kong.

—The Sarawak United Front

The doorbell sounded. Ava was so engrossed in her writing that it didn't register until the second ring. She answered the door and stood to one side as her dinner was wheeled in, tipped the server, and told him he didn't need to set the table for her.

She poured a glass of wine and carried it and the plate of spring rolls to the desk. As she sipped and munched, she reviewed what she had written. *It could be better,* she thought, *but it connects the dots and delivers a clear message.*

Ava finished the spring rolls and replaced that plate with the wok-fried beef. May Ling sometimes teased Ava about her preference for white wine, even when she was eating red meat, but this time her selection complemented the meal perfectly. The beef was sliced into uniform strips, so thin they were almost translucent, and so tender that the meat almost dissolved on her tongue. It had been fried with garlic and pepper, and the pepper had such a snap to it that sometimes it burned her mouth. The Sauvignon Blanc was the perfect accompaniment.

When Ava had finished the beef, she pushed the plate to the back of the desk, poured another glass of wine, made a couple of minor changes to the document, and hit Save.

She then turned to the lists of email addresses she'd made the night before.

She entered the Sarawak United Front website and accessed its email. Using info@sarawakfront.com as the sender, she input all the addresses on her lists into a mailing group. In the subject line of her message she wrote WE PLANTED THE BOMBS. In the body of the email, she wrote:

Tonight our organization declared war on the Chong family of Sarawak state in Borneo, by attacking them where they live and do business in Hong Kong. This is the beginning of the war—not the end.

We attach a statement that explains why we took action.

No people were injured by our bombs. We will strive to be always as careful as we continue forward.

—On behalf of the Sarawak United Front and in memory of Jamilah Daeng, whose death was caused by the Chong family

Ava went over to the window that overlooked Victoria Harbour. She sipped her wine as she thought about what she had written. *Is it wise*, she wondered, *to give them advance notice that the bombing will continue? It will make it harder if we do continue, but in the interim it should grab the public's attention and put the Chong family in the spotlight. I'm going to leave it in,* she decided. She also debated copying Bowles on the email, then decided not to. Allowing him to learn the truth from the media would have a much bigger impact.

She returned to her laptop, read everything one more time, attached the document, and, with a feeling of intense satisfaction, hit Send. Now all she had to do was wait for someone to react.

Ava checked the time, saw there was a good chance that Fai would be at her hotel, and reached for the phone. As she did, an email message arrived in her personal account. It was from Aisyah, a list of ten environmental and Indigenous rights organizations in Sarawak. *The more the merrier,* she thought.

Ava called Fai and was delighted when her lover answered with "I was just about to call you."

"You sound cheery. How was your day?"

"Terrific. We were scheduled to shoot one long and rather difficult scene, but we were able to do it in only two takes, and Lau Lau managed to film an additional scene. That puts us back on schedule. Chen is really pleased with himself, and I have to admit he's doing very well for a first-time producer."

"Surely Lau Lau should be getting the bulk of the credit."

"Oh, he is. Chen has been quick to compliment him, but to create the right environment for a director to succeed, the producer has to make sure all the pieces are in the right place at the right time. Chen has done that very well."

"I couldn't be happier to hear that."

"I know you're going to get tired of me saying this, but this is going to be a really good film. Silvana was at the top of her game again today."

"Are she and Chen still…"

"They are, and it's kind of adorable to see," Fai said. "When he came on set today, they both went out of their way to pretend there's nothing going on, but the chemistry is so obvious that even Lau Lau — who knows nothing about the other night — made a comment."

"Let's just hope it lasts until the film is completed. I wouldn't want anything to disrupt a smooth production."

"I'm not worried. Whatever happens, Silvana is a true professional," Fai said. "I'm more concerned about how you're doing. You still haven't told me why you're in Hong Kong."

Ava took a deep breath. "The people responsible for what happened in Kuching have businesses here. I'm here to hold them accountable."

"Please don't do anything dangerous."

"I won't."

"I wish I could believe that."

Ava laughed. "No, seriously, I mean it. I have a plan that will take a few days to execute, but there's very little risk attached to it."

"Even if that is true, please be careful."

"I promise I will. And now I should say goodbye, because I still have some work to do," Ava said. "Love you, and I'll call you tomorrow."

"Love you too."

Ava ended the call and then phoned Toronto. When no one answered, she checked the time and realized Mimi would already have gone to work and Derek was most likely out with the baby. She was disappointed, but given the way the rest of the night had gone, it was a minor blip. She was thinking about who else to call when a yawn overtook her and she suddenly felt fatigued. It had been a long, strenuous day. Her adrenalin had spiked when the bombs went off, but then it had gradually ebbed as the night went on, and now it was spent.

Ava was still wearing the bathrobe she had put on after her shower. She went into the bedroom, slipped off the robe, and pulled on a T-shirt. It was a bit early to go to bed, but her body was telling her she needed sleep. She thought briefly about having a nightcap but then decided she didn't need one. Instead she climbed into bed, and before she could finish replaying the day's events in her mind, she had drifted off.

28

AVA WOKE WELL BEFORE DAWN WITH THOUGHTS OF THE previous night's events racing through her head. Something felt off. She went over the details of the plan again but couldn't shake the feeling that she needed to rethink her strategy. She made herself a coffee, sat down at the desk, and reached for her phone.

"*Wei*," Sonny answered groggily.

"It's Ava. I'm sorry for calling so early."

"*Momentai*. Actually, I thought I would have heard from you before now."

"Why?"

"Didn't you see the news on Pearl TV?"

"No."

"They ran a piece on the bombings. They mentioned Bowles's car and showed footage of the building on Garden Road. It looks even worse on video," Sonny said.

"Did they mention the Sarawak United Front?" she asked.

"Yes, and a woman named Jamilah Daeng."

"That's fantastic. I wish I had seen it."

"I'm sure they'll replay it on the morning news."

"I'd like to give them something new to report," said Ava.

"Like what?"

She hesitated. "The first thing that went through my mind this morning is that we should have bombed the Chong headquarters on Jubilee Street last night. Security is sure to be intensified today."

"And you want to do it now?" Sonny asked.

"That's what I was thinking," she said. "Can you be ready in the next hour?"

"I don't see why not. And you're right about the timing. We might not get another chance."

"Is it too early to get the Toyota back?"

"I never returned it."

"What about Jimmy?"

"I doubt he's even slept yet. He phoned me after he saw the news and was very excited," Sonny said.

"Then call him, please. Let's see if we can get this done while it's still dark."

"I'll get back to you soon," he said.

Ava ended the call and opened her email. Six newspapers and Pearl TV had written to info@sarawakfront. com with questions. One of the papers was the *Sarawak Daily Journal*, which brought a smile to Ava's face. Sulaiman Chong would most certainly know what had happened in Hong Kong.

She scanned the messages. Most asked to speak directly to a representative of the organization, but the *Daily Journal* wanted to know if the Sarawak United Front was aligned with any organizations in Sarawak. They also asked if the Jamilah Daeng mentioned in the press release was the same woman who had "recently died through misadventure in

Kuching." *They may suspect we're bogus,* Ava thought, *but we're getting their attention.*

Her phone rang, and she saw it was Sonny. "Are we on?" she asked.

"I'm leaving here in five minutes to get Jimmy. We'll see you in about an hour."

"Terrific," Ava said. "Ask him to bring extra explosives. I want to make an even larger impression."

"Will do."

"I'll see you outside the Mandarin," she said, and ended the call. She finished her coffee, made another, and picked up the phone again to call Toronto.

"Hey, you're up early," Derek said when he answered.

"I thought you'd like to know that the email address you set up on the website worked very well."

"That's great, but I'm guessing you're calling to ask if I've had any luck getting into Martin Bowles's bank account."

Ava heard a touch of excitement in Derek's voice. "Yes. So tell me."

Derek paused and then said, "MLJS052274. The letters are all capitals."

"That's the password?"

"It is."

Ava wrote it down in her notebook. "I'm impressed. How did you manage to get it?" she asked.

"My software runs key names and numbers in thousands of sequences. It finally hit on M for Martin, L for Laila, J for Joshua, and S for Sarah, and Bowles was born on May 22, 1974 — 05/22/74. Chong should have been more cautious."

"And what did you discover in the account?" she asked.

"Close to fifty million U.S. dollars."

"I was hoping for something like that," Ava said.

"How much does he owe you?"

"Given our history, this may sound strange, but what he owes us is irrelevant. There's a greater good here that needs to be served. Uncle always stressed that what mattered most was not our personal feelings about a job but whether or not we had contributed to the greater good. This is one of those times."

"Then I'm even more pleased I was able to make a contribution."

"One that I should be paying you for," Ava said.

"Never," Derek said. "And Ava, don't offend me by insisting."

"Then I'll just say thank you."

"I appreciate that. You know you can call on me at any time," he said.

"I hope I don't need to," Ava said. "Love to you and Mimi."

She put her phone to one side and opened her laptop. She found the website for the Kowloon Merchants Reserve Bank, input Bowles's account number, took a deep breath, and entered the password. She stared at a balance: US$47,356,129. She opened her notebook and wrote: *Will Henry Chew help? Will Ronald Ho keep his mouth shut?*

Ava went into the bedroom to retrieve a pouch from her LV bag. It contained a dark blue Hong Kong Special Administrative Region passport that had been issued to a woman named Jennie Kwong, who looked, unsurprisingly, like Ava. In her former job, Ava had occasionally found it useful to change her identity. It had been several years since she'd felt the need, but she had made a point of keeping the passport up to date. As she thought about the money in

Bowles's bank account, it seemed that it might be a good time for Jennie to reappear. She replaced the passport in the pouch, glanced at the bedside clock, and realized she had to hurry if she was going to meet Sonny and Jimmy as planned.

Ten minutes later she was standing outside the Mandarin in the darkness of early morning, waiting for Sonny. The doorman nodded inquiringly at her, and Ava imagined he was keen to know what she was doing. She nodded back and turned away, not wanting to give him an opening for questions.

There were hardly any cars on the road. Over the next five minutes only four taxis passed the hotel from the direction Sonny would be coming. She waited another five minutes with still no sign of Sonny, then began to reach for her phone to call him. Before she could, the Toyota appeared on Connaught Road. When it stopped in front of her, Jimmy leapt out of the front passenger seat and opened the back door for her.

"Sorry we're late," Sonny said. "Jimmy wanted to add a little extra oomph to the bombs."

"That's okay. You call the shots when it comes to explosives," Ava said.

Sonny drove the car towards Des Voeux Road, which they found just as quiet as Connaught had been. When they reached the intersection with Jubilee, there wasn't another car in sight. Sonny turned onto Jubilee and slowed down to allow Ava and Jimmy to scout ahead. The street was well lit, and Ava could see the CIC Building in the near distance.

"There's a guard out front, leaning against the door," Jimmy said abruptly.

Ava hadn't seen him, and now that she did, she groaned.

"There's only one that I can see," said Sonny.

"Drive past slowly," she said. "Jimmy, take a good look at the building as we go by. Let's be sure there aren't more of them inside. Sonny, we should look straight ahead when we pass. We don't want him to think we have any interest in the building."

When they reached the end of Jubilee Street, Sonny turned onto Queen's Road and parked the car. "What did you see?" he asked Jimmy.

"The one guard standing outside, and that's all. The lights in the lobby were dimmed but I could see well enough."

"What do you think we should do?" Sonny said to Ava.

"We need to get rid of that guard," she said.

"If I stop the car in front of the building, I can't imagine he's just going to stand there while we get out. He'll likely step inside to call for help," said Sonny.

"How do you think he would react to someone simply walking along the street?" she asked.

"What are you suggesting?" asked Jimmy.

"I'll take off my hoodie so he can see that I'm a woman. If he doesn't react before I get there, I'll put him down. Then you can pop the trunk and we'll stuff him in there until we're finished. We can drop him off around the corner."

"That could work," said Jimmy.

"Is he armed?" Sonny asked.

"He has a gun, but it's holstered," said Jimmy. "He doesn't look any tougher than the guy I saw Ava take out in Sha Tin."

Sonny turned to Ava. "Boss, I don't feel easy about this."

Ava slipped the hoodie over her head. "I'm going to act like I'm lost and little tipsy. If I see him reach for a gun or a phone, I'll keep walking and meet you back at the intersection with Des Voeux."

Sonny shook his head. "I still don't like this, but I know you're going to do it anyway."

Jimmy got out of the car and peered down the street. Ava joined him a few seconds later. "He's still by himself," said Jimmy.

"Okay, here I go."

She turned the corner and started walking slowly, weaving slightly from side to side, trying not to exaggerate her supposed drunkenness. In her mind she was a woman trying to act as if she hadn't had anything to drink but was coming up a little short. The guard continued to lean against the door, facing straight ahead and not paying attention to anything on either side. Ava's running shoes didn't make any noise, and as she got closer to him, she realized he might not notice her until she was right on top of him. She didn't think that was a good idea, so when she was about twenty metres away, she said, "Excuse me, I'm lost. Can you tell me how to get to the Four Seasons Hotel from here?"

The guard seemed startled, but Ava saw him relax when he realized who had spoken.

"I was at a party and my friends told me I could walk back to the hotel, but I must have taken a wrong turn somewhere. I'm not from Hong Kong."

She was next to the guard now and didn't see any change in his demeanour.

"You shouldn't be out by yourself at this time of night. You should have taken a taxi," he said.

"I know, but I haven't seen any," she said. "Is it far to the Four Seasons?"

"No," he said, turning to point in the direction of Victoria Harbour.

Ava leapt onto his back and felt his knees start to buckle. As he tried to steady himself, she wrapped her left arm around his shoulders while her right hand searched for his carotid artery. She applied as much pressure as she could generate. He reached back and tried to throw her off, but she had a tight grip on him. He swore at her and flailed his arms, but she didn't let up. Gradually his resistance faded. When she felt his legs give way, Ava slid off his back but didn't release the pressure on his neck. It wasn't until he was on the ground and unconscious that she finally let go. She looked up and down the street, was relieved to see they were still alone, and waved towards where she'd left Jimmy.

A moment later the Toyota arrived, the trunk opened, and Sonny got out to help her load the body. In one smooth gesture he picked up the guard, carried him to the car, and laid him in the trunk.

"That was well done," Jimmy said as he emerged from the Toyota carrying four bombs.

"He didn't put up much of a fight," Ava said. "Now, let's do what we came to do."

Sonny was carrying the wrench. "Are we doing it the same way as before?"

"Yes. You should break three windows, evenly spaced out across the front, and then break the glass in the door," Jimmy said, and then looked at Ava. "Four bombs instead of two we planned on, and they're stronger than the one we used earlier. They're really going to make a mess of this place."

"That's perfect," Ava said.

29

THEY MANAGED TO REACH THE INTERSECTION OF Jubilee and Queen's Road before the bombs exploded in rapid succession. Even from that distance, the noise reached them as such a deafening roar that Ava had to cover her ears. When it subsided, she stepped out of the car and looked back at a street covered in glass, bricks, and other debris.

"There'll be nothing left of the front of that building, including the shops in that little mall," Jimmy said. "I bet we also took out part of the second floor."

Sonny got out and opened the trunk. He picked up the guard and carried him to the sidewalk, setting him down with his back against a wall. "We should get out of here," he said.

The short drive back to the Mandarin was quiet. Ava had expected to hear sirens again, but the Toyota reached the hotel without encountering any signs of the police. As the car came to a stop at the entrance, Sonny said to Ava, "Do you want me to hang on to the Toyota or should I return it?"

"Take it back. I know I've been changing my mind quite a bit these past twenty-four hours, but I think I've finally made the impact I wanted. Now I have some different levers I want to pull," she said. "Thank you both for your help."

"It was fun," said Jimmy with a smile. "I'm available whenever you need me."

"I appreciate that. And even though I know you aren't doing this for money, I'll send you a payment later today," she said. "If you don't want it, spend it on your granddaughters."

"Do you need me for anything else?" Sonny asked.

"I'm not sure, but if I do, I'll be in touch. There's a lot going on with this project. It's comforting to know you're covering my back."

"I'm there for you, boss."

"I know," she said as she opened the car door and stepped out.

Ava thought briefly about going back to bed when she returned to her suite, but her mind was once again racing and she could feel the adrenalin pumping through her system. Instead she ordered a pot of coffee from room service and sat down at the desk. She opened her laptop, found the email from Aisyah with the names of the environmental and Indigenous rights organizations in Sarawak, and made a record of them in her notebook. Then she replied to Aisyah: Thank you for this. Could you ask Celia to contact each of these organizations individually and ask them for their banking information? She should tell them she has a friend who wishes to make a contribution to their cause. Have Celia send the information to you, and then forward it to me. Please stress to her that you need this information as quickly as possible.

Next she went online to look for news about the bombings. The Kuala Lumpur newspaper had a minor mention, writing that they appeared to be the work of eco-terrorists who objected to the business practices of the Chong family of Sarawak province. The Hong Kong papers had stories about the bombings on their front pages. They weren't the major story, but the headlines, BOMBING IN HONG KONG and LOCAL BANKER BOMBED, were prominent. Both papers referenced Martin Bowles as well as the Chong family and said they had tried unsuccessfully to contact them for comment. The Sarawak United Front was said to have taken credit for the bombings. It was characterized as an environmental activist organization based in Borneo that was opposed to illegal logging in the rainforest.

Ava had saved the *Sarawak Daily Journal* for last, but before she could read it, the doorbell sounded. Two minutes later she was back at the desk with a pot of coffee. She poured a cup and accessed the *Journal*.

Across the top of the page the banner headline read: CHIEF MINISTER'S FAMILY TARGETED BY TERRORISTS. The story that followed made her smile grimly:

IT APPEARS THE ORGANIZATION THAT JUST DAYS AGO CLAIMED CREDIT FOR BOMBING A WAREHOUSE IN KUCHING, KILLING ONE INDIVIDUAL, HAS EXPANDED THEIR TERRORIST ACTIVITIES TO HONG KONG AND HAS MADE THE CHONG FAMILY A TARGET.

REPORTS FROM HONG KONG SAY THAT THE HOME OF MARTIN BOWLES AND HIS WIFE, LAILA CHONG, THE DAUGHTER OF SARAWAK'S CHIEF MINISTER SULAIMAN CHONG, WAS TARGETED LAST NIGHT IN A CAR BOMBING. FORTUNATELY THE DAMAGE WAS RESTRICTED TO THE HOME'S EXTERIOR AND THERE WERE NO HUMAN CASUALTIES. LATER IN THE EVENING, ANOTHER BOMB WAS

DETONATED AT AN OFFICE BUILDING BELONGING TO THE CHONG FAMILY. AGAIN THERE WAS ONLY PROPERTY DAMAGE AND NO LOSS OF LIFE.

CREDIT FOR THESE ATTACKS HAS BEEN CLAIMED BY THE SARAWAK UNITED FRONT, THE SAME ORGANIZATION SUSPECTED OF BEING RESPONSIBLE FOR THE WAREHOUSE BOMBING IN KUCHING. IN A STATEMENT SENT TO THE MEDIA, THE SARAWAK UNITED FRONT MADE UNSUBSTANTIATED ACCUSATIONS ABOUT THE CHONG FAMILY'S ENVIRONMENTAL STEWARDSHIP IN SARAWAK, CITING THOSE AS THE REASONS FOR THE BOMBINGS. BUT NOTICEABLY, THEY ARE NOT AT ALL CLEAR ABOUT WHAT THEY HOPE TO ACCOMPLISH WITH THEIR PROGRAM OF TERROR.

IN RESPONSE TO THE ATTACKS, AHMAD CHONG, CEO OF CHONG INDUSTRIES AND THE SON OF THE CHIEF MINISTER, SAID, "OUR FAMILY REGRETS THAT THIS TERRORIST ORGANIZATION HAS CHOSEN VIOLENCE AS A WAY OF EXPRESSING ITS DISSATISFACTION WITH THE ENVIRONMENTAL POLICIES SET BY OUR DEMOCRATICALLY ELECTED STATE LEGISLATIVE ASSEMBLY, AND BY WHICH OUR FAMILY ABIDES. WE WILL NOT YIELD TO THEIR PROGRAM OF TERROR, AND WE ARE HOPEFUL THAT THE SARAWAK CONTINGENT POLICE, WORKING CO-OPERATIVELY WITH THE ROYAL MALAYSIA POLICE AND THE HONG KONG POLICE FORCE, WILL BRING A SWIFT STOP TO THEIR MURDEROUS WAYS."

THIS NEWSPAPER HAS MADE SEVERAL UNSUCCESSFUL ATTEMPTS TO CONTACT THE SARAWAK UNITED FRONT. THE ORGANIZATION HAS NO VISIBILITY IN THE STATE AND IS UNKNOWN TO THE ENVIRONMENTAL AND INDIGENOUS RIGHTS GROUPS WE CONTACTED. LOCAL

POLICE OFFICIALS SUSPECT ITS MEMBERSHIP COULD BE DRAWN FROM INTERNATIONAL ECO-TERRORIST GROUPS OPERATING OUTSIDE MALAYSIA'S BORDERS.

This is very good, Ava thought. She returned to her emails and the questions from the media. Using Brooke's mission statement and remembering the sentiments he'd expressed in his office, Ava answered them as best she could. At the end of each reply she mentioned the Jubilee Street bombing and said the Front wouldn't be giving interviews to anyone until the issues with the Chong family had been resolved.

Now what? she thought as she sent the last message. It was just past six o'clock, too early to start making local calls. She went to the window and saw that the sun was starting to rise. An early morning run in Victoria Park was suddenly very appealing.

An hour and a half later Ava returned to her suite, sweating and with a plan firmly fixed in her mind. She took a long, leisurely shower, spent more time than usual drying and styling her hair, and then applied a touch of mascara and red lipstick. She put on a white button-down cotton shirt and black linen slacks and slid into her black pumps. *This isn't a day to look like someone who might set off bombs*, she thought.

She opened her notebook and found the number for Henry Chew at the Kowloon Light Industrial Bank.

"Mr. Chew, please. This is Ava Lee calling," she said when the receptionist answered.

"Ms. Lee," Chew said a moment later. "I didn't expect to hear from you so soon. Was there a problem with Ronald Ho?"

"No, he was entirely co-operative. Thank you for making the connection."

"It was my pleasure."

"I would appreciate it if you could do something else for me."

Chew went quiet, and Ava knew she was making him nervous. "I want to open an account with your bank," she said. "Just a standard chequing account. How long do you think that might take?"

"We could do it today," Chew said, clearly relieved.

"Excellent. What do you need from me?"

"Will it be a personal or business account?"

"Personal."

"Then I need a name, address, phone number, proof of identity, and a signed signature card," said Chew.

"I'll want to do online banking."

"Of course. Once the account is set up, we'll arrange that for you."

"If I come by the bank this morning, can we get it all organized?"

"Yes, of course," said Chew. "My morning happens to be wide open."

"I'm in Central. I can leave here within the next ten minutes," Ava said, reaching for her LV bag. She put her notebook and phone into it and left the room to head for the Star Ferry.

The ferry terminal was packed with people coming to work in Central, but the crowd began to thin near the departures area. Ava got in line and a few minutes later was on board. She had intended to sit near the rear again, but, noticing that the wind was up and the water was choppy, she took a seat near the middle that still gave her a decent view of the Hong Kong skyline. As the boat left the dock, Ava could hear the water slapping against the sides of the boat and felt the swell. She had felt sick on the ferry more than once and was wondering if she should take a taxi for the return journey when her phone rang.

"Ava Lee," she said.

"It's Jack. Can you talk?"

"Yes. I'm on the Star Ferry, but I'm alone."

"Ava, what the heck have you been up to?" he asked. "I knew you were going to go after Martin Bowles and his wife's family, but I didn't expect this."

"How much do you know?"

"I saw the news last night about Bowles's car and the office building, and now I'm looking at footage of his company headquarters blown to smithereens. I assume that you're responsible for this. Am I correct?"

"Yes. Is that a problem for you?"

"Well, no, but it is a surprise. How did you manage to arrange all that so quickly?"

"I had help from some friends."

"You have friends with very special talents," said Jack.

"Speaking of friends, could you possibly do me another favour?" she asked.

"Of course."

"Could you reach out to Martin Bowles?"

"We aren't exactly close. And I'm sure he has his hands full dealing with the fallout from those bombings," Jack said.

"I know, but you are acquaintances, and I'm sure he wouldn't snub the chairman of the Hong Kong Jockey Club's membership committee."

After a slight hesitation Jack said, "What would you like me to say to him?"

As Ava was preparing to answer, the ferry lurched and water splashed over the railing. "Jack, the ferry ride is rough this morning and it's getting noisier. Would you mind if I called you back in a couple of hours?"

"Call whenever. I'll be here," he said.

Ava gripped the railing and willed the ferry towards the Tsim Sha Tsui terminal.

The remainder of the trip took only five minutes but felt much longer. When they were safely docked, Ava sighed with relief as she stepped onto solid ground. She shuffled with the crowd out of the terminal, skirted the bus and taxi lines, and headed for Salisbury Road. Wing On Plaza was on the north side, an easy one-kilometre walk from the terminal that took her past the Peninsula Hotel.

She never walked past the Peninsula without feeling uncomfortable. It had been built in 1928 and was one of the grandest hotels in Hong Kong, but Ava's only memory of it was being asked to leave. In one of her earliest visits to Hong Kong, shortly after she had started working with Uncle, her father had invited her to join him for afternoon tea at the Peninsula. At the time Ava still dressed fairly casually, and she showed up for tea wearing open-toed sandals and shorts. She got as far as the lounge, but before she could sit down she was intercepted by a host, who politely informed her that she couldn't stay because her outfit did not meet the dress code. Marcus tried unsuccessfully to intervene, but Ava was forced to leave. She hadn't been back to the Peninsula since, but she still thought about it every time she saw the hotel.

Wing On Plaza soon came into view, and next to it was

the three-storey Kowloon Light Industrial Bank. Like the Merchants Reserve Bank, Light Industrial had a customer branch on the ground floor and its corporate offices above. Ava opened a door beside the branch entrance and climbed two flights of stairs. Henry Chew's office was directly across from the door to the stairway. Ava knocked, and a young woman opened the door and said, "Good morning, Ms. Lee."

They walked through a small outer office and entered Chew's much larger one. In addition to two rows of grey filing cabinets, a round boardroom table with eight chairs, and several bookcases, there were two sofas, a coffee table, and an enormous desk. Chew stood up when Ava entered. He was a small, well-dressed man who looked at least ten years younger than she knew him to be.

"How nice to see you again," Chew said. "Let's sit at the table. Can we get you something to drink?"

"No, thank you," Ava said as she sat down.

"I'll call for you if we need anything," Chew said to the woman.

Ava reached into her LV bag, took out the Jennie Kwong passport, and passed it to Chew. "I would like the account opened in this name."

He opened it to the photo page, then said, "This is, er, highly irregular."

"I know, and I apologize for not mentioning it when we spoke earlier," she said. "The passport is legitimate. I've used it several times in the past without difficulty."

"Does Jennie Kwong exist?"

"I'm sure a Jennie Kwong exists somewhere, but I've never met anyone by that name." Ava handed him a business card. "You can use the address of our trading office, but just the building's street number, not the floor, and you should change the last two digits of the phone number."

"Is this subterfuge really necessary?" Chew asked.

"Yes."

Chew looked uncertain as he rose to his feet. Ava wondered if he was about to become unco-operative. "I'll take the passport to my assistant. She'll input your information into our system and then I'll be back with a signature card."

"Before you go, can you tell me how long it normally takes for a wire transfer to go from one Hong Kong bank to another?"

"A few minutes, perhaps not even that. Why do you ask?"

"I'll be doing a wire transfer into this new account later today."

"We can handle it. That's business as usual for us."

"Except that I'm anticipating the wire will be for around fifty million U.S. dollars."

Chew looked at Ava with a puzzled expression. "As you know from your days working with Uncle, we have dealt with larger sums than that, but I suspect there's more you want to tell me."

"The money will be coming from an account at the Kowloon Merchants Reserve Bank, and the transfer may result in a phone call from Ronald Ho. He'll know where the money was sent and will probably ask about Jennie Kwong." she said.

"I'll tell him she's a new customer who was referred to my bank by Zhao. That should quell his curiosity."

"That would be excellent," Ava said.

Chew nodded. "Now, let me get your account set up."

30

AVA CAUGHT A TAXI ON SALISBURY ROAD AND TOOK it through the Cross-Harbour Tunnel back to Hong Kong. It had gone much easier with Henry Chew than she had anticipated, partially because he hadn't asked any questions about the money she intended to transfer. She assumed it wasn't a lack of interest on his part, but rather an understanding, acquired through years of doing business with men like Uncle and Zhao, that there were some things it was better not to question.

She had turned off her phone while she was with Chew, and when she turned it back on, she saw she had missed a call from Amanda. Ava hit her number.

"Hey, I've been trying to reach you," Amanda answered.

"I was in a meeting. What's going on?"

"You are asking *me* that?" Amanda laughed. "You certainly got the media attention you wanted. Aisyah and I saw the news this morning, and then we read about it in the *South China Morning Post*. Aisyah keeps saying she can't believe it's real, and then she breaks out in a huge grin. She's bursting to tell Celia, but I've told her she needs to restrain herself."

"Yes, we all need to show some restraint until this is over,"

Ava said. "Have you spoken to your father?"

"No, I haven't. How involved was he?"

"Only indirectly, but we couldn't have moved as quickly as we did without his help."

"He'll be pleased to know that," Amanda said.

"I have one more favour to ask of him, but I'm waiting until I've finished confirming a few other things," said Ava. "How is Aisyah coming along with the banking information I requested?"

"She's been on the phone twice with Celia since we got to the office. I know they have at least some of what you asked for."

"Excellent. Ask her to send me what she has, and to send the rest when she gets it," Ava said. "I'm heading to the hotel now. I have some work to do when I get there, and if it goes well I'll have something I need to go over with you and May Ling."

"Does May know what you've done?"

"She knew my intentions," Ava said. "But I haven't heard from her this morning, so I'm assuming she hasn't seen the news."

"Will you call to let her know?"

"Why don't you do that," Ava said.

"Sure, I'd love to."

"Good, and tell her I'll call later."

The taxi worked its way through Central to the Mandarin. On arrival, Ava wasted no time getting to her suite. She went immediately to the desk, opened her laptop, and accessed the Jennie Kwong bank account to confirm that it was active. It was, so she switched to the Kowloon Merchants Reserve website, found Bowles's account, and typed in MLJS052274.

A second later the screen showed the balance: $47,356,129. Ava took a deep breath. Now that she was in, she had to decide how much to transfer.

At minimum she was going to take the insurance money they were owed, plus the donations she intended to make to the environmental and Indigenous rights organizations identified by Aisyah. *But this isn't about what we're owed*, she thought. *This is about Jamilah and setting things right.* "Screw the Chongs," she muttered, and transferred forty-seven million dollars to Jennie Kwong. "That should get their attention."

Ava got up from the desk and went to the bathroom. When she returned a few minutes later, she checked the Kowloon Light Industrial account. The forty-seven million had been deposited. She picked up her cell and phoned Amanda.

"Hey, will you set up a conference call with May and then patch me in?" Ava asked.

"Sure. Do you want me to do it now?"

"Yes, please."

While Ava waited for the call, she opened her emails. Her mother had sent a message and Aisyah another that contained banking information for six organizations. She wrote down the details in her notebook and turned to her mother's email.

Ava, Daddy said he saw you a few nights ago at the hotel and that you looked fabulous. He is so very proud of you. He wants to have dinner with you but isn't sure you are willing. Do me a favour and call him to set something up. If you come back from Asia in the next few weeks, it may be the only chance you have to spend time with him. Hope things are going well with you, Fai, and the movie. Love, Mummy

Ava sighed. Her mother liked the idea of her daughters and her husband getting together. She had no idea how awkward it could be, and as difficult as it was for Ava, it was even worse for Marian. She was married to a senior public servant in Ottawa, and Bruce was a *gweilo* with rather narrow views of marriage. Marian had adopted some of his attitudes, and she had expressed to Ava more than once how embarrassed she felt by their complicated family structure. In fact, at the beginning of one recent visit to Ottawa, Marian had pulled Ava aside and told her that, as far as her friends were concerned, Jennie Lee was a widow.

Ava did not wish to disrespect Marcus, and having a meal with him would make her mother happy, so she replied to Jennie: Yes, I saw Daddy at the Mandarin. He looks as good as ever. I am planning to have a meal with him, Michael, and Amanda. I'll let you know how it goes. Otherwise, all is well. Love, Ava.

She clicked Send just as her phone sounded. "Hi," she answered.

"It's Amanda. I have May on the line as well."

"May, did Amanda tell you how we did?" Ava asked.

"Two buildings and a Bentley. Impressive."

"We debated doing more, but it was getting risky. Besides, I think they got the message," Ava said. "And if it wasn't loud and clear half an hour ago, it sure will be now."

"What did you do?" May asked.

"I moved forty-seven million U.S. dollars out of Martin Bowles's bank account."

"Shit!" May blurted.

"Holy mackerel, how did you do that?" asked Amanda.

"A contact of mine cracked Bowles's password, so I was

able to access his account," said Ava. "I wired the money to an account at the Kowloon Light Industrial Bank that I set up under the name Jennie Kwong. It's an alias I've used before. The bank's president, Henry Chew, knows me and was willing to go along with it. I know it sounds a touch dramatic, but I wanted to keep some distance between us and the Chongs. Now we have to decide how much of the forty-seven million we keep."

"Do you have a number in mind?" May asked.

"We agreed that three million would cover our losses, but I think I'd prefer to keep five. We'll give a million of that to Jamilah's family to secure their future, and the other million will make up for the aggravation caused by the Chongs."

"That works for me," said Amanda.

"And me," added May.

"Great. I'll transfer five million to our corporate account. I didn't want to proceed without discussing it with you first. For one thing, you might have wondered who Jennie Kwong is."

"What are you going to do with the rest of the money you took from Bowles?" Amanda asked.

"I'm going to send donations to some environmental and Indigenous rights organizations in Sarawak," Ava said, "which will leave about thirty-five million. I plan to use that as leverage to negotiate a settlement with the Chong family."

"Once we have our money, what is there to settle?" Amanda asked.

"I can't leave the Jamilah situation the way it is. The record has to be corrected. For the sake of her family's peace of mind, I want her death to be publicly identified for what it was. And then I would like to see someone held accountable."

"Do you really think you can get the Chongs to admit they had anything to do with the warehouse bombing?" May asked.

"Maybe not, but we won't know unless we press the issue," said Ava. "I guess it will come down to how badly they want their money back."

"It certainly is a lot of money," said May. "Aren't you worried they might just decide to come after you with every means at their disposal...including violence? What if they target your banker?"

"Ronald Ho, their banker, knows that the Kowloon Light Industrial Bank has strong triad connections. I'm counting on him to tell the Chongs, and I can't imagine they'd be stupid enough to mess with triads," Ava said. "As for me, aside from you and Henry Chew, no one knows anything about Jennie Kwong. If I play this correctly, I can meet with Bowles as Jennie Kwong, cut a deal, and then disappear."

"How quickly do you think you can make that happen?" May asked.

"That depends on how soon I can meet with Bowles, and how co-operative the Chongs will be."

"I wish there was something we could do to help," May said.

"If there is, believe me, I won't hesitate to ask," said Ava. "Shall we leave it at that?"

May laughed. "Go and do your thing."

"I will," Ava said. "But before I go, I have a favour to ask of Amanda."

"What is that?" Amanda said.

"Can you call my father and set up a dinner with me, Michael, and yourself?"

"What about Aisyah?"

"I would prefer it to be just family."

"I understand, and I'm sure she will as well," said Amanda. "Of course I'll call Marcus."

"Thank you. Let me know what you arrange," Ava said. "Okay, now I have wire transfers to send and phone calls to make. I'll keep both of you updated as best I can."

31

THE PHONE CALLS WERE AVA'S IMMEDIATE PRIORITY, and Jack Yee was at the top of her list.

He answered on the first ring. "Ava, I've been sitting here trying to figure out what else you might have in store for Martin Bowles."

"Nothing quite as dramatic as last night, but it might have an even bigger impact," she said. "I need to talk to him, and I would prefer to do it face to face."

"Do you want a meeting?"

"Actually, I was thinking of surprising him while he's having a coffee with someone else."

"And you think that someone else should be me?"

"Yes," she said. "I also want to create an opportunity for you to introduce me."

"Introduce you as what? A friend of the family, a former business associate, Amanda's sister-in-law?"

"Former business associate is the most neutral. But my name won't be Ava Lee," she said. "I want him to know me as Jennie Kwong."

"Ava, you're confusing me."

"I want to keep Three Sisters out of our conversation. I know that might be overly cautious, but the Chong family has a reputation for being nasty, and they have enough money to cause major problems for us," she said. "Jennie Kwong is an alias I used when I was doing business with Uncle. I have a Hong Kong passport in her name if the need arises, but I hope it won't. I'd prefer it if you could provide a background story for Jennie that Bowles can accept."

"What kind of story?"

"Tell him that you know Jennie as a debt collector and that she has strong ties to the triads. If I'm fortunate, he'll be told the same story by at least one other person he trusts. The objective, of course, is to deter him from going after Jennie Kwong."

"Why would he want to do that? I haven't seen her name associated with any of the bombings."

"Earlier this morning I took forty-seven million U.S. dollars from Martin Bowles's account with the Kowloon Merchants Reserve Bank. The money was transferred to an account in the name of Jennie Kwong. Some of the money will be used to repay Three Sisters for our losses in Sarawak, and another amount will be sent to various environmental and Indigenous rights groups in Borneo. When that's done, there'll be between thirty and forty million left in Jennie's account. I'm prepared to return it to Bowles if the family agrees to certain conditions."

Jack was silent, and Ava began to wonder if she had told him too much. "If you can't help me, I'll understand," she said as lightly as she could.

"Sorry. I'm just trying to wrap my head around this. When you took care of those problems of mine, I never asked how you resolved them; I was just grateful that you did. Now I feel like a sausage-lover getting a peek inside the meat-packing plant."

"As I said, I will understand," said Ava.

"No, it's okay. I'll help," he said quickly. "But tell me, if I can get Bowles to meet me, how will it play out?"

"I'll show up and say hello to you as an old acquaintance. You'll introduce me to Bowles and I'll ask if I can join you for a few minutes. I know that will seem rude of me, but you'll be too polite to decline. After I take a seat I'll have my conversation with Bowles. You can find an excuse to leave while I do, or you can stay. It doesn't matter to me either way. When I'm finished, I'll leave, and at that point you can tell him about my background."

"At least I won't have to invent your ties to the triads."

"Excellent. So, Jack, do we have a plan?" she asked.

"The hardest part will be getting Bowles to meet me for coffee," he said. "I'm not saying he won't, but after last night I'm sure he'll be shaken. He may not be ready to leave his house for a while."

"Do whatever you must to convince him. Who knows, he might be pleased to get away from his troubles and be with someone who can offer him support in such a difficult time."

"Okay. I'll do what I can."

"Thank you. I appreciate the effort, regardless of the result," she said. "Call me after you've spoken to him."

Ava put down the phone, closed her eyes, and pressed her neck against the back of the chair. *Am I making this too complicated?* she thought. *Why not use a simpler means of contacting Bowles? No, meeting him face to face and laying out my plans in person is the most effective option. And Jack*

*will be there to support me with a background story. This
will work.*

Ava was starting to rise from the chair when her mobile
rang. "Hello, Douglas," she answered. "You were on my list
of people to call this morning."

"I don't know if I find that flattering or frightening," he
said. "I've just finished reading, for the third time, this morning's edition of the *Sarawak Daily Journal*. The story on the
front page is astounding. Evidently the Sarawak United
Front has struck a decisive blow against the Chong family.
However, as clever as you are for using that name, and as
supportive as I am of your goals, I can't say I support your
methods. I'm assuming, of course, that you were responsible."

"I did warn you not to overreact."

"But bombs, Ms. Lee?"

"We were careful. No one was harmed," she said.

"Thank god for that, but your tactics are still quite
shocking."

"The intent *was* to shock the Chongs. And we aren't finished when it comes to that," said Ava. "Although I'm sure
you'll be relieved to know that what we have in mind doesn't
involve more explosives."

"There's more to come?"

"Most definitely."

"Can you tell me what it is?" Brooke asked.

"Not yet, but I will soon."

"Then why were you planning to call me?"

"I have been thinking about Arven Saad," she said.

"Coincidentally, so have I. What you said about him and
Commissioner Chik has stayed with me. The more I think
about it, the more likely it seems that an arrangement was

made," Brooke said. "And given Saad's position as de facto head of the Chong's timber business, it also seems likely that he authorized the attack on your warehouse."

"The question remains, what can we do about it?" Ava said.

"I'm afraid I have nothing to suggest."

"I've been mulling over a few possibilities," Ava said. "How close is Saad to the Chong family?"

After a slight hesitation, Brooke said, "As I told you previously, he's their right-hand man. Given his political responsibilities, Sulaiman has little to nothing to do with the day-to-day operations of his various businesses. Theoretically that responsibility lies with Ahmad, but his involvement can be sporadic — depending on whether there's a new woman in his life, or if he's got a new hobby. When that's the case, Saad becomes the point man. From all accounts he is very capable, and from what I've observed, he's as ruthless as the old man."

"Does that make him irreplaceable?"

"Everyone is replaceable, but I can't think of a circumstance where he would want to leave."

"What if they had a solid reason to cut him loose?"

"Such as?"

"What value does the family put on money?"

"Greed is part of the family's DNA, and with Sulaiman it's a disease," Brooke said with a laugh.

"That's what I wanted to hear."

"Why?"

"I can't tell you just yet."

"Are you always this vague?"

"No, but I'm not comfortable with discussing plans until they're set."

"Then I'll wait."

"Thank you, Douglas. I'll be in touch," Ava said, and ended the call.

It was raining outside and there was a light mist over the harbour. As Ava looked at the people scurrying along the sidewalks, she thought about her conversation with Brooke. Despite being cautiously reserved with him about her expectations, she thought she might have a plan with a chance to work.

A yawn caught her off guard, and she realized her early morning was beginning to catch up with her. Ava thought about taking a nap, then decided to keep working while she was on a roll. She returned to the desk, called room service for another pot of coffee, and returned to Jennie Kwong's bank account. She sent a transfer to the Three Sisters corporate account and then phoned Amanda.

"I just sent five million to our corporate account," Ava said.

"Great," Amanda said. "And I spoke with Marcus. He was really happy with the dinner suggestion. How does seven tonight, at Megan's Kitchen in Wan Chai, sound to you?"

"Sounds good, but your father is trying to set up a meeting for me. If it turns out to be tonight, it has to be a priority. I'll let you know as soon as I hear from him."

"Talk to you later, then," Amanda said and hung up.

Ava yawned again. *This is ridiculous*, she thought. *I need to get some sleep or I won't get through this day.* She went into the bedroom and crawled under the duvet. She thought briefly about what might lie in store for the rest of the day before sleep won out. With it came a dream.

Ava was running in Victoria Park. From the position of the sun, she guessed it was midday. It was warm, and the jogging path was so full of walkers and runners that she couldn't go more than twenty metres before encountering an obstacle. As her frustration grew, she started to consider other options. Causeway Bay was nearby, and in the past she had enjoyed a route that took her along parts of the harbour and past the Hong Kong Yacht Club. She left the jogging path and headed in the direction of Causeway. As she neared the park's western boundary, she saw a lone figure in the distance, sitting on a bench. He wore a black suit and a white shirt and was smoking. She ran towards him.

I thought I might catch you here, Uncle said as she approached.

Can I join you? she asked.

Of course. Come and sit with me.

She sat on the opposite end of the bench and took a deep breath. *Do you know what I've been up to?* she asked.

Yes. I have been keeping an eye on you. I was pleased to see you made the right decision, he said with a smile. *I am proud of you, my girl.*

All I've done is scare Martin Bowles and get my hands on some of the Chongs' money.

I think you have set the stage for success.

I wish I had your confidence, she said.

Uncle took a cigarette from his pack of Marlboros, lit it with his old Zippo lighter covered in faded black crackle, and took a deep drag. *Do you remember how I used to say that people often do the right thing for the wrong reason?* he asked.

How can I forget? It was your mantra, and I've adopted it.

Well, think about those words now. You have thirty-five million arguments to use against the Chong family.

But what if the money doesn't matter to them, or they won't do what I want?

Then use the money to make them regret that decision, he said.

How?

Uncle shook his head and turned towards her. Even though they were sitting in sunlight, his face was in shadows and his countenance was grey. *You will think of something,* he said.

You have too much confidence in me.

Only because it is justified, he said. *Do not be so hard on yourself.*

Ava saw brown eyes brimming with tenderness. She reached for his hand, but it slipped away from her. She looked into his face and shivered at the sight of tears running down his cheeks. She closed her eyes to hold in her own tears. When she opened them again, he was gone and she was in her bed, crying.

32

IT TOOK AVA SEVERAL MINUTES TO COLLECT HERSELF.
Uncle had rarely been emotional with her when he was alive,
but Ava didn't need emotional displays to know how much
he cared about her. It was something she had realized from
their earliest days working together. It was a feeling she
returned but — like Uncle — seldom voiced. Now she wished
she had done it more often.

She waited until her chest had stopped heaving and her
cheeks were dry before getting out of bed. She checked the
time; she had slept for more than an hour and felt refreshed.
She hadn't missed any calls, but now her phone was ringing.
She saw Jack Yee's name on the screen.

"Yes, Jack," she answered.

"Four o'clock in the Starbucks on the second floor of the
IFC Mall, near the harbour," he said. "It's a short cab ride
from the Mandarin."

"Wonderful," she said. "How did you persuade him?"

"It wasn't easy. I told him I was getting concerned calls
about his situation from some overzealous Jockey Club
members, and that there had been some discussion about

his continued membership. I said I didn't want it to become a problem, so the sooner we addressed it in person, the better."

"How was his mood?"

"He sounded panicked, and he kept repeating how unfair it was to have his and the Chong family name dragged through the mud. He has no idea what's going on, and for a man so used to being in control, that must be very unsettling."

"I'm pleased to hear that."

"When will you be at Starbucks?"

"Shortly after four. I'll give you a chance to get settled before I make my appearance."

"I hope he doesn't overreact."

"I'll try to keep it low-key."

"It isn't you I'm worried about," Jack said.

"I'm sure it will go well," Ava said.

I couldn't have asked for a better reaction from Bowles, she thought as her phone rang again.

"Ava Lee," she answered.

"This is Henry Chew."

"You sound perturbed," she said.

"I've just finished speaking to Ronald Ho."

"Does he know about the money taken from Martin Bowles's account?"

"He does indeed. You can't be surprised by that."

"I'm not. Did he ask about Jennie Kwong?"

"He did, and he also asked if she's connected to you," Chew said. "He isn't a stupid man; he most certainly knows how to put two and two together. Of course I denied there's a connection, except for the fact that both you and Jennie have strong ties to Zhao. I told him he needs to make clear to his clients that you and Jennie Kwong are protected by some very powerful friends."

"Did he buy that?"

"I don't know, but I kept stressing that any imprudent action on his part would be sure to infuriate Zhao. I suggested he keep his head down and let things follow their natural course. I went a bit further, in fact. Maybe I shouldn't have, but I felt he needed calming down."

"What did you say?" Ava asked, immediately anxious.

"I told him my understanding is that the money is with my bank temporarily, and that once some issues had been resolved, it will be returned," Chew said. "But I also made it clear that it isn't going to be returned until I receive specific instructions from you."

"I think you handled that very well," said Ava.

"Ava, how long do you think it will take to resolve this? The longer it drags out, the greater the chance that Ho will feel compelled to go to the banking authorities, or even the police."

"I want to end it as fast as possible. I would do it today if I could, but I suspect that I won't know where we truly stand for at least a few more days."

"But you aren't talking about weeks?"

"No."

"Okay. I can manage things from my end for a few days."

"One thing you should know," Ava said. "I've started moving money from the Jennie Kwong account. By the time I'm done, it will be about twelve million. The remainder will be left for Ho's clients — assuming that they're co-operative. And if they are, they won't be complaining about the millions that are gone, so don't worry."

"Thanks for keeping me informed."

"That's how it should be," she said. "Speak to you soon."

She glanced at the time and realized she needed to get ready for her meeting with Bowles. But first she had one more call to make.

"Hey," Amanda answered.

"It appears that seven o'clock will work for dinner. So unless you hear from me before then, I'll see you at the restaurant."

"Marcus will be happy."

"I'm sure it will be an enjoyable evening," Ava said.

Ava had never been completely open with Amanda about Marcus and doubted she ever would be. Amanda had her own relationship with her father-in-law, and it revolved around how well Michael and Marcus were getting on. Ava knew sharing her feelings would benefit no one. The only person she trusted enough to discuss the complications of her family life had been Uncle. He was a terrific listener, non-judgemental, and able to see every angle.

Ava inspected her wardrobe and decided on black slacks, a white silk blouse, and the black pumps. She added her Cartier Tank Française watch and, half an hour later, climbed into a taxi.

The IFC Mall was part of a tower complex that comprised the International Finance Centre and formed part of the waterfront skyline. The tower that housed the mall and its more than two hundred high-end stores was the smaller of the two. Ava hadn't been to the mall itself but had gone to a meeting with May Ling in Tower 2, which measured eighty-eight storeys and was the second tallest building in Hong Kong. In Chinese culture, eight is associated with wealth and fortune and is considered to be the luckiest number. But as May Ling pointed out to Ava, the top floor of the building may have been numbered eighty-eight, but the actual count was less, because the number four had been avoided. Four signifies death, so there were no floors that contained that number in the tower.

The cab arrived at the complex and Ava tipped the driver generously to make up for the short ride. She headed directly into the mall and took an escalator to the second floor. She was early, but she still looked inside the Starbucks to make sure Jack and Bowles hadn't arrived. When she saw they hadn't, she moved away from the entrance and began to window-shop. One thing Ava hadn't inherited from her mother was the shopping gene. While Jennie Lee could spend hours flitting happily from store to store, Ava could think of nothing more boring. All high-end shopping centres felt the same to her. No matter what city you were visiting, you were always sure to find a mall filled with the same stores peddling the same goods. Still, the window-shopping killed time. At ten after four Ava made her way back to Starbucks.

Jack was there, sitting at a corner table near the back of the shop with two men. Ava recognized Bowles from his photo in the Hong Kong Jockey Club file, but the other man was a mystery. He looked to be about forty and was clean-shaven, with jet-black hair combed back and hanging fashionably long to his collar. He sat with one leg crossed, and Ava saw he was wearing black Gucci loafers that matched his black silk shirt and black slacks. By comparison, Bowles looked seedy. His sandy brown hair was thinning and his cheeks were covered in stubble. He was wearing a dark grey suit and a powder-blue shirt unbuttoned halfway down his chest.

Ava watched them for a minute. Bowles was speaking to Jack, leaning forward with his head bobbing up and down. He looked intense, while Jack's expression was sympathetic as he uttered the occasional word of encouragement. The third man sat very still, his hand wrapped around a cup that he didn't move. Ava wondered if the stranger could be a bodyguard, but if he was, he was the slimmest, best-dressed, and most sophisticated-looking bodyguard she'd ever seen.

Ava took in the area. No one was hanging around outside the café, and the only other occupants were two groups of women. She assumed it was safe to approach Jack's table.

The three men didn't notice her until she was almost on top of them. Then Jack looked up at her. "Jennie, what a surprise! How long has it been, two years?"

"At least two years," she said with smile. "Do you mind if I join you?"

She sat down before Jack could answer. "I apologize if this seems rude, but I really want to speak to Mr. Bowles," she said.

Bowles and the stranger turned towards her. "Do I know you?" Bowles asked.

"No, but Jack does," Ava said, her eyes locked on Bowles. "Jack, why don't you introduce us."

"Certainly. Jennie, Martin Bowles is an acquaintance of mine through the Hong Kong Jockey Club. And this is his business associate, Arven Saad. Mr. Saad flew here from Borneo this morning to help Martin deal with a problem," Jack said. "And gentlemen, this is Jennie Kwong. She is a first-class debt collector who I needed to employ in my former business life. The reason was unfortunate, but the result was most satisfactory."

Ava looked at Saad, hoping that her surprise wasn't too obvious. As she gathered herself, she became aware that Saad was staring at her with dark brown eyes devoid of any emotion.

Bowles's jaw had dropped. "What are you doing here?" he sputtered, breaking the silence.

"I have something of yours that we need to discuss."

Bowles started to rise, but before he could, Jack got out of his chair. "I think I should leave you three alone. It seems you have some business to discuss that doesn't concern me," he said. "Martin, if you like, I'll wait outside until you and Jennie have finished."

"You have incredible nerve approaching us like this," Bowles said to Ava, still looking shocked and ignoring Jack.

"I just couldn't pass up the opportunity," she said.

Bowles shook his head, but before he could speak, Saad reached out and touched his arm. "I want to hear what she has to say." Bowles sat back in his seat and Saad stared across the table at Ava. "We're listening."

"Given Mr. Bowles's reaction, I assume you've heard from Ronald Ho and that my name was mentioned," Ava said.

"We have, and it was," Saad said, with a slight nod.

"So you know that forty-seven million dollars of Chong money is now sitting in my account."

"That's *my* money!" Bowles nearly shouted.

"My understanding is that it's your money in name only. I'm told the account is being used to disguise the money's source before it's forwarded to one of your company accounts at the HKSS Bank. It isn't money laundering in a strictly legal sense, but the intent is the same, since you're trying to hide its origin from HKSS."

"You seem to know a great deal about our business," Saad said sharply.

"We've been gathering information for only a few days, but I think we've done quite well," said Ava. "In addition to accessing your account, we've identified all your real estate holdings. And of course we also managed to learn where Mr. Bowles lives and what car he drives — or, should I say, drove."

Saad looked at Bowles, who was rising to his feet again with his fists clenched. "Martin, please don't do anything rash. As unpleasant as this is, we need to talk it through," he said.

Bowles stared daggers at Ava, and she knew he wanted to strike her. Despite Saad's intervention, she braced herself.

"Sit," Saad said, tugging at Bowles's arm.

Bowles fell into the chair and Saad turned to Ava. "You've just answered a lot of questions I had about yesterday's events, but what I don't know is who you are and why you're doing this."

Bowles pointed a finger at Ava. "You frightened the hell out of my wife and our two small children. You put people's lives at risk!"

"We wanted to get the Chong family's full attention. The fact that Mr. Saad came to Hong Kong so quickly is an indication that we were successful."

"Stealing the money would have been sufficient to accomplish that," Saad said. "Don't you think the bombs were a little excessive?"

"Perhaps, but the symbolism was important to us."

Saad cocked an eyebrow and took a sip of his coffee. For the first time he seemed to be working at appearing calm. "Might you be referring to a warehouse in Kuching that was attacked in a similar fashion about a week ago?" he said slowly.

"Yes, I'm talking about that warehouse."

"What does it have to do with us? The police have concluded that the woman who died in the explosion was responsible. The case has been closed."

"It is true that Jamilah Daeng was blamed, but I've been told that was only after you and Commissioner Chik decided to pin the bombing on her," Ava said. "Obviously, since she died in the explosion, Jamilah isn't in a position to defend herself, but the fact that you and the commissioner conspired to blame her raises a few questions. For example, why would you bother to concoct that fabrication if the Chong business empire wasn't connected to the bombing?"

"No such discussions took place, and why would they? Whatever happened at that warehouse had nothing to do with us. And believe me, Commissioner Chik doesn't need advice from me or anyone else on how to conduct police business," Saad said. Then he peered at Ava more closely before asking, "How do you know so much about the recent events in Kuching?"

"My client briefed me."

"Your client?" Saad said, his disbelief evident. "Who is this client?"

"The Sarawak United Front."

"That's the group that sent the emails libelling us," Bowles said.

"Martin, there's no such group. It doesn't exist," Saad said. "Ms. Kwong — if that's her real name — is playing games with us."

"How do you know it doesn't exist?" Ava asked, ignoring

his remark about her name but realizing there might be a problem.

"That's neither here nor there," said Saad. "What matters is that you've stolen forty-seven million dollars from us. The only question I want answered is, what do you want from us in order for you to return it?"

"I don't want to give her anything," Bowles interjected angrily. "We'll turn our lawyers loose on them and their bank. We'll go to the Hong Kong Police if we have to."

"Ahmad doesn't want this to get any messier," Saad said to him, and then turned back to Ava. "I suspect you're pleased to hear that."

Ava nodded. "I believe a quick resolution is best for everyone."

"So do I. But I'm curious to know what your next move might be if that doesn't happen?"

"I can make your money disappear in a heartbeat, and there would be no trail to follow. We could also continue to plant bombs and pepper the news media, business associates, government officials, and your banks with stories about the abuses the Chong family has heaped on Sarawak. And I guarantee you, the longer those bombs are going off, the greater the impact those stories will have."

"And you would do all that based on a mistaken belief that we had something to do with the bombing in Kuching," Saad said.

"There's no mistake."

"We could argue about that all day, but I don't see the point," said Saad. "Tell me what it is you want."

She saw Bowles's face turn red. If there had been any doubt about who was calling the shots, it was now dispelled.

Ava nodded. "First we want the police to retract their statement about the bombing in Kuching. We want Jamilah Daeng's death to be classified as a homicide and for the police to commit to a proper investigation. I don't actually expect them to conduct one, but I'll come back to that in a minute.

"Next, the company that owned the warehouse needs to be compensated for their losses. I have already sent them five million dollars from your account. And in Jamilah's name I have sent another seven million to various environmental and Indigenous rights organizations in Sarawak. We want you to acknowledge in writing that those payments were made voluntarily by you and represent fair compensation."

"Which means you're proposing to return only thirty-five million dollars of our money," Saad said.

"In most places thirty-five million dollars is a lot of money," Ava said. "And last, we believe that someone in your organization gave the order to blow up that warehouse —"

"This is absurd," Bowles interrupted.

"Let her finish," Saad said.

"Someone has to be held accountable. We don't care who it is. You can make the actual bomber the fall guy or find some mid-level employee who gave an instruction that he will claim was misinterpreted. We don't even care what they're charged with, only that their ties to the Chong family be made clear."

Saad looked at Bowles. "You know your father-in-law as well as I do. How do you think he'll react to the family name being connected to a bombing?"

"He'll be angry beyond description," Bowles said, turning to Ava. "Sulaiman Chong is a proud and powerful man. He isn't someone you want to make an enemy of, and yet that's what you seem intent on doing."

"You asked me what we want," Ava said. "The family can respond as they see fit."

Saad went still, his eyes boring into Ava's. "My boss is Ahmad Chong, Chief Minister Chong's son. I will speak to him tonight."

"Thank you. When you do, you might tell him that my client has engaged Douglas Brooke as their lawyer in Kuching. If there's a deal to be done, Mr. Brooke will be representing their interests during any negotiations and is to be given appropriate respect."

"We know Brooke. He'll get the respect he deserves," Saad said. "How will I reach you after I speak with Ahmad?"

Ava stood up. "You can send an email to info@sarawak-front.com. It will be forwarded to me. I check my email constantly. Include your phone number if you want me to call you."

"No phone number?"

"Not that I want to share."

Saad looked irritated but then flashed the hint of a smile. "Before you leave, Ms. Kwong, I have to say that your face is rather familiar. I've been trying — unsuccessfully — to put a name to it, but I have a feeling that if I search hard enough, I'll come up with it."

"My name is Jennie Kwong."

"And your client is the Sarawak United Front," Saad said. "Two lies don't cancel each other out."

33

AVA DECIDED TO WALK BACK TO THE MANDARIN. THE conversation with Saad had rattled her, but she had accomplished what she wanted, and she didn't believe that if Saad figured out her real identity it would derail her plans.

She couldn't see Jack Yee when she left the Starbucks, so she called his cellphone.

"Where are you?" he asked.

"I just left our friends. I think it went well, although Saad suspects my real name isn't Jennie Kwong. It's possible he saw a photo of me that was taken in Kuching when we visited the police headquarters. If he asks you, just say it's the only name you know me by, but given the business I'm in, you wouldn't be surprised to know that I use others," she said. "You might say that when you hired me, you heard I have a shady past, including connections with triads."

"Okay. I'm heading back to the coffee shop now," said Jack. "None of that will be a problem."

Ava smiled as she ended the call. Jack had proved to be a very competent co-conspirator. She left the IFC Mall and had begun walking back to the hotel when her phone rang.

She glanced at the screen and saw Sonny's name.

"Hey, what's up?" she answered.

"Jimmy called. One of the news outlets is reporting that the police believe the bombs were set by two men and a woman driving a blue Toyota. They're asking for anyone who might have seen them to come forward."

"That isn't surprising. The guard at the CIC Building obviously saw me, and he must have spotted the Toyota when we drove by," she said. "Where is the car now?"

"In a garage in Kowloon, getting a paint job and new licence plates."

"So the car shouldn't be a problem. That leaves the guard, but I doubt he'll be able to provide an accurate description of any of us."

"I agree, but Jimmy is still nervous. He asked if I think you have more activity in mind. I didn't know what to tell him."

"I just met with Martin Bowles and an executive from the Chong family. My hunch is they'll make a deal. But I should know for sure in a day or two."

"And if they don't?"

"There are other ways besides bombs to make the Chong family miserable. Thank Jimmy for me and ask him for his banking information. I still need to pay him."

"Will do, boss," said Sonny.

"I'll be in touch."

Ava had kept on walking while she spoke to Sonny, and a few minutes later the Mandarin came into view. The doorman nodded and tipped his hat as she went past, and it struck her that there was someone who had seen the Toyota and its occupants quite clearly — the doorman who had been on duty that morning. Could he have seen the news and made a connection? It was a long shot, but she couldn't take anything for granted.

"Excuse me," Ava said, turning back towards the doorman. "What's the name of the doorman who usually works the nightshift?"

"Wing," he said.

"When is his shift?"

"He normally works from ten to six."

"Thank you," she said.

It had been a long day. As Ava got into the elevator, she considered going to M Bar for a drink, then decided against it. There was still work to be done, and besides, she knew there would be lots of liquor at dinner.

When she got back to her suite, she checked the time and, figuring Douglas Brooke might still be in his office, dialled his number. A moment later his secretary put Ava through to him.

"I wasn't sure when I'd hear from you again," he said.

"Things are moving quickly," she said. "How flexible is your schedule?"

"You are my top priority."

"Excellent. So here's what's been going on," said Ava. "In addition to the bombings, I took forty-seven million dollars from a Chong family bank account. I met with Arven Saad and Martin Bowles a short while ago and told them we're prepared to return thirty-five million, if certain conditions are met."

Brooke didn't respond. After several seconds Ava began to wonder if he was still on the line. "Douglas, are you there?"

"Sorry, I had to pick myself up from the floor. I don't mean that literally, of course, but you do have a knack for shocking me," he said. "Did you say Arven Saad is in Hong Kong?"

"Yes. I guess the family thought the situation was important enough to send him."

"You do understand that Sulaiman Chong is a man accustomed to getting his way, yes?"

"He may be the so-called Sultan of Sarawak, but in Hong Kong he's the sultan of nothing. This is our playing field."

"You do seem to have found his vulnerability," Brooke said. "How did Bowles and Saad react to your demands?"

"Saad ran the show. I think he understood I'm serious," said Ava. "I assume he's already relayed our conversation to Ahmad and maybe even to Sulaiman. That's why I want to give you a heads-up."

"Is there a specific reason for the heads-up?"

"I told Saad you would handle any negotiations on our behalf."

"That will irk them."

"I don't care. That's the way it's going to be handled," Ava said.

"And what might these negotiations entail?"

"It's too soon to say. I have to hear back from them."

"And if they don't agree to a settlement? What happens to the money you took?" Brooke asked.

"I haven't decided. Besides, I didn't take it. A woman named Jennie Kwong did. The same woman met with Saad and Bowles. As far as they know, she's a debt collector."

"Now you're confusing me."

"Jennie and I are one and the same, except they don't know that."

"So who do the Chongs think I'm representing?"

"Jennie Kwong."

"That is clever."

"That's simply being careful," Ava said.

"What do you want me to do now?" Brooke asked.

"Nothing. You just need to wait until you hear from me. If they try to contact you directly, let me know before you talk to them."

"Okay then, I'm in waiting mode."

Ava put down the phone and walked over to the window. It was rush hour, and both the harbour and the streets of Central were active. She looked down at the boats, cars, and people scurrying around the city. In a macro sense it all seemed aimless, but every microcosm had its own energy and purpose, and in Hong Kong they had collectively built a city that in her eyes was a wonder. Ava's team hadn't built anything, but they had reached all the way across the South China Sea to get justice from a family who thought it was beyond the reach of the law. "I'll make you pay, one way or another," she said aloud.

Ava's phone rang and she groaned. Too much of the day had already been spent talking, but she knew she had to answer when she saw Jack Yee's name on the screen.

"Jack, how did it end with Bowles and Saad?" she asked.

"I don't know. Bowles was going back and forth between anger, worry, and perhaps even fear. Saad questioned me about our relationship and asked if I had always known you as Jennie Kwong. I stuck to what we agreed on."

"Including the triad ties?"

"As forcefully as I could. I told him that several men died when you were collecting the money that had been stolen from me, and that you have friends who will do anything for you."

"Then it sounds to me like it went well."

"I hope so."

"Thank you again. I'll take it from here."

"Ava, be careful."

"Always."

34

MEGAN'S KITCHEN WAS ON THE FIFTH FLOOR OF A building on Wan Chai Road called the Lucky Centre. It wasn't the type of place where Ava would have expected to find a first-class restaurant, but she trusted Amanda's judgement.

When Ava stepped out of the elevator, she was greeted by a hostess and led to a table where Amanda, Michael, and Marcus were already seated. After a round of hugs, she sat down.

"I remembered that you like to drink white wine with hotpot," Marcus said, taking a bottle of Pinot Grigio from an ice bucket. "Shall I pour?"

"Please," Ava said, failing to remember when she had ever eaten hotpot with her father. She raised her glass when he'd finished. "Good health to us all."

"How was the rest of your day?" Amanda asked.

"It went well. Your father was a huge help. I've thanked him, but you might mention that I told you how grateful I am, "Ava said.

"I don't understand why you ladies are still doing business in Borneo," Michael said. "After the fiasco in Kota Kinabalu

I thought you would sell that company and move on."

Ava looked at her half-brother. Physically he resembled their father, and like him he usually wore a suit. That evening both of them were in casual shirts — Burberry for Marcus, Lacoste for Michael — which she guessed was a practical concession to the danger of stains that accompanied hotpot. "Cutting and running isn't part of Three Sisters' corporate culture," she said. "We did talk about leaving but we weren't ready to make that decision. Now, however, we may be, but not because we feel pressured."

"Exactly. If we do leave it will be because the business doesn't fit with Three Sisters' long-term strategy," said Amanda.

Michael looked ready to argue but stopped himself when a server arrived at the table.

"Are you ready to order?"

"You take care of it. I trust your taste," Ava said to Amanda.

"Is everyone willing to try something different?" Amanda asked.

"Sure," Ava said, while Michael and Marcus nodded agreement.

Amanda picked up the menu. "We'll have cuttlefish balls, the cheese-filled meatballs, Peking duck dumplings, tofu, mushrooms, U.S. rib-eye, chive dumplings, and the Iberico pork to start."

"What kind of broths would you like?" the server asked.

"We'll have the chicken, the chili-based, and the tom yum cappuccino broth."

"Tom yum cappuccino broth?" Michael asked when the server had left.

"It's a house specialty," said Amanda.

"I'm sure it will be interesting," Marcus said, then looked at Ava. "It may not be any of my business, but I'm curious to hear what the long-term strategy for Three Sisters is. Your mother has been talking about a film you're somehow involved with that stars Pang Fai. How does that fit into your strategy?"

"There is a film being made, but the story of how that came to happen is quite long and complicated. I'm not sure I'm up to explaining it tonight."

"Your mother said it involves events in Tiananmen Square. Surely you understand how dangerous a subject that is for Beijing."

"Of course, but our film is not overtly political. It focuses on the love of a mother for her son."

"Your mother told me that Pang Fai is playing a general. Is she the mother?"

"No."

"So who is she?"

"Someone who believes that no army should ever be used to attack its own citizens."

"Ava, it sounds to me like this film will provoke the Chinese government," said Marcus.

"Daddy, it's a love story."

"Ah, our food is arriving," Amanda said.

The talk ended as three pots of broth were placed on the main table and the platters of food on smaller side tables. "It all looks good," said Ava.

They ate and drank slowly, but as the evening progressed they managed to work their way through three bottles of wine and three additional platters of food. In Ava's opinion, hotpot was the most seductive of meals, enticing her to eat far more than she could have imagined when she sat down. It was always that way. The slow pace and small portions going into the pots tricked her into thinking she was being moderate, but the portions added up. By the time the platters were empty, she had eaten enough for two.

Their conversation picked up as they ate, but there was no further mention of the film or any other Three Sisters investments. Instead Ava asked Michael about his business, and her father about his other sons. They answered at length, and during the occasional lull Amanda filled the void, talking about a film she and Michael had seen, and how excited she was about the coming weekend's horse racing in Sha Tin, where her father had an entry.

When the bill arrived, Michael and Marcus both wanted to pay, but Marcus prevailed. As he was settling the account, Ava's phone rang. Brooke's number showed on her screen.

"Excuse me. I apologize, but I have to take this call," she said, rising from her seat. She walked to the entrance and found a spot in the lobby where she could be alone. "Douglas. Have you heard from the Chongs?"

"Ahmad phoned. I had to take the call because he used a private line, and I couldn't just hang up on him. He wants to meet me tomorrow morning at their corporate offices," Brooke said.

"Was he upset?"

"He was loud, insulting, and verging on irrational," Brooke said. "He had some exceedingly nasty things to say about Jennie Kwong. Evidently you really got under Arven Saad's skin, and he in turn infected Ahmad."

"He has until tomorrow morning to calm down."

"Are you saying you want me to go?"

"Yes."

"You still haven't told me what offer is on the table."

"We're prepared to give them back thirty-five million dollars and bring an end to hostilities in exchange for the police publicly clearing Jamilah of any wrongdoing, declaring her death a homicide, and reopening the investigation into the warehouse bombing, plus the Chongs offering up someone in their organization to take the fall."

"That's a lot to swallow," Brooke said slowly.

"Will Sulaiman be there?" Ava asked, pointedly ignoring his remark.

"Ahmad didn't say, but I doubt it. They'll probably keep the old man in reserve until they really need him," Brooke said. "But a question: what if Ahmad or Sulaiman insists on speaking directly with you?"

"Tell them you're my representative and that you speak for me. I have no interest in talking to them unless they're serious about making a deal."

"I'll use that as my point of reference."

"Then good luck tomorrow, though I'm sure you'll have success," Ava said. Amanda, Michael, and Marcus arrived in the lobby. "I have to go now. Call me after the meeting."

"We were thinking of having a nightcap at M Bar. What do you think?" asked Marcus.

"I would love that," Ava said.

"I'll drive. There's room for all of us," Marcus said.

"Speaking of cars, I'm sorry for monopolizing Sonny the past few days," Ava said.

"He's your man and you're his priority," Michael said. "Like Dad, I'm just grateful that you make him available when you aren't in the city."

Marcus had parked his black BMW 7 just a short walk from the Lucky Centre. Ava and Amanda got into the back seat.

"Was that Pang Fai you were speaking to on the phone?" Marcus asked as he pulled away from the curb.

"No, it was a lawyer we've retained to handle an issue we're having in Kuching," she said.

"I have to say your mother is quite taken with Pang Fai," he said, turning his head to glance at her. "I tell her she's star-struck, but she says when she's with Fai it's like having another daughter."

"Fai enjoys her company as well," Ava said.

"Your mother does worry, though. She doesn't want to see you get hurt. She told me you were quite shaken when your relationship with that other young woman ended. What was her name, Maria?"

"Daddy, I don't mean to be rude, but I have no interest in discussing my personal relationships with you or Mummy," Ava said. "When you're in Toronto, the two of you can talk about them between yourselves as much as you want."

"Ah, sorry," he said.

Ava felt Amanda nudging her and turned to look at her sister-in-law. *Well done*, Amanda mouthed.

As Ava smiled, her phone rang, and she saw the incoming number was Fai's. *What a coincidence,* she thought. "Hi, babe. I'm in my father's car with Amanda and Michael. We're heading to the Mandarin for drinks. Can I call you later?"

"Sure. I just got back to my hotel and I won't be going anywhere. It was a long day that ended with a surprising, but happy, twist."

"Tell me," said Ava.

"Later," Fai said with a laugh. "Enjoy your family."

35

AVA SAID GOODNIGHT TO HER FAMILY IN THE ELEVATOR after they left M Bar. They had managed to get a table near a window, but the bar was crowded, and so noisy that they almost had to yell to be heard. They stayed for just one drink before making their exit.

"Will I see you tomorrow?" Amanda asked Ava.

"That depends on how the morning goes. But one way or another I'll be in touch."

"When will you be leaving Hong Kong?" Marcus asked.

"I don't know, though I can't imagine I'll be here for more than another day or two."

"Then you'll be heading back to Taipei?"

"Yes, until the filming is completed. After that, Fai and I plan to go to Shanghai and spend some time with Xu."

"So there's a chance I won't see you in Toronto."

"Unfortunately, that might be the case."

"I hope it isn't. I'd like to see you there," he said as he held out his arms. Ava stepped into them and they hugged. Her head pressed into his neck, she felt the strength of his grip and relaxed in it. She knew he loved her as she loved him, but both of them struggled to communicate their feelings. *It would be easier if we lived in a vacuum,* she thought, *instead of this web of complications.*

"If I don't see you, please enjoy your time with Mummy. And be extra nice to Marian. She often feels she's not a real part of this family," said Ava.

"I promise," Marcus said.

Ava took out her phone as soon as she was out of the elevator. She pressed Fai's number even before she got to her door and heard Fai's *wei* as she opened it. "What was so surprising about today?" she asked.

"Harris Jones."

"Who's he?"

"He writes for the *London Tribune* and is one of the most influential film critics in the world."

"I've never heard of him, but I'll take your word for it."

"He was on set today. Chen invited him to Taipei; he even offered to fly him here first-class and pay his expenses. Jones didn't accept Chen's money but he wanted to know why he was so prepared to spend it. Chen told him Lau Lau is making a film for the ages and he thought Jones would appreciate being the first person to experience it."

"Does the opinion of one critic mean that much?"

"This isn't about a finished film. Chen is being really shrewd; he's playing to Jones's large ego. Jones can't help but appreciate the opportunity he's been given to witness Lau Lau's big return," Fai said.

"And what does Chen hope to get from this? A good review?"

"Jones is a man of principle. His opinion of the film will be based on its merits," Fai said. "Chen won't try to influence him in that regard. But he will likely encourage Jones to use his connections to get *Tiananmen* included in next year's Cannes Film Festival."

"That's good news. Can I do anything to help?"

"I don't think so. It's all up to Chen and Lau Lau now. Jones is staying here for another few days, so they'll be doing everything they can to guarantee his desire to see the finished product," Fai said. "If Jones writes positively about the film and says how eager he is to see what Lau Lau has created, that will attract a tsunami of attention."

"I like seeing this strategic side of Chen."

"He's always been clever that way."

"Where is he tonight?"

"He, Lau Lau, and Jones went out for dinner. I was invited, but I didn't want to be a distraction," Fai said. "The more time Chen and Lau Lau spend alone with Jones, the better."

"I am so glad things are going well."

"How are they going on your end?" Fai asked.

"Far better than they were yesterday. And if tomorrow meets my expectations, I could be on a plane heading for Taipei the day after."

"That would make me very happy. I miss you so much."

"I can't make promises, but if my luck holds out..." Ava said, trailing off as she saw that two messages had been forwarded to her personal email account from info@sarawak-front.com. Both were from Saad, asking her to call him.

"Let's hope it does," said Fai. "We'll speak tomorrow. Love you."

"Love you too."

Ava thought about using her own phone but didn't want to risk the possibility that Saad could trace it. She knew there was a store just five minutes from the hotel that sold SIM cards and cheap pay-as-you-go phones, and decided that was the safer option.

Ava grabbed her bag and headed for the door. When she reached the lobby, she checked the time and realized the store might already be closed. She scolded herself for not thinking of that sooner and looked for someone to ask. The concierge desk wasn't staffed, but she thought the doorman might know. She headed for the entrance and saw the doorman from the night before. *Two birds, one stone,* she thought.

Ava approached the doorman with a smile, but her attention was riveted on his reaction to seeing her. "What a pleasant evening," she said.

He smiled and tipped his cap. "The weather has been good," he said.

The doorman looked relaxed, completely at ease. There was nothing in the way he was acting that suggested he connected Ava to the two men and the blue Toyota in the news. She knew it was possible he hadn't seen the reports, but if that was the case, it was unlikely he would, since the television stations were rigorous about refreshing their news cycles. In Hong Kong, today's news quickly became tomorrow's history.

"I need to buy a SIM card. I remember seeing a store on Ice House Street. Do you think it will still be open?"

"That place is out of business, but there's a 7-Eleven on Chater Road that sells cards and phones. The hotel's back entrance is on Chater, and the store is almost immediately on the left."

"Thank you," she said.

Five minutes later Ava left the 7-Eleven with a cheap phone, a phone card worth five hundred Hong Kong dollars, and two SIM cards. She waited until she got back to her room before she called Saad.

"This is Arven Saad," he answered.

"This is Jennie Kwong," she answered. "I assume you spoke to someone in Kuching?"

"That's why I'm calling."

"Douglas Brooke informed me a little while ago that he has a meeting with Ahmad Chong tomorrow morning in Kuching," she said. "I thought that was the agreed-upon process."

"A meeting is scheduled, but the family isn't happy. In fact, they find it highly insulting that you've brought a man like Brooke into the mix. They don't want him involved in this. They want to deal directly with you."

"What's their problem with Brooke?"

"The family puts tremendous value on its privacy. Brooke has a reputation for being indiscreet. That makes him unreliable."

"Mr. Saad, Douglas Brooke has been selected by my clients to be their lawyer. He is negotiating on their behalf. If an agreement can be reached, he will be the one to make sure it's papered to our satisfaction," Ava said, and then paused. "There's nothing else to discuss."

"What if the family insists that the principals negotiate in person?"

Ava went silent.

"Are you still there, Ms. Kwong?" Saad asked, in a tone that betrayed his annoyance.

"I'm still here."

"Well?"

"I was thinking. Does this mean you're inviting me to Kuching?"

"The family believes that a face-to-face meeting will be the most effective way to resolve this situation."

"Does this mean the family is prepared to agree to our conditions?"

"It means they're prepared to discuss your conditions," Saad said.

"That isn't enough."

"You know there's always give and take when it comes to negotiation, Ms. Kwong. No one ever gets everything they want, and it would be unreasonable of your clients to expect it. At the very least, you should give the family an opportunity to present their position to you personally. All they want is to understand why you're asking for certain things. They want to hear the reasons directly from you, not from some half-assed local lawyer who makes a living trading on his family's name."

"I didn't realize Douglas Brooke was such a sore point."

"If you think that highly of him, bring him to the meeting."

Ava paused to gather her thoughts. "Bottom line, is the family prepared to do a deal?"

"Yes, but not with Brooke. They want to sit across the table from you."

"Then we'll meet," Ava said.

"That's great —"

"But not in Kuching," she interrupted. "We'll meet in Hong Kong. Tell the family to send whoever they want to represent their interests."

"I'm not sure —"

"Mr. Saad, I've been doing business in Asia for a very long time. I know how it works in places like Sarawak, where the police, the politicians, and the businesspeople cover each other's backs and do favours for one another. So I'm not getting on a plane to Kuching, where I could be arrested as soon as I set foot on Malaysian soil," she said. "It's Hong Kong or nothing."

"I think your views on Sarawak are mistaken, but I will talk to the family."

"You do that."

"And if they agree to Hong Kong, when would you be ready to sit down with them?"

"My calendar is clear."

"I'll see what can be done."

"You can email or call me at this number," Ava said, and ended the call.

She took a small bottle of cognac from the minibar and emptied it into a wineglass. Then she walked to the window and stared out into the night. She hadn't expected her demands to go unchallenged, but she was surprised that Douglas Brooke was such a source of contention. She also couldn't believe they had expected her to go to Kuching. *Maybe they're hoping Jennie Kwong is ignorant of how things operate there*, she thought. *One thing is certain — I'm being tested.*

No more compromises, she decided. If Saad called back, he would have to agree to her terms. If he didn't, she would have to follow through on the threats she'd made. They would have to find a way to plant more bombs, and she would move the thirty-five million to an account that was harder to trace. She would talk to May Ling and perhaps Brenda Burgess, Three Sisters' Hong Kong lawyer, about finding a public relations company to target the Chongs.

Ava lost track of time as she stood at the window, her attention flitting between the activity in the harbour and her thoughts about what might come to pass with the Chongs. She was so absorbed that, when she heard an unfamiliar ringtone, she didn't realize it was coming from her burner phone until the fourth ring.

"This is Jennie Kwong."

"Saad again," he said. "I've spoken to the family. In the spirit of compromise, they are prepared to meet with you in Hong Kong."

"Where?"

"The corporate boardroom in the CIC Building is available. Damage from the explosion was restricted to the ground floor, and most of the debris has been cleared away. I think it would be an appropriate choice, don't you?"

"I see your point," Ava said, deciding it wasn't worth another argument. "If I agree, who will attend the meeting?"

"For certain, Ahmad Chong, Martin Bowles, and I will be there."

"What about Sulaiman Chong?"

"I doubt it, but I can't rule out the possibility."

"How will they get here?

"By private jet."

Ava did some rough calculations, then said, "I want Douglas Brooke to be there. I'll have to speak to him and get back to you."

"So we have an agreement to meet?"

"We do."

"Before you hang up, can you tell me who will be representing your team at the meeting? Is there any chance we might meet your client?"

"I'll be there and so will Douglas. Beyond that, I can't say."

36

AVA SAT WITH HER NOTEBOOK OPEN IN FRONT OF HER.
Doubt had begun to creep into her mind as soon as she hung
up from Saad. *Was I too quick to agree to meet at their office?
Perhaps I just got excited after they agreed to come to Hong
Kong. I have time to think about that,* she decided, *but first
things first.* She called Brooke.

"I didn't expect to hear from you so soon," he answered.

"There's been a change in plans. Your meeting with
Ahmad has been cancelled and replaced by one here that I
want you to attend."

"What happened?"

"Saad called to request my attendance in Kuching.
I declined but told him I would be prepared to meet in Hong
Kong. The Chongs have agreed. There's an early morning
flight from Kuching to KL, where you can catch a connection
to Hong Kong. That should get you here by early afternoon."

"Then I'll see you in Hong Kong tomorrow," Brooke said.

"Good."

"Do you think this means they're willing to do a deal?"
he asked.

"Saad thinks they are, but all I know for certain is that they're willing to talk."

Brooke paused and then said, "Are you sure you need me in Hong Kong? You're the one they want to meet with, and you certainly don't need my help with the negotiations. I've seen you in action."

"It's important to me that our agreement be properly papered. And by properly, I mean it can't be disputed in Hong Kong, Sarawak, or anywhere else for that matter. It has to be airtight."

"I'm not familiar with the intricacies of Hong Kong law."

"I have a capable lawyer here who can work with you."

"Very well. I'll be happy to work with him."

"It's a she, actually. Her name is Brenda Burgess."

Brooke sighed. "The last vestiges of male chauvinism that my wife and daughter haven't drummed out of me have just made an unwelcome appearance."

"Not to worry. Now go and book your flights. I'll arrange to have someone pick you up at the airport and I'll make a hotel arrangement," she said.

Ava put down the phone and returned to her notebook, where she made a list of people she needed to call. Brooke would arrive in Hong Kong tomorrow in the early afternoon. From a practical standpoint there was no reason to delay the meeting, since she already knew what she wanted to accomplish. But strategically it might serve her purposes to make the Chongs wait an extra day; it could put them off their game. Then again, if she moved faster, she might be able to create additional pressure.

As Ava weighed the pros and cons, an email from Brooke arrived confirming his flight schedule. She wrote back: Great timing. My friend Sonny Kwok will meet you at the airport. He'll be carrying a sign with your name on it. I'll see you when you get to the hotel. With that settled, she turned to the other calls on her list.

Auntie Grace answered the phone in Shanghai. "Ava, it's so nice to hear from you. Xu told me you and Fai might be coming to Shanghai in the next few weeks."

"That's the plan, but there are no firm dates yet."

"You know I'll be here whenever you come."

"We're looking forward to seeing you and Xu," said Ava. "Is he at home?"

"I'll get him."

"Ava, how are things going in Hong Kong?" Xu asked a moment later.

"They might come to a head in the next day or two. That's why I'm calling. I could use some help," she said. "Do you still have contacts in the Hong Kong Customs Department?"

"We wouldn't be shipping so much product there if that wasn't the case."

"And your contacts extend to Chep Lap Kok?"

"Those are especially strong, since most of our phones are transported by air," he said. "What do you need at the airport?"

"Am I correct in assuming Chep Lap Kok is also the port of landing for private planes?"

"It is. Private planes are how we move our goods. They land at the Hong Kong Business Aviation Centre. It's part of Chep Lap Kok but has its own executive terminal and a separate team to handle Customs, security, and the rest," Xu said. "What is it you need?"

"I need the flight manifest for a private jet coming in from Kuching sometime tomorrow."

"That should be easy enough. Is that all?"

"Yes."

"Do you have any additional information about the flight that I can give to Customs?" he asked.

"I expect the jet will be owned by one of the Chong family's companies, and I believe Ahmad Chong will be one of the passengers," she said.

"I'll pass that along to my contact," Xu said. "By the way, you don't have to wait until the plane lands before you know who's on it. They'll have to file a flight plan, and that normally includes a passenger list."

"The sooner I know, the better. Thank you for this, *ge ge*."

"*Momentai*. You'll hear from me tomorrow."

Ava looked at the next name on her list, then checked the time before making the call.

"This is Richard Bowlby," Brenda Burgess's husband answered.

"Richard, this is Ava Lee. I hope I'm not calling too late."

"Of course not. We're always pleased to hear from you, Ava," he said. "I assume you want to speak to Brenda?"

"Yes, but before I do, I want to thank you for your help with setting up BB Productions and the banking to support it."

"It was my pleasure, though I have to tell you I expect to be invited to the premiere of BB's first film."

"You and Brenda will be at the top of the list."

"Excellent. Now let me pass the phone to her."

"Hi, Ava," Brenda said.

"Hi, Brenda. Are you free for a few hours tomorrow afternoon? I apologize in advance for the short notice."

"What's going on?"

Ava explained the situation to Brenda in detail, from the bombing of the warehouse in Kuching to the phone call she'd just had with Douglas Brooke. When she'd finished, nearly twenty minutes later, Brenda waited several seconds before saying, "So, Jennie Kwong lives again. It's been a long time since you've used that identity. I'd almost forgotten she was part of your repertoire.... Ava, you continue to be my most interesting client."

"I'm not sure that's a good thing."

"After the fact, I always think it's a good thing. But at first blush I question whether I'm up to the challenges you throw my way."

"And in this case?"

"Oh, I think I'm up to it. I'll gladly attend the meeting, and I'll be pleased to work with Douglas Brooke on the sub-sequent paperwork."

"The meeting could be rancorous."

"After everything you've done to those people, I'd be shocked if it wasn't," Brenda said. "And that's not being criti-cal of your actions. Richard and I have known quite a few men like Sulaiman and Ahmad Chong. In many ways they're vestiges of the colonial past, typified by an overwhelming sense of entitlement. In India they're mini-rajahs and in Malaysia they're sultans. The idea that someone, particularly a woman, would oppose them so brazenly — and even worse, threaten their little empire — must be driving the Chongs mad. I expect there'll be a lot of condescension and anger thrown your way before the meeting is through."

"I can handle it."

"I know you can. I'm actually looking forward to being there to see it."

Ava smiled as she glanced at her notebook. "Brenda, there's one more thing you should know. Later tonight I'm going to transfer the thirty-five million to the BB bank account — as a precaution, nothing more. I know Chen has sole signing authority and that there are multiple layers of banks and lawyers between Richard and the account, but it would be irresponsible not to let you know."

"Why is that necessary?"

"I trust my Kowloon banker, but I also know the Chongs have strong Hong Kong connections. They could bring pressure to bear that he can't resist. I don't want to take that chance."

"I'll tell Richard. He won't mind," Brenda said. "So what time tomorrow do you think we'll be convening?"

"I'm going to say mid- to late afternoon, but I'll email you after I speak to Saad to confirm."

"I'll leave my afternoon free," Brenda said. "It will be good to see you again."

Ava thought about who to phone next and decided Saad could wait.

"Hey, boss, is everything okay?" Sonny answered.

"Things are moving along nicely. I'll be meeting with representatives of the Chong family tomorrow afternoon," she said. "But before I do, could you go to the airport to meet Douglas Brooke, the Kuching lawyer I hired? He's arriving around one p.m. on a Malaysian Air flight from Kuala Lumpur."

"No problem."

"I told him you'll be holding a sign with his name on it."

"Then I will be," said Sonny. "Where is he going to stay?"

"I'll book a room for him here at the Mandarin."

"Okay, boss," Sonny said, and hung up.

Is it time to call Saad? she thought. *No, a few more things to do first.* Ava opened her saved emails and scrolled through her correspondence with Burgess and Bowlby, until she found the message setting out the bank details for the BB Productions account in the U.K. A few minutes later, thirty-five million dollars had been transferred into it from Jennie Kwong's account. With that done, Ava wrote to Chen:

The BB bank account is going to be substantially larger tomorrow. Ignore the change. The money is being parked there until some decisions are made here.

Fai told me about Harris Jones. Sounds like a great move on your part. But then, according to Fai, you've made a lot of them lately. Keeping Lau Lau focused can't be easy. We're all so pleased you took on the task of producer. You're a natural!

Hopefully I'll be able to wrap up my business in a day or two and rejoin you in Taipei. We must have a glorious dinner when I get back. I really enjoyed our last one, particularly Silvana Foo's company. I haven't met many people so entertaining and intelligent.

Is the reference to Silvana too much? Ava thought. "Oh, what the hell," she muttered, and clicked Send.

Now it was time for Saad. Ava dialled his number.

"Yes?" he said abruptly after the first ring.

"Assuming there are no delays, my lawyer can be in Hong Kong tomorrow afternoon. Can your team be prepared to meet by four o'clock?"

"They can and they will. Are you agreeable to meeting in our boardroom in the CIC Building on Jubilee Road?"

"We are. Unless you hear otherwise, we'll see you there at four."

37

AVA WOKE AT SIX A.M. AFTER A RESTLESS NIGHT.
Despite her satisfaction with the way the evening had gone,
she couldn't stop thinking about all the things she might
have done differently. She got out of bed twice. The first
time she emailed Brenda to confirm the meeting time, and
to ask her to come to the Mandarin at three o'clock to meet
Douglas Brooke for a preliminary conversation. The second
time she checked the BB Productions bank account to make
sure the wire transfer had arrived. It had. Then she looked
at her email and saw there were messages from Chen and
her mother.

Chen had written: Great to hear from you, Ava. Dinner with
Harris Jones couldn't have gone better. Lau Lau was brilliant
when he spoke about the film, and I could see Jones was stor-
ing a lot of what he was saying for use later on. I think we've
found an important ally in him. Over after-dinner drinks—just
the two of us; no need to worry about Lau Lau, he's still dry—
Jones said we have three things going for us with this film: The
subject matter is important and will cause controversy. There
will be a real interest in seeing whether Lau Lau can still do

great work. And, of course, he mentioned Fai's growing fan base. He says there are people who would pay just to see her sitting quietly reading a book.

Glad things seem to be doing okay on your end. Hurry back to Taipei. We all miss you. I most certainly will organize another dinner. Love, Chen.

Ava noted that he hadn't mentioned Silvana Foo, but perhaps that was simply Chen being circumspect.

Jennie Lee's email was equally buoyant. Ava, your father called me after your hotpot. Thank you for doing that. He really enjoyed seeing you, and that made me very happy. I'm counting down the days until he gets here but I'm trying to keep busy. I have an appointment to get my hair done, as well as a facial. I have mah-jong games organized for the next four nights. Marian and the girls will arrive in Toronto two days before your father, so I'll have lots of time to spend alone with them. I hope things go well with Daddy and the girls. It's been some time since he saw them, and I hope they don't treat him like a stranger. I don't think Marian talks to them about him very much, but that's probably because Bruce doesn't want her to.

From what your father told me, it doesn't sound like you'll be back here when he is. I'm a little disappointed, but I understand that your life is complicated. Stay in touch and be safe. Love, Mummy

Ava replied: I enjoyed my time with Daddy as well. I'm also sure his visit will be a great success and that Marian and the girls will love being with him. Don't worry about those things. Love, Ava

After a trip to the bathroom, Ava made a coffee and sat in her usual spot by the window overlooking the harbour. The sun had risen, and even the harbour's murky waters looked inviting in the flickering light. But as she absorbed the view, her thoughts took off in sudden, unexpected directions.

If Tiananmen *is as controversial a film as Harris Jones believes, Fai might not be able to continue living in Beijing after its release. The Chinese government could make life very difficult for her. If she can't live there, where can she go that she'd be safe? There was a time when Hong Kong would have been a palatable option, but the Chinese government is tightening its grip and the region is no longer autonomous. Chen has already divested all his Beijing assets and purchased a home in Thailand — that was clever planning on his part. Why haven't I suggested to Fai that she sell her hutong house and develop an exit strategy?*

Ava felt her face flush. She had accepted from the beginning that the Chinese government would be hostile to the film. That was the main reason she had taken such care with its financing; she knew she needed to conceal the Three Sisters' involvement. In the back of her mind she had also known that Fai might be criticized for her participation, but for some reason Ava hadn't taken that thought to its logical conclusion. *Why not? Did I think Fai is too big a star to be a target of government harassment? Am I avoiding a long-term commitment to her? It's a commitment I've already made subconsciously, but I've never voiced it. We need to sort this out,* she thought. *After the filming is finished, I'll talk to Fai.*

Ava went into the bedroom and put on her running gear. Her thoughts about Fai had unnerved her and she needed to reclaim her equilibrium.

It wasn't yet crowded when she got to the park, and Ava managed to get in four quick laps before she had to start slowing down. She did one more lap and then headed for Causeway Bay. It was a complicated route from there to the Mandarin, but red lights aside, she ran it at full speed. That's what she needed to clear her head.

Forty-five minutes after getting back to the hotel, Ava walked into Café Causette feeling calmer. She ordered congee with shrimp, salty peanuts, and spring onions. *Why*, she wondered, as the server left the table, *did I just order congee?* It was something she never ate in Canada, something she never ate anywhere but in Hong Kong. Was it Uncle's way of reaching out to her?

She picked up her phone and saw she had a text from Douglas Brooke and a missed call from Xu. The text read: Flight from Kuching landed in KL on time. Flight from KL still as scheduled. Will update if there are any changes.

Ava replied: My driver, Sonny Kwok, will bring you to the Mandarin Oriental Hotel. I've reserved a room for you. I'll meet you at 3:15 in Café Causette in the hotel. BTW, I've asked Brenda Burgess, our Hong Kong lawyer, to join us.

Xu's voicemail said, "Call me. The flight plan for the plane from Kuching has been registered."

Ava smiled as she dialled Xu's number in Shanghai. She could not remember a single time he had failed her, and the first words she spoke when he answered the phone were "I just listened to your message. Thank you for this. I'm going to buy you a bottle of Johnnie Walker Blue Label at duty-free when I come to Shanghai."

"The Scotch isn't necessary, but it will be enjoyed all the same. The weather is lovely here right now. We could sip it while sitting outside by the fishpond," he said. "But about that plane — it's scheduled to land in Hong Kong around noon."

"How many passengers?"

"Six."

"Does that include the crew?"

"No."

"Do you have names?"

"Let me get the list," Xu said.

Six passengers were more than Ava had expected.

"Here I go," Xu said a moment later. "There are two Chongs, initials S and A; two Dins, initials M and J; an M. Chik; and an M. Jaffar. I hope some of those names mean something to you."

"Most of them, and I'm sure my lawyer can fill in the blanks."

"Do you need anything else from me?"

"Now that you mention it, it might be useful if I could ask another favour of Zhao. Do you have any more iPhones you can send his way?"

"No, but I do have the new Apple Watch coming off our production line this week. Tell him I'll give him first crack at them. He'll jump at the chance."

"Thanks, *ge ge*. Now I'll have to get you a whole case of Scotch."

"Just finish what you're doing there and come visit us in Shanghai when the film's done."

"I promise we will," said Ava.

She looked at the names she'd written in her notebook. It appeared that Sulaiman and Ahmad Chong were coming. That both Chongs would be on the plane didn't surprise her, but Chik's presence did. *Why would the police commissioner of Kuching be coming to Hong Kong?* she wondered. The other three names meant nothing to her.

Ava scrolled back through the list of incoming calls on her phone until she found Lydia Lazim's name.

"This is Constable Lazim," she answered.

"Lydia, this is Ava Lee. Are you free to talk?"

"For a few minutes, but not much longer, I'm afraid."

"Then I'll speak quickly. We got to Hong Kong safely, thanks to you, and we've taken action against the Chongs. Did you hear about the bombings here?"

"I did, and I assumed you were behind it."

"We were."

"I'm glad to know that."

"The family has agreed to negotiate with us. We want the truth about Jamilah's death to be made public, and we want charges brought against the people responsible —"

"I'll be shocked if either of those things happens," Lydia interrupted.

"We have a substantial amount of leverage, which we won't hesitate to use, but I'm not calling to discuss that," said Ava. "We have a meeting scheduled this afternoon with the family. They're flying in from Kuching with four other people. I think Commissioner Chik might be with them. Could you check to see if Chik is in his office today?"

"I can do that," Lydia said, almost in a whisper.

"And there two people named Din and another, named Jaffar, on the plane. Do you know who they might be?"

"Jaffar is a lawyer. The Din brothers are policemen attached to the Chief Minister's office as security."

"Would the Chief Minister normally travel with his security team?"

"I have no idea, and it isn't something I'd feel comfortable asking."

"Then don't. You've been very helpful. I don't want to create a difficult situation for you."

"But I will see if the Commissioner is here today. That's easy enough. I'll text you the information."

"Thank you, Lydia."

"Don't mention it," said Lydia. "And good luck."

Ava sat back in the chair. *Why are two policemen and Commissioner Chik on the plane? Are they really security for Sulaiman in his capacity as chief minister, or are they coming to Hong Kong for a different purpose? I need to strengthen the warning Ronald Ho gave them*, she thought. She phoned Zhao.

A gruff voice answered the phone, but when the man heard Ava's name, his tone softened. "Just one minute," he said.

"Ava, what can I do for you this time?" Zhao asked when he came on the line.

"I would appreciate another favour, and this one comes with Xu's new Apple Watches attached to it. Xu says he'll give you first crack at them this week when they come off the line."

"This has to be a substantial favour if you're dangling those watches at me," Zhao said.

"Just a two-minute phone call," Ava said. "I would appreciate it if you would contact Ronald Ho again. I have a meeting later today with the Chong family. They need to understand that Jennie Kwong — the alias I'm using in our negotiations — has your protection. I'd like you to stress that any threat to Jennie, or anyone affiliated with her, is a direct affront to you and will be dealt with accordingly."

"Jennie Kwong?"

"How Jennie came to be is a long story that's not worth

repeating now. I thought it safer to use her name rather than my own."

"It isn't like you to be worried about threats from anyone."

"I'm not concerned for myself so much as for the people working for me. The Chongs are capable of lashing out at them as a way of exacting revenge on me. I want to head that off," she said.

"I will quite gladly deliver the message, and I'll make sure Ho passes it along."

"If all goes well you won't hear from me again, so I'll thank you now for everything. I don't know how I'll repay you for all these favours," she said.

"Feel free to call me anytime. The watches and phones make us even, so you owe me nothing but the thanks you've already given."

That went well, Ava thought as she ended the call. Asking Zhao to lean harder on Ho might be unnecessary, but she didn't want the Chongs to believe they could renege on their deal. They had to accept her terms and then move on as if it had never happened.

Ava's phone sounded and she saw a text from Lydia Lazim: Commissioner Chik isn't in the office today. I was told he's travelling on official business.

Ava wondered if she should take Sonny with her to the meeting. *No,* she decided. *That would be an overreaction. His presence might be seen as a provocation.*

38

BRENDA BURGESS PHONED AVA AT TEN TO THREE. "I'M
a little early," she said. "I'm downstairs in the lobby."

"I'll be right down."

Ava applied a little lipstick, then brushed back her hair
and secured it with her lucky ivory chignon pin. Back in the
living room, she put her notebook in the LV bag and called
Douglas Brooke.

"Brenda is here. We'll meet in Café Causette in fifteen
minutes."

"See you there."

Brooke's flight had arrived on time and, when he got to
the hotel, Ava had spoken to him briefly to confirm their
meeting.

The rest of Ava's afternoon had been spent on the phone
with May Ling and Amanda. May had updated Ava and
Amanda on the happenings at PÖ — the Po siblings were
discussing launching a perfume line — and then Ava brought
up the idea of selling the furniture business in Kota Kinabalu.

"I'd like to be rid of it," May said.

"Me too," Amanda agreed.

"Then it's decided. But let's settle this dispute with the Chongs before we start negotiating with Aisyah," Ava said.

"How optimistic are you that you can do that today?" May asked.

"All the decision makers will be seated at the table, so it will depend on their willingness to be practical," Ava said. "By now Zhao should have told the Chongs' banker that Jennie Kwong is someone they need to treat with respect."

"Good luck with Jennie," May said.

"Thanks. I'll call you both when I have a better idea of how things are going to play out."

I'm blessed to be associated with so many fine people, Ava thought as she stepped into the elevator. Her partners had never failed her.

Brenda was standing near the elevator when Ava arrived in the lobby. The women shared a hug.

"Douglas Brooke is here. He'll meet us in the café in a few minutes," said Ava.

"What about the group from Kuching?"

"They landed a few hours ago. Xu phoned me after they cleared Customs."

"I did some reading about Sulaiman Chong," Brenda said as they walked towards the café. "He's quite the man — a hands-on political powerhouse, the wealthiest man in Sarawak, one of the richest in Malaysia, and now he's built a Hong Kong real estate empire that must generate a measure of respect from our local authorities."

"Are you suggesting he has ties to politicians in Hong Kong or China?"

"Many of their real estate holdings have minority partners. I didn't recognize any of the names, but I wouldn't be surprised if some were mainland Chinese. They could have direct connections, although typically they prefer to use Hong Kong intermediaries," Brenda said. "Either way, Chief Minister Chong is someone to be taken seriously."

"Believe me, I'm taking him seriously. But that doesn't mean I'm prepared to back down."

"I wouldn't expect it any other way."

Ava and Brenda took a table against the wall with a clear view of the entrance. At that time of day the café was quiet.

"How did you find Douglas Brooke?" Brenda asked after they had ordered coffee.

"We were introduced by the brother of one of our business partners. He knew Brooke in university and went to him for help when the trouble began in Kuching," said Ava. "I don't know how good a lawyer he is, but he knows how things operate in Sarawak, and he knows the Chong family. I've been satisfied with him so far."

"I'm surprised he's so willing to alienate the Chongs," Brenda said, and then quickly added, "By that I mean he's living in a rather closed society in Sarawak, a society where Sulaiman Chong has the power to reward and to punish."

"Brooke may feel insulated from the family by his family history. He's a direct descendant of the white rajahs," Ava said as she glanced at the café entrance. "And here he is now."

Brooke was wearing a freshly pressed navy-blue pinstripe suit that made him look far more impressive than Ava's first impression of him in Kuching. Ava waved at him and he nodded in recognition and walked to their table. She also saw that he wasn't as pale or frail-looking as he had been at their first meeting, and wondered if perhaps he had been hungover.

"Brenda Burgess, this is Douglas Brooke. And vice versa, of course," said Ava.

"Pleased to meet you," Brooke said to Brenda. "I'm delighted to have a partner in this adventure that Ms. Lee — or Ms. Kwong, as I'm to call her today — has embarked us on."

"Here it's Ava, but in the meeting it will be Ms. Kwong," said Ava. "As for adventure, that part has finished. Our job now is to negotiate a settlement and paper it so tightly that it defies litigation."

The server arrived at the table with a pot of coffee and two cups and saucers.

"Will you have coffee?" Ava asked Brooke.

"I'd love some."

"Could you arrange another setting, please?" Ava asked the server.

When the coffee had been poured, Ava turned to Brooke. "I'm sorry I couldn't be there to meet you when you arrived. I was involved in a discussion with my business partners that I couldn't get away from."

"It wasn't a problem. Your driver took very good care of me."

"The group from Kuching arrived around the same time as you. We haven't had a chance to discuss that," Ava said. "Do you know a man named Jaffar? I'm told he's a lawyer."

"He's the Chong family's personal attorney and has Sulaiman's complete trust. I'm not surprised Sulaiman sent him."

"Sulaiman *brought* him. The Chief Minister is here in Hong Kong, as are Ahmad, Commissioner Chik, and two members of the Minister's security team."

"Good grief! They're taking this very seriously," said Brooke.

"As they should. But tell me, why do you think Chik is here?" asked Ava.

"He could be overseeing security details, or — and I think this is more likely — he could be here to offer his opinion on revising the police statement," Brooke said.

"Maybe they think that part of our demands is negotiable," Brenda said.

"Well, it isn't," said Ava.

"What role do you want us to play?" Brenda asked.

"Be prepared for me to send questions in your direction, but otherwise I'll do the heavy lifting," Ava said, then looked at Brooke. "Assuming I can reach an understanding with Sulaiman, do you think Jaffar will present an obstacle to you and Brenda?"

"He'll do what Sulaiman tells him to do. The danger is that Sulaiman will give him haggling room by being less than exact in his instructions."

"Then it falls to me to ensure that doesn't happen," Ava said.

"I don't mean to sound pessimistic, but Sulaiman is famously obtuse. His pattern is to give what seem like clear directions while leaving room for several interpretations. That way, if things go wrong, he can always claim his wishes were misconstrued."

"In other words, he's a politician," Brenda said.

"A very talented politician, with a finely honed instinct for survival," said Brooke.

"Duly noted," said Ava as she glanced at her watch. "We should get going. I thought we would walk to the building."

"Ava, before we go, I have a slightly odd question for you," Brooke said.

"Go ahead."

"Well, you mentioned there's a small security team with Sulaiman, and I wouldn't be surprised if that was buttressed by men hired by Martin Bowles. What if they ask for ID? What happens to Jennie Kwong?"

Ava reached into her LV bag. "This is Jennie Kwong's passport, and she also has a Hong Kong ID card."

Brooke raised an eyebrow.

"Welcome to Ava's world," Brenda said with a smile.

39

THEY LEFT THE HOTEL AND EASED THEMSELVES INTO THE early pedestrian rush hour. Brenda led the way, accustomed to timing traffic lights and manoeuvring around knots of people. Ava followed alongside while Brooke struggled to keep pace, obviously a fish out of water. But even Brenda was brought to a halt when they reached Jubilee Street. Barriers manned by police officers had been erected at either side of the intersection and it was closed to traffic.

Ava approached the officers. "Are you allowing pedestrians to enter the street?" she asked. "We have a meeting in the CIC Building."

"You can go through, but we're obliged to tell you it's at your own risk," an officer said. "We can't guarantee that the area is entirely safe."

"We understand, and thank you for the warning," she said.

Ava slipped around the barrier and started down the street, past a line of dumpsters filled with debris from the explosion. Despite the best efforts of the cleanup crew, shards of glass and small pieces of wood and metal were still visible on the ground. As they neared the CIC Building, Ava saw another row of barriers with five security guards standing around them. It would have looked like a war zone if there hadn't been people in business attire coming and going from the building.

"You really did a number on this place," Brenda said quietly.

"I'm surprised the building is open," said Brooke.

"They've had two days to clean up. Besides, we blew up the lobby, that's all. I'm sure the elevators and basic services weren't damaged."

Ava had expected the guards would request their IDs, or at the very least ask what business they had in the building, but other than eyeing them they did nothing. As they entered what was left of the lobby, Ava got a better sense of the damage. A wall of plastic sheeting separated what had been the shopping mall from the main lobby; the floor was dusty and the air seemed heavy. The reception desk had been destroyed, but there was a temporary metal desk with a young woman sitting uncomfortably behind it. Ava approached her.

"We have a meeting with Mr. Bowles in the CIC conference room," she said.

"That's on the thirty-eighth floor," the woman said, pointing in the direction of the elevators. "Only two are in service, so you might have to wait."

"We don't mind."

"I thought security would be tighter," Brooke said.

"Why? They know I'm the only danger they face, and I'm going to be in the room with them."

The wait was several minutes, but after a jammed elevator emptied out, the trio stepped inside as the only passengers.

The thirty-eighth floor couldn't have been more different

from the lobby. Ava walked across rich, colourful rugs to an expansive teak reception module that had four chairs, two of which were occupied. On the wall behind the module, a sign read CIC EXECUTIVE OFFICES. On either side was a series of unidentified closed doors. One of the doors was flanked by two large men wearing jeans and zippered windbreakers. Ava saw bulges on their hips. "Do you recognize those men?" she whispered to Brooke.

"The Din brothers," he said.

"Well, at least we know where they are." Ava smiled at the receptionist. "My name is Jennie Kwong. My associates and I have an appointment with Mr. Bowles and Mr. Saad."

"They're expecting you. Just one moment," the receptionist said, picking up a phone. "They're ready for you. Let me show you the way."

The woman led them to where the Din brothers stood guard. The men glared at the trio as the receptionist knocked, waited, and then opened the door.

The conference room was smaller and more functional than Ava had expected. The walls were painted a neutral colour and the furniture consisted of a large wooden table with a dozen nondescript metal chairs set around it and two bare credenzas. Even the view was disappointing, as the windows looked out onto the neighbouring building.

Saad, Bowles, and three other men sat at one end of the table. Ava recognized Sulaiman Chong from his photos and assumed the younger of the other two was Ahmad.

"Why don't you sit over there," Saad said, pointing to the furthest point from them.

"Sure," said Ava, realizing that civility was going to be in short supply.

"The Chinese woman is Jennie Kwong," Saad said to no one in particular.

"That's me," Ava said as she sat down. "And these are Douglas Brooke and Brenda Burgess. Mr. Brooke is our legal representative and Ms. Burgess is the lawyer for Three Sisters Investments."

"I don't know why Ms. Burgess is here, but that's your business," Saad said. "Sitting with me is Sulaiman Chong, the Chief Minister of Sarawak; Ahmad Chong, the CEO of Chong Enterprises; and Mohammed Jaffar, our corporate lawyer."

Ahmad leaned forward. "Brooke, I can't understand why you agreed to work with these people," he said harshly. "They've declared war on Sarawak, and you're here in support of them? There will be consequences."

Ahmad was in his forties, Ava guessed, and a type of man she had encountered in business more often than she cared to remember. He was the son of a rich man, the heir apparent to an inherited empire rather than one he'd built, and that gave him a deep sense of entitlement. Ahmad was wearing a grey suit that looked tailor-made, with a white silk shirt and an Armani tie. His hair was combed straight back and he had a moustache that looked like a fat black caterpillar resting on his lip.

Before Brooke could react, Ava said, "We needed a lawyer, and Mr. Brooke came highly recommended as someone who is knowledgeable and unbiased. That's all there is to that. Though, I should add, he has our full protection. So whatever 'consequences' you have planned, you can forget it."

"What sort of protection are you talking about?" Ahmad snarled.

"I think you know," said Ava.

"I'd like to hear it," said Ahmad.

Ava looked at Sulaiman Chong. "I understand that Ahmad is your son, but do you think it's wise to involve him in these negotiations?"

Ahmad rose to his feet. "You bitch!" he shouted.

Ava shook her head. "Mr. Chong, either you control your son or ask him to leave. We would like to keep this professional, and his behaviour is unacceptable."

Sulaiman stared across the table at Ava. He was smaller in person than she had expected, and to Ava he looked frail, maybe even ill. But whatever physical shortcomings he might have, Sulaiman Chong made up for with eyes that bored into her with sheer hatred. "Emotions are running high on our side. Given the events of the last few days, I think you can understand why," he said in a calm and measured tone, though his eyes lost none of their intensity.

"It's been a difficult time for everyone," said Ava. "A business was destroyed, a woman murdered, and her name slandered in the media. Those involved could have struck back in kind, but they chose to take the high road. That's something for you to keep in mind."

Mohammed Jaffar leaned towards Sulaiman and shielded his mouth as he spoke to him. When Sulaiman nodded, Jaffar said to Ava, "I would like to change the subject if I may."

"Go right ahead."

Jaffar nodded. "You referred to the loss of a business, but surely the warehouse was insured?"

"Since the police have suggested that Jamilah Daeng, the employee who died from injuries suffered in the blast, was herself responsible for the attack, the insurance company says the policy is rendered null and void."

"We might be in a position to persuade the insurance company to change its position," said Jaffar.

"It doesn't matter now. The loss has already been covered with money from Mr. Bowles's account."

"And that loss was how much exactly?" asked Jaffar.

"We calculated it at five million U.S. dollars."

"But you took forty-seven million from Mr. Bowles. That should leave a balance of forty-two million," said Jaffar.

"As I told Mr. Saad yesterday, the balance is thirty-five million. The difference was donated to environmental and Indigenous rights groups in Sarawak in the name of Jamilah Daeng."

"That's crazy," Ahmad said. "They won't have a clue what to do with that kind of money."

Jaffar leaned forward to block Ahmad. "When you say 'donated,' do you mean the money has already been transferred?"

"Yes."

"We'll deal with that later. For now, let's focus on the thirty-five million," Sulaiman said to Jaffar.

The lawyer nodded. "We want it returned," he said to Ava.

"Of course you do. And you can have it. All you have to do is meet our conditions."

Sulaiman turned to Saad. "Arven, remind me. What are this woman's demands?"

Saad ran his index finger along his lips as he prepared to speak.

"Mr. Chong," Ava interrupted, "rather than have Mr. Saad recite them from memory, I will give them to you directly, so there's no chance of misunderstanding."

"If you must," Sulaiman said, his voice taking on an edge.

Until then neither Brenda nor Brooke had appeared to react to any part of the conversation. Now Brenda took a notepad from her briefcase and uncapped a pen.

"I should start by saying that if we reach an agreement here today, we want it properly documented," Ava said. "That's one reason both Ms. Burgess and Mr. Brooke are here with me. My client doesn't believe in verbal contracts or handshakes."

"I don't either, which is why Mr. Jaffar is here," Sulaiman snapped. "Now proceed."

Ava ignored that last comment and looked at each of them in turn as she laid out her demands, slowly and carefully. Bowles was visibly agitated as he listened, while the others were impassive.

When Ava finished, Jaffar spoke. "That was all very interesting, but without acknowledging there's an ounce of truth to your allegations, what evidence do you have to suggest that someone attached to the Chong organization was involved in the warehouse bombing?"

"We have a source inside the Kuching police contingent who informed us that Mr. Saad met with Commissioner Chik immediately after the bombing. The two of them concocted a story about the bombing being carried out by Jamilah on behalf of some radical environmental group, the Sarawak United Front, and then determined that Jamilah's death should be classified as the result of misadventure," she said.

"And you aren't going to tell us who this source is, are you," said Jaffar.

"No, but their credibility is impeccable," said Ava.

"And if it wasn't the woman, who did set the bombs? Did your source give you a name?"

"No, but there's only one logical conclusion."

"Are you suggesting that Mr. Saad ordered the bombing of the warehouse?"

"Maybe he didn't give the direct order, but I can imagine a scenario where he told someone the lumber business was becoming a problem and needed to be shut down. Maybe he left the details vague, or maybe he didn't. But when a life was lost, he needed to put a spin on what had happened. So they decided the blame should be attributed to Jamilah. And since she was dead, there was no one to contradict them."

Sulaiman looked at Brooke. "Douglas, are you really going to lend your support to this fantasy?"

"From what I've heard, there's substance to it. I won't dismiss it out of hand," Brooke replied.

"I have an idea," Ava said. "Why don't we ask the other participant directly?"

"What are you suggesting?" asked Sulaiman.

"Commissioner Chik flew into Hong Kong with you today. I imagine you've got him stashed away somewhere nearby. Why don't you send someone to get him?"

Ahmad's face fell, but Ava was happier to see Sulaiman flinch. It was a slight movement, just a tic of his right eyelid, but she knew she'd struck home.

There was a pause, and then Jaffar said, "Could you leave the room for a few minutes? I would like to speak to my clients in private."

40

AVA, BRENDA, AND BROOKE WERE SITTING ON A SOFA outside the conference room.

"Do you really think Chik is nearby?" Brooke asked softly.

"It makes sense to me, and Sulaiman flinched when I asked about him," Ava answered.

"You know these men, Douglas. How do you think the meeting is going?" Brenda asked.

"I thought Ava made her case very well, but I still can't imagine them voluntarily giving up anything," Brooke said, pursing his lips. "Sulaiman is accustomed to getting his way. Surely he must expect that nothing will be different here. His style is to demand and then stand firm. He believes 'compromise' is a word that describes losers. I expect that's how he'll behave —"

Brooke was interrupted by an office door opening. A man emerged, glanced at the trio on the sofa, and walked over to the conference room. One of the Din brothers opened the door for him and he disappeared inside.

"Was that Chik?" Ava asked.

"Yes. I'm surprised to see that he isn't wearing his uniform."

"That could be a message that he's here in the employ of

the Chong family, not as the police commissioner," Ava said. "Parading him in front of us could be their way of telling us he's part of their team."

"And if that is the case?" Brenda asked.

"Then there might not be a deal after all."

"I hope they're reasonable," Brenda said. "I'll support you however this turns out, but you need to know there'll be risk attached to pursuing them."

"I know, and that isn't my first choice. But it's their decision how this plays out."

They lapsed into a silence that lasted several minutes, until Brenda said, "I don't think I've ever been to a meeting in Hong Kong where I wasn't offered something to drink. If this is meant as an insult, it's trivial and small-minded."

"I guess we're not held in much esteem here," Ava said with a smile.

The minutes dragged by. Ava stared at the conference room door as she weighed Brenda's comment about risk against her own willingness to compromise.

"He's leaving," Brooke said, interrupting Ava's internal debate.

She looked across the lobby as Chik walked back to the office he'd come out of earlier. This time he didn't look in their direction, and Ava thought his manner was almost furtive.

Jaffar appeared in the doorway. "We're ready to resume," he said loudly.

Ava led Brenda and Brooke back to the conference room, where they retook their places at the table.

"I hope Commissioner Chik was forthcoming," Ava said as she sat down.

"He clarified a few things," Jaffar said matter-of-factly.

"Foremost of which is that he didn't discuss the bombing or its effects with Mr. Saad in the manner you describe."

"I don't believe that for a second," said Ava.

Sulaiman waved a hand dismissively in her direction. "We'll never agree on that topic, so there's no point talking about it further," he said. "Let's talk about money."

"I've already told you my terms. Money isn't the only consideration here today."

"We understand that you believe you have a strong hand, but we aren't convinced it's as strong as you think," said Jaffar. "You're little more than thieves, and Commissioner Chik has offered to approach the Hong Kong police to file a complaint. But for now, we prefer to keep this affair private."

"How prudent of you."

"We have our own Hong Kong lawyers. If we can't reach an accommodation, we can make life very uncomfortable for you," Jaffar said.

"And we could tie you up in court for years, using your own money," said Ava. "Even if you eventually won, you'd have to find the money, which is already offshore in a jurisdiction that looks unkindly upon illegal logging."

Jaffar looked at Sulaiman with a combination of frustration and resignation. Grim-faced, Sulaiman nodded.

"Of course, that was just a hypothetical scenario. As unhappy as it makes us, we are prepared to make you an offer to settle this matter," Jaffar said.

"What do you propose?"

"We will cover the loss of the warehouse. You said it was five million dollars. We doubt the building and the inventory were worth anything close to that, but we'll allow you to keep that amount."

Ava shook her head. "You have this backwards. I'm the one who has the money. Right now, it isn't yours to give."

Sulaiman's face tightened, and Ava knew he was starting to lose control.

Jaffar looked at Brooke and Brenda. "Mr. Brooke, Ms. Burgess, surely you both can't believe that Ms. Kwong has the right to do what she wants with money she stole."

"I'm not in a position to comment on the legality of who owns what," Brooke said.

"Neither am I, but if you negotiate in good faith with Ms. Kwong, I don't see why all the questions about the money can't be resolved," said Brenda.

Jaffar turned his attention to Ava. "We've made an offer."

"Yes, and it makes me think you aren't taking me seriously. Putting the money aside, you've made no mention of my other requests. In case you've forgotten, I want the true cause of Jamilah Daeng's death made public, and I want someone to be held accountable," she said, then turned to Brooke. "Douglas, help me with this. Under Malaysian law, if someone sets a bomb with the sole intention of destroying property but accidentally causes a death, what would the charges be?"

"At the most severe end of the spectrum, that person could be charged with murder," Brooke said carefully, looking at Jaffar. "At the most lenient, if the bomb at the warehouse was intended to damage property only, then it could be a charge of involuntary manslaughter."

"What are the penalties attached to those charges?"

"For the first it could be life imprisonment, and for the second, as little as a year or two in jail."

"Would you agree with that range?" Ava asked Jaffar.

"I'm not a criminal lawyer," he said.

"And Brooke isn't much of one either," Ahmad said, leaning forward to reinsert himself into the conversation.

"I agree with my son. To my mind, that makes any discussion about accountability pointless," said Sulaiman. "Anyway, at the end of the day it all comes down to money. So let's fix an amount and close the deal."

"Just like that?" Ava asked.

"Why not? You said you'll return thirty-five million, which means you would keep twelve," said Sulaiman. "We offered you five, but I'm prepared to meet you partway. We'll give you eight million."

"What do you say?" Jaffar asked, and then looked at Brooke and Brenda. "I think it's a fair offer, a reasonable compromise."

"It isn't my decision, and I'm not about to give my client advice in front of you," said Brooke.

"Of course not. Would you like to adjourn to another room to discuss it?" asked Jaffar.

"If my non-financial terms aren't part of the package, there's nothing to discuss," Ava said, abruptly rising to her feet.

"Are you really stuck on that?" Jaffar asked.

"Yes, I am, so why don't you discuss that with your group," she said. "We're leaving. Mr. Saad has my cell number and I'm sure one of you has Douglas's. Call either of us if you want to pursue this any further."

Ava headed for the door, followed by Brooke and Brenda. When she opened it, she was confronted by the Din brothers. Behind them she could see Chik lurking.

"You're going to regret this!" Ahmad shouted.

For a few seconds Ava thought the brothers would try to stop them from leaving. Then Jaffar said loudly, "Let them pass," and they moved aside.

Chik was only a few metres away. It was her first opportunity to really look at him. He was tall and brawny, and even in a polo shirt and grey slacks, he looked like a military man. He smiled at her grimly and held up the photo that had been taken of her at the Kuching police station. "This was just sent to me," he said. "I knew it was you, but I wanted confirmation."

"Congratulations," said Ava.

"Whether you know it or not, there's an outstanding assault charge against you in Kuching that's waiting to be exercised."

"This isn't Kuching."

"No, but our laws can be brought to bear elsewhere. You're too confident for your own good, Ava Lee."

41

THEY DIDN'T SPEAK UNTIL THEY HAD WALKED THROUGH the makeshift lobby door onto Jubilee Street. Finally Brooke broke the silence. "They know who you are."

"Knowing who I am doesn't change anything," Ava said.

"What if it means there won't be a deal?"

"Then we'll see who can inflict the most damage. I don't want it to end up like that, but if it does, I like my chances."

"Is working with her always like this?" he asked Brenda.

"Usually. Sometimes it's even crazier, but every once in a while Ava tosses an easy task our way," Brenda said. "She and her partners are my firm's favourite clients."

"Where did you learn to negotiate like that?" Brooke asked Ava as they approached the barriers at the end of the block. She slid around one and turned to face him.

"My mother was my first teacher. With the exception of food, she treated every price tag as an invitation to haggle. It was less about saving money than of getting value, and she wouldn't stop until she got it or walked away. Walking away was something she was never reluctant to do, and I saw that it often worked as a tactic.

"My other role model was my former partner, Uncle. He showed me how to operate on a larger, macro level. He taught me to think about the big picture and to start every negotiation with the best possible result as my goal. Obviously the best result isn't always possible, but he counselled me to give ground grudgingly and to have a clearly defined bottom line. When it came to that bottom line, Uncle was also very clear that if he didn't achieve his goal, there had to be consequences for the other side. My mother would walk away, but Uncle would wreak havoc."

"So you are serious about the threats you made?"

"They're promises, not threats. If they call you first — which they might — you should make it clear that if there's no deal, Martin Bowles will never be able to get in a car again without wondering if it's going to explode; none of their Hong Kong real estate holdings can have enough security to protect them; and we're prepared to spend their thirty-five million dollars connecting the Chong name to ecological destruction and genocide."

Brooke went quiet. They walked the next block in silence until Brenda asked, "Assuming you get it, how do you want us to paper the twelve million?"

"They know my real name now, but the money flowed through an account in the name of Jennie Kwong, so we need to reference that in the agreement. We could make it a payment to Jennie Kwong to the benefit of the Three Sisters for the damages incurred in Kuching. Would that work?"

"I think so. And the payment will have to be irrevocable, with Jennie and/or Three Sisters able to allocate the money as they see fit. The beneficiaries of Three Sisters' donations will have the same irrevocable rights."

"We'll have to let the recipients know that the donations are protected from seizure."

"Of course," Brenda said.

"And that we're there to provide legal or other forms of assistance if they need it."

"If I can get the other party to indemnify Three Sisters and the organizations from any claim or legal action, that will look after it."

Rush hour was in full swing, and they were quickly surrounded by a sea of people. They shuffled along in silence until the Mandarin Oriental came into view. "Do either of you want to join me in M Bar for a drink?" Ava asked.

"Yes," Brooke and Brenda said simultaneously.

Ava found a table near the window.

"It's been years since I was in Hong Kong," Brooke said as he sat down. "I've seen images of the harbourfront, but none of them do it justice. It's hard to believe how much things have changed."

"My husband says the only constant in Hong Kong is change," Brenda said. "Nothing seems to stay the same for very long."

A server arrived at the table and a moment later left with their drink orders.

"Well, all in all, how do you think the first round went?" Ava asked.

"The offer of eight million was a step in the right direction," said Brenda. "I won't be surprised if they're willing to settle at ten."

"What about the non-financial demands? It didn't seem to me that they're willing to change the story," Ava said to Brooke.

"I was thinking about that as we were walking here," he

said. "Sulaiman is fanatical about protecting his reputation. He considers himself to be Sarawak's leading citizen. He might be okay with the police changing their statement about the bombing, but I can't see him agreeing to have the Chong name associated with it in any way."

"What if we kept their name out of it but found a way to implicate Saad?"

"In the minds of the public, and even at official levels in Kuala Lumpur, Saad and the Chong family are inseparable."

Brenda turned to Ava. "Tell me, in all of this, what's most important to you, securing the money or the non-financial factors?"

"The non-financial."

"And of those, what matters most, correcting the public record about the death of your employee or seeing the Chong family vilified?"

Ava sighed, sipped some wine, and said, "Jamilah's parents believe their daughter's soul is condemned to hell because she took her own life. I can't imagine the kind of misery and pain that belief is causing them. If I can alleviate it — and nothing else — all this will have been worth it."

"I'm pleased to hear that," said Brenda.

"But it doesn't mean I'm ready to settle for only that."

"Of course not —" Brenda began, and then stopped as Brooke's phone began to ring.

Two sets of eyes watched as he took it from his pocket. "Yes, this is Douglas Brooke," he answered. He listened for several seconds and then said, "Jaffar, I'm in a bar and it's noisy. Give me a moment to walk outside so I can hear you properly." Then he covered the microphone and looked at Ava questioningly.

"Go. If he has any doubts about how determined I am, tell him I'm a crazy woman, capable of doing anything," she said.

"I'll deliver that message," he said with a smile.

"He looks slightly seedy, but his mind is sharp enough," Brenda said when Brooke had left.

Ava could see him outside the bar. "Douglas looks quite animated."

"I'm quite sure he hasn't had many opportunities to dictate to the Chong family," Brenda said.

"He's coming back."

Brooke's face was impassive as he approached. He picked up his glass of Scotch, took a long swallow, and then smiled. "Jaffar wants to reconvene. He said Sulaiman isn't convinced it's the right move, but he and Saad persuaded him to give it another go."

"What did you say?" Ava asked.

"I told him I had to talk to you."

"I'm prepared to meet, but let's not look too eager. When is he expecting an answer?"

"He said if they don't hear from us by ten o'clock, they'll start making arrangements to return to Kuching," Brooke said.

Ava checked the time. "We'll meet them at nine, but hold off calling them until eight."

"Where do you want to meet?"

"Here, at the hotel. I'll reserve one of the boardrooms next to the business centre."

"May I make a suggestion?" Brenda asked.

"Sure," Ava said.

"I agree with making them wait, but that gives us more than three hours to kill. Rather than wasting it, I'd like to suggest that Douglas and I head over to my office to begin drafting an agreement," she said. "I have a feeling you're going to get most of what you want."

"Yes, let's be positive," Ava said. "Douglas, are you okay with that?"

"Absolutely."

"I understand how you want to protect the twelve million, but I'm less sure what you want when it comes to the death," said Brenda.

"I want the police to issue a statement saying they've re-examined the evidence and have decided to reopen the investigation into the warehouse bombing. They have to state, without equivocation, that they now believe Jamilah wasn't responsible for anything that occurred and that her death is being treated as a homicide," Ava said. "They need to say, at the very least, that no environmental organization was connected to the bombing and that they now suspect it was instigated by a business rival. I also want a senior member of the department to speak to Jamilah's parents and advise them of the new findings. And last, the truth about the bombing and Jamilah's death has to be properly reported in the *Sarawak Daily Journal* and other local media."

"What about accountability?"

"On a completely practical level, I think I have to let that go. On the one hand, it would be comforting to know that justice can be won, but on the other, I suspect it might be a deal-breaker for Sulaiman. Besides, it won't really do any-thing for Jamilah or her family," Ava said. "Douglas, what do you think?"

"I agree with you. It's a laudable objective, but given the realities of what we're dealing with, I think it's unrealistic to expect that anyone will ever be charged, let alone convicted. Actually, if the case is indeed reopened, I expect it will be in name only — nothing will be investigated. I also think you're absolutely correct about Sulaiman. Even getting him to accept a vague reference to a business rival in the police statement is going to be a challenge."

"Okay, then we let it go. It will be our contribution to compromise."

"We'll proceed on that basis," Brenda said, rising from her chair. "Douglas, let's go."

"My cell will be on. Call me after you speak to Jaffar."

As they left, Ava thought about ordering another glass of wine, but decided if she wanted to stay sharp, one was enough. She felt hunger pangs and was debating ordering room service when she noted the presence of a man standing in front of her. He smiled. She guessed he was in his late thirties or early forties. He was clean-shaven, with a full head of hair, and trimly built. He wore a blue pinstripe suit with a cream shirt and sported a red Ferragamo logo tie.

"I saw you the other night when I was here with Marcus Lee and some friends."

"I'm sorry, I know Marcus, but I don't know you."

He smiled knowingly. "Marcus said you're his daughter, but none of us really believed that."

"Why not?"

"We all know he has four sons. But whether you're his daughter or his girlfriend, I would like to buy you a drink. And if that goes well, maybe we could have dinner."

Ava stiffened at the man's use of 'girlfriend.' In Hong Kong male business circles a so-called girlfriend was often paid for her company. She struggled to restrain her temper as she looked at him. "He told me you're thinking of hiring his company to manage some of your properties," she said.

"We are, but nothing has been finalized."

"I'm sure he and his sons would do a great job," she said, rising from her seat.

"You're leaving?"

"I have a meeting, and it isn't with Marcus — who does happen to be my father."

"If I gave any offence —" the man said.

"Not to worry," said Ava as she strode past him and out of the bar. As soon as she reached her room, she called Marcus's cell.

"Ava?" he answered, sounding surprised.

"Apologies to Elizabeth for calling at this time, but I was just approached by one of the men who were with you the other night in M Bar," she said.

"You sound angry."

"Are you still thinking of doing business with them?"

"Yes."

"Do me a favour and don't," she said. "And when they ask you why, tell them your daughter — who is definitely not your girlfriend — didn't appreciate being hit on in M Bar. He stopped short of asking how much I charge for an evening, but not by much. Is that reason enough?"

"More than enough."

"Thank you, Daddy."

42

AFTER SPEAKING TO HER FATHER, AVA SANK INTO THE chair at the desk. She knew she might have overreacted to the drink-and-dinner proposition, but there was no doubting the guy's underlying assumption. It was insulting to both her and Marcus, and she didn't know which angered her the most. Still, she knew she could have let it go and not involved Marcus.

Her reaction was a sign that she was on edge. She needed to get the business with the Chongs resolved and put behind her. With that front of mind, she called the business centre to book a boardroom for nine o'clock. Next she phoned Brenda's cell.

"I didn't expect to hear from you so soon," Brenda answered.

"I wanted to confirm that we have a boardroom reserved for nine o'clock," said Ava. "Why don't we meet at eight-thirty to go over our strategy. Call me from the lobby when you get to the hotel."

"Okay. I'll tell Douglas."

As Ava hung up, her hunger pangs returned. She reached

for a menu and a moment later was ordering a cheeseburger and fries from room service. It wasn't her typical Hong Kong meal, but she had a craving.

While she waited for her food, Ava opened her notebook and wrote *Terms and Conditions* across the top of a blank page. *What am I really prepared to settle for?* she thought. The twelve million was a given. None of that was going to be returned, and she had to ensure that Brenda's document completely shielded Three Sisters and the organizations in Sarawak she'd given money to from any legal action aimed at reclaiming it.

She was sure Sulaiman would agree to have Jamilah's death reclassified as a homicide. There was no cost attached to that unless Saad or a Chong business was directly implicated, and that wasn't going to happen.

Would Sulaiman agree to the police saying they believed the warehouse bombing was the work of a business rival? If no rivals were named, why should the Chongs care? Except she imagined they would care if Brooke was correct about the public assuming they were behind the bombing. But it was a point Ava wasn't ready to concede.

What about the *Sarawak Daily Journal* and the other media? Would Sulaiman resist their reporting that the police had changed their position? Ava had little doubt that his influence over the media was close to absolute, but she expected him to say otherwise.

Given Ava's willingness to concede on someone's being held accountable, she thought everything else she wanted would be a reasonable ask. But even if she got agreement and they made the money work, there was one last thing she couldn't ignore. Ava, Amanda, May Ling, and all Three

Sisters' employees and businesses, including the furniture factory in Kota Kinabalu, could still be at risk. She had no doubts that the Chong family was vengeful. Once their money had been returned and they were safely back in Kuching, thoughts of payback would begin to surface. How could she minimize the risk they posed?

She reached for her phone and called Kowloon.

"Ava, your ears must be burning," Zhao said when he answered.

"Why's that?"

"I'm with Uncle Fong and some other old friends. We were just talking about your adventures with Uncle."

"If you don't mind, I'd like to speak to Fong for a minute," she said.

"Ava, I didn't know you were in Hong Kong," Fong said seconds later.

"I'm just passing through on some quick business."

"Zhao mentioned something about that, but he's too discreet to provide any details."

"It's nothing worth mentioning," she said. "How are you? Staying out of trouble?"

"I haven't been to Macau in almost a year, if that's what you mean. And I've actually been able to save a good part of the money you send me every month. I can't remember the last time I had so much cash on hand."

Ava laughed. Uncle Fong was addicted to gambling, and over the years he had left most of his money on the gaming tables in Macau. He had been Uncle's oldest friend and a cohort in the Fanling triads, which Uncle had headed for decades. When Uncle died, one of his requests to Ava had been that she make Fong's later years free of money worries.

She had honoured that request, and she also made sure
Sonny checked in on him once a week. "Then the next time
I'm in Hong Kong, you can take me out to dinner," she said.

"I'd like nothing better. . . . Now I'm passing you back to
Zhao."

"What can I do for you this evening?" Zhao asked.

"I apologize for bothering you again, but I need one last
favour. I know I said that before, but this time I swear I mean
it," she said.

Zhao laughed. "What do you need me to do?"

"I know you've spoken to Ronald Ho on my behalf.
Although I trust that he's passed along your messages,
I think I need to go one step further. And there will never
be a better opportunity than tonight."

43

BRENDA BURGESS PHONED AVA FROM THE HOTEL LOBBY at eight-thirty exactly. Ava gave her the room number and stood in the hallway to meet her and Brooke.

After talking to Zhao, she had eaten dinner, spoken to Fai, changed her clothes, and spent some time reviewing what she had written in her notebook. She was keen to see what Brooke and Brenda had come up with, and how it would fit with the direction she had decided to take.

Brenda waved at Ava as she and Brooke got out of the elevator. Ava took a few steps towards them. "I'm sorry for rushing you like this," she said. "Were you able to pull something together?"

"It turned out we're a pretty good team. I don't think we did too badly," Brenda said.

Ava led them into the suite. Brenda reached into her briefcase and placed two pieces of paper on the coffee table. "It's concise, but I think it gets to the core of what you want. By the time we've finished boilerplating it, the final document will run to about ten pages."

Ava picked up the top sheet. "While I read this, please help yourselves to whatever you want from the minibar. There's also water on the desk, and the coffee machine makes a good brew."

"I'll get some water," Brenda said.

"Nothing for me," said Brooke.

Ava could feel Brooke's eyes on her as she began to read, which made her slightly uncomfortable. Brenda must have sensed the awkwardness. "Douglas, come and join me at the window. The harbourfront is particularly beautiful tonight."

The draft was in point form. Ava scanned it quickly and then went back through it more thoroughly. "If they agree to this, I can't see any way they can reclaim any part of the twelve million," she said.

Brenda turned away from the window. "Yes. We're requesting indemnities for everyone we could think of. But you still have to give us the names and contact information for the organizations you sent money to, so we can add those details."

"I will, after we get an agreement," said Ava. "But I see you didn't list the conditions we want them to meet before we send back the thirty-five million."

"Douglas and I discussed that. Our opinion is that they're best left out until we know what's decided. We did start putting them on paper, but we stopped when we realized it's better for you to continue expressing them verbally."

"I think you're right. Besides, I've decided to back off on a few of those demands if we can get a quick deal that's going to stick."

"In this case, I think having some measure of flexibility is a shrewd tactic," Brenda said.

"Well, Uncle used to say that when you corner a rat, you

leave him no choice but to attack you. You need to give the rat a sense that all isn't lost, and that there is a way out for him. Of course, there really isn't, but by the time he realizes it, you've got what you wanted. I haven't always followed that advice, but this is one occasion when I think the strength of the rat makes it appropriate."

Brenda looked at her watch. "If you want us to be in the boardroom when they arrive, we should probably head down there now."

"Did you bring copies of this draft?"

"We did."

"Don't hand them out until we have an overall agreement."

"Okay."

Ava stood up. "Let's go."

They rode the elevator to the second floor in silence, then entered the business centre, where Ava identified herself and was directed to the meeting room. It was slightly smaller than she had expected, with ten chairs set around a rectangular table. On a side table were bottles of water and pop, an ice bucket, and two Thermoses containing coffee and hot water.

"At least we can be polite and offer them refreshments," Brenda said.

"And we will," said Ava. "As far as seating goes, we'll take this end and put them at the other. If only the four of them come, that will leave some space between us."

"I can't imagine they'll bring Chik and Saad," Brooke said.

"If they do, it won't change anything," said Ava. "Douglas, would you mind standing at the door so we know when they arrive?"

"Not at all."

Brenda waited until Brooke had left before leaning towards Ava. "You seem tense. I'm not accustomed to seeing you like this."

"I want to end this tonight," Ava said. "I don't want to spend any more time with these people than I absolutely have to. I don't want them in my life, or in the lives of anyone I care about."

"You said upstairs that you're prepared to back off on some demands. How far will you go?"

"I'm not going to roll over, but if they're reasonable, then I will be as well."

"And if they're not?"

"Then we'll go to war," said Ava.

Brooke stuck his head inside the room. "They're coming. Sulaiman, Saad, Bowles, Ahmad, Jaffar, and the Din brothers."

"Make sure the brothers stay outside," said Ava.

Ava heard Brooke greeting them, and then he stepped inside with the others trailing behind. "Please sit at the other end. There are drinks on the table," she said.

She searched their faces as they walked to the far side of the room and took their seats. Bowles looked nervous, maybe even worried. *That's logical*, she thought, *given that he's the only one who lives in Hong Kong and has the most to lose if a deal isn't reached.* Jaffar and Saad seemed calm. Ahmad Chong's brow was furrowed and his mouth tightly set, as if he was preparing for a fight. Sulaiman looked angry, and as he sat down he stared at her with as much hatred as she could ever remember being cast in her direction.

Jaffar took a single sheet of paper from his briefcase and placed it on the table in front of him. "We have reviewed everything that we discussed with you earlier. While we are ready to make further concessions, we need you to confirm that there is willingness to compromise on your side as well."

"We are prepared to listen with an open mind. Beyond that we won't make a commitment," Ava said.

"We didn't come here to have you waste our time," Ahmad snapped.

"Let us not prejudge Ms. Lee's response," Jaffar said, and then smiled at her. "You don't object to me calling you Ms. Lee now?"

"Of course not."

"Get on with this," Sulaiman said to his lawyer. "And Ahmad, you stay quiet until he's finished."

"Very well," said Jaffar. "My clients are prepared to concede the twelve million dollars you have already laid claim to, but with one caveat."

"Caveat?" Ava asked.

"If we can get your insurance company to honour your policy, we believe that money should be reimbursed to us. In other words, you get the twelve million, but no more. So if you can recover three, four, or five million you will hand it over to us."

"What actions are you proposing that would persuade the insurance company to make a payment?" she asked.

"We consulted with Commissioner Chik —" Jaffar began.

"He thinks he can find a justification for reopening the investigation," Sulaiman interrupted. "He's reluctant to do so, but —"

"But he isn't doing it under duress. He admits that some facts may have been inadvertently missed or examined too hastily," Jaffar quickly added. "So any reluctance he has isn't because he thinks the force deliberately miscast its original opinion. It's more a matter of how the public will perceive reopening of the case. The Commissioner is justifiably proud of his force's reputation, and he doesn't want to see it tarnished."

"Are you saying that he'll reopen the case but doesn't want the public to know about it?"

"The police will make some kind of announcement, but he doesn't want to blow it out of proportion."

"Let me explain my sense of proportion," Ava said, her voice tightening. "As I have told my colleagues, Jamilah Daeng's parents belong to a church that believes people who kill themselves are condemned to hell for all eternity. As was explained to me, this means that not only do they have to bear the loss of their daughter in this physical world, all hope of meeting her again in the afterlife has also been crushed. So her parents have been doubly hurt, and it's a pain that will likely increase rather than diminish over the years."

"What can we do about that?" Sulaiman asked.

"I want Commissioner Chik to call the family personally to tell them her death has now been classified as a murder, not accidental suicide. And I want him to apologize to them for the error," Ava said. "Next, I want a banner headline on the front page of the *Sarawak Daily Journal* that states the same thing, and a front-page story that says the police now consider the bombing of our warehouse to have been the work of a business rival, and that neither Jamilah nor any environmental organization was involved in any way. I would expect every other media outlet in Sarawak to be given the same information and told to run stories however they see fit."

Jaffar shook his head. "The Commissioner might be

willing to call the parents, but for the rest of it —"

"I don't expect a real investigation. Tell him that. He can make the announcement and then do nothing," Ava said. "The police might have to endure a day or two of mild embarrassment, but it will pass. But I am firm on what I want to see declared publicly."

"We don't control the news media," Sulaiman said.

"I don't believe you. But even if that's true, pay them to run the stories. It will cost you a pittance compared to the thirty-five million you'll lose otherwise."

"It really means that much to you?" Jaffar asked.

"Yes. It's my deal-breaker."

Jaffar cupped his hand over his mouth and whispered something to Sulaiman. The Chief Minister nodded, then looked at Ava.

"You said before that you want some reference made about the Chong organization," Jaffer said.

"Perhaps that isn't necessary."

"What?" Sulaiman shouted, looking confused. "What are you playing at?"

"I'm not playing at anything. I'm being practical. I want to leave here tonight with a deal," said Ava. "I've been told that you're protective of your family's reputation. I respect that."

"You'll be satisfied with the announcement of an investigation and a phone call to the dead woman's parents?" Jaffar asked.

"The announcement has to set the record straight and be fully reported in the local media."

"Your position is noted," said Jaffar. "Now, about the money. Do you accept our proposal with regard to a potential insurance payment?"

"My initial instinct is to say no, because I don't want to extend my dealings with you past next week, and I don't want you involved in our business, even peripherally," Ava said. "But I acknowledge there is a fairness element to consider. So, if our claim is settled, we'll return that money to you. We'll forward it to you through Mr. Brooke's office."

"How will we know if you get paid?" Ahmad asked.

"Don't insult me. I know how to honour an agreement," Ava said sharply.

"I'll trust you to do the right thing," Sulaiman said to Ava, glancing angrily at his son.

"Thank you," Ava said and leaned towards the Chief Minister. "As I see it, we have waived our demand to have someone made accountable for the bombing, and we have agreed to exclude the Chong name from any police communications concerning it. Further, we have just committed to handing over to you several million dollars of insurance money. What I would like to know is what we're going to get in return."

Sulaiman looked questioningly at Saad and then Jaffar.

"We should do it," Saad said.

"I agree," added Jaffar.

Sulaiman bit his lower lip, but then he slapped his palm on the table. "We will agree to everything else you have asked for," he said. "Now what?"

"We have to paper the agreement," Ava said calmly, showing no emotion. "My lawyers have already started putting something together. Perhaps Mr. Jaffar could meet with them separately, either here or in Ms. Burgess's office, to come up with a draft. I don't see why we can't have something to read and sign by tomorrow."

Sulaiman started to respond, but his attention was diverted by shouts and thuds coming from the other side of the door.

"What's going on?" Bowles said, getting to his feet and taking a step towards the door. Before he got there, it was thrown open.

Sonny stood in the doorway, holding one of the Din brothers by the throat.

"You can put him down now," Ava said.

Sonny nodded, dropped the brother, and stepped to one side.

"We told the man we're here to have a chat. I guess he didn't believe us," Zhao said as he stepped into the room. Behind him, pale and visibly sweating, was Ronald Ho.

44

ZHAO'S DRAMATIC ENTRANCE HAD SHOCKED THE room into silence. Tall and lean, Zhao was wearing a navy-blue silk shirt with grey slacks. His silver hair was braided down his back, and he looked at them through lightly tinted red glasses. All told, he was a magnetic figure.

"I hope I'm not too early," he said to Ava.

"Your timing is perfect," she said.

"Did you get the deal you wanted?"

"Yes, we have reached an understanding."

He took the chair next to Ava, which left the seat next to Ahmad Chong for Ho.

Zhao smiled across the table. "My name is Zhao. I am a long-time friend and occasional business partner of Ms. Lee's," he said. "She invited me to join you for a few minutes, and I brought Ronald Ho with me in case there was any doubt about my status. Ho, tell your acquaintances who I am."

The banker licked his lips and swallowed. "Mr. Zhao is the leader of the largest triad gang in Kowloon."

"Actually, it's now the largest triad gang in all of Hong Kong. And the only reason that should be important to you is that I'm prepared to commit those resources to support Ms. Lee," Zhao said. "She told me earlier about what she hoped to achieve here today, and now that she's apparently done it, I'm here to put my chop on it."

"I have no idea what you could be talking about," Sulaiman said, his voice steady but his eyes flitting back and forth from Ava to Zhao.

"It's very simple. From this moment on, Ava and anyone directly or indirectly connected to her who is affected by the agreement you've reached is off-limits to you. Ava, do you want to elaborate?"

"Yes, I do. Nothing untoward is to happen to any of my partners, businesses, or employees, or the organizations in Sarawak that received the donations, or the lawyers — including Douglas. And when I say nothing, I don't just mean physical harm or threats. There are to be no lawsuits, no attempts to intimidate, no 'accidents' — nothing."

"And if anything does happen, you will answer to us. We may be based here, but there isn't a single part of Asia we can't reach," Zhao said. "All it will take is a phone call from Ms. Lee. And in case you're stupid enough to think you can finesse us, the results will be catastrophic."

"These threats are totally unnecessary," Jaffar said.

"Who are you?" Zhao asked.

"I'm Mr. Chong's lawyer."

"Will you be involved in writing the final agreement between Ava and your clients?"

"That is the plan."

"As you're doing it, remember that everything you commit to had better be honoured," said Zhao. "So if you think you can phrase things in a way that gives your clients wiggle room, don't bother. If there's a problem later, we'll hold you to blame."

Ava smiled at Zhao. "Thank you for coming here at such short notice. You truly are a good friend," she said, and then looked at the Chongs. "I invited Zhao because I sensed your doubt about my connections. I hope this makes things clear."

"As Jaffar said, this was unnecessary. But things are clear," Sulaiman said.

"Excellent," Ava said. "So with that, I think we're finished. Brenda and Douglas and Mr. Jaffar have work to do, and we should let them get started."

"We're ready to spend the next few hours here, if that's okay with you," Brenda said to Jaffar. "We can go over what's been decided and lay out the general terms of the agreement. Once that's done, Douglas and I can meet at my office in the morning and boilerplate it for you to review. With any luck, we can wrap things up by tomorrow afternoon. Does that work for you?"

"That's fine."

Ava stood up and looked at Sulaiman. "Did Commissioner Chik come to the Mandarin with you?"

"No, he's at his hotel."

"The sooner you get him started on what he has to do, and the sooner it's publicized, the sooner you'll get your money. If you move quickly, there's no reason you can't have it back within forty-eight hours."

"We don't need to be told what to do or when to do it," Sulaiman said.

"Of course you don't," Ava said and smiled. "Zhao, I think it's time for us to leave."

When she reached the door, she could see Sonny chatting

with four other men, while the Din brothers stood nearby with their backs pressed against the wall. "I didn't realize you'd brought so many men," she said to Zhao.

He laughed. "All I really needed was Sonny, but in our business there's no such thing as being too careful."

"Would you like to join me for a drink?" she asked.

"No thank you, Ava. I still have business to do in Kowloon. Thanks to you, I have several shipments of new iPhones scheduled to arrive, and we need to finalize distribution," he said. "But I'm going to leave my men here until your lawyers are finished inside. We don't want any last-minute changes of heart."

"Sonny is going to stay."

"My men will keep him company. Besides, a couple of them have never met him, and they're thrilled to have the chance. Sonny is a bit of a legend in Kowloon."

Ava nodded and walked over to Sonny. She reached up and kissed him on the cheek. "Thanks for the help. Zhao's men are going to stay here with you until the lawyers are finished. When they are, make sure Brenda gets home safely. You and I will talk tomorrow."

"Congratulations, boss."

"I didn't do it alone. Without you, Jimmy, and Zhao, it wouldn't have happened."

Sonny looked slightly embarrassed, but Ava touched him lightly on the arm. "We'll talk tomorrow," she repeated.

Ava walked with Zhao to the elevators. "Thanks again for all this," she said.

"I'm here any time you need me," he said. "Give Xu my regards when you see him."

Ava reached her room a few minutes later and immediately

took out her phone. In rapid succession she called May Ling, Amanda, and Xu to report on how the day had gone. It wasn't something she would have done normally until the deal was signed, but she had rarely felt so confident of an outcome.

Amanda asked if she could pass on the news to Chi-Tze and Aisyah. After a slight hesitation, Ava gave her the go-ahead.

Xu asked if Zhao had been as helpful as she'd hoped for. When she told him about Zhao's personal intervention at the meeting, he said, "I'm going to put him at the top of my list when it comes to all my new products. I appreciate someone who does a favour for a fair price and then goes beyond the expected and asks for nothing in return. Now, when will we see you and Fai? Auntie Grace mentions your visit every day."

"If we can wrap up things here tomorrow, I'll head for Taipei either tomorrow night or the day after. When I get there, I'll have some idea how close Lau Lau is to finishing the film. Then I'll let you know."

Ava's last call was to Fai. But first she showered, poured a glass of cognac, and propped herself up on the bed with a mound of pillows.

"*Wei*," Fai answered. She sounded choked up.

"Are you crying?" Ava asked.

"I have been. I'm getting over it now."

"What happened?"

"No, you go first. How was your day?"

"It went well. In fact, very well. I expect we'll sign an agreement tomorrow, and then I'll be heading to the airport to get the first plane I can to Taipei," Ava said quickly, her concern about Fai cutting short any details.

"That's wonderful."

"But what's going on with you? You're making me nervous."

"Oh, don't be. There's nothing to worry about. In fact, when you get here, we should celebrate," Fai said. "That's why I've been crying. They're tears of joy."

"I don't understand."

"Of course you don't. I'm sorry for jumping all over the place. Let me gather myself," Fai said, and put down her phone.

Ava pulled her knees to her chest and closed her eyes. Despite Fai's assurances, she couldn't help feeling that something was going wrong.

"I'm back," Fai said finally.

"What's happened?" Ava asked, more loudly than she intended.

"Four hours ago, Lau Lau invited me, Chen, Harris Jones, and Silvana to a room in his hotel that he and his editor were using as a cutting room," Fai said. "Without any of us knowing, they'd been working there night after night to assemble the footage into a rough cut. I'm sure neither of them has slept more than a few hours a night since we got here, because they've basically been creating the film as we've gone along. What usually takes months of work in post-production, they've been doing on the fly. It isn't a finished product, but the entire framework — the major scenes and the thrust of the film — is all there to see."

"Has Lau Lau finished shooting?"

"Not yet, but the hard work is done. We'll wrap in the next day or two."

"And what you saw is good?" asked Ava.

"No. It's magnificent."

"I am so pleased to hear that."

"Ava, you have no idea," Fai said. "*Tiananmen* is the finest film Lau Lau has ever made. It will be his masterpiece. When we finished watching the rough cut, Silvana and I were in tears. And Chen was speechless, which for him is a rarity."

"What about Harris Jones?"

"After the film ended he was quiet for a moment. And then he stood up and bowed to Lau Lau. He said, 'I've always believed you're a genius. This is the proof. The world must see this film, and I'll do everything I can to make that possible.'"

Ava found herself blinking back tears as well. Business concerns aside, she had always thought that bringing Clark Po's work to the broadest possible market was something to be proud of. Could *Tiananmen* be more than that?

"Do you think Lau Lau would allow me to see the rough cut too?" she asked.

"He can hardly wait. You're the reason it exists."

ACKNOWLEDGEMENTS

THE PLOTS FOR MY BOOKS COME TO ME IN MANY different ways; the plot for *The Sultan of Sarawak* is the second that was suggested to me by a reader. I was in Westport, Ontario, five or six years ago, taking part in a wonderful day-long author's event, when I was approached by a man. He thrust a book into my hands and told me he thought its subject — illegal logging in Borneo and the laundering of money that flowed from it — was a perfect job for Ava to tackle. It took me a while to embrace his idea, but eventually I did. This novel is the result.

Embarrassingly, I don't know the man's name. I looked for him via Facebook several years ago and he did contact me, but between changing email addresses and my general incompetence with anything social media related, I lost it. So, this is very large thanks to someone who is currently anonymous. Hopefully he'll read this book and contact me so I can send him something appropriate.

As with all my books, I had a bevy of first readers who kindly provided me with feedback and corrections. A thank you again to Carol Shetler, Robin Spano, John Kruihtof,

Ashok Ramchandani, Lam Lau, and my first reader of first readers, my wife Lorraine.

This is also the first book that I've done with my new agent, Alexandra Machinist of ICM. Alexandra, who works out of New York City, negotiated a three-book deal with House of Anansi, and I really appreciated her efforts and the results. So, thanks, Alexandra.

Doug Richmond, who is now fittingly Senior Editor at Anansi, molded a rather fat manuscript into shape, and as always made the experience for me as stress-free as it can be. Thank you, Doug.

This was, alas, the last book that Anansi's managing editor, Maria Golikova had a hand in. She has moved on to other pastures. I wish her well but will miss her professionalism and enthusiasm.

IAN HAMILTON is the acclaimed author of fourteen books in the Ava Lee series, three in the Lost Decades of Uncle Chow Tung series, and the standalone novel *Bonnie Jack*. His books have been shortlisted for numerous prizes, including the Arthur Ellis Award, the Barry Award, and the Lambda Literary Prize, and are national bestsellers. BBC Culture named Hamilton one of the ten mystery/crime writers from the last thirty years who should be on your bookshelf. The Ava Lee series is being adapted for television.

NOW AVAILABLE
from House of Anansi Press
The Ava Lee series

Prequel and Book 1　　**Book 2**　　**Book 3**　　**Book 4**

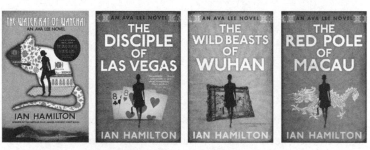

Book 5　　**Book 6**　　**Book 7**　　**Book 8**

Book 9　　**Book 10**　　**Book 11**　　**Book 12**　　**Book 13**

www.houseofanansi.com • www.facebook.com/avaleenovels
www.ianhamiltonbooks.com • www.twitter.com/avaleebooks

ALSO AVAILABLE
from House of Anansi Press

The Lost Decades of Uncle Chow Tung

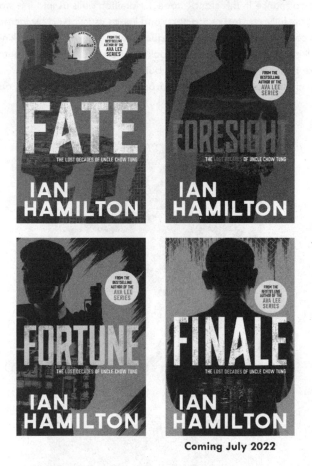

Coming July 2022

ALSO AVAILABLE
from House of Anansi Press

"Hamilton, author of the Ava Lee mystery series, turns in a stellar performance in this stand-alone...Hamilton pulls us into the story with carefully crafted characters, and keeps us involved by increasing the complexity of the tale: introducing a mystery here, uncorking a shocking revelation there. The book is a departure from the author's more traditional mystery fiction, but his fans will find much here that is familiar: realistic dialogue, characters they can care about, and a gripping story."—*Booklist*

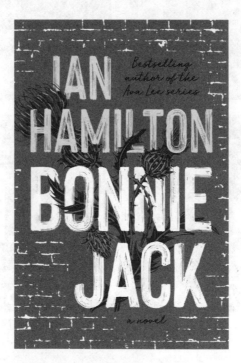

www.houseofanansi.com
www.ianhamiltonbooks.com

PRAISE FOR IAN HAMILTON AND THE AVA LEE SERIES

PRAISE FOR *THE WATER RAT OF WANCHAI*
WINNER OF THE ARTHUR ELLIS AWARD FOR BEST FIRST NOVEL

"Ian Hamilton's *The Water Rat of Wanchai* is a smart, action-packed thriller of the first order, and Ava Lee, a gay Asian-Canadian forensics accountant with a razor-sharp mind and highly developed martial arts skills, is a protagonist to be reckoned with. We were impressed by Hamilton's tight plotting; his well-rendered settings, from the glitz of Bangkok to the grit of Guyana; and his ability to portray a wide range of sharply individualized characters in clean but sophisticated prose." —Judges' Citation, Arthur Ellis Award for Best First Novel

"Ava Lee is tough, fearless, quirky, and resourceful, and she has more— well, you know—than a dozen male detectives I can think of... Hamilton has created a true original in Ava Lee." —Linwood Barclay, author of *No Time for Goodbye*

"If the other novels [in the series] are half as good as this debut by Ian Hamilton, then readers are going to celebrate. Hamilton has created a marvellous character in Ava Lee...This is a terrific story that's certain to be on the Arthur Ellis Best First Novel list." —*Globe and Mail*

"[Ava Lee's] lethal knowledge...torques up her sex appeal to the approximate level of a female lead in a Quentin Tarantino film." —*National Post*

"The heroine in *The Water Rat of Wanchai* by Ian Hamilton sounds too good to be true, but the heroics work better that way...formidable...The story breezes along with something close to total clarity...Ava is unbeatable at just about everything. Just wait for her to roll out her bak mei against the bad guys. She's perfect. She's fast." —*Toronto Star*

"Seldom does one get a thriller about white-collar crime, with an intelligent, independent lesbian and Asian protagonist. It's also rare to find a book with such interesting and exotic settings...Readers will find great amusement in Ava's unconventional ways and will certainly enjoy accompanying her on her travels." — *Literaturkurier*

PRAISE FOR *THE DISCIPLE OF LAS VEGAS*
FINALIST, BARRY AWARD FOR BEST ORIGINAL TRADE PAPERBACK

"I started to read *The Disciple of Las Vegas* at around ten at night. And I did something I have only done with two other books (Cormac McCarthy's *The Road* and Douglas Coupland's *Player One*): I read the novel in one sitting. Ava Lee is too cool. She wonderfully straddles two worlds and two identities. She does some dastardly things and still remains our hero thanks to the charm Ian Hamilton has given her on the printed page. It would take a female George Clooney to portray her in a film. The action and plot move quickly and with power. Wow. A punch to the ear, indeed." — J. J. Lee, author of *The Measure of a Man*

"I loved *The Water Rat of Wanchai*, the first novel featuring Ava Lee. Now, Ava and Uncle make a return that's even better...Simply irresistible." — Margaret Cannon, *Globe and Mail*

"This is slick, fast-moving escapism reminiscent of Ian Fleming, with more to come in what shapes up as a high-energy, high-concept series." — *Booklist*

"Fast paced...Enough personal depth to lift this thriller above solely action-oriented fare." — *Publishers Weekly*

"Lee is a hugely original creation, and Hamilton packs his adventure with interesting facts and plenty of action." — *Irish Independent*

"Hamilton makes each page crackle with the kind of energy that could easily jump to the movie screen...This riveting read will keep you up late at night." — *Penthouse*

"Hamilton gives his reader plenty to think about...Entertaining."
— *Kitchener-Waterloo Record*

PRAISE FOR *THE WILD BEASTS OF WUHAN*
LAMBDA LITERARY AWARD FINALIST: LESBIAN MYSTERY

"Smart and savvy Ava Lee returns in this slick mystery set in the rarefied world of high art...[A] great caper tale. Hamilton has great fun chasing villains and tossing clues about. *The Wild Beasts of Wuhan* is the best Ava Lee novel yet, and promises more and better to come."
— Margaret Cannon, *Globe and Mail*

"One of my favourite new mystery series, perfect escapism."
— *National Post*

"As a mystery lover, I'm devouring each book as it comes out...What I love in the novels: The constant travel, the high-stakes negotiation, and Ava's willingness to go into battle against formidable opponents, using only her martial arts skills to defend herself...If you want a great read and an education in high-level business dealings, Ian Hamilton is an author to watch." — *Toronto Star*

"Fast-paced and very entertaining." — *Montreal Gazette*

"Ava Lee is definitely a winner." — *Saskatoon Star Phoenix*

"*The Wild Beasts of Wuhan* is an entertaining dip into potentially fatal worlds of artistic skulduggery." — *Sudbury Star*

"Hamilton uses Ava's investigations as comprehensive and intriguing mechanisms for plot and character development." — *Quill & Quire*

"You haven't seen cold and calculating until you've double-crossed this number cruncher. Another strong entry from Arthur Ellis Award–winner Hamilton." — *Booklist*

"An intelligent kick-ass heroine anchors Canadian author Hamilton's excellent third novel featuring forensic accountant Ava Lee...Clearly conversant with the art world, Hamilton makes the intricacies of forgery as interesting as a Ponzi scheme." — *Publishers Weekly*, *Starred Review*

"A lively series about Ava Lee, a sexy forensic financial investigator." — *Tampa Bay Times*

"This book is miles from the ordinary. The main character, Ava Lee is 'the whole package.'" — *Minneapolis Star Tribune*

"A strong heroine is challenged to discover the details of an intercontinental art scheme. Although Hamilton's star Ava Lee is technically a forensic accountant, she's more badass private investigator than desk jockey." — *Kirkus Reviews*

PRAISE FOR *THE RED POLE OF MACAU*

"Ava Lee returns as one of crime fiction's most intriguing characters. *The Red Pole of Macau* is the best page-turner of the season from the hottest writer in the business!" — John Lawrence Reynolds, author of *Beach Strip*

"Ava Lee, that wily, wonderful hunter of nasty business brutes, is back in her best adventure ever...If you haven't yet discovered Ava Lee, start here." — *Globe and Mail*

"The best in the series so far." — *London Free Press*

"Ava [Lee] is a character we all could use at one time or another. Failing that, we follow her in her best adventure yet." — *Hamilton Spectator*

"A romp of a story with a terrific heroine." — *Saskatoon Star Phoenix*

"Fast-paced... The action unfolds like a well-oiled action-flick."
— *Kitchener-Waterloo Record*

"A change of pace for our girl [Ava Lee]... Suspenseful." — *Toronto Star*

"Hamilton packs tremendous potential in his heroine... A refreshingly relevant series. This reader will happily pay House of Anansi for the fifth installment." — *Canadian Literature*

PRAISE FOR *THE SCOTTISH BANKER OF SURABAYA*

"Hamilton deepens Ava's character, and imbues her with greater mettle and emotional fire, to the extent that book five is his best, most memorable, to date." — *National Post*

"In today's crowded mystery market, it's no easy feat coming up with a protagonist who stands out from the pack. But Ian Hamilton has made a great job of it with his Ava Lee books. Young, stylish, Chinese Canadian, lesbian, and a brilliant forensic accountant, Ava is as complex a character as you could want... [A] highly addictive series... Hamilton knows how to keep the pages turning. He eases us into the seemingly tame world of white-collar crime, then raises the stakes, bringing the action to its peak with an intensity and violence that's stomach-churning. His Ava Lee is a winner and a welcome addition to the world of strong female avengers." — *NOW Magazine*

"Most of the series' success rests in Hamilton's tight plotting, attention to detail, and complex powerhouse of a heroine: strong but vulnerable, capable but not impervious... With their tight plotting and crackerjack heroine, Hamilton's novels are the sort of crowd-pleasing, narrative-focused fiction we find all too rarely in this country." — *Quill & Quire*

"Ava is such a cool character, intelligent, Chinese Canadian, unconventional, and original... Irresistible." — *Owen Sound Sun Times*

"Ava may be the most chic figure in crime fiction." — *Hamilton Spectator*

"The series as a whole is as good as the modern thriller genre gets." — *The Cord*

PRAISE FOR *THE KING OF SHANGHAI*

"The only thing scarier than being ripped off for a few million bucks is being the guy who took it and having Ava Lee on your tail. If Hamilton's kick-ass forensic accountant has your number, it's up." — Linwood Barclay

"One of Ian Hamilton's best." — *Globe and Mail*

"Brilliant, sexy, and formidably martial arts-trained forensic accountant Ava Lee is back in her seventh adventure (after *The Two Sisters of Borneo*)... Ever since his dazzling surprise debut with *The Water Rat of Wanchai*, Hamilton has propelled Ava along through the series with expanded storytelling and nuanced character development: there's always something new to discover about Ava. Fast-paced suspense, exotic locales, and a rich cast of characters (some, like Ava's driver, Sonny, are both dangerous and lovable) make for yet another hugely entertaining hit." — *Publishers Weekly*, *Starred review*

"A luxurious sense of place... Hamilton's knack for creating fascinating detail will keep readers hooked... Good fun for those who like to combine crime fiction with armchair travelling." — *Booklist*

"Ava would be a sure thing to whip everybody, Putin included, at the negotiating table." — *Toronto Star*

"After six novels starring Chinese Canadian Ava Lee and her perilously thrilling exploits, best-selling Canadian author Ian Hamilton has jolted his creation out of what wasn't even yet a rut and hurled her abruptly into a new circumstance, with fresh ambitions." — *London Free Press*

"It's a measure of Hamilton's quality as a thriller writer that he compels your attention even before he starts ratcheting up the suspense."
— *Regina Leader Post*

"An unputdownable book that I would highly recommend for all."
— *Words of Mystery*

"Ava is as powerful and brilliant as ever." — *Literary Treats*

PRAISE FOR *THE PRINCELING OF NANJING*
NATIONAL BESTSELLER
A KOBO BEST BOOK OF THE YEAR

"The reader is offered plenty of Ava in full flower as the Chinese Canadian glamour puss who happens to be gay, whip smart, and unafraid of whatever dangers come her way." — *Toronto Star*

"Hamilton's Chinese Canadian heroine is one of a kind … [An] exotic thriller that also offers a fascinating inside look at fiscal misconduct in China … As a unique series character, Ava Lee's become indispensable." — *Calgary Herald*

"Ava Lee has a new business, a new look, and, most important, a new triad boss to appreciate her particular financial talents … We know that Ava will come up with a plan and Hamilton will come up with a twist." — *Globe and Mail*

"Like the best series writers — Ian Rankin and Peter Robinson come to mind — Hamilton manages to … keep the Ava Lee books fresh … A compulsive read, a page-turner of the old school … *The Princeling of Nanjing* is a welcome return of an old favourite, and bodes well for future books." — *Quill & Quire*

"Hamilton uses his people and plot to examine Chinese class and power structures that open opportunities for massive depravities and corruptions." — *London Free Press*

"As usual with a Hamilton-Lee novel, matters take a decided twist as the plot unrolls." — *Owen Sound Times*

"One of those grip-tight novels that makes one read 'just one more chapter' and you discover it's 3 a.m. The novel is built on complicated webs artfully woven into clear, magnetic storytelling. Author Ian Hamilton delivers the intrigue within complex and relentless webs in high style and once again proves that everyone, once in their lives, needs an Ava Lee at their backs." — *Canadian Mystery Reviews*

"The best of the Ava Lee series to date…*Princeling* features several chapters of pure, unadulterated financial sleuthing, which both gave me some nerdy feels and tickled my puzzle-loving mind." — *Literary Treats*

"*The Princeling of Nanjing* was another addition to the Ava Lee series that did not disappoint." — *Words of Mystery*

PRAISE FOR *THE COUTURIER OF MILAN*
NATIONAL BESTSELLER

"The latest in the excellent series starring Ava Lee, businesswoman extraordinaire, *The Couturier of Milan* is another winner for Ian Hamilton…The novel is a hoot. At a point where most crime series start to run out of steam, Ava Lee just keeps rolling on." — *Globe and Mail*

"In Ava Lee, Ian Hamilton has created a crime fighter who breaks the mould with every new book (and, frankly, with every new chapter)." — CBC Books

"The pleasure in following Ava's clever plans for countering the bad guys remains as ever a persuasive attraction." — *Toronto Star*

"Fashionably fierce forensics…But Hamilton has built around Ava Lee an award-winning series that absorbs intriguing aspects of both Asian and Canadian cultures." — *London Free Press*

PRAISE FOR *THE IMAM OF TAWI-TAWI*

"The best of the series so far." — *Globe and Mail*

"One of his best...Tightly plotted and quick-moving, this is a spare yet terrifically suspenseful novel." — *Publishers Weekly*

"Combines lots of action with Ava's acute intelligence and ability to solve even the most complex problems." — *Literary Hub*

"Fast-paced, smoothly written, and fun." — *London Free Press*

"An engrossing novel." — *Reviewing the Evidence*

"Hamilton's rapid-fire storytelling moves the tale along at breakneck speed, as Ava globe-trots to put clues together. Hamilton has always had a knack for combing Fleming-style descriptors with modern storytelling devices and character beats, and this book is no different." — *The Mind Reels*

"An engaging and compelling mystery." — *Literary Treats*

PRAISE FOR *THE GODDESS OF YANTAI*
NATIONAL BESTSELLER

"Ava at her most intimate and vulnerable." — *Toronto Star*

"This time, [Ava's] crusade is personal, and so is her outrage." — *London Free Press*

"In *The Goddess of Yantai*...Ava's personal and professional lives collide in a manner that shakes the usually unflappable character." — *Quill & Quire*

"Told in his typical punchy and forthright style, Hamilton's latest thriller is a rapid-fire read that leaves the reader breathless and eagerly anticipating the next installment... This is a series of books that just seems to get better and better."— *The Mind Reels*

"I wanted to just rip through this book... If you love great writing, an intense pace, and a bit of a thrill, then [the Ava Lee novels] are perfect for you."— *Reading on the Run*

"Action packed and thrilling."— *Words of Mystery*

PRAISE FOR *THE MOUNTAIN MASTER OF SHA TIN*

"Whether it's the triad plot lines or the elegant detective skills of Lee, Ian Hamilton has managed to maintain a freshness to his stories. *The Mountain Master of Sha Tin* is as slick and smart as *The Water Rat of Wanchai*, the first Ava Lee novel... This is one of Canada's best series by one of our best writers."— *Globe and Mail*

"Propulsive."— *London Free Press*

"Hamilton's punchy, fast-paced style has woven a tapestry in over a dozen novels that have introduced us to a variety of characters... This novel, like the previous tales, rockets along."— *The Mind Reels*

"Hamilton provides a fascinating peek into a disturbingly glamorous world."— *Publishers Weekly*

"Another action-packed entry in a solid series."— *Booklist*

PRAISE FOR *THE DIAMOND QUEEN OF SINGAPORE*

"With crisp, taut storytelling, Hamilton whips us around the globe with his captivating prose that delivers like a phoenix strike... Hamilton's

Fleming-esque style of description elicits images and sensations that bring Ava's realm to colourful, glittering life... The perfect summer read, completely engaging, entertaining, and unputdownable." — *The Mind Reels*

"Hamilton takes great care to make sure that the Ava Lee universe and the characters feel authentic, and it especially shows in this book... I'm looking forward to the next book and to seeing Ava take on an even bigger opponent." — *Words of Mystery*

"Another fantastic addition to Hamilton's box of jewels." — *The Bowed Bookshelf*